W9-CXY-662

Further praise for *Flatbellies*

"Equal parts *Stand by Me* and *Missing Links*, *Flatbellies* . . . is a rollicking, lyrical tale of teen angst, rebellions and redemption set in the mid-1960s. . . . Propelled by seamless, sophisticated writing, unpredictable plot twists and well-developed characters, *Flatbellies* blends its robust morality tale with a touching, quirky love story and a healthy dose of beer-fueled humor. . . . A fast-paced, entertaining story that seizes and surprises the reader from its opening paragraph, *Flatbellies* is a rare delight, an emotional, heartwarming testament to the strength of the human spirit and our grand game's magical ability to mold and forge the characters of those who play it."

—James McCarten, GolfWeb at PGAtour.com

"Each generation tends to produce at least one or two good coming-of-age novels. The better ones reflect their particular social history, and also repeat some eternal verities. For the first phase of Boomers, those born in the first five years or so after World War II, *Flatbellies* nicely fills that niche. . . . As the story unfolds, Hollingsworth touches upon some fond and deep memories about life in the mid-1960s in Middle America. . . . There's much to enjoy in this engaging new novel."

—Fritz Schranck, [Delaware] *Cape Gazette*

"The skillfully crafted characters . . . enter their senior years dedicated to achieving the impossible, but love, loss and life keep getting in the way."

—Carol J. Burr, *Sooner Magazine*

"A charming and beautifully written new golf novel joining the elite coming of age stories of a generation. Set in a small Oklahoma town in the mid-1960s, it is a memorable and moving tale of the struggles and accomplishments of a high-school golf team and its quest to win the state championship."

—Golfread.com

FLATBELLIES

It's not about golf.
It's about life.

A. B. HOLLINGSWORTH

W. W. Norton & Company
New York London

Copyright © 2001 Clock Tower Press
First published as a Norton paperback 2003

This book is a work of fiction. Although the story may be set in the context of actual historical events and figures, the principal characters in this story are products of the author's imagination. Any similarity to actual persons is purely coincidental.

All rights reserved.
Reprinted with permission of Clock Tower Press.
Printed in the United States of America

Library of Congress Cataloging-in-Publication Data

Hollingsworth, Alan, 1949
Flatbellies / by Alan Hollingsworth
p. cm.
ISBN 1-58536-038-4
1. High school students—Fiction. 2. Golf tournaments—Fiction. 3. School sports—Fiction. 4. Teenage boys—Fiction. 5. Oklahoma—Fiction. I. Title.
PS33558.O34975 F58 2001
813'.6—dc21 00-067086

ISBN 0-393-32420-6 pbk.

W. W. Norton & Company, Inc.
500 Fifth Avenue, New York, N.Y. 10110
www.wwnorton.com

W. W. Norton & Company Ltd.
Castle House, 75/76 Wells Street, London W1T 3QT

1 2 3 4 5 6 7 8 9 0

For

F. W. Hollingsworth, M.D.
(1919-2000)

who spared the rod when he had both opportunity and reason to do otherwise

FLATBELLIES

1961

Kyle DeHart opened his eyes and shook himself free of the murky green water that always tried to suffocate him during sleep. But today held bright hopes. A new game was about to unfurl, and every 12-year-old knew that a great moment in sports could be a rocket to glory. The fuel for that rocket? It was one of Godzilla's golf clubs Kyle had smuggled the night before, now taped like a booster to the crossbar of his metallic blue Schwinn Traveler.

Between the springs of the bunk above, held in place by little metal bars across her face, nestled the fourth grade photo of Gail Perdue. Like an imprisoned angel, she stared down at him every night and every morning, never blinking, never looking away. Her spooky father had rejected the school photographer's version, taking her instead to a professional where the hallowed glow about her head was captured in the portrait, as it should be.

In a way, she was indeed a prisoner. In exile. Before she left for her seven years in California, Gail set their wedding day for February 14, 1972. He pressed his fingers against her radiant face in the crinkled photo, feeling a toasty flush in his own face before letting his hand drop to his side.

Reaching beneath the bed, he fumbled with the push buttons on the suitcase-sized box where the loose end of the tape reel was clicking in cadence. Slicker than snot, he thought, to be commandeering the first tape recorder in El Viento. He prayed his scheme would work. The popping sound of the STOP button brought the clickety-clack of the spinning reel to silence. Surely the machine would not burn out by running all night, every night, while he was in the process of becoming a genius. Having discovered subliminal learning from his Weekly Reader, *Kyle was excited about his academic prospects next fall.*

The subliminal strategy was easy. With his 45s on the tape, it was like *going to sleep with the radio on. Thirty minutes into the tape, he had slipped next year's geometry formulas between tunes. He knew it was working when, last Tuesday, he was singing "oo-ee-oo-ah-ah" and suddenly Area=πr^2 popped into his head for a sandwiched second before "walla-walla-bing-bang."*

Deeper into the tape, he had recorded his mother's old 78s, which included some of the songs he would be playing this summer in Oklahoma City's Junior Symphony. The debate over his chosen instrument—he wanted to play drums, his mother insisted on anything but—led to the Battle of '59, which ended with the Treaty of '61. He would play the xylophone. So he had recorded the "Comedians' Gallop" for subconscious benefit, in case he needed to accompany circus acrobats or Ed Sullivan's jugglers some day in order to earn a living. Later in the tape, deep in sleep, the Drinking Song from some Italian opera played while his whispered recordings of English grammar rules were superimposed over the oompahs. By the time "Ave Maria" brought it on home with world geography, he was a sleeping human sponge, soaking subliminal messages into every brain cell.

The 27 seconds he spent dressing in blue jeans, white tee shirt, Keds hightops and a red baseball cap crowned at the top and creased at the sides, was a defined unit of time, standardized by every boy in America who wore the same uniform—with permissible variations in cap color—every summer day. But there was a peculiar twist today. Through the magic of iron-on technology, Kyle's tee shirt was emblazoned with a rubberized New York Yankees logo covering the front. The world of plain white tee shirts would be stunned.

It was time to sneak by Godzilla, alias Leonard DeHart, M.D. His technique was flawless. As usual, he was strangely compelled to look at Gail's picture, and then take several breaths before he was able to leave his room.

Avoiding the stairs that squeaked—numbers two, five, nine, and eleven—he slipped to the landing on the first floor, then approached his father's study where outstretched legs appeared through the doorjambs.

If the magazine were being held at eye level, he would be safe. As he spotted Popular Science, *a small monthly that provided limited but adequate coverage for a decent blockade, he realized he could steal home. He crept by the study door, and then picked up the pace to slide safely into the kitchen.*

In the pantry, he grabbed his daily can of shoestring potatoes, but avoided the new electric can opener, favoring the quieter manual method. He squeezed the opened can like Popeye before he poured the potato sticks into his mouth, allowing some of his breakfast to fall on the floor where the family wiener dog, Squirt, shared in the spoils.

As the chomped shoestrings traveled down his gullet like the Sailor Man's spinach, he could feel his biceps enlarge, and he always made a muscle to confirm the impression. He looked to the corner to toss his empty can in the garbage, but the wastebasket was full. Uh-oh. He had forgotten again.

He looked around, confirming silence while planning a rapid escape through the back door. The crrreak of the chair in the study let him know that Godzilla was emerging from the water, and Kyle wasted little time getting outside. Exits somehow provided the entrance of power.

From the edge of the back porch, he flew toward the shrubs faster than a speeding bullet, able to feel the red cape flapping in the breeze. Tumbling through the base of the vast hedge, he scampered to the alley where he parked his bike for getaways. Secured with duct tape, the glistening silver shaft of his father's pirated golf club nestled parallel with the metallic blue crossbar. Mounting the saddle, he began to charge for safety at the neighboring Justice castle. The outside screen door slammed shut. The monster was completely out of the water, standing on the beach.

"Kyle!" it yelled.

He pedaled faster.

"Kyle DeHart, don't you go gallivanting off now. You get back here and take out the trash!"

He could feel the flames from Godzilla's mouth nipping at his fanny. Only two more lawns to cross before he reached the Justice's moat.

"Kyle, for cryin' out loud! If I've told you once, I've told you a thousand times..."

...Doc Jody was in the front yard, hitting fly balls to son Jay, short for Jacob (though the Biblical rendering rarely prevailed). Mama Justice sat on the front porch of their yellow brick home in a flowered sundress, fanning herself with the newspaper.

Jay had spent the standard 27 seconds as well this morning donning blue jeans, Keds hightops, a red baseball cap, bill creased with perfect side flaps, and the only other tee shirt in civilization with a rubberized Yankee logo.

The Justice castle oozed the sounds of summer through its screened windows. You were likely to hear Dizzy Dean singing songs to Pee Wee Reese during the ballgames by day, while Gary Moore sent his guests with Secrets out the door with 50 bucks and a pack of Winstons by night.

From the back bedroom window, Kyle could hear Jay's college brother Josh, short for Joshua, crooning to the company of his twanging banjo, with Tom Dooley's lyrical fate spilling into the alley.

"Kyle, get out there and snag some flies with Jay," said Doc Jody, his smooth bass voice enough to inspire leaping, superhuman catches.

Kyle and Jay traded licks on each other's arms then turned to face the hitter. There they were, Mantle and Maris in the outfield, the boys of summer.

Mama Justice rested her newspaper in her lap and smiled at the Yankee outfield. Kyle figured that she sensed their destiny, and that her grin revealed how happy she'd be someday, boasting that she knew them back in the little leagues.

Doc Jody tossed one up with his left hand and hit a pop fly using only his right hand on the bat.

"Mantle is backing up," yelled Kyle.

"Maris calls for it," Jay replied.

"Mantle leaps..."

"Maris has it," said Jay, as he caught the ball with a crowd-pleasing jump then fell to the ground. He held his glove in the air to show the grandstands that he'd made the catch.

Kyle helped him to his feet as they prepared for the next hit. Line drives, grounders, pop flies, it didn't matter—Jay Justice grabbed eight out of ten balls. For Kyle, swallowing these stats helped secure their friendship.

"You men better be getting to the country club," Doc Jody said. "Don't you start at ten o'clock?"

"Yeah," said Kyle, "and we still have to go pick up Peachy."

Jay nodded in agreement.

"Well, go to the den and grab a club out of my bag, Jay. Use the six-iron."

"I'll need an extra one, Dad," replied Jay. "Peachy's dad won't let him touch his clubs."

Jay lifted his red cap and brushed his palm across the stubble of a blonde burr. Kyle no longer submitted to the first day of summer sheep shearing as in years past. He liked his brown locks year round, and it had nothing to do with the girls and their itchy fingers.

As the ballplayers walked toward the outside door of the den, a room converted from a one-car garage, Doc Jody eased up behind and put his arms around their shoulders. "Let the game of golf teach you well," he said. "You win only when you lose yourself in the game. Relax and enjoy the walk."

Every now and then, Doc Jody would say goofy stuff like that.

As they tossed their ball gloves on the sofa, Kyle noticed the trophy wall. He had seen the wall hundreds of times, but he never really paid attention to Doc Jody's jam-packed golden golfers. He quickly counted 12 men swinging clubs on the top shelf, and then multiplied by four shelves to guess 48 total. He thought about his puny bowling trophies at home, and how he spaced them carefully between model cars, his collection of Famous Monsters of Filmland magazines, and a plastic heart that opened up to reveal the valves and stuff, just to fill one shelf. One short shelf.

Jay emerged from a closet with two clubs. "Let's go." He handed one of the irons to Kyle.

As they pedaled their bikes down the driveway, Kyle glanced back at a waving Doc Jody and a smiling Mama Justice on the top step of the front porch. One neat thing about living in El Viento was that things never changed...

...Peachy didn't live in the same neighborhood. In fact, he didn't live in a neighborhood at all. Rather, he and his dad resided on the outskirts of town,

hidden from the road by a fortress of evergreens. His great stone house, large and sprawling, had a regulation pool table and everything, including a poker room with a bar and wood-paneled walls covered with framed photos of ladies in their pajamas.

Peachy was the son of Peach Waterman, a mysterious town personality whose name alone set the adults to whispering. The senior Peach was rarely at home, so the boys walked in after no one answered the doorbell. They gawked at a four-foot statue of a lady whose bathrobe had slipped to her waist while carrying a jug on her shoulder. Risking the possible threat of eternal damnation, Chipper limited his stare to three seconds. One thousand one, one thousand two, one thou...

"Heyyy, you peckerwoods up there...we're downstairs." Peachy's voice rumbled out of the basement game room like a belch.

Walking down to the poker room, they were greeted by a musty odor and muffled speech. "I'm telling you, Mansfield is bigger," said one voice.

"Is not," said another.

"Is so," said the first.

Peachy was hosting one of his games with older boys, judging from the unfamiliar gravel voices. "Mansfield is 40-19-35½, and Monroe's only 37-24-37."

"You dumb shits," interjected the higher voice of Peachy, "the first number is just the inches around. You don't know who's the biggest unless you know the cup size. The cups are like batteries, from double-A to D. But I'm bettin' Mansfield is a triple-D, and I'll betcha five dollars."

"Oh, yeah, well how you gonna find out?" asked a deeper voice. "They don't give out cup sizes. It must be privileged information, or somethin' like that."

"Hey, guys," Kyle interrupted with an awkward squeak as he entered the poker room. Jay was two steps behind.

Peachy stood up and saluted the two as they entered the room. The older boys at the table didn't bother to look, tapping their cigars into ashtrays. After pushing his glasses back up over the bump on his nose, Peachy laid down his cigar and retrieved a red rabbit's foot from his jeans pocket. He stroked it three times, kissed it, stared at the ceiling, then stroked it again three times in the opposite direction. "Come on, baby, don't fail me now." He put the charm back in his pocket and sat down. Kyle noted Peachy's white tee shirt, without the Yankee logo.

Suddenly, Peachy locked into a staring contest with one of the older boys who was holding his fanned cards just beneath his eyes. Peachy needed nothing more than the eyes. The elder Peach had schooled the younger artist in the science of reading human beings. Every gesture had meaning unique for that particular individual, but the universal gesture was the pupils of the eyes. Peachy said his old man taught him that pupils dilate with pleasure and that this was an involuntary reflex, crossing all boundaries of biology. Dilated pupils meant the person was sitting on a good hand. Kyle thought it was cool-deluxe to have a dad who could teach you neat stuff like that.

"Hot diggity dog shit, I got you," yelled Peachy, throwing down his cards while raking in the loot. After taking a drag on his cigar, he pointed his circled lips toward the ceiling like a wolf howling at the moon, then blew a perfect smoke ring.

"C'mon, Peachy, we're gonna be late," said Kyle.

"Sure, sure. Gentlemen, it's been a pleasure. Feel free to stay and make yourselves at home. I've gotta leave for an hour or so to keep these morons happy..."

...Upon arriving at the country club, Kyle noticed that the kids at the top of the hill formed sort of a firing squad with rifles aimed at a lone figure. As the three friends reached halfway between the condemned soul and the line of executioners, Kyle turned around and stared at this poor old man who had more wrinkles than Boris Karloff wore in The Mummy.

The sunlight hit Methuselah as if a giant magnifying glass were focusing beams onto pure white hair. Bent forward at the waist, shoulders hunched, the man held his chin way out, reminding Kyle of a cartoon turtle attempting to stand on its hind legs.

"Get in line, fellas," said the fossil in a crackling drawl. "We just now commenced."

Kyle scanned the row of blue-jeaned kids as the three of them fell into the uniformed ranks. No girls. About 20 boys formed the line. Half he knew, while the rest were from the other grade schools. As expected, he and Jay were the only two boys wearing tee shirts with Yankee logos.

"Look how the Vardon grip has the pinky of your right hand overlapping the forefinger of your left," the old man said.

Kyle spotted the legendary L.K. Taylor from Madison School and was amazed that the great athlete had chosen to attend this first day of golf in the history of the Summer Recreation program at El Viento, Oklahoma. "L.K." stood for "Long Knock," a nickname born when a 323-foot home run sailed over the fence, smashing the windshield of the principal's Studebaker, all in regulation American Legion play. Most of the town believed it to be the longest home run by a sixth grader in the country, or at least in Oklahoma. And everyone knew L.K. would someday be a professional athlete, probably in all three sports—football, basketball and baseball.

"Hey," Kyle said under his breath to Jay, "get a load of L.K. Taylor. What's he doin' here? Golf isn't really a sport, is it?" After all, Kyle and his friends had only signed up because Archery and Diving were full, whereas Golf conveniently had three spots open.

"According to Webster's," Jay began, "a sport is a physical activity engaged in for pleasure."

"Oh, cut the friggin' crap, egghead," interrupted Peachy. "If that's the definition of a sport, then screwin' would be in the Olympics. Do they have Olympic golf? Hell, no. Case closed."

Peachy was right. Golf was more like a hobby, a recreation for old men.

"Then why," replied Jay, "are there pictures or references to golf on 26 pages out of 144 in the first issue of Sports Illustrated, *August 16, 1954?"*

Jay was right. Jay knew the facts and it was hard to argue with the facts. Of course, it was pretty darn hard to argue with Jay on anything. Sports Illustrated *would never give that much attention to a hobby.*

While the three of them fiddled with their grips, Kyle decided to think of the question as being true sports versus nonsports. When it came to true sports, Jay was the best athlete at Hightower, the grade school serving the new addition of town. On the other hand, Kyle excelled in nonsports. He could outswim, out-bowl, and out-Ping-Pong Jay, allowing a balance in their friendship. Given a choice, though, he would have preferred the blessing of true sports. As he thought more about the distinction between true sports and nonsports, the difference occurred to him: true sports were the ones that made the girls squeal.

"Head down, left arm straight...head down, left arm straight," the old man was saying over and over as the kids took practice swings at imaginary golf balls.

"Hey, Kyle, grip down on the club more like this," directed Peachy, quickly to assume expertise in this nonsport he had played for only five minutes. In truth, Peachy was still looking for a sport that would not humiliate him.

"Hey, hey, the Peach is going to be the next Arnie," he sneered. As he took his gangly swings, it seemed as though each extremity hated the others, flailing in different directions, until the clubhead finally scooped the ground.

"You, son, you've got a good swing," shouted the old-timer, as best as his quivering voice allowed. "Step out front here and let the other boys see."

Peachy began a confident stride toward the white-haired man.

"No, not you, sonny. That young fella' behind you."

Peachy scowled at the old man, then let his solo middle finger make a careful adjustment on his horned rims so that only Peachy's two friends appreciated a masterful flipping of the bird.

Everyone turned to look at a new kid as he stepped to the front. He had a burr haircut, with white scars coursing through the dark stubble of his scalp. Kyle thought it odd that he didn't wear a baseball cap, and that he kept his hair so short, almost as if he were showing off the scars. As the kid reached the old man, he turned where everyone could see at once that he had a black eye.

"Nice shiner," said Peachy.

"Who's that?" Kyle asked.

"He moved to town a few months ago," began Jay. Kyle and Peachy huddled close. "His name's Buster Nelson."

"Looks like a hood to me," said Peachy.

"I don't think so," Kyle replied. "Not with that haircut."

"Get this," Jay said. "He's a boxer."

"A boxer," cried the other two in unison. "Who does he box? Where? No one boxes!"

"I hear his dad teaches him to box, so he doesn't have time for other sports."

"I don't believe it," grumbled Peachy. "I say he's a hood, probably a street fighter. A boxer with gloves shouldn't get a shiner like that. At least not a kid boxer. I don't get it."

Kyle watched the instructor place a real golf ball at the feet of Buster the boxer. The entire row of prospective golfers then saw the kid lift a shot into the air with a swing nearly as smooth as the old geezer's.

"I'll be a monkey's friggin' uncle," whined Peachy. "Did you see that? The Peach doesn't believe it. That kid has played golf before. No one can step up there and hit balls like that." Peachy began practice swinging and swaying more feverishly in anticipation of his first crack at a ball. Then he looked up at the old man.

"Hey, gramps, when are we gonna hit some balls?"

Oh, God, thought Kyle. Did Peachy really call the old man "Gramps"?

With white hair gleaming and close-set eyes sparkling through wire spectacles, the old man trudged up the hill directly toward Peachy, then squared his stance. He smiled, and Kyle exhaled.

Peachy tried to smile back, but it wasn't easy, emerging as a smirk that could rip cellophane off a new deck of cards.

"I'll repeat my introduction for those of you who may not have heard. My name is Ethan Ashbrook." He smiled again at Peachy. "I've been playing golf here since the club opened in '29. Like I was saying, the summer recreation folks are letting me teach golf so as to get you kids interested in commencin' the sport. There's no sport that reflects the game of life better than golf. First and foremost, it takes self-discipline." He stared at Peachy, this time without smiling, with the sort of scary look that only old people can give just by being old.

For the first time in history, Kyle saw Peachy lose the stare contest and lower his head to the ground. But Peachy caught himself and quickly assumed a cocky, fidgety pose, flexing imaginary muscles.

Ethan Ashbrook poured some golf balls out of a large pail, and began hitting them toward a distant flag at the base of the hill. His rhythmic swing was identical each time, like the pendulum of a clock that sent each ball soaring the exact same trajectory toward the flag.

"Golf is unique," he continued while swinging away. "It's pretty much a

solo sport and your success will be based on whether you're a friend to yourself, or whether you become your own worst enemy."

Kyle wasn't sure he liked the sound of "solo sport."

"There's plenty of trouble on a course," Mr. Ashbrook said. "You can avoid it, recover from it, or let it ruin your game. That gol' dern trouble is always there, and you'll not get through a round without looking it straight in the eyes."

"Sounds like a real blast," cracked Peachy.

"Yeah," replied Kyle, "I thought we were here to have fun. This is starting to sound like church." He wondered if there was predestination in golf.

"Cool it guys," Jay said, "you're getting loud."

"Go read a book, Univac," countered Peachy.

A gust of wind broke the morning calm and ripped the baseball caps from the boys' heads. Caught in the dusty gale, the caps began to roll along the hilltop like tumbleweeds as the boys zigzagged to recapture their most prized possessions.

"That old south wind commences in the morning after sunrise, and dies down again after sunset. It'll always be there, so you have to learn how to play with it. Not against it. Just you and the elements." The old man stroked more shots toward the flag as he spoke, unfazed by the obvious hurricane.

As Mr. Asbrook continued the sermon on boundaries, hazards, and penalties, Kyle opted for faraway thoughts of Gail. He often pondered her flight from El Viento. First, the cars parked in front of her house, then the men in cowboy hats and string ties leading her father to the '58 white Ford Galaxy with the search light on the dashboard. Her mother crying. Gail being brave, not crying, her snow-white hair brushed by the wind. He had offered flowers picked from his mother's garden. Gail gave him her school picture in return, then pulled him behind the moving van. "Do you want to kiss me goodbye?" she asked. As he leaned in for his first kiss, she pushed him away and mocked, "You didn't say the magic words."

"The magic words?" he asked, startled.

"If you say, 'I love you,' then everything you do after is okay."

So he said, "I love you," and he meant it. Then, the kiss.

"Now you're my one true love," she said, "and you must wait for me to come back. Do you promise?"

"I promise," he said, with all his heart...

..."We're going to commence hitting some real shots," Mr. Ashbrook said. "I've given you each 10 balls, now we'll aim them toward the flagstick. Don't go too fast because I want to watch each of you. Check your feet. Are they set apart about as wide as your shoulders?" He watched Peachy spread his feet a little farther apart, overestimating the shoulder factor.

He set his own stance, then placed the clubhead behind the ball.

"...and keep those knees bent just a little...ball in line with your left heel...now just like the practice swings, keep your left arm straight as you bring 'er back, head down...bring 'er back, now...swing."

Kyle felt the pop of metal club against the ball and was startled to see it airborne. A 100-yard marker was planted beside the flagstick, and his ball scooted on past—well over 323 feet. Longer than L.K.'s legendary home run. Farther than a football field. Able to leap tall buildings. It made his biceps bulge and it felt great.

A THUD, then 'aw shit,' came from behind him. As Kyle spun around to look at Peachy's shot, a dust cloud blew into his face with the prevailing winds. His eyes were forced shut by the grit, and he began to spit mud. He could hear Peachy saying, "The grip is loose on this club. The Peach needs a new club."

"Jiminy Christmas, Peachy, did you set off a grenade?" asked Kyle, still wiping the dirt from his face onto his prized tee shirt.

After nine attempts to launch the perfect shot, one ball remaining, he heard a girl's voice from the street behind. "Hey, are you guys gonna teach us to play golf?" It was Kelly, Jay's steady girlfriend, getting off a bicycle-built-for-two, along with a new girlfriend. A cute, new girlfriend.

"Hey, Kelly, baby, waddya say?" drooled Peachy. "Who's your good lookin' friend?"

"She's too good lookin' for you, Peachy," Kelly replied with a cool reserved just for him. "So, how do you guys like golf? Jay? Kyle?"

The two boys looked at each other for the response. Peachy went back to raising puffs of dirt.

"Spit it out, boys," Kelly said, as she put her hands on her shapely hips. Kyle wondered if the buttons on her blouse would pop. She had changed so much during this past school year.

"Yeah, we like it fine," said Jay.

"Okay so far," added Kyle.

Jay had lucked out finding Kelly. She was a regular pal, and it confused Kyle as to whether being a pal might be more important than worshipping a goddess. He had been Jay's original best friend for as long as either of them could remember, long before Peachy joined them. After all, their doctor dads were partners, and they would be, too. After Kelly came along, the duo became a trio, and when the trio played, Peachy was excluded.

Kyle pictured the day it would be a permanent double date, after Gail returned from California. But Kelly didn't seem to approve of the idea, any more than she approved of Peachy. She seemed to have a sixth sense, so it was puzzling when she said Gail was "different." Finding the perfect match for him seemed to be a consuming pastime for Kelly.

"We're supposed to be on our way to water ballet," Kelly said, her eyes

darting between her girlfriend and Kyle, making a silent introduction. "We signed up for golf but there weren't enough for a girls' class. So ya'll have to teach us later. Right, Amy?"

Kyle squinted into the sun to get a better look at the other girl.

"Kyle, this is Amy. She just moved to town and she's in our grade."

"Hi, Amy," he nodded, lifting his cap and smoothing his hair against the wind.

"Hi, Kyle. Nice to meet you." Her voice was like a musical tone, incredibly rich, like the difference those long hollow tubes make converting a xylophone to a marimba.

Holding his baseball cap to block the sun, he finally got a good look at the new girl. She was a looker supreme. Standing by the tandem bicycle, wearing white shorts and a pink blouse tied at the waist, she stretched one arm toward him to shake hands.

What? He couldn't believe it. She was 20 feet away. He had never seen a girl offer her hand before. Did she really expect him to walk all the way over to shake? The gold streaks of her hair were catching the sunlight, and the wind formed teasing fingers in the lighter shade of blonde about her face. She was staring directly at him, smiling, hand outstretched, dangling, waiting.

He felt his feet carrying him toward her, and he could see that her deep green eyes were about the same color of the country club pool before they painted it blue. Freckles dusted her cheeks made full by dimples—not single-point dimples like a dart would make pressed against flesh, but line-dimples forming cute little creases. He reached for her hand, and they shook. She had a surprisingly strong grip that made his biceps bulge. More than when he ate his shoestring potatoes. More than Popeye's spinach. It was a long 20 feet back to his place in line.

"Listen, Kelly," said Jay, "we'll meet ya'll at the pool when we finish, okay?"

Even if this was a deliberate setup by Kelly and Jay, Kyle was game.

"Okay, but let's see you guys hit one first."

Kyle turned toward the girls. Amy's smile broadened, and Kelly was already beaming. He waited until the other kids finished their attempts then addressed the final ball.

"...just you and elements," echoed the voice of Mr. Ashbrook, "...plenty of trouble on a course...compete only against yourself..."

All eyes were riveted on him as he began his final shot. He could almost hear the applause, and through the ovation, he imagined a distant...squealing.

Another glance at Amy...then the swing.

It felt good. A scoop of turf lifted out of the ground as the ball soared toward the flagstick. A dust cloud rose where the ball hit first, then the shot bounced left and right before landing squarely at the base of the flagstick. A metal CLUNK signaled contact.

"Ooooo," squealed the girls. "You hit the flag, Kyle." He turned to see Amy clap her hands once, then hold them together, church-steepled near the V of her neck. She took one step forward, then stopped, hesitating, like she wanted to rush to his side, but couldn't.

Maybe golf was a true sport after all.

"Good shot," said Jay. "It's sort of a hole-in-one." He patted Kyle on the shoulder.

"Lucky stiff," chimed Peachy.

Kyle stretched to every bit of his four-feet-eleven-and-a-half-inches. He flipped the golf club in the air, one-half-turn, catching it by the head like it was the most natural thing in the world for a true athlete to do.

With a fake calm that implied he did this most every day, he began to brush away the turf stuck to the clubhead. He grinned and nodded to Amy, then looked down at the sole of the club and saw a number through the dirt. It was his lucky number 7.

"Great shot, Kyle," he heard Amy say.

1966

On a right-muggy day in April, with promised showers holding back as teasing vapor, Kyle "Chipper" DeHart ushered the team to the fifth tee box. Not the entire golf team, but three out of five.

Missing but accounted for at baseball practice was L.K. Taylor, jock supreme-o, Yankee hatchling, muscled mammoth, due to join them in a jiffy. They would then feel a wee bit smaller but a whole lot safer.

And Buster Nelson? Who knew? After his red-faced attempt to turn his driver into a slinky by wrapping it around a sapling on the fourth hole, Buster left his one-under status boiling on the course where the scintillating fumes—in spite of his subpar round—joined the vaporous threats in the sky. From there he had simmered off to the conniption colony, short fuse city, timebombsville.

That left three for now.

"So there you have it," Peach said. "The friggin' point of living is to get back to where we don't know the difference between so-called good and evil. The Bible calls it 'Paradise' straight out, and I'm talking about your sumbitchin' King James."

"Oh, you're so full of it," replied Chipper. "You're twisting everything around. Jiminy Christmas."

"Hey, peckerhead, take it up with Moses. He wrote it, not me. The world was perfecto before the broad muffed her apple test. Ya'll are missing the whole point of the Bible which, by the way, pardon my French, is a crock of bullshit for reality. I mean, if we have to die because of this Adam and Eve crap, why do animals have to die? Tell me that, why don't you?"

"Easy does it," cautioned Jay, who never liked stepping on the toes of the Almighty. Not even the little toes.

"But the symbolism is there," continued Peachy. "If we were all naked again and no one cared..."

"Shut up and hit the ball, Peachy, you've got honors," said Chipper.

Jay hadn't waited for Peachy to clam up before starting to the tee box. As he walked, he smoothed white zinc oxide ointment on his nose.

"Let's not hippety-hop so fast, froggy gremlin. The Peach here is the man. I'm up, not you. You screwed the pooch on that last hole."

"You're right, Peachy," said Chipper. "You do win one every now and then. You're up."

Peachy Waterman Jr. brushed the sandy bangs from his forehead, but the defiant mop toppled back to cover the horned rims that he finger-nudged over the bump on his nose. "Fuggin'-A," he said. "The Peach is hot."

He strutted to the tee box clutching his 6-iron. Not a confident stride but more of a screwball swagger. It seemed to Chipper that Peachy was always navigating through a minefield laced with hidden banana peels.

Peachy was especially snide today because of an incident at the first hole. Chipper had ordered him to back off and leave the escaped convict's garb—two striped shirts—hanging on the dead limbs of the cedar where the boys had spotted the bounty. Escapees from the adjacent federal prison grounds were common, so Peachy vowed to capture souvenirs another day.

"Genesis two-seventeen. Look it up, dipshits."

"Shut up and hit the ball, Peachy."

Some days, like today, Chipper couldn't stand to watch Peachy swing. It was ugly. Hideous. Irritating. An insult to the notion of athletic grace, making it even harder to defend golf as a sport. Rather than witness this blasphemy of the sacred history of the game, Chipper covered his eyes with his cupped hand. Peeking between his fingers, he saw Jay do the same, anticipating Peachy's misfire.

Clunk.

But the familiar sound was followed by an unfamiliar ka-boom!—the sound of a one-megaton cherry bomb. Chipper jerked his fingers from his eyes, halfway expecting to see a mushroom cloud.

The door to a metal toolshed 50 feet away in the rough flew open, and a shirtless man in prison-striped trousers emerged, both his bare arms reaching for the sky.

"Holy mother of shit," yelled Peachy, backing away, dropping his 6-iron. "I hit the...What the...?"

A second convict followed the first one out of the darkened doorway, his arms fired upward as well, searching for similar mercy.

"Oh my God," said Jay.

"Uh-oh...uh-oh," Chipper said as he noticed an evolving expression on the prisoners' faces—from initial fear to pleasant realization. Their arms dropped slowly to their sides as they sneered broken-toothed grins of relief toward each other.

"Fight or flight?" asked Jay under his breath.

"What?"

"Fight or flight? You know, adrenaline. Do we fight or do we run?"

Chipper scanned the golf course. It was nearly empty, as usual. Three golfers versus two felons. One was fat with spindly arms, but the other was lean and muscled.

Both convicts reached to the waistbands of their trousers at the same time that they began walking toward the golfers. Knife-like weapons appeared in their hands. The muscled jailbird with an eagle tattooed on his hairy chest smiled—at Chipper, it seemed.

Peachy bolted. No surprise.

The score was even now—two on two—but he and Jay were without weapons. "Fight or flight?" whispered Jay.

The golf course was their land, their homestead, and these rattlesnake varmints would never take that away. If they gave in now, how could the place ever be safe for women and children?

As if Matt Dillon himself began to tug at Chipper's arm, he felt his hand reaching for his Wilson Staff Aqua-Tite Strata-Bloc driver, carefully removing it from his bag and applying an extra-tight Vardon grip. Jay followed suit, selecting one of his long irons as a weapon.

Of course, the coward option was still open.

Chipper didn't want to die, not even a glorious death because, quite simply, he had more to say. More to do. He was wondering about the notion that an entire lifetime passed before your eyes during such moments. This did not occur. Instead, as he prepared for blood, with his raised arms reverberating with each explosive beat of his heart, a resurrected memory powered its way into his brain—a misty morning, five years ago, when he and the team first held these weapons in their hands, the summer after sixth grade. And those few holy hours, on a day that anointed him for predestined glory (he was sure) were squashed into the next few seconds. And it was the remembrance of his consecration that assured him that it was not his time to die...that he could defend his land...and make the world safe...

Chipper...no, all the way back to Kyle. Nickname christenings in sports were common, good or bad. In this case, Chipper was a badge Kyle wore with pride. After all, fate could have just as easily dropped a zinger on him like Hacker DeHart, Bunker DeHart, or even Duffer DeHart.

All the way back to Chipper...tumbling in chilly green water that soaked his lungs into a soppy sponge...then sneaking away to Jay's house where they borrowed a couple of Doc Jody's clubs...off to lasso Peachy on their way to that first golf lesson from Mr. Ashbrook...the surprise of seeing the great L.K. Taylor...Buster the boxer...the perfect shot with his own magical 7-iron...meeting Amy for the first time...Kelly. Then, departing from the events of that special day, an apparition began to rise out of the murky green swamp. Hands folded at chest level with angelic calm, head cocked to one side with a quizzical look, long-forgotten Gail Perdue whispered through her sweetly parted lips: "Destiny, Kyle. Remember our destiny."

Chipper's spell broke when he heard thundering footsteps and clattering golf clubs, mixed with guttural sounds of a striking warrior. The mammoth L.K. was pulling his newfangled Ping putter from his bag as he ran through Chipper and Jay toward the outlaws. As L.K. swung the putter above his head, letting it fly like a whirlybird, Chipper could hear the swooshing of parted air as the gold head of the putter crunched with a thud against the eagle tattoo of the hairy chest of the lean convict.

The two outlaws skedaddled out-of-bounds on Number 9 with L.K. Taylor bird-dogging their every step.

Chipper held his driver like an unfired rifle on his shoulder. Jay did the same with his 2-iron.

"Well, cut my legs off and call me Shorty," Chipper said.

"Call me dazzled," said Jay.

"Yeah, we're two lucky, dazzled sumbitches."

The next day, near dusk, Chipper sat alone in his Thunderbird, its front headlights pointing a determined path to the first tee box while the triplet taillights wasted their red streams on the empty parking lot behind. Peachy's mug was on the front page of the El Viento *Tribune*, splayed now across the steering wheel, a few imagined canary feathers clinging to the corner of his snarly smile, poster boy for Circumstance over Virtue.

After Peachy's tail-tucked sprint the day before, he had called

Freddy Ray and Bubba—Peachy knew all the cops by their first names, and they his—to alert the police of the escapees. By the time the law arrived, L.K. had cornered the two jailbreakers against the chain-link fence that surrounded the buffalo preserve on north Country Club Road.

Peachy accepted all the credit without so much as a blink. Chipper read the headline for the zillionth time as his eyelids fought to close:

Shank Mistaken for Gun Shot
Shocks Escapees from Shed

L.K. wouldn't mind the misplaced glory. After all, his name graced sports pages at least every week the year round, often in the big city newspapers as well.

Knowing that the story would be repeated for years with conflicting accounts, Chipper silently rehearsed his version—with only slight augmentation as to his own key role. Then, in a moment of mystic peculiarity, he felt his eyelids flutter shut, conjuring a substitute front page photo, perhaps born out of yesterday's dalliance with the Hereafter: a snapshot of him and his golfing pals reveling in victory on the first tee box, a trophy of gold nestled in the grass, teammates' captured smiles betraying ageless joy. When he believed his eyes to be open again, he could still visualize the trophied image, a mirage of sorts. The portrait was so real that he totally erased the convict yarn, consumed by a weighty premonition of events that would demand much more than a few measly, conflicting accounts. Rather, happenings just around the corner, but oh-so-far-reaching that flesh would be added to this dry-boned village every time the townsfolk uttered the words, "Remember when...?"

And a quiet voice urged him to take note, turn tales into testimony, and provide a passageway unto the second and third generations.

One

The majestic elm on the first hole was split down the middle, some said due to a lightning strike that divided the trunk eons ago. One-half grew straight with a celestial reach, while the other half bowed into an archway across the tee box as if groping for the turf. From the crown of the arch hung a section of logging chain, topped by a splintered sign with faded letters: "When this chain is parallel to the ground, it is too windy to play golf."

School was out, and two months had slipped by since Chipper's mirage on this very soil. With triple-digit heat for 10 straight days, and now the morning winds peppering his face with the gritty topsoil blown from Chief Crazy Hawk's adjacent land, Chipper could hear only a single tune:

We gotta get outta this place...

L.K. had completed his jump, setting the chain in motion with a swat eight inches above the free tip, followed as usual by Jay's airborne effort that grabbed the tip and stilled it again. Buster never joined the ritual and was cleaning dirt from the face of an iron, using a wooden tee to plow out the grooves.

"Go for it, Chipper," L.K. yelled. "You can do it, buddy."

"Come on, Chipper, today's the day," added Jay.

"Bet you miss," said Peachy.

Chipper looked beyond Jay and L.K., at the men lining up their putts on the nearby fourth green. Their brightly colored Banlon shirts were loose at the armbands, but stretched tight at the bellies. Skinny calves beneath Bermuda shorts could not hold up the socks that were intended to match the Banlons. Orange socks went with an orange shirt, light yellow was a shade away from cream, bright red struggled with crimson, and green declared all-out war with turquoise.

The foursome routinely puffed on stogies (or held a "chaw in jaw"), rambled nonstop about the glory of Dubya-Dubya-Two when men were men, and grumbled about the pantywaists in Washington who were too scared to stamp out Communism, all while playing lousy golf.

The mouthpiece for the group was Sarge, looking splendid in orange-on-orange today. Chipper noticed Sarge's cheek was puffed to the point of explosion by a wad of chewing tobacco. Golf held many mysteries, but one of the greatest was how Sarge could possibly visualize the ball as he putted, since his stomach bloated well into the calculated line of vision.

As his pals continued to cheer, Chipper noticed Sarge hesitate on his putt and glare at the boys, waiting for the noise to die down. Rather than honor Sarge's putt, Chipper saluted with an impish grin and began his run for the chain. Perhaps today was the day. He had never reached it before. He pushed off from earth so hard he was certain he altered the planet's orbit around the sun, if only a fraction. A boosting groan added extra inches to his leap. His hand stretched like Silly Putty for the metal links, but he felt only the shielding cushion of air that spelled "choke."

As he fell to the ground, he heard Jay, L.K., and Peachy in collective sympathy: "You're almost there, Chipper. I mean it, man. You've gotta be only a quarter inch away." "Next time, buddy, next time." "I knew you'd miss."

With his five feet eleven and three-fourths inches, and no growth for the past year, Chipper knew the only variable was the oomph in his spring. Jay was only five feet ten and could do it. L.K. was six-foot-four with long, thick muscles, so it was almost effortless. He would simply have to muster more oomph.

Chipper rose to dust himself off, noticing from one corner of his eye that Sarge remained on the fourth green along with his squad, all hands on all hips. Chipper joined the rest of the golf team at the bench, turning his back on Sarge and company.

"Hey, Peachy, your turn, man," hollered L.K., choking back laughter. The others joined in, feigning encouragement, knowing Peachy would barely leave the ground.

"Jump, Peachy, jump...jump, Peachy, jump," chanted L.K. as if cheering a basketball tip-off. Jay followed suit. As Chipper joined them in the cheer, he looked back at the grouch-bags. Sarge tucked his hands in his armpits as he crossed his arms and rested his elbows on the tabletop of his stomach where it curved out from the chest.

"Jump, Peachy, jump...jump, Peachy, jump." L.K. motioned for Peachy to back up for a longer run prior to takeoff, knowing such a move had little to offer.

"Jump, Peachy, jump. Jump, Peachy, jump."

With the determined look of a world-class high jumper, Peachy began his sprint toward the chain. At the critical point where he planted his foot for the leap, Peachy's knee buckled. His other leg saved him from a complete fall, but the overcompensation sent him in flailing gyrations, charging toward the team, unable to stop. As Chipper braced to grab him, he caught only the look of terror in Peachy's eyes prior to impact. Like a bowling ball picking up the 7-10 split, Peachy took out both Chipper and Jay, as the three of them fell against the wooden bench, tipping it backward and spilling them onto the fringe of the fourth green.

As Chipper looked up from the ground, a huge orange sphere hovered above like a hot air balloon.

"You fuggin' flatbellies are too damned loud," scolded Sarge. "Golf's supposed to be quiet, so you girls better learn to shut yer fuggin' traps."

The hideous sound of a loogie in its birth canal began to gurgle in Sarge's throat. Even though Chipper couldn't see Sarge's face around the orange horizon, he knew it would be disgusting. *Ptoooey!* A large wad of tobacco juice landed on the ground between Peachy and Chipper. They both wiped away stray drops of the spit-juice combo that hit their faces.

Jay, unscathed, was first to his feet and first to apologize. "Sorry, Sarge, we got carried away."

"Yeah, sorry," added Chipper, not quite so sincere, still feeling the poison on his cheek even after the tobacco juice was wiped away. He gave Peachy his hand and lifted him to join the others. "You okay, Peachy?"

"You bet. The Peach is always okay."

They watched Sarge turn and start to waddle away. Peachy was uncharacteristically quiet. For a while.

"Hey, Sarge," Peachy called after him. The Sarge paused and turned his head. "I hear you broke a hundred for the first time last week. How's it feel to master the game?"

"You're a smart ass, Peachy Waterman. A smart ass just like your old man." Sarge pointed his putter at Peachy. "You screw with me, and I'll kick your butt."

Peachy yelled back, "Wha'd you say? I couldn't hear ya'. You say you wanna kiss my *butt?*" Then Peachy turned around, bent over, and pointed to his own rump. But Sarge had already turned to walk away.

Two

After watching Sarge and his troupe mosey out of sight, Chipper directed his attention to the Chief's house. A museum of dilapidated farm equipment surrounded the unpainted dwelling, nearly hidden from view by weed trees and wild-growing shrubs. The house on this one-man reservation, complete with a windmill missing most of its blades, was situated on a gentle rise, about a football field from the golf course. Chipper could only imagine the value of hundreds, if not thousands, of golf balls that rested beyond that barbed wire property line, which served as out-of-bounds for holes Number 1 and Number 2.

No one knew if he was a real Indian chief or not, but whenever he surfaced on the front porch of his two-story ramshackle house, toting his .22 rifle loaded with bacon rinds, the authenticity of his title really didn't matter much. Chipper wondered about the improbability of bacon bits traveling through the barrel of a .22, but the story had been told for years as if it were true. And, given the choice of facing Chief Crazy Hawk and his bacon rinds, or wading the creeks in order to restock their golf ball supply, the team would always pick the creeks, complete with broken glass and water moccasins.

"What do you figure Mr. Ashbrook wants with us?" asked L.K. as he milked the grip on his driver, veins bulging all the way up his arms.

"Betcha it's just another one of Ethan's sermons," said Peachy.

"He wants to talk to us about our season," Chipper said, liaison to the team, since fate had placed his locker in the clubhouse next to Mr. Ashbrook's.

"What's to say? We did great," began Jay. "Best in school history.

Our 15 and 4 in match play was a 78.947 win percentage...rounded down."

"And friggin' conference champs," added Peachy. "What more do you want?"

"Yeah, five returning lettermen," said L.K. "Even Peachy finally lettered. Makes you wonder."

"Screw you, L.K. The Peach is on a roll. My letter will be the same friggin' size as yours."

L.K. laughed.

Chipper felt sick to his stomach. He had lettered this season as a junior, but he wasn't yet a true letterman. He still had to be initiated, and the Letterman's Club fights weren't scheduled until August, right before the school year.

L.K. and Jay were already initiated, having lettered in the true sports as freshmen. Buster had lettered in golf as a sophomore, but missed initiation last year for unknown reasons. Rumors circulated about his hands being registered, or something like that. Chipper had slipped onto the A-team this year as fourth man while Peachy played a precarious fifth.

Chipper, Peachy, and Buster would all have to fight this August. As a would-be lover, the fight was an unthinkable rendezvous for Chipper. Sixteen-ounce gloves, the river bottom, bloodletting or a knockout for the finale, the whole thing made him sick. But he knew he would never be able to wear the letterman's jacket without proving he could fight to the finish.

Chipper spotted the white-haired old man trudging up the concrete stairs of the basement pro shop. "Hup two, guys," he said to the rest of the team. "Here he comes."

"Well, goody gumdrops," sneered Peachy.

The closer Mr. Ashbrook shuffled to the practice tee, the more each golfer assumed attention. Even Peachy. By the time Mr. Ashbrook was within whisper distance, all five of them were statues.

"At ease, fellas." He grinned as he studied them head to toe. After inspection, he struck a match to light his pipe. Chipper noticed that the knuckles of his hands seemed more gnarled than before.

"Two shots...per man...per round."

"What's that, sir?" asked Chipper, since Mr. Ashbrook was staring mostly at him.

"Two shots...per man...per round. That's the difference between you fellas and those Castlemont rich kids who are having their picture made right now with the state championship trophy."

"But, sir, there were four teams ahead of us at state," L.K. said.

"We lost by 20 shots."

"Just plain malarkey. You're looking at it wrong, son."

"Mr. Ashbrook's right," said Jay. "Our low fourball, that's leaving Peachy's score out, averaged 308. That's a 77 average per player. If each man shot two less on the three rounds, we'd have won state by four strokes."

"Jay," asked the white-haired mentor, "can you get two strokes off your game?" Jay nodded yes.

"L.K.?"

Another nod.

"Buster? Chipper?"

Mr. Ashbrook hesitated a moment. "Peachy?"

Everyone knew Peachy was slippery in medal play where each stroke counted, jinxed by a shank—a near-grounder squirting extreme right—which could send his score skyrocketing on a single hole. This plague was fatal in medal tournaments like conference and state where, fortunately, only the lowest four scores counted. Individual contests against other high schools were match play, using five-man teams in pairings, so a shank-induced triple bogey would cause Peachy to lose only that particular hole. Peachy could hit his irons for weeks without a shank, but when it descended like a fog, the shank was there to rule. And it might last for several days. L.K. would say, "Peachy's having his period." Peachy admitted it was a curse.

"Sure, Peachy can shave two points," offered Chipper. "He can get rid of 10 shots a round, because we're gonna get rid of the shank this summer."

"The Peach'll be hell on wheels without the shank."

In truth, even without the shank, Peachy struggled to break 80. "Good. That's good," Mr. Ashbrook said with a conciliatory tone. "Before you fellas hit away, I want to mention something."

He puffed at his pipe, but gave it a quizzical look when no smoke returned. As he tried to light it again his match refused to stay lit, the south wind gaining momentum, blasting heat and dirt against their skin.

"Huddle 'round, fellas. Block that wind for me."

The five young golfers moved in close. Maybe closer than they'd ever been to Mr. Ashbrook before, because Chipper had never noticed how his cool blue eyes sank so deep into their sockets. Each boy stood shoulder to shoulder as the old man continued with repeated match strikes.

"It's not so easy as it sounds for you to trim two shots, but I'm going to tell you the secret how. Huddle closer...that darned wind."

Their semicircled accordion could squeeze no tighter. Chipper felt the sweat of Peachy's arm on one side and Jay's on the other. In the summer, they played shirtless, much to the dismay of adult club members.

"We Okies made it through the dust bowl..."

With peripheral vision, Chipper watched Peachy to make sure he didn't start rolling his eyes or fidgeting.

"...because we stuck together. It was not, mind you, every man for himself. We shared, we worked, we encouraged..."

Still no smart aleck remark by Peachy.

"...and we didn't just survive, we thrived. We're stronger now, and we did it through teamwork. Teamwork. That's the secret."

The match lit, and the tobacco glowed while the golfers stood their ground. Ethan Ashbrook scanned the row as he talked.

"I'm always spoutin' off 'bout golf being a sport for individuals, but I see something special in you fellas. If you build each other up, support each other, you might discover a sort of...chemistry. A sort of...magical bond that changes your game. Maybe as much as two strokes per man per round."

Chipper loved the word 'magical.'

"I've spent the past five years with each of you teaching fundamentals. But golf instruction is overrated, my friends. After all, who taught the old masters? Why, no one. Think about it. They taught themselves. You're beyond me crabbing at you now as you shoot for a new level. Beyond good. Beyond excellent. To the mental game. That's what I'm talking about, fellas. The mental game that comes from the spirit...the magic...of teamwork. I've not given a squat for team golf...that is, until I had the privilege of schooling you five. So now, make the five become one."

Chipper was inspired. He knew he could never be competitive as an individual in golf, but he could help fuse this team into a magical bond. Each man had his role in life, and Chipper felt his was often determined by moments like this.

"Now let's see you fellas hit some."

"On the tee, playing first man for El Viento High School...Jay Justice," mocked Peachy, as if the practice tee had suddenly become the state tournament.

Jay addressed his drive with perfect calm, as if the wind weren't even blowing. Blonde-haired and fair-skinned, he was the only team member always in headgear—today a boating hat with the rim turned down—and always with white zinc oxide plastered on his nose. Using this careful regimen, he would tan until his skin was darker than his hair. If he ever strayed, though, it was lobster city. He hit a gentle fade up the left side of the fairway such that the crosswind actually added distance, coaxing the ball to the right side of the fairway, 290 yards from the tee.

"Perfect drive, Jay," said Mr. Ashbrook, followed by the others who copied the compliment.

"Next up, second man, L.K. Taylor, a golf ball's worst nightmare," Peachy said.

L.K. didn't have to worry about the wind. The power of his drives cut through the atmosphere, ignoring resistance. Unfortunately, his skills took a precipitous drop after the power drive which, of course, was no good to him on the par 3s.

Watching L.K. swing at the ball always reminded Chipper of Babe Ruth as he pointed his club skyward, predicting a home run over the center field wall. L.K.'s bone structure wasn't really that big, but his jam-packed muscles made him seem invincible. A decathlete as opposed to a shot-putter. L.K.'s old man was the shot-putter type, and he ridiculed golf as a sissy sport. L.K. didn't act like he cared. In spite of apparent testosterone poisoning, L.K. barely needed to shave his snowplow jaw that flared at the sides, and his voice was as high as Dennis Day on the Jack Benny Show. Chipper found this mismatch difficult to understand.

L.K. blasted a high, long drive up the center of the fairway. He stood motionless in his follow-through, the sunlight tinting his short kinky hair in various shades of copper and brown.

"Just under 320," he said.

Buster nodded in agreement with the distance call.

"Hit 'em Buster." Peachy the announcer was carefully polite.

Buster teed the ball and stretched his wiry frame. He began his Big Bad Wolf huffing and puffing as he worked himself into a frenzy. Buster hated the ball. When his scowling face turned red, it was time to start his backswing. Perfect swing—crack—perfect drive. If it weren't for his temper costing him three or four shots a round, he'd probably be first man, figured Chipper. And no one could judge distances like Buster, even on courses he had never played before.

Buster brushed his straight black hair out of his eyes. He had the longest hair on the team, conveniently covering his scalp scars, keeping it one-sixteenth of an inch shorter than expulsion during the school year. Chipper noticed how his face stayed a bit red even when he wasn't swinging at the ball. Buster's skin was bumpy, not with pimples, just a sheet of little lumps that would camouflage any zit. And for some reason, his left eyelid drooped a little more than the right.

"Great shot, Buster," said Mr. Ashbrook. Buster rarely made eye contact with the other players, but Chipper often noticed that he would look directly at Mr. Ashbrook, and then it didn't seem that his face was quite as red.

"I didn't hit it exactly square," he said. For Buster, that was a lengthy discourse.

"And now, hitting fourth for El Viento," began Peachy, "that man with the golden 7-iron, that scrambler who can get down in two from any fringe, the only man who threatens par without ever hitting a green in regulation...Chipper DeHart."

Chipper addressed the ball with his 2-wood. Mr. Ashbrook and the others chuckled at Peachy, but the words rang true. He would rather be chipping from the fringe for a birdie than facing a long putt.

Unlike Jay who had the control and finesse to play the wind for extra distance, Chipper had to do the exact opposite, drawing into the crosswind when going west, then fading against the gusts coming east. Fighting the wind trimmed his distance, but allowed him to hug the fairways. And, after all, he didn't really need to hit the greens in regulation anyway. Up and in. Again and again.

A respectable drive landed him 260 yards from the tee, barely in the left rough.

"And now," L.K. said, "hitting his Shirley Temple slice..."

"Screw you, L.K.," Peachy replied as he put his wooden tee in the ground. Everyone laughed. That is, everyone except Buster who never really found Peachy to be that amusing.

Peachy's swing was a conglomerate violation of all known golfing principles. As Jay would put it, The Swing was a marvel of modern physics: for every action, there is an equal and opposite reaction. Or even algebra: a negative multiplied by a negative equals a positive. For L.K., it was a challenge to fight back the laughter before Peachy hit the ball. And for Chipper, it was orchestrated chaos that contained a hidden flaw...a flaw that needed to be exorcised.

Peachy brushed back his sandy bangs from the rim of his glasses. With mole-like eyes, he was one of those rare people who actually looked better with the magnifying power of lenses. Peachy had one of those mushy bodies where there's not an ounce of fat, but no identifiable muscles either. As he addressed the ball, his sly grin disappeared, and it almost seemed that he took the game seriously.

Everyone knew what to anticipate, but it was still amazing each and every time. With his left wrist cocked upward overriding the grip, and his left shoulder pulled up Quasimodo-style toward his ear, he would pause with the clubhead at the ball for five to ten seconds, a long five to ten seconds, motionless. Who knew what was going through his head at this point? Then, Peachy would raise the clubhead straight up, take it back at a right angle parallel to the ground, then forward, then up and back down, very, very slowly to the ball. His teammates accused him of making a sign of the cross, but Peachy would always protest.

Chipper theorized that Peachy tacked on new rituals to his swing, hoping for a better outcome, but he never shed the old ones. Not so long ago the clubhead simply went up and down. Now the multidirectional water-witching was established as the norm, and Chipper was noticing a new direction of the club, a small circle at the top of the cross, before Peachy brought the club face to the ball.

The first hint that Peachy's swing was finally underway was a nearly imperceptible wiggle of his butt to the left, which probably cost him 20 yards in distance in that it led to the infamous 'wiggle to the right,' which was far more perceptible, if not outright laughable.

An overextended backswing would twist his head around like an owl, then the downswing, which was followed by the traditional "Awshit." And finally, a posed follow-through as if a gallery of 10,000 were watching him at the Master's. "I missed it," he would say to explain either the direction, or the distance, or both.

And now, Peachy's drive began. Quasimodo. Pause. Cross with a circle at the top. Wiggle to the left. Wiggle to the right. Backswing brings club shaft within a hair of twisted head. Downswing. *Crack.* "Awshit." Master's pose.

The ball went perfectly up the middle, unaffected by the wind, farther than Chipper's drive.

"Fair. Just fair," came Peachy's response.

It was a marvel of modern physics. Or algebra. Or as Chipper believed, Peachy was quite simply a guy who was, on occasion, visited by Lady Luck.

Three

No girls allowed. At least not until after 5:00 PM. Such was the official policy of the El Viento Country Club, a rule that Amy vowed to change someday. Chipper had to remind his girlfriend, frequently, that Tuesday was Ladies' Day, and that she should be pleased with this designation. After all, there wasn't a Men's Day. Amy didn't bite on this line of reasoning.

She would play her 18 in the evenings, often coming in under 90. Her scores beat Peachy's with increasing frequency, especially if he had the curse. After winning Ladies' A Flight last year in the club tournament, she planned to move up to Championship Flight this year.

Chipper thought her knowledge of the game was eerie, like with club selection where she seemed to know his game better than he did. When Amy said, "Hit the 4-iron," he would hit the four and she would be right.

Chipper shot his average 78 earlier in the day, unable to shave two strokes in spite of Mr. Ashbrook's inspirational pep talk. He was looking forward to a sunset round with Amy, Jay, and Kelly. No wind. No pressure.

"Jay, how'd you shoot today, hon?" Kelly asked from the open window of her car.

"73, with two double bogeys."

"Gee, must have had some birds, huh?"

Kelly pulled her clubs, all six of them, from her yellow Volkswagen, then started walking toward Jay. They deep-kissed. Right there by the first tee box.

"How'd you do, Chipper?" Kelly asked after she surfaced for air.

"78. Six bogeys and the rest pars."

Chipper smiled as Amy's red Corvair pulled up beside the Volkswagen.

"Sounds like you had a better day than Amy," she said in warning, as he watched his girlfriend step from her car and pull the strap of her plaid golf bag onto her shoulder. He didn't understand. Amy hadn't even played golf yet today.

As she got closer, Chipper could see that her eyes were red. Contact lenses again, he thought. He gave her a peck on the cheek, not to be totally outdone by Jay. Jay and Kelly could wrap themselves up in an exchange of saliva sure to gross out every adult at the country club, and most of the kids. But that was as risqué as they got. Light petting. No beer.

"What's wrong, Amy?"

"Nothing."

She sounded strained.

"No, really. What's wrong?"

"I said...'nothing.'"

"Kelly said you had a bad day."

Amy smelled like the roses that grew by her front porch. He hugged her, then pulled her head to his shoulder, stroking her hair, right down to the Breck flip.

"Nothing, I tell you. Let's play some golf."

"Jay and I are playing our own twosome," announced Kelly. "We'll start on number 1, and you two start on 5."

Uh-oh, thought Chipper. Some pregame planning had occurred.

Jay shrugged his shoulders to declare innocence, then he and Kelly locked arms and strolled toward the wooden bench near the number 1 tee.

Amy pulled away, banging Chipper in the knee with her golf bag as she spun around toward the fifth tee.

"You sure you're okay?" he called out after her. She threw her clubs down on the tee box, metal rattling like a monkey shaking its cage at the zoo. *What was going on? She was always in a good mood. Always. This was bizarre.*

"I haven't done anything, have I?" he asked.

"Nope, *not a thing*, Chipper."

Amy pulled out an iron and addressed the ball. Chipper loved this point in her swing. She had cute curves and, with her fanny sticking out, knees bent, poised for the swing, she reminded him of a ballerina starting a plié. The corners of her mouth turned up naturally, so it was hard to tell when she was really smiling. Her summer tan seemed to last all year, and no matter how she wore her golden hair—today with a pink headband—she always looked luscious.

He had never seen her swing with so much force. The ball shot from the tee and headed beyond the green.

"Too much club, Amy."

"I hit the 3-iron, like I always do here," she snapped.

Chipper's tee ball landed on the fringe. As they walked down the fairway, he took Amy's hand in his, but he felt a gnawing in his stomach. What the heck was going on?

"Chipper, we've gone steady for three years now. Right?"

"Right."

"And we really dated off and on for two years before that. As much as you can date at that age. And I put up with all the girls chasing you..."

"What do you mean 'chasing me'? The boys were after you like hotdogs looking for a bun."

"But they leave me alone now that we go steady. The girls don't do that. They still flirt with you. I understand. I mean who can resist your dark, wavy hair and those Bambi eyes? I know all that, and I know you've been true to me."

"So what's this about, Amy?"

"It's about us, Chipper. It's about love, and it's about commitment. I don't mean marriage so much right now. You know Jay and Kelly talk marriage all the time, and I never ask that of you. I may or may not want it some day, but I'd never ask it. I'd do anything for you, and I see myself as your perfect partner."

"I agree, Amy."

"You've got so many talents, Chipper. You've got brains, you're a leader, you're creative...you're really going to do something big someday, I just know it."

He nodded his head in agreement.

"But do you know that you need me?"

"Of course, I know it."

"But do you really, really know it? For example, do you remember how you got in trouble, you and Peachy, when we were broken up that time? There's something in your system, Chipper. You take risks, you take chances. When we're together, you don't. Am I right?"

"You're right, Amy. Everything you're saying is true. That's why I love you. You make me want to do the right thing."

"I'll be your partner, Chipper, always at your side. That's commitment, sweetie, with an eye to the future. But you never talk about the future."

"Is that what this is all about? That I don't talk about the future?" He felt defensive, but he held back. *What started all this? She was fine 24 hours ago. What happened?*

"I think about the future all the time," he said.

"Sure, you do. You think about being senior class president next year, you think about being Big Man on Campus the year after that, you think about medical school, and on and on. But, Chipper, where am I? You have incredible dreams, incredible goals, but am I there? And do you even wonder about *my* dreams?"

Amy pulled away to enter the trees for her next shot. Chipper felt like a jury had just convened and convicted him. And, in spite of the Supreme Court's 5-4 decision two weeks ago, no one had bothered to read him his rights. Something had to be deeper, and darker, than dreams and commitment to make Amy this upset.

She pulled a pitching wedge from her bag, and started to chip back to the green, but couldn't get the shot off. Chipper watched her try to figure out how to play the ball. But before she made her backswing, she had to wipe something from her eyes. Surely, not tears. Amy Valente never cried. Oh, there was that one time when she talked about her dad leaving and how tough it was being the only girl in school whose parents were divorced. Jeez, anyone would cry at that. She was only seven at the time her father vanished. And she never saw the guy again. No, it couldn't be tears. Probably, it was those newfangled contact lenses. No one could brave the Dust Bowl with plastic in their eyes.

Four

Day 19 with thermometers above the sizzle-mark. No rain, and none in sight. Odd-even water rationing had been converted to zero outdoor watering. Worst of all, a burn ban had forced cancellation of the country club's annual Fourth of July fireworks display, a celebration so deep-rooted in the hearts of El Viento's youth that Chipper feared an uprising, if not outright anarchy.

In spite of the midmorning breeze gaining strength, Chipper felt like he was wearing three layers of wool. *I gotta get out of this place*, he thought.

Why had Peachy wanted to meet him here in the deserted parking lot of the high school? As he stood on the hot asphalt, leaning against the open door of his Thunderbird, he felt like a Pillsbury muffin on one of those baking trays, expanding in the oven with time-lapse photography.

The squealing tires of Peachy's red Corvette spinning into the parking lot signaled the alarm that the muffin was fully baked. After skidding to a stop, the driver's door flew open and the defiant melody of Lovin' Spoonful's "Summer in the City" poured onto the baking tray, along with Peachy.

"Get your clubs outta your trunk!" he yelled.

"What?"

"Your bag. Get it out of your trunk."

Sometimes it was easier not to ask.

"Now, take your irons out," Peachy said as he ducked his head back into the Stingray.

"Sweet mother in heaven!" Chipper said as he watched Peachy emerge with major league contraband. "What in the world is that?"

The missile would have passed for army surplus if it weren't for the red, white, and blue decorations.

"It's the star-spangled friggin' banner," Peachy replied. "Fifty balls of light will explode out of this baby."

"What the..."

"I'll be damned if those commie pinkos at city hall are gonna destroy another American institution. We're gonna have our own July Fourth celebration."

"How...where?"

"Poor little Gus was working the register at the pro shop and, well, all the keys are kept there, you know. And, so, here we are. The sumbitches were gonna spoil anyway, so I took one."

"Peachy, you stole it?"

"Not stole, my friend. I'm fighting for liberty. Fighting for the right to celebrate this great fuggin' country."

Peachy cradled his shady symbol of liberty as he made the transfer from his car to Chipper's golf bag, then he stuffed the rocket into the bag like ramrodding a cannon.

"So why drag me to jail with you, Mr. Freedom Fighter?"

"Here's the deal, Chipper. Keep cool, my boy. Take this sumbitchin' rocket to my locker at the country club. You know the combination."

"Why don't *you* do it?"

"The old man just popped in unannounced. He came back into town early for the father-son tourney this afternoon. When he pulls his tricky shit, like coming home early, he white-gloves my car."

"White gloves?"

"Yeah, you know. He checks every square inch for dirt. Or, so he says. But we both know he's looking for the old booze-ola, or rubbers, or both. My ass'd be grass if he caught me stealin'...uh, if he found this rocket in my possession."

"When are you planning this so-called celebration?" Chipper asked. "And do you know how to set this sucker off?"

"Elementary, my dear Chipper. A piece of guttering, bury it in the ground. Dumbshit Gus is gonna take care of the preparations after sundown tonight. In the rough on the first hole, I figure. That way, all the kids in town can watch it from their cars on Country Club Road."

"What! You're telling everybody in town?"

"Back off, now. I'm not tellin' anything about who or what. I'm taking full responsibility. And I'm taking full credit when the sumbitch lights up the sky. I won't mention the whole golf team is out there, helping, and it'll be too dark to see us."

"The whole golf team? What are you talking about?

"Teamwork, Chipper. Didn't you listen to Mr. Ashbrook's sermon? You know full well we got some serious problems on this team. Now I don't want to mention anyone's name, like Buster Nelson, the friggin' asshole. But we're one helluva long way from that magical bond shit Mr. Ashbrook was blabbering about with his verbal diarrhea. We need to do this, Chipper. We need to do it...for the team's sake."

Peachy could make sense out of the most garbled state of affairs. And Chipper felt a deep sense of responsibility for finding ways that the team could unify. This moment wasn't about transfer of hot property. It was Peachy seeking Chipper's blessing. Leadership carried a burden, clearly, with such weighty decisions.

"I'll have the team there," Chipper said with a sigh, only halfway relieved about his choice.

"Great. I knew you'd do it."

John Sebastian was still singing on the radio: *Walkin' on the sidewalk, hotter than a match head...*

"When should I tell everyone to be there?"

"Nine-fifteen tonight. It'll be good and dark by then."

Peachy strutted back to the red Vette, while Chipper lifted the loaded cannon into his trunk.

"And don't forget," Peachy added, "the tourney starts at noon today. Act like nothin's happening."

Before the Vette pulled away, Chipper gestured for his friend to roll down the driver-side window.

"Hey, Peachy, one question. Why didn't you smuggle this thing to your locker yourself?"

Through his carnival huckster's grin, Peachy replied, "Teamwork, lad...it's the magic of teamwork." Then he rolled up his window, smothering Sebastian: *In the sum*——.

Five

The shot ricocheted off Hacker's tree, then the foursome hit the dirt to save their lives, though Chipper was dying mostly of embarrassment. Once again, it was the Father-Son Tournament, and Chipper's dad had just teed off.

"Hit another one, Leonard," offered Doc Jody, Jay's dad.

Chipper remained silent. Hacker's tree was in the middle of the fairway creek, below the elevated first tee box and well out of the way of decent golfers.

After adding his mulligan shot as a donation to Chief Crazy Hawk's stockpile out-of-bounds, Leonard DeHart, M.D., finally hit a playable drive. For Chipper, it was torture.

Jody Justice teed his ball. 'Suave and de-boner,' Peachy would say about the Doc, but clearly he was the coolest dad in El Viento. Chipper always figured if he could somehow get into Sherman and Peabody's "Way-Back Machine" and travel back 30 years to when Doc Jody was a teenager, they probably would've been friends, cruising the strip, talking about girls and stuff.

"Lenny, we've got unlimited mulligans today," Doc Jody said. "Don't you agree?"

"Sure do," replied Chipper's dad.

Chipper tried to laugh.

Dr. Justice's swing was as polished as anyone on the PGA Tour. He had been club champion every year he had entered the contest. Needless to say, Doc Jody and Jay were a cinch for the Father-Son trophy. Doc Jody cracked a textbook drive over 300 yards, fairway perfect.

As Chipper approached the tee, he turned and spotted Peachy and his dad—the real Peach Waterman—getting ready to tee off as a lonely twosome following the DeHart-Justice foursome. Chipper felt horrible.

With club rules mandating five maximum per group, Peachy and his dad would be sequestered, just like the entire town would have voted it. Chipper turned to his father, "Hey, Dad, let's let the Watermans play with us. There's no one else waiting to tee off."

"No sixsomes, Kyle," grumbled his father. "Hit your drive."

Chipper knew it was more complicated than the rule about no more than five players per group. It was about Peach Waterman. It was about the new gold Cadillac every year, the young girlfriends draped in diamonds, the red Corvette Stingray for Peachy's sixteenth birthday, and the globe-trotting—which left Peachy Junior at home to fend for himself. And the adults would chant in unison: "No visible sign of income."

Chipper nodded to Peachy Junior, adding an index-fingered wave with a quarter-twist of the wrist that only teenaged boys could master. Peachy signaled back.

"Hit the ball, Kyle," growled his dad.

Chipper closed his waving hand into a fist, a fist he had to relax before he could slip into his pocket for a wooden tee. He powered his drive down the left center of the fairway, 270 yards off the tee as measured by a struggling baby cedar nearby.

"Imagine what I'd do with a driver," he pronounced to the open air, loud enough for the ears of his father whose third drive had fallen 40 yards short of Chipper's. He had a knack for ignoring the truth about the 2-wood. And the truth was that he didn't have enough control to use a driver.

Jay smiled at his dad as he teed his ball. Doc Jody had a pipe in one corner of his mouth, but he smiled back with the other corner.

Chipper wished his dad would, for once, give him a smile like that, a smile that said, "All is well." Then, as if he were psychic, Doc Jody took the pipe from his mouth, and used both corners to deliver just such a smile to Chipper. All was well.

Jay's drive landed even with his father's, both of them looking at birdie potential. "Hey, Pop," said Jay, "one of us should get the eagle."

Doc Jody didn't seem to hear his son. He winked at Chipper, then turned to big Peach and little Peachy and said, "Mr. Waterman, you fellas go ahead and hit, then join us, why don't you?"

Chipper's dad mumbled something under his breath about the dregs of society and the burden of public scrutiny. Chipper felt warm inside.

"Peachy, what's happenin', man?" asked Chipper, with a conscious effort to spill no beans regarding proposed rocket trajectories later tonight.

"Not much." He added in a whisper, "Gettin' any?"

"Naw."

"How 'bout you, Jay? How's the angle of your dangle?"

"Zero."

Peachy's dad stepped toward the tee. Chipper had never been this close to the real Peach Waterman before. He was a big, imposing man, with wavy black hair combed straight back with more than a dab of Brylcreem. He looked right through, or beyond, every other person on the first tee box. But he shook Doc Jody's hand, then hit a fairly good drive.

"The old man's a hacker," Peachy said, not too far removed from that designation himself. "I'll wax his butt."

"Peachy, the Father-Son Tournament means you team up with your father, not against him," Chipper said. "No one's gonna beat the Justice team, but you might take the handicap trophy."

"Screw that crap." Peachy pushed his glasses up and brushed away his bangs. "I'll sandbag a few holes, let the old man up the ante, then plaster him on the back nine."

Quasimodo. Pause. Cross with a circle at the top. Wiggle to the left. Wiggle to the right. Backswing with overswing. Downswing. *Crack*. "Awshit!" Master's pose. Duck hook out-of-bounds onto Chief Crazy Hawk's property. Peachy grinned at Chipper as if to say, 'It's all part of the strategy.'

Peachy's next drive stayed in bounds, so the sixsome began their march down the fairway. Jay's dad carried his bag on his shoulder like one of the boys, and Peach Waterman drove an electric cart for himself and his son. Chipper's dad pulled his bag on a two-wheeler cart used mostly by the ladies, the old men, and the hackers. It was humiliating.

With the Watermans in their cart and the Justices ten paces ahead, Chipper was facing inevitable conversation with his father. This close, there was always tension even before the words began.

"Kyle, I've been thinking."

Uh-oh.

"You ought to consider professional golf as a career."

Chipper fought back the laughter, then immediately began to feel knots in his stomach. How could his dad be so distanced from reality? He took his 7-iron out of the bag and began to use it like a walking stick.

"Why, I read the other day that if a fella shoots even par on the tour, he'll make $20,000 a year. Now that's a good living."

"Uh, Dad, I've never shot even par in my life."

"Well, for crying out loud," his father's voice began to rise, "you shoot in the seventies. What does it take to get on down to par?"

Chipper began to pound the 7-iron on the fairway as he walked.

"That's at El Viento, Dad. I know every blade of grass on this course. When we compete in the city, it's more like high seventies and low eighties. The only ones on the team good enough for college golf are Jay and L.K., and maybe Buster if he'd cool down. As far as the pros go, jeez, Ritchie Cosgrove from Castlemont has been breaking par since he was 14. Maybe two or three others in the state. Maybe Jay..."

"Well, son, one excels where one spends their time and effort. You live on this golf course. Every time your mother and I plan something, you go traipsing off to play golf. I don't see your getting into medical school. You haven't done anything constructive all summer and, frankly, we're a little concerned."

Clouds of dust were starting to appear where Chipper was slamming the 7-iron into the ground. "I make straight A's, Dad," he replied through clenched teeth. "Remember?"

"Well, when I was your age, I was working as an assistant in a hospital lab during the summer and had my own chemistry set in the basement. I spent my summers..."

Chipper couldn't take it anymore. "Hit your ball, Dad, you're furthest from the green of the whole group."

Two awkward practice swings preceded his father's real stroke, which dribbled 50 yards down the fairway.

Chipper grinned.

Six

On the final hole of play in the Father-Son tournament, Chipper was at his favorite position, alone on the fringe. With his lucky 7-iron in hand, he was both oracle and king, predicting as well as commanding only two more strokes. Chip. Putt. Round ended.

"Nice round, Chipper," said Doc Jody who had been keeping his score. "I've got you down for a five over 77. Right?"

"Yes, sir. 71s for you and Jay?"

"Correct."

As they signed each other's cards, Chipper looked across the green to see little Peachy pulling a wad of bills from his money clip and counting out an untold fortune for his father.

A gentle arm enveloped Chipper in a hug, and Doc Jody said, "Sorry your dad got called to the hospital. And after only three holes."

"Aw, it's okay. I'm used to it."

He had learned years ago that the sick and suffering always took precedence over family obligations. But then again, Doc Jody always seemed to be around for Jay. His dad once said it was because Doc Jody sent his sick patients to specialists in the city, or else asked *him*, Chipper's father, to manage them. The implication was that Doc Jody didn't pull his fair share of the partnership, but no one else in El Viento ever implied, even remotely, that Doc Jody was anything but a saint. He even spent three weeks each year doing missionary medical work in the jungles of Central America. Chipper considered him a second father.

Doc Jody threw his other arm around Jay and walked both boys to the edge of the golf course near Country Club Road. "Well, men, I guess you've heard I lost the battle to expand this course to a full 18 holes."

"Yes, sir," said Jay, "we heard. I guess being on the City Council doesn't mean you always get your way."

"No, son, it doesn't. People are funny when it comes to a profit. As long as I've been on the Council, I've never been as angry as when they sold out to those developers."

Doc Jody's voice was strained.

"Dammit," he said, as if the vote had just taken place. "We've got the hospital and clinic grounds butting against the north side of the course, the federal prison on the west, and the Chief's land on the south—and he'll never sell. The only way to expand was east, and now that opportunity is lost forever."

Doc Jody, with both arms still around the boys, stared wistfully toward the east where the lumber frames of new houses were springing up to mark the expansion of El Viento.

"When you men grow up, if you decide to stay in El Viento, you'll probably be city leaders, you know." He hugged them closer, while Jay and Chipper checked out their destiny with a knowing glance to each other. "Promise me you'll keep working to find the land to make an 18-hole course. There's a lot more important things in life than turning a profit."

Chipper loved missions.

"And while you're at it, the day I die, give me a 21-gun salute by teeing off into that housing development." Doc Jody smiled at them and walked away. Chipper noticed how straight-backed he walked, trim as a teenager. Everyone said his hair used to be blonde, like Jay's, when he was a kid. But now it was mixed, like the color of a sand trap after rain drags in dirt from the edges.

"Let's play some Horse," suggested Chipper.

"Where do you want to start?" Jay asked.

"How 'bout on the fourth hole. I don't see anyone coming up the fairway."

Horse was a game they had borrowed from driveway basketball years ago, applying the same basic rules to golf with a few minor adjustments. It was a two-man game, and a private game for Chipper and Jay.

One player would pick a difficult or nearly impossible lie away from the green, then try to get to the cup in the fewest shots. The other player had to do the same, from the exact same lie.

"You first," Jay said.

Both boys carried junker 5-irons for the game since club damage was expected. Chipper set his ball beneath a wooden bench so there couldn't be a follow-through. With a short, chopping swing, he sent the ball scooting across the green to the far side fringe. Up and in, he would get a three.

Jay put his ball in the same dirt under the bench, studied the situation for a moment, then lay down on his belly with his golf club turned around like a pool cue. With an eight-ball-in-the-corner-pocket approach, he shot from beneath the bench. His ball stopped three feet from the cup.

The rules were loose in Horse.

Chipper's shot from the fringe was close, but Jay sunk his putt for a winning two.

"That makes me H," said Chipper.

"So...penny for your thoughts."

The rules of the game included the command to answer the penny question immediately, like a word association test, and the winner of each letter asked first.

"Del Crandall."

"Del Crandall? The ball player?"

"Yeah. Did you ever wonder why he was my favorite player?" asked Chipper.

"I just assumed 'cause he was a catcher and you were a catcher."

"Why not Yogi Berra then, the catcher for the Yankees, our favorite team? Why a catcher for the Milwaukee Braves?"

"I don't know. I never thought about it," said Jay.

Chipper planted his 5-iron in the ground like the staff Moses used in the Ten Commandments movie. "How many times in the history of baseball has a player hit a game-ending grand slam homer on a three and two pitch with two outs, bottom of the ninth, with his team trailing by three runs?"

"Once," Jay answered without hesitation. "In 1955. Del Crandall."

"Correct, as usual."

"And that's why he's your favorite player?"

"Yup. A good player, not a great player, but a good player who did what no one else has done. It's a storybook ending," Chipper said, "and it's only happened once. Most people are surprised by that."

"Yeah, but a lot of that is luck. Homers are hit every day in baseball. Del Crandall happened to be in the right place at the right time."

Chipper raised and lowered his staff back to the earth. "The point is that he prepared. He was ready for the moment."

"Huh?"

"I figure it's my duty. I gotta get prepared 'cause I think there's a moment out there for me. I don't know if other people feel like that or not. Do you, Jay?"

Jay cocked his head then said, "No. I don't think so. Dad tells me life is about service to others. Just service. The more you give, the more you get."

For Chipper, lives of quiet service sounded dangerously close to lives of quiet desperation described by that Walden goofball they studied in English last year. He needed more than that. If that two-out-bottom-of-the-ninth moment ever came and he wasn't prepared, he wouldn't be able to forgive himself.

"Uh-oh," Jay said. "I just thought about our 9:15 rendezvous with our friend, the klepto-pyromaniac. We're supposed to be at my house for dinner with Kelly and Amy at 8:30. I'd better call home pretty quick."

"Yeah, make up some excuse. The rocket'll only last a second, so we should make it by 9:30 easy."

Sunset was still a half-hour away when Chipper spotted Gus, Peachy's toady sidekick, walking up the #1 rough with what looked like a posthole digger.

Seven

All five golfers huddled around the launch site in the rough on Number 1, near the out-of-bounds barbed wire fence. Chipper could only imagine the number of cars with doused headlights that were lined up on Country Club Road, each auto filled with teenagers seeking more, perhaps, than renewed patriotism. Peachy presented the weaponry to Chipper who started to say a few words but stopped when he felt something wet on the shaft of the rocket.

"Peachy! What did you get on this thing? It's wet."

"Aw, it's nothing. Just spilled a little beer. It spewed when I used my church key."

"Let me see that," Jay said, taking the rocket from Chipper. "The propellant is in the shaft. It doesn't feel too wet. How long ago did you spill your beer on it, Peachy?"

"Just a few minutes ago. It wasn't very much."

"I guess it's okay," said Jay, with the pyrotechnical authority of a 17-year-old genius. "The star case is pretty dry, so the gunpowder ought to be okay."

"It's fine," Peachy said. "Stick it down the hole."

"Saltpeter, sulfur, and charcoal, Peachy. With other stuff for the colors. It won't work if the shaft is wet."

"Saltpeter?" Peachy said. "Hope I didn't get any on me. I sure don't want my shaft to malfunction."

"Saltpeter is just potassium nitrate," Jay explained. "And all that stuff about boner prevention is a bunch of hooey."

"Excuse me, Mr. Wizard, I forgot to study my fuggin' chemistry book before I left the house tonight."

"Come on, you dipshits, cut the crap," L.K. said, apparently with subzero interest in the ceremony. Buster nodded in agreement.

"In the words of our immortal hero, Alan Shepard, to Mission Control," Peachy said, "Why don't you fix your little problem and light this candle?'"

In an effort at crowd control, Chipper said, "Let me have the rocket."

He took the treasure and raised it slowly to the night, a thin slice of moon allowing a pitch-black sky. A dying breeze still fanned the trees on the hot, deserted course. "We dedicate this summer," Chipper began, trying to avoid sounding too corny, "and all next year, to golf and this team. Next spring...we'll be state champions. Two shots...per man...per round."

He lowered the rocket to the ground, chanting: "Two shots, per man, per round." And the others joined him: "Two shots, per man, per round."

He coaxed the shaft into the cylindrical launching pad, then pushed the support stick into the base of the hole.

"Two shots, per man, per round."

Striking a match, he grabbed the end of the fuse and held the fire inches away, allowing the team to exchange glances as they continued to chant: "Two shots, per man, per round."

Match touched fuse, and the team scattered in five directions while the hissing sound predicted a spectacular display. Liftoff began with a scorching sound but no visible trail. Chipper raised his eyes to the night sky, waiting for the natural stars to be joined by these chemical fireballs.

But the explosion occurred only 20 feet in the air, forcing Chipper's eyes back to earth in horror as each red, white, and blue glowing star was ablaze as it hit the ground, starting one fire per star per millisecond. There were at least 50 fires raging within a twitch of time.

"Holy mother of Christ!" screamed Peachy, closest to the action.

Communal cursing followed immediately. Chipper briefly noticed a stream of headlights in the distance making swift exodus.

Like Keystone Cops, all five boys began running in circles, stomping out fires with their feet in fast motion. One man per fire, only a few seconds per fire, before moving to the next one. And in the short time that passed, fires that were 30 seconds old grew to a diameter of three feet. Just when Chipper thought they might be making headway, with 10 or 12 fires left, the most horrible sight in his young life struck him senseless. It had to be an optical illusion. But it wasn't. The remaining fires were on the opposite side of the barbed wire fence—on Chief Crazy Hawk's property!

In moments of crisis, Chipper remembered that some men have superhuman strength, and that 98-pound weaklings can lift automobiles off their wives pinned beneath, and all that sort of thing. With a run usually reserved for the logging chain, Chipper flew over the top of the barbed wire fence in a high jump well above five feet. He barrel-rolled along the ground after impact, stopping just short of the biggest fire. Golf balls were everywhere, like an Easter egg hunt, but there was no time for that.

As if by reflex, Jay flew over the top wire, then L.K., then Buster, and they began stomping on fires now five and six feet in diameter. Progress was not so easy to measure any more.

Chipper looked up about every tenth stomp to see if the lights were coming on at Crazy Hawk's house a hundred yards away. The house stayed dark. The cursing was muffled now, and each boy continued in silent stomping to avoid waking the Chief.

Peachy was on the other side of the barbed wire, facing his nemesis.

"Peachy, don't jump," Chipper said in a whispered yell. "Come on through the wire. We need help."

Spreading two of the middle wires carefully, Peachy threw one of his legs to the other side in a crouched position. But as he lifted his in-bounds leg, he lost his footing and became trapped by the barbed wires, spinning in suspension like a human shish kebab, lighted by the nearby flames.

"Mother fuggin' sonuva bitch, goddam mother fuggin' sonuva bitch!" screamed Peachy at the top of his lungs.

The porch lights came on at the dwelling of Chief Crazy Hawk.

Chipper left his fire and ran to Peachy's rescue, stabilizing, then spreading the barbed wires. Peachy fell to the ground, groping for his dislodged glasses, discovering in the process the slew of golf balls. As he began stuffing the bounty into his pockets, Chipper grabbed him by the arm and lifted him off the ground.

"Forget 'em!" Chipper yelled. "Help us stomp out the fires!"

"For chrissakes," whined Peachy.

He dragged Peachy toward the flames of the largest remaining fire, closest to the Chief's house. The porch lights were on, but still no sign of the Chief.

Jay, Buster, and L.K. were closing in on their final fires, leaving only the giant bonfire where Chipper and Peachy were stomping. Chipper could smell the burning rubber of his Converse high-tops as he crushed the fire beneath, sparks flying from under his feet. The heat was intense, and the fire was growing. He glanced every two seconds toward the empty porch of the Chief's house.

One by one, Jay and the others finished their fires and raced to the master fire to help Chipper and Peachy extinguish the flames. With five boys stomping around the perimeter of the fire in a war dance, chanting quiet obscenities, the diameter of the blaze began to shrink from ten feet, to seven, then three.

A loud pop split the night air. Chipper thought they'd been shot. Not yet. A screen door had slammed shut, and Chief Crazy Hawk was standing on his porch, rifle in hand.

Though Chipper thought the team was already at the max, they flew into faster motion, their 10 little feet turning flames to cinders swifter than any previous fire-squelching in recorded history. Just like the 98-pound guy who lifted the car off his wife.

The Chief began walking down the porch steps. The fire diameter continued to shrink until the golfers were stomping on each other's feet. As Jay converted the last flame to embers, Chipper yelled, "Let's get the hell outta here!"

All five boys hit the ground at once, snaking their way through the tall grass in a military belly-crawl toward the safety of the fence and the golf course beyond.

Chipper looked over his shoulder and saw the Chief still walking toward them. Without moonlight, there was only a man and his rifle silhouetted by the porch light behind. Chipper whispered to himself, "Oh, God, get us out of this alive. I'll never do anything this stupid again."

From Peachy came, "Shit, oh dear, oh shit, oh dear." And from Jay, "There's only 25 feet to the fence. We'll make it in 17 seconds." Buster and L.K. slithered ahead in silence.

"Fe Fi Fuggin' Fum...I'll blow the ass off a white man's son."

It was the Chief. Closer.

"Fe Fi Fuggin' Fum...I'll blow the ass off a white man's son." Closer still.

Ten feet from the fence, Chipper turned again to see the Chief pause and raise his rifle. He wondered if bacon rinds could kill. But how did they know for sure it would be bacon rinds? Bullets were just as likely.

"Fe Fi Fuggin' Fum..."

In the blackness of the moment, a new light appeared. Flames at the feet of the Chief. It was the master fire, starting up again from its glowing embers.

As the Chief lowered his rifle and began to stomp out the flames, Chipper sprang to his feet and ran full tilt boogie for the fence. Before he realized what was happening, he landed on the other side. The anchoring thuds of L.K., Buster, and Jay followed in rapid succession. Peachy wiggled through the wire and joined the others.

Within a jiffy, all five boys sprang to their feet, and began zigzagging back up the Number 1 fairway like jackrabbits.

Eight

After dinner they adjourned to the den, only to find out that Candid Camera was a rerun. Doc Jody saw this as his cue to crank up the player piano. Chipper never wanted to leave the Justice's den, once settled, that is. Certainly, he didn't want to leave tonight, so soon after the star-spangled inferno.

Doc Jody's favorite old-time song was "Heart of My Heart," and he would always start the sing-alongs with this piano roll, spurning the automatic switch in favor of the pedals.

Chipper put his arm around Amy's shoulder. She sneaked her arm around his waist in return. Jay and Kelly did the same, French-kissing for two seconds while Doc Jody lowered his head to light his pipe. Mama Justice appeared from the kitchen, removed her ruffled apron, and placed it on Doc Jody's chair as she joined the choir. Her hair was jet black, like Kelly's, only sprayed to a perfect helmet, while Kelly's flowed with the wind. Chipper couldn't help but compare her to television mom Donna Stone. After all, Doc Jody resembled Dr. Stone. Then again, the hair colors didn't match, so maybe it was something else entirely.

Amy brushed a strand of blonde hair from her eyes and placed her shiny lips to Chipper's ear in a whisper. He felt the tingles all the way down.

"Look how Jay's parents smile at each other, after all these years," she cooed.

Indeed, Chipper always noticed that Mama Justice and Doc Jody had a locked-on smile built for two, kind of like they shared a secret, and no one else was allowed in on it. And that's the way he and Amy would be, probably, 20 or so years from now. He thought Amy must have been dreaming the same thing because he found himself looking right through her deep green eyes, and he could see his reflection in her dark, widened pupils.

Heart
of my
heart
brings back
those
memories

The words scrolled on the piano roll as all six began to sing, some off key and some on.

...kids...
...corner...
...street...
...rough...
...ready...

Doc Jody would always slow the tempo lever at this point.

But oh,
how we
could
harmonize

Up tempo.

The phone rang and Mama Justice walked to the other side of the den to answer. Chipper barely noticed her as he continued singing with the others.

...heart...
...friends...
...dearer...
...bad...
...part...

Mama Justice's voice cut through the finale, "Chipper, it's for you. They asked for Kyle."

Chipper's heart stopped. Only his parents called him Kyle, and Mama Justice wouldn't refer to his parents as 'they.' He let go of Amy and started for the phone. It had to be the police.

...tear...
...glisten...
...listen...
...gang...
...heart...

"Hello?"

"Kyle?" He didn't recognize the girl's voice, with its soft beckoning tone.

"Yes?"

"I've loved you...always loved you...from afar." Click. Dial tone.

He cast a scornful glance at the telephone receiver in case Amy was looking.

"Prank call, I guess," he managed.

Amy was always able to pierce his armor with a stare, and she was puncturing him now with a look he had seen only once before, at the golf course two weeks ago, fifth hole, the day she was having contact lens trouble.

It was almost as if she could hear a stranger knocking at the door.

Nine

After the hundredth—no, thousandth—lifetime miss on the logging chain jump, Chipper caught his breath on the first tee with Jay, Buster, and L.K. Peachy was late.

The rarest sort of day had dawned at the El Viento Country Club. No wind. Not a breath. A downpour two days earlier had ended the triple-digit thermal siege at 22 days, a few scorchers shy of a Dust Bowl record set in the '30s. The fairways had a unique green tint, and the creeks were full.

Squealing tires broke the calm as Peachy's red Stingray turned into the parking lot, then fishtailed on the gravel until the car slid into line with Chipper's '60 white Thunderbird, Jay's ancient Buick named Old Blue, and L.K.'s white-on-yellow '55 Chevy. Buster usually hitched a ride or walked.

"Hey, peckerheads," shouted Peachy as he jumped from his car, "gotta new trick to show you."

"What's he up to now?" Jay asked.

Peachy tossed his golf bag in line with the others already in a row on the tee box.

"The Peach can pass out anytime he wants," he announced, beaming with pride. "On command, whenever the need arises."

"Now there's a real useful tool," replied Jay.

"Hey, Peachy, can you make it permanent," added L.K., "like where you never wake up?"

"Learned it from the piece I went out with last night," Peachy said, unfazed by the ridicule. "Out-of-town chick, friend of one of my dad's girlfriends. Whoa, what a night; but that's another story."

"Okay, mister cocksman," L.K. said, "show us your new trick."

Chipper remained silent, intrigued by his wacky friend.

Peachy was wearing the team uniform of Madras shorts and no shirt, but he pushed up imaginary sleeves on his bare arms for dramatic effect. "Gentlemen...observe."

He began inhaling and exhaling deeply, lifting himself upright with each inspiration, bending over at the waist with each expiration. Deep and fast. Over and over.

The rest of the team snickered at this casualty-of-common-sense. All except Chipper.

The sound of air whooshing in and out of Peachy's lungs carried far and loud on this rare windless day.

Breaking the rhythm, Peachy stood erect at the end of a huge inspiration, then held his breath. Fists were clenched and eyes were shut. His face turned red, then purple, then his eyeballs popped out, looking to explode. Finally, the bug-eyes rolled back in his head, and he fell flat to earth in a lifeless lump.

Chipper hurried to his side and waited for movement. The others—even Buster—gathered around. Buster tapped his toe against Peachy's side, then kicked harder as if testing the tires on a used car. Peachy didn't budge. In fact, his mouth hung open, and he was drooling.

"Look at his hand twitching," Chipper said, the first to diagnose that Peachy was alive.

"Yeah, the leg on that side is twitching, too," added Jay.

"Dumbshit," Buster said walking away.

Peachy's eyes opened, and he shook himself awake as easy as getting out of bed in the morning. He hopped to his feet. "Pretty cool, huh?"

"Yeah, neat," said Chipper.

"Gimme a break," L.K. said. "You're full of it."

"How do you do it?" Chipper asked, amazed that a person could alter their level of consciousness so easily.

"Don't do it, Chipper," advised Jay. "You'll destroy brain cells. Peachy doesn't have anything to lose."

"Hey, the Peach is fine, man." He took Chipper aside and explained the art and science of hyperventilation, followed by blocked expiration through skillful positioning of tongue against throat, imagining that you're trying to exhale into your brain. Chipper was fascinated.

Peachy did his trick two more times, proving that, indeed, the methodology was sound and the harmful effects were nil.

Chipper braced himself, bent at the waist, hands on knees. He began the rite, according to instruction. In and out deep breaths. Wait for the tingle. In and out. Would he be able to feel it? In and out, as deep as he could, to the point he felt his lungs might burst. Then he felt it...a tingling of his brain just like Peachy had described. One more inspiration and *hold*. With the base of his tongue thrust back against his throat, he pushed with his stomach muscles against his closed airway. Dots appeared before his eyes, and then...he felt warm all over...

The golf course was deserted, except for Chipper on the seventh green, wind blowing with the strength of a cyclone. But everything was orange. No other colors. How did he get from the first tee to the seventh green? As he stooped to putt, the wind lifted his ball right off the orange green, and he found himself clinging to the flagstick to keep from being blown away. His body was parallel to the ground. It was too windy to play golf...

Then, more tingles. As he looked at the blue sky from the ground, he saw sunlight bouncing off the white hair of an old man stooped over him. The wind was gone.

"You okay, son?" asked Mr. Ashbrook. "Chipper?"

He raised himself to a sitting position and the team helped him get to his feet. He was back on the first tee.

"Yeah, sure, I'm okay," he lied, as the picture became increasingly clear.

"You'd better take these salt tablets, son. It's only ten o'clock and it's already ninety degrees out here."

Chipper glanced at Peachy who immediately looked down and started fiddling with the grip on his club. Chipper knew instantly that Mr. Ashbrook had seen the harebrained stunt but probably not the part involving Peachy. How did he let Peachy get him into these situations?

"Chipper, you and the team come on over to the practice tee," Mr. Ashbrook said. "I want to show you something."

"Are you all right?" Jay asked.

"I guess."

"I was gonna do it, too," Jay said. "Right after you did."

Chipper knew that his friend would never try anything so stupid. It was friendly support—so typical of Jay.

Mr. Ashbrook teed a ball for a practice shot, but rather than swinging away, he pulled a second ball from his pocket and began massaging it as he crouched near the ground.

With Mr. Ashbrook preoccupied, Peachy began pooching out his stomach and walking around like he was pregnant. It was a sign that

Sarge was nearby. Sure enough, Chipper could spot the red belly-ball, centered among Sarge's arms and legs, at the north end of the course, floating up along Number 9 rough. The boys were laughing quietly. Even Buster.

When Mr. Ashbrook stood up, Peachy sucked in his stomach and the laughing stopped in a heartbeat.

Lo and behold, it was a sight none of them had ever witnessed before. The second ball was balanced perfectly on top of the first!

Mouths wide open, they each took a step forward in disbelief. More cautious steps forward. Then they dropped to their knees for a closer look. Unbelievable. One golf ball balanced on top of the other.

"Okay, Mr. Ashbrook, we give up. What's the trick? Did you use glue or gum or what?"

"No trick, Peachy. It's for real."

They couldn't move their eyes.

"It's a lesson I can only teach when it's perfectly still outside, and you know we don't get many perfectly still days at El Viento." They nodded in agreement.

"Life is a series of hazards, fellas. It's not about *what if* you meet troubles. It's about *when* you meet them. I'd say that's the secret of life, as a matter of fact. Now as to the *meaning* of life...I'll leave that to the men of the cloth. But I can describe the secret, and the secret is being prepared for trouble and responding to it in the right way."

Chipper wasn't exactly sure what the old man meant. For one thing, he had made it 17 long years without any major trouble whatsoever, so did this sermon really apply here?

Mr. Ashbrook gripped what appeared to be his 7-iron and started to address the double-bubble-ball. Then he stopped and told Jay to remove his cap. The other boys were already capless.

This is crazy, thought Chipper, *what is going on?*

With his feet planted and his knobby knees almost touching, Mr. Ashbrook used his skinny arms to place his iron behind the lowest ball.

"When the world is still, fellas, develop those aspects of your character that you'll need when some cockamamie trouble comes a-knocking. If you're ready, then you won't see it as trouble at all."

And with those words, he cracked a perfect shot into the practice range. But...there was only one ball flying from the tee! Chipper and the others looked at Mr. Ashbrook who was looking toward heaven.

"Catch the second ball in your cap, Jay," the old man said, completely calm.

Chipper looked skyward and saw that the second ball had gone straight up in the air from the launching pad, and was now headed back to earth.

Jay had to run only a few steps to catch it in his cap. Mr. Ashbrook watched him from his follow-through position. The group was awestruck, speechless, save for a few "unbelievables," "my goshes," and one "son-of-a-motherin-bitch."

"I call it the rocket shot," said the old man.

The day's round was delayed. Taking advantage of the still air for balancing golf balls, all five team members practiced the rocket shot. For Chipper, the 7-iron worked best, swinging away at the lower ball, pretending that the top ball wasn't even there. Jay perfected the technique first, describing the probable physics behind golf ball balancing, including a recitation of the various numbers of dimples in balls by different manufacturers. Then he began to mutter something about practicing trouble shots 30 minutes every day for the rest of his life. L.K. tried to see how high he could get the top ball to go, while Buster pounded his club into the ground each time the trick didn't work just perfectly.

Peachy never could get the trick to work, so he excused himself to the pro shop where he tried to entice the entering golfers with the wager that he could balance one golf ball on top of the other. Apparently, they had seen the trick because he reported no takers. After that, Peachy resorted to luring bettors on the wager that he could pass out on command. Still no takers, he returned to the first tee box, voicing his outrage with the "chickenshit members of this country club."

Ten

Buster's birdie putt on the first hole defied gravity, hovering on the rim of the cup. Clocks around the world stopped, awaiting his response.

"Of all the damn days for that shithead south wind to be gone," he growled through clenched teeth, "it would have to be with my ball on the south lip."

Chipper wondered how far Buster would throw his putter.

Buster reared back to launch the javelin, but caught himself. He started to throw again. Caught himself again. Finally, he walked over to his golf bag, slammed his putter inside and headed for the next tee.

L.K.'s putt for par missed by a mile.

"Drive for show, putt for dough," whispered Peachy.

Indeed, L.K.'s drive had been humongous, almost 400 yards, landing in one of the many charred circles of grass left from last week's July Fourth fires, the mysterious black spots still punctuating the landscape both in-bounds and out-of-bounds. The black spot was, of course, the pirate's symbol of impending death, and Chipper tried his best not to be superstitious. L.K. had pulled his approach, flubbed two chip shots, then two-putted for the bogey.

Maybe they'd spent too much time goofing around with the rocket shot.

"You're up, Jay," Chipper said. "Birdie wins it."

The second hole was the highest point on the course, a north-south hill margined by two creeks that were usually dry in July. Today, they were overflowing.

One dead, gnarled tree, called the Hanging Tree, marked the second tee box. The only dead tree on the course had been left as sort of a landmark. Rumor held that a pro named Johnny Revolta had played the course in 1935, back when there were sand greens, and that he had broken the wooden shaft of his driver against the tree after hitting his tee shot out-of-bounds.

Similar to the first hole, Number 2 butted against Chief Crazy Hawk's out-of-bounds fence on the left. Chipper wondered if out-of-bounds was as dangerous back then. Did the Chief's father, or grandfather, live there? Probably so, since the out-of-bounds fence for Numbers 1 and 2 was also the edge of the '89 Land Run, and the Chief's land was not opened, remaining as one boundary of Indian Territory. Chipper could almost picture teepees out in the field being bombarded by golf balls, particularly the one hit by Johnny Revolta, who then broke his driver on the Hanging Tree.

Jay's drive was ideal, as usual.

"Nice shot, Jay," Chipper said. "Buster, you hit next, you were awful close to the birdie."

Buster walked to the tee box as if he were the only person on the course. No words. No eye contact.

Though Peachy knew his limit with L.K., he was empty-headed as to those same limits with Buster. It didn't really matter. Buster took out his anger exclusively on inanimate objects.

"Heard you had a date last weekend, Buster," began Peachy.

"Uh-huh." Buster readjusted his teed ball and looked down the fairway.

"Carol Austin?"

"Uh-huh."

"What did you use for wheels, man, a bicycle? Or did you walk?"

Chipper started to get nervous and cast a warning glance at Mr. Bright Red Corvette Stingray.

"My dad's pickup."

Again, Buster readjusted his teed ball and took his stance.

"Hmm, I bet your date was impressed."

Buster glared at Peachy, then looked back at his ball.

"Well, Carol's a cute little filly," continued Peachy. "I've thought about asking her out myself."

Since Buster routinely huffed and puffed before starting his backswing, Chipper didn't give it much thought when the huffing and puffing began. But Buster didn't swing. And Peachy continued.

"I hear she puts out."

Buster's face turned crimson and his daggered eyes were pointed at Peachy.

"So, Buster, did you get in her pants?"

Buster raised his driver into the air like a butcher hunkering to slice a side of beef with one fell swoop. With his black hair forming pointed fingers on his lumpy red forehead, covering the one droopy eyelid, Buster the boxer let out a savage war cry that would have curdled Geronimo's blood as he began charging toward Peachy, sword held high.

Peachy began running in circles, bobbing and weaving between the other members of the team.

"I'm gonna kill you, you son of a bitch," were the only intelligible words coming from Buster. Most of the sounds were grunts.

"Somebody get him! He's crazy!" pleaded Peachy, scooting in and out of his friends.

The thought to help did occur to Chipper, especially since he had never seen Buster attack before. It had been a long time coming, though, and Peachy deserved it.

Buster caught Peachy at the Hanging Tree and pinned him against the trunk, using the shaft of his driver to press against Peachy's throat, cutting off the squawk.

Peachy's mole-like eyes were bigger than earlier today during the pass-out exhibition, his glasses smashed on the ground. His flailing arms tried to reach Buster without success, as the dead limbs of the Hanging Tree enveloped them both. Buster was relentless. When Peachy's face changed from scarlet red to deep purple and his eyes were one step from blowing their sockets, L.K. intervened. His long muscular arms surrounded Buster from behind, lifting his feet off the ground.

"All right," L.K. said. "Enough, please." Boxer or not, Buster knew he was no match for L.K.

Buster looked at Peachy's so-called friends, Chipper and Jay, apparently to see how they would side.

"He deserved it, Buster," Chipper said.

"Yeah, I just hope his larynx is okay," added Jay.

Peachy rolled on the ground, groaning and clutching his throat.

Buster calmly put his driver back in his bag and began walking toward the clubhouse.

"Don't screw with me anymore, Peachy Waterman, you fuckjaw," he said over his shoulder.

Peachy was starting to whisper now with a raspy effort. Chipper knew trouble was lurking any time Peachy attempted speech. Rushing to Peachy's side, he said quietly, "Apologize, man. You were way out of line."

Peachy looked back with pitiful eyes that said, *Please, no.*

But Chipper cupped his hand around Peachy's throat and said it again: "Apologize."

"I'm sorry," came his half-hearted reply.

It was a first.

"He can't hear you. Say it louder."

"I'm sorry."

This time, Buster turned and nodded recognition of the marginal apology.

"Think I'll play by myself, starting over on Number 1," he said. "I shoulda had a birdie anyway."

"I'll play with you, Buster," offered Chipper.

"No, thanks. I'll play it alone."

Eleven

Sunset would hold off for a few more holes while they waited for the girls. Peachy was home nursing a sore throat, probably with his father's best brandy, or his worst moonshine. Buster left after his solo 18 holes, claiming one of his best rounds ever, a three under 69. Chipper could see L.K. in the distance, wading the creeks for golf balls.

Jay selected the next lie on the asphalt sidewalk by the clubhouse and chipped it to the fringe. Chipper followed with a closer shot, 15 feet from the pin. After Chipper won the hole, he said, "Penny for your thoughts."

"I was just wondering about Buster's benefactor."

"Benefactor?"

"Yeah, you figured he had a benefactor, didn't you?"

"No. I mean, well, maybe..." stumbled Chipper. "You think somebody pays for his golf?"

"Sure. You don't see Buster down there wading the creeks for balls, do you? L.K.'s dad won't give him a dime for golf, but Buster's dad doesn't *have* a dime to give. Have you ever seen him?"

"Yeah," replied Chipper. "His old man looks like a wino or something."

"Well, have you ever seen Buster buy a golf ball? The new bag, his replacements for broken clubs, membership fees. The guy's got to have a benefactor."

"Sort of like *The Millionaire*, huh? But who?

"Well, I say its Mr. Ashbrook," Jay said.

"What? Why?"

"I don't know; just a feeling. Who did Mr. Ashbrook spend the most time with when we were little? Who does Buster open up to? Watch them."

"I will. Too bad L.K. doesn't have a benefactor, down there having to wade the creeks.

The silence that followed indicated to Chipper that both boys were thinking about the luxuries of being doctors' sons. All of life's necessities, like golf balls, were put on the monthly club statement where Chipper's dad could complain about it.

"Look at that front coming in," said Chipper. "I knew today was too good to be true."

A bank of dark thunderclouds lined the northwestern sky in sharp contrast to the bright blue above.

"Supposed to be a 30-degree drop in temperature and maybe a tornado warning," said Jay. "Boy, that squall line looks mean. Should be about a half hour away."

Chipper picked the next lie on the fringe of the green, then mandated left-handed play, toe of the club pointed down. He lost the hole.

"I'm Horse."

"Penny for your thoughts."

"So, Jay, are you and Kelly doing it yet?" Chipper figured he might catch him off guard.

"Nope. Close, but no. We're not going to do it until we're married. You know that."

"I know. Just asking. Gotta check every few months...or weeks."

Jay laughed as he took a handkerchief from his pocket and wiped the white zinc oxide from his nose. The evening sun disappeared prematurely behind the storm front.

"How about you two?"

"Same here. We're waiting. Amy makes sure of that. I don't think she gets as hot as Kelly. I've been thinking though..."

"Yesss?"

"Maybe Kelly gets turned on because she knows you're gonna get married. Now that I've mentioned marriage to Amy..."

"I heard that you *barely* mentioned it," Jay said, "in a kinda, sorta way."

"Well, I thought it was pretty darned solid," Chipper replied.

"Kelly said Amy said that you always put in a qualifying adverb, or adjective, as the case might be."

"Well, I didn't mean to sound so..."

"Take it from me, Chipper, I wouldn't plan on Amy getting all hot and bothered for your body until you get rid of those adjectives and adverbs."

"Amy said that, did she?"

"Just some friendly advice. Clean up your grammar."

Chipper paused at the sound of distant thunder and watched the glow of hidden lightning roll through the clouds. Maybe Jay was onto something.

"Jay, you remember that part in *Shenandoah* last year when Jimmy Stewart was talking to that guy who's about to marry his daughter?"

"Yes. Doug McClure's his name."

"Whoever. You remember what Jimmy asks him? He asks him if he *likes* the daughter. Jimmy knows the guy loves her, but what he really wants to know is that he likes her. Remember that?"

"Sure."

"That was pretty cool," Chipper said. "I've thought about that line a lot. You gotta like your wife, not just love her."

"Okay, so what's your point?"

"I like Amy. I mean I really like her."

"Hey, you handsome studs," interrupted a voice from the parking lot. It was Kelly. Amy was with her, smiling like the good old days.

"You conceited farts," Kelly said. "*Both* of you turned around."

"Sorry we're late," Amy added.

Kelly locked onto her boyfriend's lips. Finally, she released and swatted Jay on the butt.

Amy and Chipper hugged and exchanged a short, friendly kiss.

"Love you."

"Love you, back."

"This front's moving fast, so it'll be too dark to play," Jay said. "Let's putt around a little, then go riding around before the storm hits."

The girls said okay.

"Did you hear about Amy's 39 yesterday?" Kelly asked the boys.

"Only about a thousand times," joked Chipper. "It was from the ladies' tees, after all." A 39 was in Chipper's range, a bit disconcerting. Amy's previous record was 43. Quite a jump, he thought.

"I also took a mulligan on my first drive," she said, almost as a courtesy to Chipper.

He was relieved.

The four of them began to putt, but Jay and Kelly spent more time kissing than putting, so they were off within minutes to the back seat of Old Blue in the parking lot.

"Amy, I'm real proud of your 39. I didn't mean to make fun."

"Thanks, Chipper. I appreciate that."

Amy continued putting as she talked, her cute little fanny sticking out as she addressed the ball. And those tan legs coming out of those oh-so-white and oh-so-short shorts. When she turned around, getting ready to stroke the ball again, her pink blouse ballooned open in front revealing the lace top of her bra.

"Amy, no more adjectives or adverbs," he announced.

"What? What in the world?"

"No more adjectives or adverbs. I love you, unqualified. I want to marry you, unqualified. And more important..." he added to appease even Jimmy Stewart, "I like you, too."

Amy dropped her putter and placed her hands on her hips. Chipper didn't know what to expect, then she said, "I love you" in a way he had never heard before. She dropped her hands to her side and started walking toward him, looking serious, eye-to-eye. He looked to see if her pupils were dilated, the poker clue a la Peachy.

Chipper was holding the flagstick, but he let it go as her body touched his.

"Do you mean it, Chipper?"

"Yes, I do." At this moment, there was no doubt in Chipper's mind, and he knew he couldn't wait for the back seat of a car.

She put her hands around his back then slid them down onto his rear, pulling him close to her soft tummy before entering into a deep kiss, tongues waggling around each other. When he came up for air, Chipper looked for a soft place for them to lie down.

The bunker. After all, the course was empty, and the clubhouse was closed.

Taking her hand, he led her to the edge of the sand and they both jumped down the incline, landing bottoms first. He rolled on top of her, and she didn't resist. In fact, he could feel her pressing back to meet each of his thrusts. And her kisses were no longer dutiful—she was enjoying it, taking the fullness of his tongue, in and out, with caution tossed out-of-bounds.

Remembering his father's admonition never to go below the waist—what a stupid thing to tell your son—Chipper immediately began groping for the top button to undo her shorts. It was on the side and he released the barrier in a jiffy, with no resistance from Amy, and without stopping his personal best in the long kiss event.

But her zipper was stuck, covered with sand, and he felt her hand against his, moving him away. Chipper assumed that meant the limit, but he was wrong. She was brushing the sand away from her zipper, trying to help. And his longest kiss continued as Amy struggled with the zipper, the delay torturing Chipper, still thrusting against her.

He put his hand on the outside of her short shorts, and she put hers on the outside of his Bermudas, stroking him in rhythm with each thrust as he dug into the sand with his golf cleats for traction. Good thing he just bought new cleats, he thought, right before the moment of climax. He burst with convulsive, unqualified "I love yous," grabbed her in a tight squeeze, then did a log-roll with her to the edge of the sand trap where they gasped for air.

Amy snuggled up and whispered "I love you" over and over. For the first time, he realized the storm was all around them. How could he not have heard the thunder?

A cold wind was making the logging chain creak on the first tee, and the sky had a greenish, unearthly cast, while lightning strikes were visible everywhere. No rain yet.

Chipper was startled by a giggle, not so far away. Then two people giggling. He and Amy crawled to the crest of the bunker and peeked over the top. Kelly and Jay were in another one across the green, staring back. Kelly jumped out of their bunker, dragging Jay behind.

"We came back to get you two out of the storm," she said, "but didn't see you. Fortunately, Chipper, we could hear you. Louder than thunder, so to speak. From the sound of things, you ought to have a wet spot on your shorts."

Only Kelly could be so comfortably risqué discussing wet spots. He couldn't see well in near darkness, but the cool spot said she was right, and he was both embarrassed and pleased at the same time.

The wind was roaring now, and he felt the first drops of rain on his forehead.

"C'mon, let's get outta here," he said.

Kelly gave a helping hand to Amy, and the girls took off running to the car to avoid the certain downpour. Jay helped Chipper out and the two of them followed.

Chipper wasn't sure why he turned around, probably to get a last look at the storm, but what he saw unnerved him.

Standing against the trunk of a large elm tree, not 10 feet from the sand trap where he and Amy had just been frolicking, was a ghost, or an angel, illuminated by the lightning strikes. On closer look, it was a young girl in some sort of white, flimsy gown that was rippling in the wind, revealing the contours of her body, while her long hair blew parallel to the ground.

Chipper's heart skipped a beat as he looked away, hoping she would disappear. Perhaps the image wasn't even real. After all, this was a particularly spooky storm.

When he looked back again, she was still there, motionless, staring at him.

He wanted desperately to call out to her, to rescue her from the storm, but he said nothing. Jay was walking ahead, and the girls were already out of sight.

He looked back a third time, and she raised her open palm to him as if he were supposed to join her in a walk up the ladder to heaven. Chipper froze. It was raining harder now, but the rain didn't seem to be touching her. For the first time in his life, he felt something brewing inside more powerful than he thought possible, more consuming than he could imagine. And he felt his feet starting to walk in her direction.

"Chipper, hurry your butt *up*. Come on!" It was Jay, yelling through the rain.

Maybe it was Jay that touched his arm. Whatever it was, he tore himself from the radiant spirit and fled to the car. Who would help her now? Lightning brightened the sky, followed by crackling thunder, and the heavy downpour began.

The whole world was storming.

Twelve

July 14, 1966: Ever since President Johnson gave the orders last month to bomb North Vietnam, this thing is starting to bug me. Hope it doesn't interfere with college and medical school, or worse, my pledging Sigma Chi. Jay sank a 15-foot putt today to win the club championship (probably the first of many). He beat Buster by two strokes, and L.K. was third. I won A-flight with a 76 and Peachy won B-flight with 82. All in all, the team took the top three spots in championship flight, plus we have the champs in the top three flights! (Boy, are the adults ever p.o.'d.) Amy was runner-up in Ladies' Championship Flight with an 81. She's getting pretty salty. Over and out.

Chipper had kept his log faithfully since the fourth grade, believing that someday the revelation of its contents would be important as his destiny unfolded.

As he started out the door of his room for the awards dinner, he could hear his two younger sisters squabbling over rights to the new pink princess phone. It had an extra-long extension cord and was to be shared equally among the three of them, meaning fifty-fifty for the girls.

Avoiding the creaky steps on the way to the first floor, he eased down the stairway intending a silent exit. But step number three issued a surprise squeak.

"Kyle, are you still here?" came his mother's voice from the library.

Trapped like a rat.

"Yeah, Mother. I'm in a hurry. Gotta pick up Amy."

"Before you go..."

Her voice was getting closer as she rounded the corner to skewer him at the base of the stairs. Although he was wary of the wide perimeter of thin ice around her feet, you couldn't argue her good looks, as mothers go. Friends introduced her saying, "Isn't she the spitting image of Maureen O'Hara?"—whoever *that* was. Chipper knew that this leading-lady exterior, however, didn't tell the whole story. After all, the other moms didn't appear on television to discuss the Great Books, the other moms didn't run for State Representative, and there was only one Concertmistress for the Oklahoma City Symphony. As a young woman, she had wanted to go to medical school. But Chipper's dad said, "No wife of mine is going to be a doctor," so she became a medical technologist and founded a national organization for women in medicine, Lambda Alpha Beta (LAB). Meanwhile—the best Chipper could tell—his dad treated sore throats.

"...I've been looking at these college brochures, Kyle, and I think your SAT scores will get you into Harvard or Yale as pre-med."

"Mother, we've been through that already. You know I want to go to OU, pledge Sigma Chi, and root for Sooner football. Jay's parents say OU is just fine, and Jay is tons smarter than I am."

He was the first to admit that his college bias was due, in no small part, to the fact that Doc Jody had taken Jay and him to all the Sooner home games, stopping first at the Sigma Chi house for alumnae lunch, ever since the boys became best friends in the first grade.

"You have so much more potential than a state university can meet, Kyle," his mom continued, one hand resting on her hip, the other holding an assortment of boring brochures. In her gold lamé slim jims, white blouse, and long dark hair pulled back in a trademark bun, she was definitely Hollywood, and convincing. But not convincing enough. Chipper could be as stubborn as he needed to be.

It was time for the 'hometown defense,' cleverly concocted to ward off these attempts by his mother to force him to ivy-covered walls when, in fact, he saw his future in a land where there were no walls—California. By claiming undying allegiance to El Viento, he could appeal to her sense of family ties, wait for the pressure to ease, then let the winds come sweep him off the plains to the beach of an endless summer.

"If OU was good enough for you and Dad, then it's good enough for me. Besides, what do I need with a Harvard degree in El Viento?"

"You don't have to stay in El Viento, Kyle, you can do anything you want."

"But why would I want to leave here? Jay and I plan to take over the clinic when we get out of medical school. We're gonna build a cart path from the clinic's back door to the Number 8 tee box. That way we can get in at least nine holes at the end of each day. What more do you need than a golf course in your backyard?"

He tried to work his way around her at the base of the stairs, but she wouldn't budge. The hand holding the brochures moved to her hip. Now both her hands dug into the gold lamé.

"You're wasting your time on that golf course, Kyle. Summer is a time to enrich your mind. I used to read one book a week when I was your age, and I worked full-time in the business office of my boarding school."

"Okay, Mother, I'll read one book a week."

"That's not the point, and you know it. You're not being productive. You're not working, you're not studying...your mind is idle."

He turned to face her, annoyed by the burial of his straight-A record. "My mind is not idle, Mother. It's working all the time. It never stops!" He was almost yelling.

"Is that Kyle I hear?" came the voice of his father. Chipper's mind took flight to the comfort of the Justices' den and Doc Jody singing "Heart of My Heart." He hurried out the back door while his mother glared at him as if he'd just flunked out of school.

As the door began to shut, he knew it would chop off his father's words: "Just when in tarnation does he plan to take out the trash? I'm getting sick and tired of his lollygagging..."

Slam.

"So, who do you think you'll have to fight, Chipper?" Jay asked, already seated at the banquet table with Kelly.

"Don't know. Don't give it much thought," he lied as he pulled out the folding chair for Amy. The thought of Letterman's Club initiation sickened him, pressing heavier each day. The aroma of fried chicken, baked beans, and potato salad suddenly lost its appeal.

"Why don't you have L.K. give you some pointers?" Jay suggested.

Although Buster was the boxer, he had yet to endure Letterman's initiation. On the other hand, L.K.'s fight was legendary.

Chipper had clung to the hope that L.K. would run for president of the Letterman's Club this year, imparting the power to set up, or rig, the boxing matches. But L.K. decided against political office, leaving Chipper's fate to a stranger. And a permanent fate it would be. Entire reputations were made or ruined by the outcome of the Letterman's

Club fights, as the initiates were divided, for life, into two groups—winners and losers.

The story of L.K.'s fight proved the point. Thought to be a gentle giant, L.K. was matched two summers ago against the meanest athlete in El Viento, a Negro called "L.D." Washington. L.D. was a packed mass of huge, knotted muscles, spoke with grunts rather than words, and scared the students and teachers alike with a murderous stare molded onto his face. When L.K. was matched against L.D., it was generally accepted that L.K.'s reach advantage would be useless, and that death would lurk within the bout. However, L.K.'s thunderous assault shocked the Letterman's Club world, and L.D. Washington was pummeled into unconsciousness in the first round.

L.K.'s legend grew even further when L.D. Washington, a few days later, threatened retaliation with a switchblade, backed by a gang of his thug-friends, bringing the town of El Viento as close to a race riot as ever in its history. L.K. was fearless as he walked straight up to Washington, took away the knife, forced him into a half nelson, then flattened him on the ground. The gang backed away while L.D. Washington grunted obscenities, vowing to get even. But he never did. He couldn't. He was a loser...for life. In fact, he slithered away from El Viento in humiliation and was never heard from again. Such was the power of the Letterman's Club fights.

"I've already asked him," Chipper replied. "L.K. says he'll work with me next week before he goes to baseball camp."

"Where are you going to work out?" asked Jay, fully aware that Chipper's mother was about to have a stroke over this fighting business, and would never allow training at the DeHart household.

"Oh...I dunno. Maybe at his house."

He was honored that the great L.K. would spend time teaching him to fight, that they would actually put on gloves together, and that some of L.K. might rub off on him. Watch out, L.D. Washington, wherever you are!

"That'd be pretty unusual," Jay said. "L.K. *never* invites anyone to his house."

Jay was right. In all these years of playing golf together, no one had been inside L.K.'s home. Maybe L.K. was trying to shield his friends from the forbidding father, a colossal man who could eclipse the sun. Mr. Taylor was captain of the guards at the federal prison on the outskirts of El Viento, and it was easy to understand why prisoners, as well as guards, would fear him.

"I guess we'll just...uh, work out...here at the country club."

Chipper envied Jay, having fought and won already. Two years ago, in a preliminary bout before the great L.K.-L.D. match, Jay had bloodied the mouth of a sprinter, ending the match in the second round. Matches rarely went the full three rounds, and were decided by bloodshed or a knockout, with the Letterman's Club President having the final decision to call the fight. No referees were needed.

"You ought to work out in one of the sand traps, Chipper," said Jay. "That would be most like the river bottom."

"Chipper's *already* been working out in the sand traps," Kelly added. The two girls exchanged glances and held back the giggles.

He felt his face flush. Amy's cheeks looked a little red too, but maybe it was the makeup that she really didn't need. Amy was dressed tonight in her favorite color pink, a wide headband matching her sleeveless dress, and her large green eyes a little larger and a little darker than usual. Her long golden hair was the color of Oklahoma wheat when the sun's shining, and tonight she held it away from her inviting face by the pink headband. He could almost forget about the Letterman's Club fights.

"Ooooh, you two are just about the cutest couple I've ever seen," squealed the voice of an elderly lady coming off the buffet line. With white cotton candy hair and leathered skin, she was recognizable to Chipper only as one of the many nameless patrons of the golf course.

"Why, Amy, aren't you just the loveliest thing all gussied up?" she continued. "And Chipper, you've got your dad's tall and dark, and your mother's handsome. I was noticing you kids as you went through the line. Young people are so attractive these days."

Her voice trailed as she walked to another table without ever introducing herself. The four of them laughed. Unknown adults addressed you by your first name in El Viento on a regular basis.

"There's L.K.," Kelly said, pointing to the food line. "Is that a date he's with?"

The foursome rubbernecked to get a better look at this rare event.

"Naw," said Jay, "that's Buster's date, Carol Austin. L.K. gave them a ride."

"Oh, she's kinda cute," Kelly said, a pretty good judge of both looks and character. "It would take a special girl to date Buster."

"I like Buster..." began Chipper.

"I didn't mean it that way. It's just...well...he's different. That temper...gosh. Oh, well, I'm glad he has a girlfriend. Who is she, anyway? I thought I knew everyone."

"She's a hot little junior high chick, a ninth grader," interrupted Peachy as he started to put his plate beside Kelly.

"Don't you eat beside me, Peachy Waterman," scolded Kelly. "Go to the other side of the table and spread your bullshit there. Where'd you come from? I shoulda smelled you coming."

"Aw, cool it, Kelly. I'm moving." Pretending hurt, he circled to the other side. "Gus and I were at that other table when y'all came in."

Gus Stufflebean, Peachy's part-time shadow and occasional conscience, followed the leader and put his plate down beside Kelly. As a thirteen-year-old, he knew to keep quiet with the big kids.

"I know all about Carol Austin from Gus here," continued Peachy. "They're in the same grade. Got her bazookas in the fourth grade and now has the best body in next year's freshman class." Peachy reported this with the smug confidence that these facts clearly summed up the dear girl's entire life. "I was gonna ask her out until I found out what a nut case Buster really is."

"I thought you only dated real women, Peachy," needled Kelly. "You know, the twenty-one year-old divorcées, go-go dancers and the like." Jay squirmed at his girlfriend's brash style at times, and this was one of those times. "You two behave," he ordered.

Buster, his date, and L.K. approached the table. L.K. sat down beside Peachy, as if to relieve Buster of the responsibility of filling the chair next to his nemesis. Buster remained at the end of the table, awkwardly shifting his stares, finally opening his mouth to speak.

"Team...this is Carol." Buster looked at his date, as if he had rehearsed this a hundred times. "Carol, this is the team."

Chipper was happy to hear Buster use the word "team." Maybe this was progress.

"Pleased to meet you, Carol," Amy said, the first to acknowledge. "This is my boyfriend Chipper. That's Jay, and this is Kelly. Peachy's right there and I guess you know Gus."

Carol's face looked a little sour at the name of Peachy, but she brightened again to see her classmate Gus. She was cuter than Chipper expected, with light brown hair in a bubble, brown eyes, and just a little over five feet tall. Her white blouse was buttoned tightly at her neck. After Peachy's introductory description, Chipper did his best not to look at her chest.

"Here, Carol, come sit by me," Kelly said. "Gus, you'll have to move down two seats."

Gus let out a junior high groan and obeyed.

"It's nice to meet all of you," Carol said in a soft tone. Kelly liked her immediately and gave an approving look to the rest of the table to let them know to behave accordingly.

The buffet line was shrinking as most patrons were seated now at the 20 or so folding tables. The west wall of the clubhouse dining room had been renovated recently with large picture windows, allowing a panoramic view of the course.

The jukebox in a dark corner was loaded with 45s, many of which were supplied by Amy, perhaps one of the strongest devotees to teen dancing in the country. Fast dance, slow dance, Swim, Watusi, Frug, Hully-Gully, or the Jerk, it didn't matter—Amy loved it all. And she looked great doing it all. Chipper danced out of duty, but enjoyed slow dancing the most. Far and away the most adept dancer on the golf team was, unbelievably, Peachy. Somehow, the rhythm, the melody—something—pulled together Peachy's usual chaotic motions into slick choreography, giving him this singular talent to prompt the envy of his colleagues.

Amy had taken it upon herself to update the jukebox repertoire. Chipper was impressed by, and strangely attracted to, Amy's talent for tackling a job like this, becoming guardian of the jukebox. Most people just accepted whatever records happened to be in the machine, but Amy had contacted the distributor and had made arrangements with the country club to be the caretaker. She claimed to have bigger plans yet.

"Where's your date, L.K.?" teased Kelly, forever the matchmaker.

"Aw, you know I don't date much, Kelly."

"Believe me, I know a whole lot of girls who would love to go out with you."

L.K. blushed, rubbing the back of his head with his catcher's mitt hand. "Well, I need to wade the creeks after dinner anyway. I'm about outta balls. I doubt any of those girls would want to wade the creeks with me."

"Oh, I don't know about that," Kelly said. "I can think of several."

Chipper looked across the room at the new panoramic windows. More than two hours of daylight were left, and the busybody lady with cotton candy hair was lowering the shades to block the glare of the evening sun. The gray-hairs called these shades isinglass curtains since they rolled right down, like in the song, but Jay would always point out that true isinglass was a gelatin sheet made from the air bladders of sturgeons, completely unrelated to the sun shades at the country club.

Chipper spotted Mr. Ashbrook across the room, slowly making his way toward their table, his bony hands balancing a paper plate and iced tea. He wasn't smiling. The board meeting must have ended, given the last minute rush at the buffet by Sarge and his squad, along with other alleged leaders of the country club.

"There's a seat across from me, Mr. Ashbrook," Gus shouted, flashing his silver-toothed smile.

"Well, folks, I'm pretty darned flustered," he said. "The board just voted..."

Sarge interrupted by bellying up to the end of the table, causing Mr. Ashbrook to cut short his concern. "Me-oh-my, if it ain't the flatbellies all sittin' together, so sweet."

Even in a plaid cotton shirt, Sarge's stomach was a natural wonder, thought Chipper. The squares of plaid were stretched into parallelograms and trapezoids near the button line.

"Have you punks heard?" Sarge paused for a moment, and Mr. Ashbrook's expression indicated with a nod that Sarge was about to finish the sentence that the old man had started.

"The board has voted, and now it's official. No more flatbellies in the club tournament from now on." Sarge grinned, proud to be the bearer of bad tidings. He puffed up what little chest he still had, staring directly at Peachy who had won B-flight, the same flight in which Sarge had finished a distant third. No trophies were awarded for third place.

Chipper broke the silence. "Uh, Sarge, how did the board define a flatbelly?"

"You little high school weenies, that's how."

"Well, Sarge, correct me if I'm wrong," began Chipper with patronizing caution, "but since all of us are seniors this fall, we'll have graduated by the time of the next club tournament. We'll still be able to play."

Sarge's smile disappeared, replaced by a childish frown that precedes a cry when candy is confiscated. He waddled away to the group's laughter.

But Mr. Ashbrook didn't laugh. "I don't like it, fellas. Not one bit." Chipper was embarrassed he had been so flippant. "I've got some good B-team golfers, like Gus here, who need to play in every tournament they can. It's a sad day when people commence to punish the youngsters because they can't come to grips with their own middle age. All I've got to say is if they can't handle middle age, then they better hang on tight for the bumpy ride into old age."

Chipper couldn't relate. It was all years and years away. But he felt sad for Mr. Ashbrook who had probably not been old forever.

Sometimes, especially when Peachy and Gus were together, Chipper could feel Peachy's snarly smile through the back of his head. And he felt it now. When he turned to greet the familiar sneer, Peachy pulled a door key from his shirt pocket, holding it for Chipper's eyes only.

Peachy leaned across the table and whispered, "After the trophy bullshit is over."

Thirteen

Chipper fidgeted in his chair, anticipating Peachy's next step. No doubt his friend possessed the lost key to the legendary clubroom, a secret hideaway Peachy had long insisted to be in the bowels of the building. No doubt, since Gus worked the cash register at the pro shop, he was privy to the location of the key, allowing Peachy to target the prize. Only one more trophy presentation to go before Peachy would confirm Chipper's hunch.

Amy's runner-up trophy was the same size as Chipper's trophy for winning A-flight. Most guys had to beat girls at everything from miniature golf to bowling, but he was A-okay with it all. Then again, what if she were to actually beat him someday?

Peachy, Buster, and L.K. all sat clutching their trophies, while Kelly continued to chat with Carol, trying to make her feel welcome in the group. Chipper noticed how the shy ninth-grader would look back toward Buster and smile repeatedly, softly touching his arm, as if she needed to make sure he was still there.

"And now before I present the final trophy," said Carl Dresden, "I would like to make the following observation..."

Mr. Dresden was the club pro and high school golf coach, at least for now. The position seemed to change every few years. He was a likable sort, with greasy dark hair, deep acne scars, younger than their parents, but still old. Occasionally, he had a few good pointers but... Mr. Ashbrook had been around forever.

"It has come to my attention," continued Dresden, "that we have a newcomer to the club championship. The record number of club championships, of course, belongs to this young man's father. But Doc Jody is away again on his medical missionary trip, this year in the Yucatan peninsula. I guess if he stayed put here in El Viento, he would win every year."

There were a few chuckles. The mere mention of Doc Jody's name was enough to bring a smile, so it didn't take much to nudge it into laughter.

"But there comes a time when the father steps aside for the son, and I am pleased to announce this year's club champion is Jay Justice. Jay, come up here and get your trophy, son."

As the clapping began, Peachy rose to launch a standing ovation, but the crowd manipulation failed and he sank back to his seat without a trace of embarrassment.

Jay brushed back his blond locks as he approached the trophy table, his strong jaw thrust forward and his nose peeling thick clumps of skin.

"I expect this is the first of many club championships for Jay," Mr. Dresden said, "not to mention other championships. We're looking forward to Jay's performance next golf season, especially at the state level. If he can whip the Cosgrove kid from Castlemont, Jay might just take it all. Then El Viento will have its first state high school champion."

Chipper was royally peeved that the *coach* wasn't mentioning next year's *team*.

Jay whispered something to Dresden.

"Jay, here, has just reminded me that our boys have a pretty fair chance at the team trophy, too. Let's hear it for Jay now."

Again, Peachy popped up like a piece of toast, this time with bootlick Gus. Undaunted by previous failure, Peachy tried to incite riot through whoops and hollers. Chipper joined them, signaling the others at the table to rise. The entire crowd stood to their feet in polite applause, more subdued than the winners' table.

After the ceremony, the team and their girls clustered at the jukebox until the last adult was gone. Gus was looking guilty.

"I know what you're thinking, Jay," Peachy said, "...Chipper...thou shalt not steal, and crap like that. Well, I'm not stealing. Gus is going to put the key back tonight, right where he got it, *after* we inspect the secret room."

As Peachy led the expedition down an isolated hallway at the north end of the dining hall, Chipper had the feeling that his friend had made the trip before. Thus, the bravado.

At the end of the hall, Peachy inserted the key and opened a ho-hum door that Chipper had never even noticed before. Single file, with Peachy in the lead, the nine explorers started down the stairs. Only the light from above helped guide them into the darkness.

Once they were all on the same level in the secret room, Peachy flipped on the lights.

It was spectacular.

The entire chamber, about the size of the pro shop, was lined with slot machines. Chipper had never seen a real slot machine before, only in the movies and on television. Most of the machines were for nickels and dimes, but a few used quarters. Peachy walked directly to a quarter machine, pulling out a handful of more change than anyone ever carried, confirming Chipper's impression that this was not Peachy's first entry to the secret tomb.

"Now let me tell you about these hypocritical assholes," said Peachy. The others were touching and stroking the machines to see if they were real. "Every other year about election time, Sheriff Kipler leads a raid on this place. Or what they call a raid. They put the slots in a big pile, take a picture for the front page of the *Tribune*, then put the slots back where they belong, right here. The church folk think it's wonderful, lard-ass Kipler gets reelected, and it's business as usual."

Peachy continued to stuff riches into the machine two bits at a time, pulling the handle over and over. The others milled around the room, gawking at the bar, the bottles of whisky, the ashtrays full of cigarette and cigar butts. Three game tables with green felt tops and strange markings were positioned around the room, each with a low overhanging light. Paintings of dogs playing poker covered the walls above the slot machines. In fact, the room was a fairly good replica of Peachy's basement.

Chipper's eye was drawn to a bookshelf, mostly empty, but home to a few tarnished trophies. He opened a door at the base of the shelves and discovered an old, dusty scrapbook propped up in the space. Some letters were missing on the cover, but he could still read: El Vi nto G lf and C ntry C b.

"Amy, look at this."

"What?"

They took the book out of the shelf, brushed off the cobwebs, and sat down together on a sofa. Flipping back the cover, they saw orange newspaper clippings so old they crumbled like wheat flakes. Chipper went right to the date of the first clipping: May 2, 1929.

He didn't recognize any of the people in the pictures, or the names, so he continued turning. A front page of the *Daily Oklahoman* with a picture of an oil derrick stopped him cold.

"Look!"

"Unbelievable," she said.

"Hey, guys, look at this," he called to the rest of the group. They began to huddle around, though Peachy continued pouring quarters into his seductress. "Look at the date."

August 7, 1935.

"Now the picture."

It was a golfer, swinging a club at the base of an oil derrick, standing inside the black latticework. Another golfer, resting his arm on his bag, stood beside the first. The State Capitol was in the background.

"Now the caption." His heart was racing.

Perennial state amateur golf champion, Ethan Ashbrook, performs his trick rocket shot to promote the PGA Championship to be held this week at Twin Hills Country Club in Oklahoma City, while favorite Tommy Armour looks on (see related story).

Chipper's silent reading was well ahead of the others, as he was already into the story where it described the rocket shot, placing one ball on top of the other, then hitting the bottom ball. Apparently, in 1935, Mr. Ashbrook's trick shot was so well mastered that the top ball went straight up in the air and down again, without ever hitting the sides of the oil derrick.

"Unbelievable."

"Perennial state amateur champ."

"What does perennial mean?"

"It means happening over and over."

"Why didn't he go pro?"

"He was famous."

"He's been doing that rocket shot for years."

The group muttered in amazement, reading the story over and over, repeating their comments.

"Why didn't he go pro?"

"The rocket shot."

"Without hitting the sides of the derrick."

"As Tommy Armour looks on."

"That was the PGA that Johnny Revolta won," said Jay.

"The guy that broke his club on the Hanging Tree?"

"Yeah. He beat Tommy Armour five and four. It was match play back then."

Chipper snapped the group to attention: "We better get outta here before we get caught."

"I'm already outta here," L.K. said as he started for the stairs. "I've gotta wade the creeks before dark."

The others followed, knowing they would never dare to enter this sanctuary again. Except for Peachy, probably.

"I knew the old man used to be good..." started Peachy.

"What do you mean, 'used to be'?" said Chipper. "He still beats your butt."

"I mean really good. I had no idea."

They shook their heads in disbelief and marched up the stairs. Peachy made a quick dash back to a slot machine for a final play. After yanking the handle, bells started to ring followed by clinking coins dropping into the winner's cup. Peachy filled his pockets with quarters, claiming a small fortune, then joined the rest of the group as they climbed the stairs.

Topside, Amy insisted that Peachy use his jackpot quarters to play the jukebox. He agreed after minor protest. Gus scampered off to return the magic key to the pro shop. Buster and Carol seemed uncomfortable remaining with the group, but Kelly offered to take them home if L.K. was too long in the creeks.

Chipper wandered to the panoramic windows overlooking the course. The top rim of the sun was still peeking above the hill, and he could see L.K. fishing out his new golf ball supply a hundred yards away in the creek on Number 1 where the cattails grew so thick.

He heard the jukebox click into gear, followed by the Platters singing, "I Loved You a Thousand Times." Although it was the flipside of a bigger hit, "Thousand Times," was Amy's number one favorite dancing song because of the swing rhythm that could spin her around Chipper in a customized jitterbug while he struggled for survival. She also liked the words:

I had to write one thousand times
That I love you...

She liked to remind him of his 'Do you want to go steady?' note that Mrs. Harrison intercepted in the seventh grade and posted on the bulletin board.

Amy danced over to Chipper, rocking her shoulders up and down like pistons in a two-cylinder engine, dragging Chipper onto the dance floor.

The three couples, plus Peachy, had the joint to themselves. Peachy didn't need a partner as he twirled in 360s, dipped to the ground, and demonstrated once again that he was king of the hop.

Buster and Carol joined in on the second song, "Only You," also by the Platters, but a slow dance. By the second beat of the song, Jay and Kelly were locked in a wet kiss that wouldn't stop. Peachy fox-trotted by himself, holding an imaginary partner and mimicking the kisses of

Jay and Kelly. Amy snuggled up to Chipper as they stepped softly to the music:

Only you can make this world seem right

The screaming was almost imperceptible, probably not even real. But there was no way to turn down the jukebox to tell for sure.

The Platters sang on, unfazed.

Again. Louder. It was real. A bone-chilling cry like a man being tortured with a red-hot poker through the eye socket.

Chipper ran to the panorama windows and looked out on the course. Nothing. The others grouped beside him.

"Oh my God, look!" Amy shouted.

Rolling on the ground, screaming, near the creek on Number 1 was the invincible L.K. Taylor, his legs covered by a tangled mass of snakes, writhing, jaws attached. He was grabbing them in each hand, squeezing, while one, no two, even more, latched-on near his feet. As L.K. pulled the upper two snakes off, Chipper could see their gaping mouths were white inside. *Cottonmouths!*

"Amy, run to the pro shop and see if Gus is still there," ordered Chipper as the group began to stumble over themselves to offer help. "They keep a snakebite kit under the register. And call an ambulance."

Amy was gone.

Chipper led the charge out the clubhouse door, running beneath the logging chain on the Number 1 tee box, down to the creek. The screams were getting louder.

Fourteen

Chipper couldn't believe he was about to cut into human flesh.

"Connect the holes," he heard Jay call out. "Join the fang marks with your cut."

He looked at L.K. lying in the Number 1 fairway near one of the burnt circles of grass, groaning helplessly. "My legs, oh goddam, my legs are on fire!" he roared between moans.

With only one tourniquet in the snakebite kit, already applied to L.K.'s right leg, Chipper used Amy's pink headband as a garter on L.K.'s other muscular thigh, hoping to halt the spreading poison. The venom had to be extracted immediately.

The others huddled in close as Chipper placed the knife blade near L.K.'s calf.

"I'm sorry, L.K., I gotta do it. Hang on."

As he pressed on the blade, he was surprised at the thickness of the skin. L.K. yelled, but not a whole lot louder than before. A red pin-stripe path connected the fang dots, but Chipper had to repeat his stroke two more times before the skin separated, exposing the yellow fat beneath. He was astonished at the steadiness of his own hand, especially since he thought his heart was about to pound its way out of his chest.

"Here's the suction thing," said Amy, keeper of the snakebite kit. She crouched down beside Chipper and handed him a red rubber bulb, which looked like a grenade in his palm.

"My legs, oh my legs, they're on fucking fire. Stop the fire...please, someone stop the fire."

Chipper placed the mouth of the bulb over the cut, but the dried rubber cracked in his hand as he squeezed. This red grenade was a dud.

He looked first at Amy, then at Jay, scanned the audience, then turned back to Jay.

"It's in the Crotalidae family, pit-vipers," Jay said. "The poison is a neurotoxin that's neutralized by digestive juices. You'll be safe if you suck it out."

Chipper wanted to disappear in a puff of smoke. This was an awful dream and maybe he would wake up soon. Making the cut hadn't been that big of a deal. He would gladly open the other bites if someone else would just...He looked around for volunteers. If someone else would just...Peachy's eyes, then Buster's, then the girls' darted away as he tried to trap their stares. If someone else would...

Chipper placed his mouth around the bloody gash and sealed his lips to the skin. The warm, salty taste was followed by an aroma that reminded him of the dead game birds that he was forced to carry on his father's hunting trips. He sucked until his cheeks hurt, then spit red juice on the ground.

"Are you sure that's safe, whiz kid?" Peachy asked in cross-examination of Jay.

Chipper went back to extracting the bloody poison.

"Yeah, as long as you don't have cuts in your mouth," Jay replied.

Chipper stopped sucking for a moment, then resumed rescue, unable to remember any cuts or canker sores.

"Chipper, move on to the next one," Amy urged. "The rest of the bites are starting to turn purple."

He jumped to L.K.'s other thigh where the pink headband held the poison in check. Crouching down, he cut into the final two bites. L.K. seemed to be moaning less, but breathing worse.

Chipper alternated mouth-suction between the two openings, trying to fight back the nausea that was getting stronger by the minute.

"Amy, what ambulance did you call?" Jay asked.

"Harper's."

"Good. They're pretty quick."

"Harper's Funeral Home and Ambulance Service," Peachy said sarcastically. "Now *there's* a racket. Drive the ambulance fast or slow, you get the body, you make the dough."

Chipper took a mouthful of bloody toxins and spit toward Peachy. He followed with a scowl that sent the motor-mouth slinking to the back of the crowd.

L.K. was no longer making words, just grunts and groans. Beads of sweat were starting to form over his entire body, while his breathing was faster and shallower.

Chipper attacked the last bite with vengeance. He was a pro now, three snake bites to his credit. Cut, suck, spit, suck, spit. Pretty much routine. He could hear the sound of Harper's ambulance in the distance.

And he could see his picture on the front of the *Tribune*. Suck, spit, suck, spit. Just like when Peachy made the front page last spring after his shanked tee shot hit the tool shed. 'Shank Mistaken for Gunshot Shocks Escapees from Shed,' he remembered. Suck, spit, suck, spit. Only this time, the glory would be well deserved, given his heroic role in securing L.K.'s future page in sports history. Suck, spit, suck, spit.

L.K.'s breathing was starting to get scary, like he wasn't even bothering to fill his lungs. His chest muscles were heaving up and down, but the amount of air whooshing seemed small—as worthless as the cracked red rubber grenade that wouldn't suck poison.

Harper's ambulance passed through the parking lot gate and down the Number 1 fairway.

Chipper noticed that little red polka dots were starting to break out around each bite, while L.K.'s legs were starting to swell...a lot. L.K. was drenched in sweat, gasping for air, when the ambulance stopped beside them.

The attendant, Slim Harper himself, jumped out, pulling a stretcher out of the back.

But before they could load L.K., his muscles began to twitch, ever so faintly at first, then hard like a seizure—like Jay's beloved dog Jasper after he ate rat poison, just before he died.

Jay, Peachy, Buster, and Chipper lifted the convulsing L.K. onto the stretcher while Slim Harper guided them through the back of the ambulance. They wanted to accompany Slim to the hospital, but Slim started raving about liability and lawsuits and the like. He told them all to get the hell out of his ambulance.

Carol began to cry when L.K. started to convulse. Up until then, Kelly and Amy were fine, but now all three girls were wiping tears away.

Chipper kept spitting long after L.K. was loaded into the ambulance. His lips were numb, as though a dentist had given him Novocain. Even though his saliva was finally clear, he could still taste the blood...and smell the dead game birds.

"How much venom do you suppose I got out?" Chipper asked Jay.

"You can get about 50% out of each bite."

"So that means L.K. has four half-bites, which is still two full bites.

Can two full cottonmouth bites kill you, Jay?"

"If four cottonmouths emptied their entire storage into L.K., then you removed half, well, L.K. could have as much as 300 milligrams still left. Even for someone L.K's size, 40 or 50 milligrams can be fatal."

Chipper cleared his throat. "Isn't there an antidote or something?"

"Yeah, there should have been some in the snakebite kit, but the kit was too old. My dad gave me a booklet to read when I was in the sixth grade called, 'Antivenin Polyvalent,' so the stuff's been available since 1961, at least. I'm sure the hospital will have some."

He was not surprised that Jay remembered every detail of a booklet given to him five years ago. For Jay, memory was a chip shot.

Chipper put his arm around Amy's shoulders. "You were pretty slick," she whispered.

As he watched the ambulance leave its dust trail up the center of the fairway toward the Number 1 tee box, he could only think of the poison still in L.K., perhaps seven times the fatal dose.

Fifteen

Peachy stood near the trophy wall, his elbow resting on a shelf, fingers dangling, while his other hand was flipping and catching one of Doc Jody's smaller golf trophies.

"Hard to believe it's been a week since L.K. was bit," he said.

"Six days actually," corrected Jay, seated at the player piano bench. "And Peachy, put my dad's trophy down, would you?"

Peachy continued to launch the golden statue higher and higher with each flip. He didn't frequent the Justice's den very often, and when he did, he seemed out of place. Or so it seemed to Chipper who stared at the swirling, spinning golfer-on-pedestal as it fell back into Peachy's palm over and over.

Chipper lifted his feet onto the couch and twisted into recline, folding his arms above his head. "L.K.'s not gonna die," he proclaimed.

"Oh, yeah? How do you know?" asked Peachy.

"'Cause God's not gonna let him," answered Jay.

"Yeah," agreed Chipper.

"Oh, brother," moaned Peachy. "Here I am with two science nuts, and you're tellin' me God's gonna decide this deal?"

"Hey, bozo, you don't use science to prove or disprove God," Chipper said. "That's like using a yardstick to measure the wind."

"Yeah, leave your atheistic junk outside this house, Peachy...and put my dad's trophy down!"

"I'm not an atheist. I'm agnostic."

"Same difference."

"Is not."

"Anyway, it's all predetermined that L.K.'s gonna live," said Chipper.

"Oh, that's right, Mister Presby-fuggin'-terian. It's all about predestination—astrology plus God minus common sense. That's some equation."

"Bug off. Besides," Chipper said, "my dad got the word from one of the specialists in the city who says they're gonna see today if L.K. can breathe on his own."

"Is he in an iron lung or what?" asked Peachy.

"No, some kinda machine breathes for him. He's got a tracheotomy and everything. Still no visitors, though."

"That was pretty cool of your dad to ride all the way to the city in the ambulance with L.K.," Jay said. Chipper stretched a little taller on the couch. He couldn't remember anyone describing his dad as 'cool'.

After all, Jay's dad was the ultimate in cool—a four-sport, four-year letterman in high school, a BMOC at Oklahoma University, then on to medical school where he became Doc Jody. But he grew up with a group of fatherless thugs before a solo event launched a turnaround. Chipper knew the story by heart, and it spooked him still.

Three of Jody's friends picked him up one night in a borrowed car, stolen actually, and the oldest, at fifteen, was driving with a six-pack between his legs. After Jody, they picked up an older girl, Jerri Sue Thackery, a dark-haired beauty who at sixteen was a Homecoming Queen with a yearning for adventure. As the driver tried to open a beer between his legs, he lost control of the car and crashed into a telephone pole. Jerri Sue was married to a wheelchair after that, supposedly still alive 30 years later in some nursing home, having the mind of a three-year-old. None of the boys were injured, but the three besides Doc Jody all died within 10 years—suicide, murder, and alcoholism.

Chipper figured that Doc dedicated his life to being the perfect pop after that, and the ideal citizen. Every time Doc Jody spoke of our debt to society, Chipper pictured Jerri Sue Thackery drooling in her wheelchair, and he knew exactly what Doc Jody was talking about.

And the secret of happiness, according to Doc Jody, was giving. Giving time to your family, giving money to your church, giving encouragement to your friends. Giving. Giving. Giving. Chipper sort of figured that Doc Jody got a little carried away, because the Justices lived in a house half the size of his own, yet Doc Jody and his dad were partners.

"For the last time, Peachy, put the trophy *down.*"

"Ah, don't get your balls in an uproar."

No wonder Jay was so selfless, thought Chipper. After all, Jay had every reason to be a conceited jerk. Good looks, money, coordination, and brains out the ears. In a big city, these things would be attributes, but in El Viento they were liabilities if you didn't humble yourself before the powers that ran the town—and the powers that ran the town were the kids without the looks, the money, the coordination, or the brains. What the power mongers did have was a survival instinct, and their secret to survival was not being prepared for trouble—it was causing trouble. Like the time that Crawdad Malone punched Jay in the face 16 times, counting each punch as he went. He explained that he was celebrating his birthday, and he wanted to knock Jay's 16 lights out since Crawdad didn't have a mother to bake a cake with candles.

Jay had to be especially careful because he was a bona fide genius. Back in the fourth grade, the teachers put Jay on display once at a high school assembly. They did this, Chipper reasoned, just to humiliate the older kids into studying. Jay spoke without notes on the methods used to date the universe. This included stuff like radioactive decay of uranium in meteorites, as well as color-magnitude diagrams of star clusters, or something like that. It was a bust. No one had a clue what Jay was talking about, including the teachers.

However, Mrs. Forehand, the fourth grade teacher, knew Jay was unique. She talked Mama Justice into dragging Jay to Dallas for special testing. Chipper remembered the day when all the fuss ended.

He was spending the night at Jay's when Doc Jody found out about the testing results and ordered it all to stop. "No one's going to make a freak out of my son," "no special schools," and "they'll ruin him," were the phrases that leaked through the bedroom walls. With ears pressed against the plaster, Chipper and Jay heard Doc Jody at his angriest that night. And they heard Doc Jody say their greatest challenge as parents was going to be raising a normal kid in the face of a 184 IQ.

"One hundred eighty-four? Isn't that like a genius?" Chipper asked Jay that night.

"Shhh," replied the genius, "Please, don't ever tell anyone." And they didn't. Except for Kelly and Amy.

Chipper could sniff chocolate chip cookies at 20 yards, and the odor sweeping down the steps to the den made saliva squirt at the sides of his mouth. Kelly had commandeered the kitchen while Jay's mom was out. Usually, Amy assisted but she was shopping with her mom.

"So, it's really from what your dad says that makes you think L.K. is going to live?" asked Peachy.

"Yep." Chipper was enjoying the pride that comes with being the point person with direct information from the doctors. Doc Jody was still in Mexico or Central America, wherever Yucatan was, so his own dad was suddenly a key player in the survival of L.K. Even though the city specialists were really the lifesavers, they relayed their information to Doctor DeHart. "They've had to operate on his legs, though, to relieve pressure or something."

"I hope it doesn't hurt his pro career," Jay said. "There were supposed to be scouts from the Reds and the Yankees this summer at the Chandler Baseball Camp."

"Let's just hope he lives," replied Chipper.

"Yeah, you're right," Jay said. "What was I thinking?"

"I'll say," offered an offended Peachy, never missing an opportunity for a late tackle. "What were you thinking?"

"Chipper, get your butt in here," hollered Kelly from the kitchen. "Help me with these cookies."

"Jay's right here," he replied, shirking to the dutiful boyfriend.

"Do your ears lap over?" she yelled back. "I believe I said 'Chipper.'"

He trudged up the steps to the kitchen and began helping Kelly shift cookies from the tray to a serving plate.

The fluorescent light on Kelly's black hair gave it a purple cast, like the feathers on the blackbirds that hung out on the golf course. Her full eyebrows and generous curves offered the Annette look that was Mouseketeer-perfect for Jay.

Chipper was always amazed at her logic and her ability to size people up, qualities completely separate from her C-plus average. She provided a nice balance for Jay who was so smart he didn't really have room in his brain for day-to-day common sense.

"I'm glad you and Amy are doing so well," she said, with a probing quality that left the sentence hanging in midair for a reply.

"Yeah, great," said Chipper, feeling the need to be brief.

Kelly moved close to his side, where she lowered her voice to a whisper.

"So, Chipper, did you ever wonder why I picked Jay instead of you?"

"No...not really." He felt uncomfortable, as if the teacher were about to pass out graded exams. "Well, I guess maybe I did wonder."

"You must have known I thought about it."

"Uh...yeah, I suppose."

"I've watched you and Jay since we were kids. A girl couldn't help but daydream about waking up to those Doctor Zhivago eyes and having those same eyes on her babies."

Chipper felt like the graded exam was about to be passed out, with his a big fat F. Don't give me my paper, he thought.

"So, why Jay?" he asked.

"I need to be needed, that's all. And Jay needs me. When Jay tees off, he's walking up the fairway to get his ball in the cup in the fewest number of strokes. He's thinking about the green and the flagstick. When you tee off, you're walking up the fairway because there's something out there for you—I've never understood what that something is, but I don't think it has anything to do with a green, a flagstick, or even a next shot. With Jay, for all of his brains, he still needs me to tell him where and when it's time to tee off. From then on, he takes care of everything. But you...you need someone to walk with you every step of the way. You need Amy."

Chipper was beyond confused. Kelly was addressing a problem that didn't exist.

"Amy and I are doing just great, Kelly. I'm not sure what you're getting at."

"You have one too many girls after you, and I don't want you to blow it."

Kelly looked at him quietly for a moment then tilted her head to one side. "I love you like a brother, Chipper."

"I love you, too."

The crash from the den was followed by the most startling shout of the century: "God dammit, Peachy, you son of a bitch, you broke my dad's trophy!"

Chipper felt a new expression on his face, and when he looked at Kelly, she was as wide-eyed as he, staring back. Jay had never cussed in his life. A little glue would fix it, and Doc Jody wouldn't care. What in heaven's name was wrong with Jay?

Sixteen

Chipper decided to squeeze in the back five holes before sunset, even if he did have to play alone.

What had Kelly been rambling about? Playing golf as though there were no greens or flagsticks? She wasn't making sense. At least Jay had seemed normal again after his stunning outburst.

The sun was slipping below the semicircled trees around the seventh green, forcing long shadows to creep toward him up the fairway in fingers. Chipper knew he would have to hurry to finish before dark.

As he pulled his 4-iron from the bag, he turned toward the seventh green. He couldn't believe what he saw. He shook his head, shut his eyes and opened them again, but the girl was still there. Where did she come from?

She looked quite young, but how could he tell from 185 yards? She was standing in the middle of the green, motionless, with one arm parallel to the ground, holding the flagstick.

In a white shirt and white shorts, she didn't have the curves for him to guess her age. Maybe twelve, maybe seventeen. Her hair was so blonde it was Clorox white, hanging to the middle of her back, shining bright even in the shadows.

As he teed the ball, she remained frozen. What now? He couldn't tee off with her standing on the green. He looked around as if someone might help him with his dilemma: the lady or the tee shot. The course was deserted. He started to yell at her, but his voice box jammed. This was too spooky.

With his 4-iron in his right hand he tried to wave her off the green with his left. Somehow, he knew she was planted.

Then a little motion. With one hand still holding the flagstick, she waved him on with her free arm. She was telling him to go ahead and hit. He couldn't read an expression on her face, so he laughed to himself to calm his nerves as she beckoned him.

He addressed the ball thinking it might scare her off the green, but she didn't budge. *Oh well*, he thought, *I never get that close to the pin anyway. She'll move if I do*. And he swatted the ball.

He was immediately relieved that he pulled it left. The ball hit on the fringe. She was like a statue.

As he walked down the fairway, his heart was pounding twice to every step, while the clanking sound of the golf clubs on his shoulder kept the cadence. Her dark eyes were enormous, and her lips were full and colored with a light frost lipstick. Golden brown skin seemed a sharp contrast to her all-white outfit and her snow-white hair. He was still trying to guess her age since her hips were narrow and she had a boyish chest, a testimony to the purity of this angelic figure.

Oh, my gosh. It couldn't be. But as he stared harder, she began to grin, barely. And he knew the answer before he asked.

"Gail?"

She smiled.

"I hear they call you 'Chipper' now. So I figured the safest place for me was close to the pin."

He laughed, not wanting to accept a put-down, even in jest. After all, he had lettered.

He wasn't sure what to do next. His feet seemed nailed to the fringe. "When did you...do you live here...like permanent?"

"We'll have plenty of time for that later, Kyle. I mean...Chipper." She laughed, almost to tease, though he knew better. "Let me see your stuff, Kyle. Let me see why they changed your name."

He was trembling inside, but here was a show-off opportunity that only happened in dreams. His childhood love was asking him to do what he did best. He could hear the Lovin' Spoonfuls playing in his head:

Custom made for a daydreamin' boy

Pulling the lucky 7-iron from his bag, he addressed the ball, noting the break in the green. Gail Perdue turned to face him, still with one hand on the flagstick. The butterflies were swarming inside to the point he feared choking on their wings as they flew out of his throat.

With pendulum precision, he lifted the ball toward the hole. It was going to be close. He could feel it the second the ball took off. The chip broke left like he calculated, bounced, and settled into a slow roll...curling right for the cup. He was going to hole-out, he was certain. The pride began to swell inside.

"Pull the pin," he called in his excitement.

But Gail didn't move.

When the perfect shot reached the edge of the cup, she pushed the flagstick forward like a throttle, stopping the ball on the lip.

"You didn't say the magic words." She wasn't smiling, and Chipper felt both fear and frustration twisted tightly together to form a rope of anger.

"Magic words? What are you talking about...magic words?"

"You don't remember, do you?" She seemed to be looking right through him. Still no smile.

He walked toward her, gripping his 7-iron for comfort. He wanted to bolt from the spot, so he didn't understand why his feet were carrying him to her threshold.

"You don't remember the magic words, 'I love you'? And that if you say the magic words, then everything after that will be okay? If you would have said the magic words...*Kyle*...I would have let your shot go in."

His anger melted, and a puzzling force seemed to be taking hold of him. He didn't understand it; he could only feel its pull. And he had never felt anything this powerful before.

"Can you say the magic words, Kyle? Can you?"

His throat was paralyzed, and he began to shake.

"No, you can't, can you? You can't keep that promise any more than you can keep the promise to save your class ring for me." Her voice changed from teasing to disappointment, as her gorgeous eyes began to look so very sad. She dropped her head to the ground, then lifted her eyes partway back up into Chipper's.

"That was years ago, Gail. We were just kids."

"Were we? So kids can break promises, but adults can't? And when do kids become adults? I promised to wait for you, to save myself for you. It's only been seven years, Kyle. Seven years. Now I'm back for you."

He was suffocating. He tried to take deep breaths. He thought of fairways without greens or flagsticks then he tried to think of Amy.

"I know where your class ring is," she continued, "so go on your way. I'm sure you think you're in love, so I won't interfere. I won't need to...because you will remember."

He wanted to reach out and hold her, to tell her "I love you," to tell her that he always kept his promises, that everything would be all right, just like before. But he didn't. He couldn't. Something held him in check.

And while he stared into her eyes, a most remarkable thing occurred. Without a crying sound, not even a whimper, and without changing her calm expression, her eyes filled with tears.

"You will remember," she repeated.

Then she turned away and walked into the darkness of the semicircle thicket of elms, all leaning to the north.

Seventeen

Blowing the ink from his fountain pen dry before he closed the logbook, Chipper read the morning entry:

July 31, 1966: Big day today. L.K. comes home, at least he's being moved to the El Viento Hospital. Also, Doc Jody comes home from Yucatan. Amy's okay now that I've told her about Gail. No wonder everyone's been so goofy lately. Wonder why no one would tell me she's back. Lovin' Spoonful's "Did You Ever Have to Make Up Your Mind?" never made it to the top (peaked at number 2). Over and out.

It was unusual for him to add to his log in the morning, but the day was going to be chock-full, and he never liked to miss an entry. Moments had to be snared on the spot lest posterity be denied precision.

The ambulance was scheduled to deliver L.K. to the local hospital before noon, so Chipper volunteered to corral the team as a welcoming committee. Closing the logbook, he primed himself to leave his room by using the deep breathing drill proven to melt the invisible barrier constructed years long past. He could hear his father in the downstairs study, rustling the newspaper, getting ready to remind him about the garbage. How did his father always know when he was in a hurry?

Peachy and Jay sat with Chipper on the hood of his white Thunderbird at the ambulance entrance of the hospital. Buster couldn't keep still, throwing gravel aimlessly into the wheat field that separated the hospital from the golf course. They had been waiting an hour, and still no sign of L.K.

Chipper grew up in the hospital so the countless visits blurred together, indistinguishable. That is, except the time his dad dragged him to the morgue to look at a dead kid.

The kid had been riding his bike on Birch Street when he was struck and killed instantly by an elderly motorist. Chipper remembered seeing the kid like it was yesterday. All purple and swollen and bloody. Chipper hadn't known him that well, but he had traded baseball cards with him only a few weeks before the accident. Two Whitey Fords and a Nellie Fox for one Del Crandall in return. He couldn't recognize the kid that night. He looked more like an alien. Chipper had been asking for a new bike for Christmas when the kid was killed, so he figured this was his dad's incomparable way of saying no. After all, his dad didn't explain why he made his fifth-grade son look at a dead kid. But then, the weeks passed, and a metallic blue Schwinn Traveler with chrome fenders was waiting for him on a merry Christmas morning.

"Here he comes," shouted Peachy.

They jumped from the hood of the car and began scurrying around the entrance like a colony of ants after a cherry bomb explosion. Slim Harper's rig pulled within inches of their legs before backing, turning around, then bringing the rear of the ambulance to the entrance. Peachy couldn't wait, so he began fiddling with the latch on the back of the ambulance. Slim slapped his hands away.

"Easy does it," Peachy said, flicking his nose with his thumb as if he were ready to spar.

"Back away, boys," said Slim.

The twin doors flew open, and in the darkened rear of the ambulance, they could barely see L.K.

"Hey, peewees," whispered the great athlete, "I'm home."

Chipper could barely contain himself. "Hey, man, we knew you'd make it."

"Welcome home, L.K."

"Yeah, stud, glad you get to see my fuggin' face again."

Chipper helped Slim pull the stretcher out in the sunlight. L.K.'s eyes were sunken and his cheeks were hollow, but other than that, he looked pretty much okay. A white blanket covered him from the waist down.

The team helped Slim roll L.K. inside the hospital where a nurse directed them to room number 16. L.K.'s parents were waiting for him there. His gigantic dad put one hand on L.K.'s shoulder, while the mom started to cry.

As Mr. Taylor helped Slim lift the patient off the stretcher onto the bed, the blanket fell to the floor, revealing both of L.K.'s legs mummified in white bandages.

"Be careful, he can't bear weight yet!" thundered L.K.'s dad. They positioned the athlete in bed, his mother still crying, L.K. panting for air as if the room were full of smoke.

L.K. turned his head on the pillow and stared at Chipper. Lifting one arm off the sheets, he reached to shake Chipper's hand. Chipper lumbered to the bedside where they clasped in a shake that lasted until L.K. said, "Thanks."

The front page of the *Tribune* be damned...hell, this was the nitty-gritty, a truly bitchin' moment.

"Dad," L.K. said, "this is Chipper, Dr. DeHart's son. He's the one who saved my life."

The towering father stretched his huge hand toward Chipper, like one of those Kodiak grizzlies right before the kill. Chipper let go of L.K.'s hand, then felt his fist melt into the giant paw of Mr. Taylor. L.K.'s dad didn't say one single word. Not a thank you. Not a nod. Not a grunt. He didn't even change the growling expression on his face. Chipper couldn't believe it. Maybe the *Tribune* should have run a story after all. Maybe this stone-cold giant needed to read in the newspaper how close his son came to death...how the venom removed at creekside by Chipper DeHart made the difference.

Chipper felt himself starting to pant, as if the air were mountaintop thin. He was compelled to break the silence, hoping to force L.K.'s dad to release the handshake.

"Everything's gonna be all right," he managed. "Just like it used to be."

L.K.'s dad freed Chipper's hand and slowly lowered his fierce eyes to the ground. L.K.'s mom turned her tears to the window.

Eighteen

"Only a couple of weeks left before the fights," spouted Peachy. "I've been working out. Shadow boxing, you know, stuff like that."

Chipper was sick. He had been counting on L.K. to help him. Now what? They said it would be weeks before L.K. was walking again. To make matters worse, the new president of Letterman's Club was Tucker Doogan, a near thug who once eyeballed Amy for a girlfriend and, as a corollary, hated Chipper's guts. And Tucker would be dictator, the absolute monarch, who matched the fighters, sealing their lifetime reputations.

"Jay, how 'bout some advice?" Chipper asked.

"Jog," he said. "Don't worry about fighting skills. With those heavy gloves and the river bottom for a ring, it's the fighter with optimal lungs that wins."

Buster was mute, as usual. He seemed calmer the past few weeks, probably since he and Carol were going steady now. Chipper had warned Peachy not to use the phrase 'robbing the cradle' and all was well. So far.

"I still think we can get in 18 if we walk fast and don't fool around," Chipper said.

"Naw, 13 at the most," Peachy replied. "We spent a lot of time at the hospital."

Chipper teed his ball.

"Hit one for L.K.," said Jay.

As he took his stance, addressing his 2-wood to the ball, he heard a distinctive rumble, a familiar sound, though he had never heard it on the golf course. He stepped away from the ball and turned to follow the reverberations in the parking lot. The others were already looking, mouths open in both fear and surprise.

When Chipper spotted the all-black '40 Ford with the chopped top and tinted windows, he knew they were being visited by the closest thing to a functional hell in El Viento. He backed off the tee box and whispered to the others. "Don't stare."

Jay had nicknamed the black Ford the Carsophagus, by switching the first 's' and the 'c' of sarcophagus. Chipper liked the word because it sounded like 'esophagus,' and he found it easy to picture the Carsophagus, with its man-eater grill of silver incisors, chewing up cars and people, swallowing the bloody, chromic mush.

The Carsophagus was so loud that Chipper could feel the vibrations. He looked down to see if his ball was wobbling on the wooden tee. A row of blackbirds resting on a telephone wire above the parking lot flew off in unison.

The Carsophagus moved slowly into the parking lot, as close to the first tee as it could get. The cable barricade offered little security, however, as the driver could go anywhere he wanted.

"Act nonchalant," said Chipper.

"Nonchalant, shit. I'm gettin' the hell outta here," Peachy squeaked. "What's he doing at the country club? Isn't there any safe fuggin' place in this town anymore?"

"Keep cool, Peachy, don't move," added Jay. "This has nothing to do with us."

In his lifetime, Chipper had managed only one good look at the driver, Jessie Ogle, the most ferocious street fighter in Oklahoma. He looked so much like a missing link that the boys in town quietly referred to him as the Neanderthal. Jay had been quick to point out that the correct pronunciation was Neander*tal*, the silent 'h' having been dropped in modern German when referring to the Neander Valley where the first bones were found. So Neanderthal became Neander Tall, which was gradually shortened to Neander T, and that's how the boys discussed him, in whispers, when the coast was clear and when listeners had lifetime commitments to secrecy and honor.

Chipper remembered every detail from his one sighting. Neander T's forehead sloped back from a brow so prominent it would keep his face dry in a spring rain, or keep the blood out of his gorilla eyes, whatever the need might be. His lips were fat and surrounded by a beard so thick it made his shaved jaw blue. His hairline started low, werewolf style, and he arranged the greasy black tangles straight back. Deep pits and scars punctuated the oily skin of his cheeks. But he was mostly remembered (indeed famous) for his huge arms that were the size of L.K.'s thighs.

Because the chopped top and tinted windows on his car concealed his head while driving, he was identifiable only by the enormous left arm, which hung like a ham out the side of the Carsophagus. And on that left arm, deltoid level, was the tattoo of a scorpion.

Rumor had it—according to Peachy—that the scorpion tattoo was fluorescent, that it would glow in the dark if there were a black light. Whenever Neander T wanted to fight, it was said he would go to the Grease Pit in the city—a bar with a black light—to find a worthy opponent, with the glowing scorpion floating like a green neon bulb through the dark crowd, tail curled and ready to strike.

Jay called it all baloney and said the rumor probably got started because real scorpions actually do fluoresce and that's how scorpion hunters and collectors find them without getting stung, by using black lights.

Many allegations circulated about Neander T, and they were spoken like truth, though no one knew for sure. Developmental highlights included being tossed out of ninth grade for decking the football coach during practice, breaking the coach's jaw, thus ending a barbaric sports career. The father was as mean as the son until Neander T beat his old man to a pulp when the kid was fourteen, right in the middle of the mother's graveside services. His antics in street fights were often recounted by eyewitnesses, though Chipper had never met a true eyewitness. But the story that sounded true and made him sick to his stomach was Neander T's nasty habit of putting his defeated rival's front teeth on the bumper of the Carsophagus while holding onto the poor soul's hair, then stomping on the victim's head, causing his teeth to explode.

Why was he here? What business could he possibly have at a golf course? He was supposed to be cruising the streets of Oklahoma City and Tulsa looking for like-minded monsters so he could practice his technique of dental extraction.

Chipper tried not to stare, but he couldn't help sneaking quick glimpses of the idling car, especially the bumper where there might be a whole row of teeth marks. The others were doing the same. The Carsophagus didn't move. Nonchalance was starting to wear thin.

To show the others that they couldn't live in fear, Chipper stepped back onto the tee box and tried to pretend Neander T wasn't breathing fire down their necks.

The golf ball was still perched on the wooden tee, surviving the earthquake's vibrations. Chipper addressed the shot, giving one last look to his comrades-in-group-terror. They were frozen, speechless, a long stretch from nonchalance.

He felt his arms were wooden as he tried to start his backswing. Nothing moved. He tried again. Still nothing. Then he pictured Amy standing there, watching him shake like a mouse in the presence of a mountain lion. He felt the backswing begin, slowly at first, then upward until it gained the necessary momentum, then down. Crack. The ball dribbled off the tee and bounced hippity-hop until it plopped in the creek below, about the spot where L.K. had been bitten.

The pitch of the rumble began to change, prompting Chipper to sneak a look at the parking lot. Through the threatening windows, he could see only a frightening silhouette. The Carsophagus was backing up, ever so slowly. He could breathe again. The black Ford with the man-eater grill crept in reverse, shifted gears, then idled slowly out of the parking lot.

"Sumbitch, fuggin' asshole," mumbled Peachy. "I hate that goddam fugger."

"Take a mulligan," offered Jay.

"Yeah, hit another," added tight-lipped Buster.

Nineteen

Playing 18 holes after an encounter with Neander T was no easy feat. But afterward, near dusk, Jay and Chipper settled down to a game of Horse on the ninth green.

Jay chipped first with his eyes shut, the ball intentionally stymied behind a small tree, but he stopped his shot eight feet from the hole. Chipper's attempt to duplicate failed miserably when his shot hit the tree square.

"Penny for your thoughts," said Jay.

Before Chipper could answer, Carl Dresden, the club pro and sometime-coach, emerged from the basement pro shop and hollered at the boys, his hand cupped to the side of his mouth: "Jay? Telephone call for you."

What sort of phone call would interrupt a golf game?

Jay looked in Dresden's direction, puzzled at first, then resigned. He walked calmly toward the pro shop. As he started down the concrete stairs, Mr. Dresden put his arm around Jay's shoulder and led him through the door.

It was odd for Mr. Dresden, usually aloof, to throw his arm around anyone. Chipper shrugged and went back to knocking the ball about the green. He dropped his junker 5-iron used in Horse and pulled out the lucky 7-iron to practice chipping. Mr. Ashbrook encouraged him to practice his drives, to learn better control, so he could capture the distance of the driver rather than his 2-wood. But Chipper liked doing what he did best, and it was more fun to play around at the short game where no one could compete, not even Jay.

Less than five minutes passed before Jay stormed out of the pro shop, up the stairs, marching toward his golf bag by the ninth green. Something was wrong. Something was *terribly* wrong. Jay's eyes were puffy red, and he wasn't looking anywhere but at his golf bag as he charged across the green. He didn't even look at Chipper.

"What's wrong, Jay?"

No answer.

Jay lifted his bag, then slammed its bottom to the ground before hoisting it onto his shoulder. He started back to the pro shop, but stopped suddenly, frozen.

"What's wrong?" Chipper asked again.

His friend turned in slow motion, wearing a scary look, still not making eye contact, sort of the groping stare of the blind. He began walking, slower than before, away from the pro shop, to the edge of the course near the parking lot.

What the hell was going on? Chipper was afraid to say or do anything. He had never seen Jay like this in all the years he had known him.

Jay threw his clubs on the ground, metal clattering, then he yanked out his driver. He pulled out a ball and teed it up facing the opposite direction from the golf course. His face was redder than Oklahoma clay as he put the driver to the ball.

Chipper remained paralyzed.

A powerful swing sent Jay's cannon shot soaring out of the parking lot, over Country Club Road, and into the new housing development across the street. A loud thud signaled contact with lumber.

"One," Jay shouted angrily.

Chipper took a few steps forward, then stopped. Jay was going to do it again. He aimed another ball at the future residential area, where 2 x 4 frames decorated the landscape that might have been another nine holes for the golf course.

"Two," yelled Jay as he whacked the next shot, which ended with a loud pop, rather than the dull thud of the first.

He wasn't stopping. He put down a third ball, wiping away tears as he addressed the shot.

"Three," he shouted, as the crack of the club against the ball was echoed by another pop from the development.

Chipper had to force his mouth closed. It couldn't be. It just couldn't be happening.

Jay retrieved more balls from his bag, hitting them one after another toward Doc Jody's nemesis.

"Four."

"Five."

"Six."

Chipper inched toward Jay, lifting his own clubs onto his shoulder.

"Seven."

"Eight."

Jay was sobbing now, wiping away tears so heavy he could barely see to swing.

It was impossible. It couldn't be true. This was all a dream.

"Nine."

"Ten."

"Eleven."

Chipper finally managed to speak as he came close. "A twenty-one gun salute?"

Jay looked at him a moment, then started bawling again. Chipper felt the same tears welling inside. He swallowed over and over to get the painful knot out of his throat. They couldn't both be crying.

"Twelve."

"Thirteen."

"Fourteen."

Jay went back to his bag for more balls, but the pouch was empty. He kicked the bag, crying and shouting simultaneously. "Nice reward from God for the missionary work," he said. "Nice goddam reward, and now I'm outta balls."

"What happened?" Chipper asked. "How'd it happen?"

"Thunderstorm out of Mexico. They think lightning hit the plane or something. Everyone's dead."

Jay grabbed his stomach and bent over at the waist, crying. He suddenly fell to the ground.

"Oh, Daddy," he sobbed. "Oh, Daddy, come back home. Please come home. I'm sorry."

Chipper walked to his side, but remained at a loss. He stood still for a moment, squelching tears of his own. After all, he had just lost a father, too. What could he do to help? He reached in the pouch of his own bag for more balls. He offered them to Jay who shook his head 'no.'

Chipper pulled the 2-wood from his bag, hesitated, then pushed it back in. Bringing out his untouched driver, he teed the ball just as Jay had done.

"Fifteen," he said as he powered a drive into the neighborhood.

"Sixteen."

"Seventeen."

"Eighteen."

Jay was curling up like a roly-poly.

"Nineteen."

"Twenty."

"Twenty-one."

Jay stopped crying, coiled so tightly on the ground that Chipper wondered whether there was anything or anyone that could pry his friend open again.

Twenty

For the first time anyone could remember in El Viento, flags had been flown at half-mast for one of its own private citizens. In the two weeks following the funeral, Chipper had written a letter to Mama Justice telling her what Doc Jody meant to him and how he would carry part of Doc with him for the rest of his life. Mama Justice told him it was the nicest note she received out of hundreds and that Chipper had been given a special blessing with words. "Special blessing" had a magic of its own for Chipper, and those two measly words began to haunt him.

As he loaded his clubs in the trunk of his car, Chipper heard the crunching footsteps of cleats on gravel and turned to see Mr. Ashbrook pulling his two-wheeler cart. Chipper waved and nodded, causing the old master to alter his doddering course toward the Thunderbird.

"What have you heard from Jay?" asked Mr. Ashbrook.

"Still nothing. Stays in his room all the time. Kelly goes in, but says he's like a robot. She can't figure it out either. But he won't talk to any of us guys."

Chipper was both hurt and puzzled by this stony severance from his best friend.

"He'll snap out of it," Mr. Ashbrook said, with the sort of assurance that Chipper longed to hear.

"Yeah, he's got to. Says he's never gonna play golf again."

"Oh, I wouldn't worry about that. Time has a way of taking care of these things. How 'bout L.K.?"

"Not much better, Mr. Ashbrook. The team is droppin' like flies."

"How so?"

"I was at the hospital one day when they changed his dressings. They had to remove a whole bunch of dead muscle from his legs, you know. It was like both calves were filleted open. Grossed me out."

"What about sports? Do they say?"

"Yeah. 'Unlikely' is what they say."

"Unlikely?" Mr. Ashbrook lit his pipe and puffed a few times. "Did you ever watch Ron Stevens play golf?"

"Yes, sir."

"Notice anything funny about his swing?"

"No, sir. A bit choppy is all. Shoots pretty good, doesn't he?"

"A seven handicap is pretty good, all right, but he's got another handicap and it's beneath those long pants he always wears when he plays."

"Oh?"

"Lost his leg in the war, right below the knee. He's got a wooden leg."

"Wow."

"My point bein' if L.K. can walk, he can play golf. The other sports may be out, but not golf. Not if he can walk."

Chipper was, in fact, on his way to L.K.'s house at this very moment, having been summoned by the formerly great athlete to be the first friend ever to cross the threshold of the Taylor home. Chipper didn't know why L.K. wanted him to visit, but he couldn't wait to share the inspirational news of Ron Stevens's wooden leg.

Chipper hopped in the front seat of his car and spoke to Mr. Ashbrook through the open window. "Thanks a lot. I'll tell all this stuff to L.K."

The old man smiled.

Chipper's first expedition to Reformatory Plaza revealed a square drive surrounded by eight modest homes, identical except for the trimmings. These were the homes of the prison elite, completely isolated from the goings-on at El Viento.

The wood siding of L.K.'s house was yellow, with white trim around the windows. Chipper noticed that Mrs. Taylor's flower boxes were unique in this dreary eight-house community, and she had stuffed them with white and yellow flowers that looked like daisies or something.

He couldn't believe he was about to become the first to set foot in the Taylor household, excepting the three Taylors, that is. Before he rang the bell, the door opened a bit, then all the way. Mrs. Taylor appeared in a yellow housedress splattered with cheery white flowers, a notable contrast to her sad and sunken eyes, though she still managed a smile.

"Please come in, Chipper," she said, faltering in her words. "Have a cookie." She seemed to have rehearsed the baked goods offering.

Before he could get his paw on the first chocolate chip, he heard L.K.'s strained voice in the darkened living room, "Come in and sit down, buddy."

Taking a chomp out of the cookie, he eased into an armchair, visualizing L.K. better now that his eyes were adjusting to the dark. He thought it peculiar that the drapes would be closed on such a sunny day.

L.K. was wearing the uniform of the golf team: Bermuda shorts and no shirt. His chest and arms seemed to be bulging more than usual, but his calves were the shockeroo, scrawny to the point of polio legs, with vertical strips of white tape on each.

Chipper must have been staring because L.K. said, "The open areas are just about closed in. The skin is coming together like a zipper."

Embarrassed, Chipper looked up and away. Mrs. Taylor had disappeared, though she couldn't be far away in such a small house.

"I'm sorry I can't help you get ready for the lettermen's initiation."

"Oh, that's okay." It wasn't okay, but he said it anyway. "Amy's been on me every day to jog. In fact, she's been riding her bike beside me. Jay told me early on that your lungs were more important than boxing skills."

"And how is Jay, anyway?"

"No change. Hermit city. I can't figure it out."

L.K. groaned some as he moved his legs, then let out a sigh. "How many more days to lettermen's?"

"One week, three days, seven hours. Can you make it?"

He hoped L.K. could be there, like the big brother he never had, the guy that would protect you if things got really bad.

"I'll try, but I don't think I'll be able to maneuver on the river bottom. My crutches will sink in the sand, you know."

They stared at each other in silence for a moment. Chipper was disappointed, and he started to feel his stomach knot.

"Chipper, there's one thing besides improving wind that'll help you in the fights."

"What's that?" he asked, his pulse jump-starting.

"Whether or not you can psyche yourself up. What do you plan to do for that?"

"I hadn't really thought about it. I'm pretty afraid of losing. That oughta count for something."

L.K.'s face hardened and his lips grew tight. "It doesn't count for shit."

Chipper arched his back and sat a little straighter in the chair.

"I want you to think about this, buddy. I want you to think about the thing that makes you the angriest."

Chipper's mind was blank.

"I want you to be angry, Chipper. Not all the time. In fact, not a moment before the fight. But the second you put on the gloves, I want you to think about the thing that makes you the angriest, the thing that pisses you off like you've never been pissed before." L.K.'s voice was fuming more and more with every word. "So what is it, Chipper? What makes you the angriest?"

"I guess Doc Jody getting killed," he replied.

"What?" L.K. said loudly.

"I said...Doc Jody getting killed."

"So, who are you mad at? Huh?" L.K. tightened his fists as his voice grew louder.

"No one."

"Bullshit! Who are you mad at?"

"I dunno. There's no one to be mad at. Things happen."

"Bullshit, Chipper. Bullshit!" L.K. lifted one of his crutches and started shaking it at Chipper. "Tell me who you're mad at!"

"I'm mad at God!" Chipper shouted. "God! Okay?" He felt his voice quiver and he swallowed hard, waiting for the lightning to strike. "I'm mad at God."

"Damn right you are," said L.K., his voice softening now. "Damn right you are." He set the crutch back down by his side.

"Everything all right in there?" It was L.K.'s mother, calling from a nearby room.

"Everything's okay, Mom."

"I'm sorry. I didn't mean to be so loud," said Chipper.

"No, you're not sorry," L.K. said. "Don't take it back. You needed to say it, and you needed to say it loud."

"I've never said that before."

"Well, when you meet that sumbitch at the river bottom in two weeks, you just remember how angry you are about that. You think about Doc Jody, then punch the asshole's lights out." L.K.'s frown melted, and he let out a raspy chuckle.

Chipper wished L.K. could be there at the river bottom.

"So, L.K., I've got a question for you."

"Yeah?"

"What were you thinking when you whipped L.D. Washington? What were you angry about?"

L.K. leaned back in his chair and seemed to drift off to the moon. His eyes rolled up to the ceiling for at least 30 seconds before answering.

"I was thinking about my brother, and the fact he'd never see me play sports."

Stunned, Chipper said, "You had a brother?"

"I *have* a brother." L.K. said.

Chipper was speechless.

Recognizing the bombshell, L.K. continued. "Older brother, five years older. He's got muscular dystrophy. Symptoms started when he was four, and he's been in bed now for eight years. They say he'll get pneumonia some time and die. He was already walking funny as early as I can remember, but he was born normal."

"I'm sorry, L.K. I didn't know. Where does he...I mean...where is he?"

L.K.'s look was piercing, and he clenched his teeth so that the muscles on the side of his snowplow jaw began to bulge.

"No one else knows. You're the first. Dad's tried to keep it a secret. It's damn near killed my mom to see Dad so embarrassed by his own son."

Chipper began to twist and fidget, wondering if he was hearing more than he should.

"I'm fed up now, though," said L.K. "I'm not keeping it a secret anymore. I always thought that Benny would get to see me on TV, you know, playing college sports, then professional. But not anymore." He looked down at his legs. "Now Benny and I are two of a kind. He's heredity and I'm environment."

Chipper looked around to make sure L.K.'s dad wasn't nearby. Then again, how could anyone that size hide?

L.K. grabbed his crutches and carefully stood to walk. He did pretty well, shuffling down a hallway that was darker even than the living room. Turning over his shoulder, he silently commanded Chipper to follow.

As soon as L.K. twisted the bedroom doorknob, Chipper knew he was in for a shock. This could be worse than the dead kid in the morgue. A hospital disinfectant smell came pouring out of the cracked door.

"Benny? You awake? I want you to meet someone."

A guttural noise came from the corner where he could see a large bed with side rails, and a lump covered by sheets.

He followed L.K. two paces behind as they approached the bed. Slits of light penetrated the Venetian blinds, forming stripes on the face of a horribly emaciated boy. His eyes were half closed, no stockpiled energy left to open them all the way. He looked ten years old. It was hard to believe he was twenty-two.

L.K. lifted the sheets part way. Chipper had guessed right. This was worse than the morgue. He wondered how the human body could get so contorted, especially if the kid was born normal.

"Shake hands, Benny. This is my friend."

Somewhere out of the twisted limbs, a skinny arm emerged. Chipper couldn't imagine room for a muscle in this bony branch, skin wrapped so tight it was blotchy red with tension.

Chipper groped through the side rails until he found the sticks of a hand that could barely open for a handshake. Once he got in the groove of the bones, he was careful not to apply any pressure.

"This is Chipper. This is the guy that saved my life."

Benny's eyelids opened, and Chipper felt a gentle squeeze on his hand. He nodded and Benny returned the gesture. Even the white skin of his face was stretched tight, paper-thin. It looked like the corners of his mouth would rip if he tried to smile. The burr haircut only made it worse.

Chipper felt himself pulling away, chilled to his core. L.K. put the cover back over Benny, talked for a moment with his brother, then guided Chipper out of the room, allowing Benny to drift back to sleep.

Walking to the living room, Chipper asked, "So you were mad at God, too, huh? I mean when you were fighting L.D. Washington?"

"Oh, no, not at all."

Chipper cocked his head, wondering what he had missed.

"I'd never known my brother any way but crippled."

"So what were you mad at? Who were you mad at when you fought?"

L.K. stopped cold and turned around to face Chipper. He raised one eyebrow and answered, "My old man."

Chipper gulped.

"My father refused to let Benny go outside. As soon as it got to where my brother couldn't walk anymore, Dad just parked him in the bedroom. In fact, we moved to El Viento at the same time Benny became bedfast, so no one here even knows about him. Dad said it was a job promotion by moving to this new prison, but I knew he wanted to keep Benny hidden from everybody.

"When I fought L.D. Washington, I was furious...furious that the old man wouldn't bring Benny to any of my sporting events. He could have, you know. All it would've taken is a wheelchair." L.K.'s jaw muscles twitched as the boys got closer to the front door. "So much for the great L.K. getting to thrill his big brother by being on television. Now Benny will never see me play anything—not football, not basketball, not baseball." L.K. let out a forced laugh. "And they don't show college golf on television, as if I'll even be able to do that."

"Sure you'll do it. Did you know Roger Stevens has a wooden leg?" Chipper announced with inspiration.

L.K. looked at him like he was the biggest dumbshit in the world.

"Now if you'd told me he has *two* wooden legs, I'd be impressed," L.K. said. "Okay, Chipper, I'll admit it: I'm mad at God, too. I wasn't then, but I am now. I feel like my life just ended prematurely."

No one was telling him so, but Chipper knew it was time to go. He kept on walking through the living room then pushed the screen door open, turning for one final question. "So what's harder, being mad at your father or mad at God?"

L.K. looked tired; the champion in early retirement. Four-sport letterman, all-state in the three sports already, the same predicted for next year. It was all over now.

"I dunno," he said. "All I know is that I see the old man every day. I don't see God much at all."

Chipper nodded and turned to the driveway where his Thunderbird waited. Halfway down the sidewalk he heard L.K. call to him, "Hey, I almost forgot, buddy. When I get where I can walk, will you help me with my short game? You know, chip and putt, down in two...just like you?"

"You bet, L.K." He swallowed hard.

Twenty-one

Chipper wasn't sure how she'd found out he was at L.K.'s house. People didn't accidentally drive by Reformatory Square. She must have followed him, and in the short time he was visiting with L.K., put the note under his wiper blade:

Kyle—

Meet me at the bowling alley—now! (Lane 7)

Gail

The bowling alley was at the town's outskirts on his way back home, but Amy was expecting him at 7:30 for his three-mile jog.

He hadn't talked to Gail in a full month, not since that evening on the seventh green, but he'd heard plenty. Fall classes hadn't even started, and she was already the most popular girl in school. Every hound dog in town was after her, and the girls were predicting she'd be head cheerleader. Only Kelly and Amy seemed concerned. Rumors linked her to three different guys already, but Chipper dismissed it as speculation. No one had actually seen her on a date.

Up the road, he saw the neon bowling ball and the lighted pins that fell over and over as the ball rolled across the sign.

I don't have time. Amy might find out. Kelly would kill me. I didn't bowl anymore. He thought of a dozen reasons not to stop, then felt his hands turn the steering wheel into the bowling alley parking lot.

As he opened the swinging glass doors, he considered an about-face, but he moved ahead. He reached to loosen his collar, but he was wearing a polo shirt and the collar was wide open.

Standing on Lane 7 with her back to him was Gail. Snowy blond hair hung to the middle of her back. She looked like a camp counselor in white shorts, white shirt, white socks, and bowling shoes. She held the ball to her chest, began her delivery toward the foul line, then let it go. She hit the head pin straight on, but left the 8-10 split.

When she turned around, she caught his eye and waved. She pointed back and forth between him and a pair of bowling shoes, indicating that she had already made the arrangements.

He looked to see who would testify against him. Only four of the sixteen lanes were occupied, and the bowlers were unknowns. Forcing himself into a casual stroll, he approached Lane 7.

"Size ten," he said, taking the shoes from her hand. "How'd you know?"

"I sized you up at the golf course that day."

"Oh," he said with caution. "Good guess."

He looked into her brown doe-eyes, which needed no makeup, and he wondered if those long lashes caused a breeze when she fluttered them like she was doing now.

"Kyle, I'm sorry if you felt pressured when we talked last."

"Oh, no, not at all," he lied.

"I know I came on strong. I guess I realized it when you never called me after that. It's just that I had waited so long for you that..." She cut herself short. "Oh, well, what's done is done. I just wanted you to come here today and help me celebrate my birthday."

"Your birthday?"

"Don't you remember? It's exactly six months to the day after yours. I think that means something." She smiled.

The next thing he knew he was lacing up the green, white, and red clown shoes. They were too loose. He wore a size nine, but he didn't want to hurt her feelings.

"Well, happy birthday," he offered, feeling a trickle of sweat leave his armpit and roll down his side. "Uh, Gail, why are you here alone? Why aren't you celebrating with friends or your family?"

Dumbshit, he thought, *why'd you mention her family?* Crazy rumors were always spinning about her dad, including one that he'd killed himself in California. In a prison, no less.

"My mom and I will celebrate tonight. You know my parents were divorced while we were in Los Angeles. My birthday is very special to me, and I wanted you to be the one."

An identical trickle of sweat left his opposite armpit and dripped into his shirt.

"I'm sorry, I...I can't stay very long," he said trying to hide the strain in his voice. "Really...I mean it."

He bowled 142 in the first game, 125 in the second game, and was working on a spare in the eighth frame of the third game. Time could really fly. He rolled a strike.

"Oooo," she squealed, clapping her hands.

He hadn't lost the old touch. He couldn't remember why he had stopped bowling. Gail was starting to loosen up, and he was enjoying himself.

Suddenly, he looked beyond Gail to see the doors of the bowling alley fly open and three lettermen in their jackets burst through in a flying wedge, with President Tucker Doogan in the lead.

Gail looked over her shoulder and said, "Oh, no, Kyle. Those boys are so ridiculous. Don't let them bully you, okay?"

He wasn't even thinking in terms of allowing such an opportunity. He was thinking more along the lines of a rapid exit out the side door, since all three lettermen were glaring at him as they marched.

The flying wedge stopped behind the plastic seats. Tucker's moon face and hooked nose made him look like an owl, especially with the slow and deliberate blinking of his round eyes. But with his muscles exceeding the legal limit packed onto a six-foot-three-inch frame, he was one scary sumbitchin' owl.

He raised one arm with index finger extended, and began curling the finger over and over toward himself. The 'follow me' command was clear. His two henchmen smiled.

Chipper could almost hear the other prisoners banging their cups against the bars of their cells as he made the long journey to the death chamber, exiting the bowling alley with the entourage, sandwiched between two lackeys, led by Tucker Doogan. Chipper never looked back at Gail.

In the alley outside, Tucker pushed him against the building, looking down on him, spitting in anger as he yelled, "You're not gonna steal another one from me, you candy ass son-of-a-bitch. You understand?"

"Tucker, what exactly is a candy ass?" Sometimes, Chipper couldn't control his mouth, especially when threatened.

"You wanna know what a candy ass is? I'll tell you what it is, you pissant jerk-off. It's you and your rich-ass, pretty-boy, fuggin' golf friends. That's what it is. Golf isn't even a goddam sport. I can't believe they let you candy asses letter."

"Well, Tucker, let me tell you something. I'm not trying to steal Gail. We're old friends, that's all. Amy and I are still going steady. In fact, I'm supposed to be there right now." He looked at his watch to add an element of authenticity to his statement, hoping the official nature of his itinerary today would scare away these three hungry gorillas.

Tucker's face got real close. "Let me offer your candy ass some advice. You stay away from Gail...period!" With the word "period," he poked his finger into Chipper's chest and the reflex was automatic—he shoved Tucker away.

Before he knew what happened, Tucker lifted him by his neck against the wall. His feet no longer touched the ground.

"You wanna fight me? Let's do it right here and now. Eddie and Homer won't interfere. When you push me, you better be ready to back it up. Fuggin' pity that your old buddy L.K. isn't gonna be much help protecting you candy ass golfers anymore."

"I'm not stupid enough to fight you, Tucker," Chipper grunted. "It's not an even match."

He felt his feet touch the ground again as his stretchy polo shirt pulled out of his Bermudas.

"Yeah, well, I may just have to fight you myself at the initiation."

Chipper knew an idle threat when he heard one. Only the new initiates to Lettermen's Club would fight. Tucker had lettered years ago, probably shortly after birth. Chipper also knew that idle threats signaled a downscaling of tension—this sixth sense was highly developed in the candy asses that grew up in El Viento.

"Never, never, never—do you hear me?—never do I want to see you with Gail again."

"Fine, Tucker, fine."

In one transient second of bravery, Chipper brushed through the circle of letter jackets, walked away with feigned calm, changed his shoes without a word to Gail, and headed home. That is, to Amy's house.

It was time to jog.

Amy never looked so good. Her hair was in a ponytail, swaying back and forth in rhythm with her hips as she pedaled her bicycle. He jogged behind.

Realizing the bowling alley fiasco was going to be community knowledge, he had told Amy everything. "Gail set you up," she had said. "Baloney," he had replied.

"We've hit the two-mile point," she said over her shoulder.

Good lungs are more important than good punches. Think about what makes you the angriest. Think about Doc Jody. Think about Tucker Doogan.

His wind was harder to come by now, and his chest was cramping along with his right side. He needed to swallow, but his tongue was sticking to the roof of his mouth. Unfortunately, he had one more mile to go. Golfers were in terrible shape.

"Come on, baby, you can do it."

At the sound of her word 'baby,' Chipper began to hear the Beach Boys' "Don't Worry Baby" in his head, and he started mouthing the words as he ran.

People would tell the stories of this year's initiation for one full year afterward, until the new recruits next year. And if the story was particularly good or bloody or gory, then it would be told for generations to come.

He pictured Tucker Doogan as an old man with a grandchild sitting on his knee, both of them laughing with delight at the story of how President Doogan arranged candy ass Chipper DeHart to fight a guy twice his size back in '66, and how the candy ass golfer got the living crap beat out of him. Then he pictured his own grandchildren hearing the same story, whereupon he doubled his jogging speed.

"Slow down," said Amy, as he passed her bicycle. "You're going to kill yourself."

"That's what I'm trying to avoid," he called back.

At the finish line, Amy jumped off her bike and let it drop to the street. She ran to him as he fell on the front lawn of her house. In front of God and, omigosh, the entire neighborhood, she dogpiled on top of him and they squirmed in their sweat, kissing between breaths. "I love you, baby," she said, "and I'll love you after the fights."

...but I keep thinking
Something's bound to go wrong.

Twenty-two

Spartacus looked between the bars of the gladiator pit to see the bloodthirsty crowd gathering in the arena. In a way, he was already relieved that he would not have to wake up to another morning of fear.

Tucker Doogan and his two henchmen were perched on the bleachers, preparing to offer thumbs up or thumbs down, either to continue or stop each and every pummeling. As straightforward as it would seem, sometimes a knockout or hemorrhage was a judgment call.

Torrential rains had forced the initiation indoors for the first time that anyone could remember. Chipper saw it as a disaster. The mushy sand of the river bottom would have softened the power of the punches, but now solid footing would ensure mega-crunches. The importance of lung capacity had diminished, while the need for fighting skills had increased, all due to a rare August thunderstorm.

When the rain started early in the morning, Chipper hoped for a cancellation, but only for a second. This was an event that *had* to take place.

In the face of crisis, President Tucker Doogan had pulled a coup by getting the keys to the gymnasium of the old high school that had been closed five years earlier for integration. Judging from the cobwebs in the gladiator pit, Chipper figured it hadn't been used since.

The initiates were huddled together in a subterranean locker room that emptied directly up a concrete stairwell to the gymnasium floor. Through the iron bars at the top of the stairwell, Chipper watched the Lettermen's Club members form a human rope around the rectangular mat in the middle of the floor. He couldn't see whether L.K. had made it or not. He shrank back into the locker room where the two dozen initiates sat on rotting wooden benches. It was easy to pick out the golfers. All three of them had pearly-white left hands, protected from the sun by their leather golf gloves. Peachy was the only restless initiate in the group, pacing back and forth in front of an emergency exit door. Buster sat on one end of the bench, his head buried in his hands.

What a great position Buster was in, thought Chipper, knowing he had the boxing skills to wreck his opponent. The only empty spot was next to Buster, so Chipper joined him, assuming a similar pose with his head buried in his hands.

The crowd was getting louder outside, and he could hear certain phrases above the drone. "Better than the river bottom," "Beat the living shit out of him," and "Murder the bastard" were just a few.

Chipper scanned the initiates, making mental notes of the ones he thought he could whip. Ten for sure, thanks to track and tennis, six others would be about even, and eight would kill him. He calculated the mortality odds to be one in three.

No one knew the pairings until they were announced with the start of each fight. Anyone was possible, even Buster or Peachy. Maybe Buster would go light on him.

"Hey, Buster," he began, only halfway joking, "if they put us together, promise not to kill me."

Buster didn't move or respond. Chipper figured he was in some sort of prebout trance. Maybe he should try the same.

Tucker Doogan appeared in the doorway. "First fight...Billy Ray Donner and Junior Russell."

"That Tucker's a son of a bitch," whispered Chipper to a mute Buster.

Billy Ray and Junior were best friends, both sophomore basketball stars. Billy Ray was white and Junior was colored. Chipper watched the shock register on their faces as they began to rise to the occasion. As they walked out the door to the stairwell, Junior wrapped his long black arm around Billy Ray's white shoulders.

The crowd noise swelled within seconds, timed with the boxers' emergence onto the gymnasium floor. Chipper once again scanned the subterranean initiates, noting the saucer eyes on each and every one of the boys.

"Oh shit, oh shit, oh shit," Peachy murmured from over near the emergency exit door. Buster's head didn't move from his hands.

Chipper felt his arm muscles tense. He tried to relax, only to feel knots form in his biceps anyway. He was glad he had eaten a can of shoestring potatoes just before leaving home. He needed the extra energy.

A whistle sounded, and the crowd noise escalated off the scale. The fight had started. He could hear the softer sound of rapid-fire boxing gloves fill those second-long gaps in the mob noise. Like waves crashing on a beach, the volume of the crowd went up and down in rhythm with the punches being thrown. He could almost picture the fight, and it was pretty easy to tell that one of the boys was losing ground, probably lily-white Billy Ray.

Finally, a huge groan was followed by a return to hushed mutterings. It was over.

One of the initiates near the door jumped up to sneak a peek, then rushed back to his bench. "Billy Ray's down," he whispered.

Peachy was starting to fiddle with the iron bar on the exit door as he paced. Buster was in a hypnotic state. As each fight was announced, Chipper was disappointed he wasn't next. He wanted to get this behind him, but it was clear Tucker wanted him to suffer as long as possible.

He caught the eye of Tim Richardson, a wide receiver and long distance runner, who seemed to be staring back at him. Tim was a nice guy, always friendly, but flawed, in that he was a friend of Tucker Doogan. Chipper couldn't remember if he'd considered Tim on the 'even' list or the 'death' list of potential pairings, but it should have been the latter. At six-foot-three and state runner-up in the mile, he had both the reach and the wind advantage.

"Peachy Waterman and Buster Nelson," came Tucker's voice from the door.

"Oh, shit!" yelled Peachy as he began to claw at the exit door. It was locked. Buster didn't move.

"Peachy Waterman and Buster Nelson. Get your candy asses out here."

Peachy spun around from the door with terror in his eyes. As he tried to take his glasses off, he fumbled them to the ground. He groped about the floor, finally locating his lenses after no one canceled the fight due to his blindness.

As Peachy stood back up, he stared wide-eyed at Chipper as if to say, "Save me." Then he bent over at the waist, hands on his knees, and began taking huge deep breaths, over and over, faster and faster.

"What the...?" whispered Chipper to himself. "He's not going to..."

Deeper breaths, faster and faster, finally reaching the climax where Peachy stood up straight, held his breath and waited for his eyes to roll back in his head.

Chipper jumped from the bench, flew to Peachy's side and threw his arm around his friend's shoulders. Hoping to fake a nonchalant slug of encouragement, he pounded on Peachy's back, shouting, "Go do it, man. You can do it." On his third blow to Peachy's back, the captured air was expelled just in time to sabotage his friend's attempt at a self-imposed blackout.

Peachy staggered a few steps, put his head down for a second, then raised back up. "I'm still seeing spots," he said.

Chipper looked up to see Buster head out the door, past Tucker Doogan who was still waiting on Peachy.

"You sonuva bitch," Peachy whispered, "I was trying..."

"I know what you were trying to do, man. Now cut the crap and get out there. If you have to, fall down dead the first time he makes contact. No one will think twice. That's what they're expecting anyway."

With that, Peachy handed Chipper his glasses, brushed his thumb against his nose and headed for the door. He scowled at Chipper one more time before he turned into the stairwell.

The other initiates dropped their eyes back to the ground, apparently relieved that they didn't have to fight Buster.

Rather than take his seat on the bench, Chipper eased to the stairwell as soon as the coast was clear. The initiates who had already fought joined the crowd of spectators, making the bodies so dense that Chipper couldn't see anything on the mat.

The whistle blew and the crowd began rioting again. Chipper could barely see Peachy's head bobbing above the crowd, but he couldn't see the shorter Buster who was probably crouched down in the attack position. Peachy's sandy hair seemed to be popping up like a cork on a fishing line, first in one place, then another. As the laughter started, Chipper realized that Peachy was running and jumping in order to stay out of reach of Buster, like Curly in the movie where the Three Stooges get in the fight racket.

Oh, my God, thought Chipper, as the laughter got louder. *Peachy, do something. Anything.*

The bloodthirsty cheers stopped. It was all laughter now. And it appeared Peachy was still running in circles around the ring, Buster hot on his trail.

Like switching channels on the radio, the laughter turned to a collective gasp, then silence. He edged to the front of the stairwell to get a better look, but he still couldn't see what happened. Everyone in the gym was dead quiet. He turned to the bleachers. Tucker Doogan stood up and gave the thumbs down sign. The fight was over in 30 seconds.

Though he still couldn't see the mat, Chipper assumed Peachy had listened to his advice and had taken the fall. His friend was probably lying spread-eagled on the mat right now, faking a coma.

When he spotted Peachy dancing about the ring, arms forming a V in the air, he thought he was dreaming. This couldn't be real. As the crowd backed away from the mat, Chipper could see between the legs that a few guys were huddled around Buster who was flat on his back. Chipper squeezed his eyes closed, then opened them again to the same image. What in the world had happened?

Nobody paid attention to Peachy prancing around the ring with his gloves locked above his head. All eyes were on Buster, the former boxer.

Eight fights and several eternities later, only four initiates remained in the dungeon, Chipper among them.

"Lloyd McCutcheon versus Barry Little," bellowed Tucker's voice from the doorway.

That sonuva bitch, thought Chipper. *Saved me for last, and against Tim Richardson, Mr. Wide-Receiver-State-Contender-in-the-Mile. I'm one dead golfer.*

Tucker smirked and walked out the doorway.

Chipper looked over at Tim who stared back without fear. His acne scars were deeper and his eyes more fierce than Chipper remembered. Tim's hands curled up into fists and he began to pound them on his kneecaps. No words were spoken.

Chipper's stomach felt like he had just swallowed razor blades. But the more he thought about waiting in this hellhole the past hour and a half, the more he sizzled and the less he thought about the razor blades slicing up his stomach. The last fight was supposed to be the main attraction, the two toughest athletes to be initiated, like the time L.K. fought L.D. And here he was, being served up as the main attraction, or more like the main *course*.

The whistle blew and the cheering and jeering began for the next-to-last fight.

Now, for his mental weaponry. He thought about Doc Jody, and the unfairness of it all. *Serving God in some godforsaken country, only to be killed by an act of Nature. But didn't the Bible say God had authority over Nature? Was there a better time to exercise that authority?* He pictured the plane being struck by lightning, then plowing to earth as a fiery ball, a comet careening from the night sky as testimony to the fact that God doesn't bother to intervene. And not only Doc Jody. Just look at pro golfer Tony Lema dying last month in a plane crash right after winning the Oklahoma City Open. Stuff like that happened all the time. And he pictured the fiery comet over and over and over.

The sound of the ravenous masses outside seemed to be fading away.

The fiery comet wouldn't stop. It kept crashing to earth. *One snap of His fingers would have stopped the tragedy, but He didn't even take the effort to snap. Why bother being Ruler of the Universe if you don't do something to correct the things that go wrong? Maybe He just created everything, and now He sits back for a good laugh. Maybe He hasn't snapped His fingers since the beginning of time. What a gyp. What a gyp for Doc Jody*. The fiery comet slammed to earth again.

He barely heard Tucker Doogan call his name. He was in a fog. The nervousness was gone.

He looked up at Tucker's owlish grin, the funny round mouth with that overhanging beak of a nose. He wanted to punch Tucker's lights out, and he felt his hands scrunching up into fists as he walked toward the door. *Why'd he have to live in a town with bullies like Tucker Doogan and monsters like Neander T, anyway? Couldn't a guy feel safe in his own hometown?*

One snap of His fingers and the comet would stop, but there was no snap. Only a fiery explosion and death.

The crowd hushed to a dull roar as it parted like the Red Sea, allowing him onto the mat. Eddie and Homer, the henchmen, were in each corner, removing the gloves from the last two gladiators.

He hadn't looked at his opponent since that moment in the dungeon when they realized their destiny. *Fuggin' goddam Wide-Receiver-State-Contender-in-the-Mile. Why'd the football team get all the glory anyway? They never won more than two or three games a year, and the girls still squealed. And here the golf team might take state—the real state—only one class of golf for all of Oklahoma. No breaks like playing schools your own size, then winning only two or three games, with the girls still squealing. The golfers were after a real state championship. Who even knew they were contenders? Why'd he let birdbrains like Tucker Doogan call them 'candy asses?'*

As he stood in the corner, he felt Homer grab his right arm, shove on a boxing glove, then lace it up. He didn't even look down until Homer started on the other arm. He watched his pearly-white left hand disappear into the huge brown glove. He knew he wasn't completely numb because he could feel the vibrations of the laces as Homer pulled them through the eyelets and tied them into a knot.

Tim Richardson was across the ring, sparring with an imaginary opponent, his black greasy hair slapping him in the forehead as he hopped around.

The comet was headed to earth again, and each time it crashed, Chipper got madder and madder.

A large form was making its way to the front row. Crutches were beating back smaller spectators until the great athlete made his appearance at ringside. Chipper felt the power of his presence, as each and every one of his own muscles grew larger and stronger. L.K. nodded and winked.

Homer led him to the center of the ring where Richardson was making screwball faces and banging his gloves together.

Chipper thought of Amy and all the help she provided for this historic moment. He pictured her watching him now, and it seemed to ignite his spirit every bit as much as L.K. being at ringside. He thought of L.K.'s brother Benny and what a gyp it was that L.K.'s dad refused to bring him out in the open, and how Benny would never see his amazing brother play college or professional ball. *One snap of His fingers. Why wasn't there even one snap of His fingers?* He thought of Doc Jody at the player piano with Mama Justice taking off her apron to sing by his side. And now she was on her own. And now they were on their own—Jay and Chipper—who'd they turn to now? *One snap of His fingers. One lousy snap of His fingers. One friggin' goddam mothering snap...*

The whistle blew.

Chipper clicked on a mental metronome and felt his hands start to pound away, every punch making contact. The crowd was louder than he had heard it all day. He couldn't believe he was not receiving any punishment at all. Glancing blows barely touched him as his rapid-fire staccato technique secured an assault that didn't seem penetrable.

He didn't need a fancy hook or an uppercut or a simple one-two. He decided in advance to punch like a jackhammer with the rhythm of the "Comedians' Gallop" while listening to the tune in his head. In his Junior Symphony days he could race through the song on his xylophone. Now, it was finally paying off. Richardson backed away, probably stunned by the walloping. The footballer was getting pulverized.

He couldn't believe how easy it was. The only pain he felt so far was a deep ache in his upper arms. In fact, it felt good to unleash. He'd underestimated himself.

Then, in a vision, a dream come true, he witnessed the miraculous. Richardson's nose was bleeding. Not profusely, but with a steady trickle of beautiful bright red blood coming from one nostril. *He'd done it. He'd won.*

He stopped blasting Richardson and backed away, pointing with one glove at the blood, turning over his shoulder to gloat at Tucker Doogan who would be forced to call the fight. Thumbs down, it would be. Richardson to the showers. A great victory for golf over football, or for boxing, or whatever this was.

Tucker Doogan rose to his feet in the bleachers, arms at his side, foiled by a candy ass golfer. Then Tucker raised one hand slowly with his thumb parallel to the ground in neutral position. With his arm extended like Heil Hitler, he flipped his thumb straight up in the air—the fight would go on. *The fight would go on?*

Chipper's heart stopped. He'd already relaxed, letting his arms fall to his side. He was puffing so hard he thought his lungs were about to pop. As he tried to raise his arms again, he realized they were made of lead.

His eyes met L.K.'s at ringside. L.K. looked furious as he turned to Tucker in the bleachers and yelled, "What d'you think that is, Doogan, red snot? Call the goddam fight!"

Chipper turned to his opponent, but was met by the brown blur of a boxing glove that sent him stumbling back into the arms of the ringside crowd. He shook it off—it wasn't all that painful—and headed back to the center of the ring. But he still couldn't lift his hundred-pound arms, not even enough to protect his face. He was gasping for air. Dull punches, one after another, whipped his skull around like those bobbing-head dogs in car windows.

Blow after blow sent him repeatedly to ringside, only to have the crowd push him back to the center. If he were registering a single punch, he didn't know it. He could only tell he'd become a human punching bag, one whop per second per face.

The crowd noise turned into a peculiar buzz as his peripheral vision began to darken. Through a tunnel, he could see brown boxing gloves headed like freight trains for his face. Over and over.

He tried to listen for the "Comedians' Gallop" in his head, but it was gone. He wanted more than anything to lie down and sleep, but he refused to drop. The massacre of his face continued.

Then there was silence. Breaking the tranquility was a loud crack that accompanied a funny thud on his nose. The pounding was gone. He had to breathe through his mouth, and he felt a warm salty fluid on his lips that he licked away. Looking down to the ground, he could see the tips of his tennis shoes as if they were ten feet away. Red drops were gathering on the rubber toes. He reached to his face with his boxing gloves and saw blood streaming down his forearms onto his tee shirt. Funny, there wasn't any pain.

He thought he saw L.K. grab his arm and unlace his gloves. But the image disappeared. He knew he hadn't passed out because he could feel his feet take floating steps across the gymnasium floor, like the moving sidewalk in the funhouse at the fair. And he could hear conversation.

"L.K., is that you?"

"Yeah, it's me, Chipper. You were unbelievable."

"I'm seeing all white, L.K. I don't see anything but white." He was getting scared.

"You'll be all right. You've just got the blind staggers. They'll be over in a minute. You're a fuggin' machine, man. You took one helluva lot of blows. Never went down to the mat. Never seen anybody take punishment like that without going down for the count. And everyone knows Richardson bled first. That goddam Tucker. If I had my strength back, I'd bust his wimpy ass to pieces."

Chipper felt someone hand him a towel to cover his nose.

"Uh, Chipper, I'm gonna take you to the emergency room," L.K. said. "I think you're going to need a little work on that nose."

Twenty-three

Amy pulled the ice pack away from his bandaged nose. She was gorgeous beyond belief. Jeans, sweatshirt, hair in curlers. Tonight, a fetching vision.

"Gotta grab more from the ice box," she said, rising from the couch. Like the Justices' den used to be, Amy's living room had become the most relaxing place on earth. And right now, Chipper was loosey-goosey, relaxed, and relieved.

He watched her curvy hips sashay into the kitchen; listened to the clunking of ice cascading into the sink; then greeted her face with a smile as she rounded the corner again.

"You're going to be fine, Chipper. Omar Sharif would still look good with a crooked nose. How's your mom taking it?"

"Not too well. Especially the nose part. She won't even discuss it."

"She was just afraid for you."

"Too afraid. It had to happen. I had to fight."

Amy plopped down beside him on the sofa, rolled onto one hip and threw the other leg over between his legs. She stroked the hair from his eyes and kissed him on the cheek.

"I love you," she said.

"I love you, too."

She held the ice pack to his nose. His injured face was so tender now, he couldn't imagine that it had ever been numb only hours ago when the break occurred. He hadn't even required local anesthesia when Dr. Bennett straightened it the best he could.

"So what did you hear about the Buster-Peachy fight?" Chipper asked. "It's still hard to believe."

"I know. The way Carol told me, Buster was chasing Peachy around the ring in circles. Everyone was laughing."

"I know. I could hear it."

"All of a sudden," Amy said, "Peachy plants one foot, spins 180 degrees and throws one wild punch. No aim, no technique, just one punch. It hit Buster square in the face, a complete accident. The next thing everyone knew, Buster was out cold. One goofy punch."

"Pure luck and pure Peachy," Chipper said shaking his head. "How's Buster taking it?"

"Carol's really worried. You know Buster can barely tolerate Peachy anyway."

"Jiminy, the team is in an awful tailspin. Jay's in solitary confinement, L.K.'s on crutches, and we may never hear from Buster again. That's our three top men."

"Don't worry, baby," Amy said soothingly. "Jay will come around. L.K. will get better. And Buster...well, we can hope. He must be terribly humiliated right now."

He touched two fingers to his lips then transferred the kiss to Amy. She took his hand and kissed his fingertips, then his knuckles.

"You know what we ought to do, Chipper?"

"What?"

"We ought to double with Buster and Carol. You know he only has his father's crummy truck part-time. We need to make him feel like part of the team. We can't afford to lose him, or her."

"You're right."

As she went back to kissing his knuckles one by one, she fluttered her lashes in rhythm with each smooch. He felt her leg moving up and down against his, ever so slightly.

"Have you heard any more talk about my fight?" he asked.

"No, only from L.K. And you know what he said already."

"I know, but sometimes the same people tell different versions on these things."

She smiled. "Well, L.K. said there were two distinct fights. You were clearly the winner in the first, then you were unbelievable in the second."

"Nicely put, Amy. I was the slugger in the first and the sluggee in the second. And he slugged me worse than I slugged him."

"But L.K. said no one had any idea you could punch that hard or that fast. Then, in the second half, no one could believe you stayed on your feet. The way L.K. described it, it was like you were out there with a mission. Some reason more than just getting initiated."

She held his sore hand with both of hers, pausing to kiss his knuckles every few seconds. Then she moved his hand to her chest and held it there for a moment, before flattening his palm against her blouse and her soft breast.

He loved the way Amy could take him out of the loss column.

Twenty-four

With school starting soon, Chipper's short game lessons with L.K. would be trimmed through the tyranny of homework. The last few weeks, however, had improved L.K.'s down-in-two percentage from lousy to okay—a long way from Chipper's near-perfect, but still enough to clip two strokes per round from L.K.'s score.

"You're on your own after today," Chipper told him. "You're doing great."

"Thanks. Picturing that basketball goal on the green as a target really did the trick on my chips. Then that new rhythm on my short putts...well, buddy, I'm much obliged."

Although L.K. looked like a spindly-legged sparrow, he could walk without crutches and was counting on a full golf swing within the month. In the meantime, Chipper thought he walked like Grandpappy Amos of *The Real McCoys*. This sidelining handicap had provided L.K. an interlude of focus on his short game that would never have come naturally for the power-hitter.

"Chippin' around the green like this reminds me of playing Horse with Jay."

"Still no squeak from him?"

"Nope. Only his mom and Kelly talk to him. He's still not leaving the house. Kelly bought his school supplies for him."

"Man, I don't get it."

"Me neither. It's been a month."

L.K. lifted a chip onto the green, then watched it curl slowly to leave a tap-in.

"Doc Jody was like a father to me," said Chipper. "I wanted to be just like him. He was kinda my definition of a real man."

"I'm not so sure there is a definition of a real man, buddy. Manhood is a pretty weird deal."

Chipper thought it odd that the great L.K. would seem befuddled by such a piddly issue, magnified only in the minds of candy asses.

"Jay told me once about a story in *National Geographic*," he said, "where a Melanesian proves his manhood by tying ropes to his ankles, then plunging off a 65-foot tower. The ropes catch him before he hits the ground. Bingo. He's a man."

"What the hell's a Melanesian?"

"Beats me. Some crazy islanders in the Pacific, I guess. That's not the point. I kinda figured I'd feel like a man after the lettermen's fights, but I don't."

"Hey, you got a crooked nose out of it."

"Yeah, the crooked badge of courage. But I feel the same."

"Well, I'm not so sure I can help you on this one. I used to think it was all about being a good jock. Now I don't know what to think."

"You've still got golf."

L.K. looked up from his tap-in shot, face blank, as if every muscle had been paralyzed by pygmy darts. "Yeah, I guess...I still have golf."

"Well, does your dad ever say anything about it?" Chipper asked, having heard L.K.'s dad described as a man's man—a war hero, a football star, everything.

"Dad doesn't say much about anything." L.K. launched another chip onto the putting green, the ball rolling within 18 inches of the cup. "I guess he just says to stand up for what you believe. That's it. Standing up for what you believe."

Wouldn't work, Chipper quickly thought. *Women should stand up for what they believe, too.*

"You know, Jay used to say that God is the model, but Amy says God isn't one sex or the other."

"You're getting yourself all confused, Chipper. What difference does it make?" L.K. hobbled onto the green and sank his putt. "I can tell you one thing, though. God isn't the model around our house."

"No?"

"Absolutely not. We don't go to church, at least not any more. And the word 'God' is taboo."

Chipper realized how little he knew about L.K. After the hidden brother stunt, what else did he have up his sleeve?

L.K. took a few practice swings as if chipping for real, then paused. "Let me tell you about the last time my family went to church."

Chipper could feel his ears go Dumbo.

"Mom used to read the Bible and pray out loud at suppertime that Benny would be healed. Dad didn't say shit about it, but he went quietly to church every Sunday. We all did, including Benny. When I was about five or six, the doctor said Benny wouldn't be walking anymore...not ever. We went to church the next week, just the folks and me, Benny back at home in his new wheelchair. He coulda gone with us, but Dad said no."

Chipper reached for his 7-iron and began practice swinging with L.K. They looked like two clocks on the fringe with pendulums going at different speeds.

"We sat there on Communion Sunday," continued L.K., "and I remember the preacher's sermon being something about prayer, and about how God always answers every one of our prayers. All of a sudden, my dad stands up in the middle of the sermon. Mind you, the preacher is ranting and raving about something, but he doesn't skip a beat as Dad stands up. The old man doesn't say a word, but I remember the whole place staring at him, including the preacher who starts to get a real nervous look in his eye.

"Dad steps into the aisle and walks directly up to the Communion table. I swear, I thought he was going to drop to his knees and beg God to heal Benny. After all, it was always Mom doing the praying. For all I knew, Dad had never prayed for Benny to be healed."

"What happened?" asked Chipper, halting his golf-club pendulum. He noted a strained look on L.K.'s face, then his teammate's pendulum stopped as well.

"So, he roars in that big booming voice of his, 'Bullshit! It's all goddam bullshit!' Then he raises his fist and lowers it, *kaboom*, on the Communion tray, little glasses of grape juice flying everywhere. And he keeps pounding until the glasses are broken into smithereens and his fist is bleeding all over the place. Mom screamed and rushed me out of the church. Dad was gone for days. I just figured God struck him dead on the spot. But he came home with his right fist all bandaged. Mom hasn't read the Bible or prayed since, best I can tell. You can still see all the little scars from the broken Communion glasses along the edge of Dad's fist."

Chipper felt as if his lower jaw was dragging on the ground.

"Now tell me, buddy," L.K. asked, "do you call that a man? Well, I don't."

Twenty-five

FALL 1966

Senior status bestowed locker choices, permitting Chipper to be next to Amy who was next to Kelly who had secured a slot for Jay. One week of classes was gone, though, and still no sign of Jay.

After sliding his Literature text on the top shelf, Chipper closed the metal door and turned to Amy while spinning his combination lock. "So, when were you gonna tell me about the 79 you shot yesterday?"

"How'd you know?"

"I heard it in the clubhouse. All the women were just ga-ga-gooey about it. Congratulations."

This was scary. Amy was in his territory now. It didn't seem right for a girl to be shooting as well as a guy...if golf was *truly* a sport.

"A few good shots, a lotta luck," she said.

"Oh, yeah, well maybe we'll pass you off as a guy next spring and you can play on the team."

Amy put her hands on her hips and glared. She could see right through his sarcastic snarl, so he backtracked without her having to say a word.

"I mean, the team's in trouble, Amy. Nothing against you."

"I should hope not."

"Buster and Peachy don't speak. L.K. can't take a full swing yet, and Jay...well, who knows?"

"The season is six months away, babe. Everything will work out. By the way, Buster didn't make a locker request, so I did some finagling and put him two doors down from Peachy. Not too close, not too far."

Chipper was ashamed he was bugged about Amy's 79. Embarrassed even that he'd whined about the team. Amy never moaned or groaned. She made things happen.

As they started down the hall, hand in hand, Amy's tone changed.

"Chipper, I have to talk to you about something I heard this morning in physics class."

Uh-oh.

"There are some rumors. I know they can't be true because I know where you are every minute of the day, but they're still going around."

"Rumors?"

"Yeah, rumors."

"What kind of rumors?"

"About Gail Perdue."

He felt the need to check his collar for lipstick at the mere mention of her name. "What about Gail?"

"She claims to be...she's saying that she and you are carrying on. Privately."

"Baloney!" He was outraged. Not that the thought didn't cross his mind, but he had never so much as smiled at her. He hadn't even talked to her since the night after lettermen's fights, after he left Amy's, when she called to talk about his loss. He was peeved in a really big way, informing her that he had technically lost, but that he'd drawn first blood. She had asked for the name of his opponent, whereupon she kept talking about how ugly Tim Richardson was and how she didn't know how a girl could stand to kiss him. After that, communication was zippo.

"I know it's not true, babe. I trust you, and I love you. I just don't understand why she's saying those things. Do you?"

"I have no idea, Amy. I swear. I think she may be a little...off." He had told Amy about the night at the bowling alley but not about the phone calls, notes on his car, sudden appearances, and so forth, leading up to the lettermen's initiation. But for some reason, everything stopped after the fights. He didn't believe he had encouraged Gail at all.

"Okay. I guess," Amy said. "It's just so weird."

"It was a great summer," he said. "Best ever. You're my only love, and I..."

"Oh, my gosh," she interrupted. "Look at this!"

Jay the Hermit was strolling toward them with Kelly. Her face was beaming, but Kelly could smile like Miss America through a hailstorm. Jay looked like a corpse, tan long gone, leaving his naturally pasty skin for the world to see. Raccoon eyes were cast to the ground as he shuffle-stepped.

Chipper approached cautiously, then threw one arm around Jay's shoulders.

"Welcome back, stud."

Amy kissed him on the cheek.

Jay stood like a dead man, propped up against his eternal desire to lie in peace.

"No need to push things," Amy said. "We love you and we're glad you're back." She kissed him again.

Kelly nodded approval to Amy with one of those girly telepathic messages that indicated that Amy ranked right up there next to Freud in her psychiatric insight and brilliance.

"Yeah, no rush," blurted Chipper. "Golf season doesn't start 'til March."

Jay's eyes lifted from the floor, while Amy turned to scowl at Chipper.

"No golf," Jay said.

"Not now, maybe. I understand. Really I do." He tried to sound empathetic.

Jay started to walk away.

"We can start slow," suggested Chipper as he took Jay's arm. "By playing Horse, maybe."

"No golf," Jay repeated, recoiling.

Chipper reached for Jay again, catching a glimpse of Kelly and Amy shaking their heads 'no.'

He ignored them both. "Jay, remember me? I'm your best friend. I just wanna..."

"Bug off, Chipper. Keep the hell away from me with that golf crap."

The stake pierced his heart so deeply that he felt blood squirt out of the holes both in front and back. And he let his friend go.

Twenty-six

"So who gives a rip fart if Jay doesn't play on the team next spring? That means I'll get to play in the state fourball. The Peach's score will finally count."

"I can't believe I'm hearing you right, Peachy," Chipper said. "This is Jay you're talking about. Your so-called friend, you twit."

"Hey, all for one, and that one is me, Chipper my boy. I can't help it if Doc Jody got killed and it screwed Jay up."

"Listen, dipshit, did it ever occur to you that we can never *never* win state if both of *our* scores count? We need three guys near par and the fourth man in the 70s. Your fuggin' 85, God willing you don't shank your way to 95, ain't gonna cut the mustard."

"But the Peach will have played. I'm sick of being some asshole's caddy every year. I wanna play with the big boys."

"Peachy, I'm gonna pretend we never had this conversation, okay? I'm gonna forget I ever heard those words come from that poop chute you call a mouth."

"Suit yourself."

Sometimes, Peachy begged to be strangled.

As the Corvette spun onto Country Club Drive, Chipper switched topics to the manhood debate of two weeks ago with L.K. Peachy raised his banner on this cause by stating that in the great scheme of what makes a man, men were the screwers and women were the screwees. Case closed.

"Speaking of screwing...did you hear that Tim Richardson is poking Gail Perdue?"

"What?" Chipper hit his head on the roof of the Stingray as he flew from his seat. "Bullcrap! Who said so?"

"Got it from the horse's mouth."

"Horse's ass, you mean. Gail told me he was the ugliest sonuva bitch she'd ever seen."

"Hey, you don't screw with your face."

"Stop it, Peachy. That really pisses me off when guys start that locker room crap and destroy girls' reputations. Especially Gail, godammit."

Peachy hung a sharp louie, fishtailing into Tate's Drive-in, teen central for El Viento. Barely above an idle, they joined the line of cars creeping through the hangout like a parade of snails searching for mates. Peachy held his left arm out the window and maintained a perpetual wave, lest someone think him conceited or less than cool. He was, of course, both, but the nonstop wave was pure Peach. Chipper looked straight ahead and pretended to smile, never looking to either side for fear he would see Gail with Tim Richardson, his archenemy in the lettermen's initiation rite.

"I don't believe it. I just don't believe it."

"Believe what you like, oh naive one. Most of us ain't virgins, you know. Unlike you and Jay, the Hardy Boys."

How he wished Amy was here right now. For some reason, he felt a rope inside being tied into knots, and he needed her to keep the knots out.

"I saw Richardson earlier today," continued Peachy. "He told me the whole story. That's why I'm telling you."

"Why do you feel I need to know?"

"He claims Gail called him the night after lettermen's initiation."

Chipper gulped to clear the expanding balloon in his throat. Gail called him that night, too, almost relishing the fact that he'd been beaten to a pulp, and asking for the name of his conqueror.

"He says she talked a lot about the fights, then she asked him out."

"She asked him? I don't believe it."

"Not only did she ask him...he says she was the horniest girl he'd ever seen. Scored the first night. And, man, is Tucker Doogan ever pissed at his old buddy."

Chipper thought he was going to explode, but the entire teen population was watching them as they crawled through the drive-in at three miles per hour.

"I thought we might see them here," Peachy said, laughing as he goosed the Corvette from the exit, leaving rubber as they headed toward the bowling alley, the western boundary of traditional cruising in El Viento.

"I hope we don't see them," Chipper said, "that is, if they're really dating. I still think Tim's making it up."

"What are you gonna do if we find them? Whomp his ass?" Peachy laughed again, causing Chipper to clench his fists in remembrance of the pounding he took.

"Listen, jerk-face, you won your fight by a fluke. Don't go talking about how tough you are."

"Oooo, touchy, touchy. I didn't say a thing about me or my glorious fight. Feeling a bit tense, are we? If I didn't know better, I'd say you were jealous. I don't blame you. I'd like to bang Gail, too."

Chipper reached for Peachy's throat to make his point. "Shut up about Gail, Peachy. Do you understand?"

Peachy didn't say a word, but his eyes opened wider than his mouth in a look of surprise, then realization, followed by a knowing smile. It was as though Peachy could see right through him, as if he could read his mind, think every thought, and it was clear that Peachy knew how much he longed for Gail, how much he thought about her, and how much he was fighting the impulse to run to her.

"Hey, man, the Peach says you need a beer." Placing the Schlitz malt liquor between his legs, he punched two openings in the can and handed it to Chipper. The bubbling and burning funneled down his throat and chest, and within minutes the knots in the rope began to untie.

Twenty-seven

Chipper often felt that fate twittered about him like a butterfly. Yet the quickest clasp of his fingers never could trap the elusive wings. He knew he would claim the bounty someday, so he stood alert to any clue that might play a role in his destiny.

Case in point was his roll-of-the-dice clubhouse locker location next to their mentor, Mr. Ashbrook. The old gent was always spewing savvy that seemed short on words and long on experience, but clearly designed by Providence for his youthful ears.

Chipper watched him now as he applied talcum powder to every crease of his decaying body, filling nostrils with the threat of an explosive sneeze.

"So, Jay said that, did he?" Mr. Ashbrook asked.

"Yeah, and I don't get it. It's like he's a total stranger."

The old man shook his head as he slapped clouds of powder into his armpits. "Was Jay acting strange at all before his dad was killed?"

"No, sir," he answered. No thought needed here. Jay never acted funny. Wait a minute..."You know, though, one thing was kinda weird."

"Yes?"

"Right before the accident, Peachy was in the Justice's den fooling around with one of Doc Jody's golf trophies. Jay went nuts when Peachy broke it, like I've never seen before. But now that I think about it, Jay was already peeved before that. Just watching Peachy flip that trophy was bugging him real bad."

"Interesting," the old man replied. "Anything else?"

Chipper looked away as Mr. Ashbrook began the ceremonial powdering of the groins.

"Maybe. I've replayed everything with Jay over and over now that I've seen what this has done to him. It didn't seem strange at the time, but Jay said something, just minutes after he learned about the plane crash, something that strikes me funny now."

"Oh? What?"

"He said, 'Daddy, come back home. Please come home...I'm sorry.' It's odd that he said, 'I'm sorry'."

Mr. Ashbrook's eyes brightened, and it seemed that he smiled. It wasn't easy to be sure about the smile since his wrinkles hung vertical like drapes, so any horizontal motion was as subtle as a cat sneaking behind the curtains.

Mr. Ashbrook lit his pipe and turned buck naked toward Chipper, his body covered with fine white powder that screamed for a feather duster. Indeed, he *was* smiling. But why?

"Young man, I'm going to tell you a story, then you make of it what you will."

Chipper worried that this moment might provide a glimpse of his destiny, and that the revelation would be poisoned by having to remember Mr. Ashbrook standing there like a skinned chicken breast rolled in breadcrumbs, smoking his pipe.

"Chipper, I could've joined the PGA back in 1916 when they started it. I knew 'Long Jim' Barnes, Fred McLeod, Jock Hutchinson, all of them back then. Even played with Walter Hagen and Gene Sarazen a time or two."

"Wow." He couldn't wait to tell the others.

"Oh, no need for commotion. The golf world was pretty small back then. Tournament prizes were lousy. No television, you know. I had a new wife, and I could actually make more money at my dry cleaning business here in El Viento than winning on the tour."

"So you didn't even try?"

"As a matter of fact, I did try, 'cause it wasn't about money. Willa, that was my wife's name, she didn't want to be separated, so she went on the circuit with me. Late fall, 1917, I planned a big showing at a tourney in Kansas City, right before my application to the PGA. But Willa found out she was pregnant, and she'd heard that the influenza was looking bad for the winter and that several people had already died in Kansas City."

"So what happened?"

"I was young and all full of piss and vinegar. I dragged Willa with me to Kansas City against her better judgment. I won the tournament, but she caught the flu. She was the first Okie to die in the epidemic that hit the country in '18. Our unborn baby went with her. It's been 48 years and I miss her every day."

"I'm sorry," offered Chipper, with the stuffiness you have when someone springs a zinger on you.

"Couldn't play golf after that. Sure as shootin', I felt I'd caused it with my own hand. What made it even worse were the other 48 folks that died right here in El Viento. Their kinfolk would stare at me on the street, figurin' that I'd hand-carried the influenza to El Viento on purpose. Lost my business as a result, and went to work on the Rock Island after that."

Yikes, thought Chipper. He had crossed a barbed-wire fence, and he needed to get back to the other side. But as he looked at Mr. Ashbrook, he wondered if the kindly gent had ever realized his destiny. Or would he be lying on a cold slab soon with butterflies mocking him as they flew about his waxen face.

"But you made it back to golf. How?"

Mr. Ashbrook stepped into a pair of enormous striped boxer shorts clipping at his knees, offering little contribution to dignity.

"I'm going to tell you seven magic words, Chipper. Try them out on Jay, and though I'm not sure what's eating at his soul, remember my story. These seven words helped me considerable."

Even the word 'seven' was magic to Chipper, and he could feel his heart begin to race. Mr. Ashbrook began curling his index finger, indicating Chipper to come closer, as if these glowing words might lose their brilliance if transmitted too far through the air.

As the old master whispered the phrase into his ear, Chipper felt shivers down his neck and spine. Not that the seven magic words were profound—in fact, Chipper wasn't even sure what they meant, but as the gooseflesh spread to his arms and the back of his legs, Chipper had the overpowering feeling that while Mr. Ashbrook had never realized his personal golf destiny, he had just passed the baton to the fourth man on the golf team.

[illegible]

[illegible]

[illegible]

[illegible]

[illegible]

[illegible]

[illegible]

[illegible]

[illegible]

Twenty-eight

A week passed before Chipper was granted an audience with the reclusive Jay. But one-word answers were getting nowhere.

Jay was at his bedroom desk, eyes fixed on the nothingness of its surface, while Chipper bounced nervously on the edge of the bed, alternating his gaze between the window and the untouched golf clubs in the corner. Amy had coached Chipper beforehand to avoid the word "golf" at the risk of execution—if not by Jay, then by her.

The seven words had to be timed right, and now was not the time. The phrase seemed empty as Chipper repeated the words in his head so he wouldn't screw it up. He needed a shrewd lead-in.

"Hey, uh, Jay. Have you ever seen Mr. Ashbrook naked?"

"Nope."

"Well, not a pretty sight."

"Oh?"

Chipper could still smell the talcum. "I guess I didn't realize that all our hair was gonna turn gray and fall out some day. And brother, do I mean *all.*"

He yucked a little to elicit a response, but Jay was dead.

"Yeah, did you know he almost joined the PG..." He caught himself. 'G' stood for 'golf', the taboo word. "Uh, he almost...well, he...uh...was married once. How 'bout that? His wife died in the flu epidemic of 1918."

"Oh?"

Chipper went on to tell the story, dancing around the G-word. And when Jay appeared unmoved, Chipper felt himself embellishing the story with details pulled from thin air, hoping to stir a silenced heart, describing the beautiful young Willa with hair of shimmering gold that made the young men of the era denounce their birthrights just for one stroke of her tresses. He related his own vision of the beauty, now ravaged by protracted pneumonia compounding the flu. Her sunken cheeks, her hollow eyes, her hair falling out in golden clumps, matted by the sweat of a torturing fever. And the unborn baby's cries for help deep inside the mother's womb, pleading for escape to the outside air. It was a masterpiece of a story and, perhaps, somewhere in proximity to the actual truth.

"You know," said Chipper, "the day that...that the plane went down, you said something I didn't understand. You said, 'I'm sorry'."

Jay looked up from his desk and stared at the blank spot on his wall where Arnold Palmer's poster used to hang. He remained silent.

"It didn't make any sense to me then, so I just thought I'd mention it now."

Chipper could see from the side that Jay's lower lip was quivering like the diving board at the pool after a back flip.

"I guess I kinda wondered what you meant, 'cause if a best friend can't..."

Jay burst forth with a torrential rain of tears, sobbing so loud it seemed that the room was vibrating. It was as if Hoover Dam gave way, allowing Lake Mead to gush itself back into the Colorado River. Chipper froze as Jay buried his head on his desk to muffle the wailing.

"I *am* sorry," Jay cried. "I'm so, so sorry."

He continued his agonizing apology over and over into the pool of anguish collecting on his desktop. "I'm sorry, I'm sorry."

"For what?" Chipper finally managed. "What are you sorry for?"

After being asked several times, Jay finally lifted his head toward Chipper, eyes acid red, and said, "For killing my father."

Chipper gasped. "For *what?*"

"For killing Dad."

"What are you talking about? Are you crazy?"

"I might as well have been flying that plane myself."

"Jay, you're not making any sense."

"I killed him sure as the world. I should be the dead one. It should've been me."

"What are you saying?"

"The mission trip. They overbooked the number of doctors, so Dad asked me to go in his place. As a construction worker. They needed workers."

"So you didn't go. So what? You don't know anything about construction anyway."

"Don't you see?" Jay wiped his eyes to stop crying, but began sobbing again. "Dad wanted me to go really bad. We had an argument, worst we've ever had. I demanded to stay, so he gave up on me. I've never told anyone the real reason I didn't want to go."

Chipper was almost afraid to probe any further. "What do you mean?"

Jay hung his head as far as his neck would reach. "I wanted to win the club championship," he confessed. "Dad always won. If he was out of the country...and I was here...well..." He shook his head sadly. "I won the trophy all right. I really won it." And he cried some more.

"Oh, Jay. It's not your fault."

"I never even said goodbye to him the day he left." Jay put his face back in the cradle of his folded arms on the desktop, taking deep breaths that were useless for stopping these tears.

"You're not responsible for your dad's accident anymore than Mr. Ashbrook is for his wife dying."

Chipper rose from the bedside and set his open palm on his friend's shoulder. It was time to pass the baton. "Mr. Ashbrook told me a saying that got him back in the saddle. Wanna hear it?"

Jay didn't move.

Hoping the majesty of the secret phrase would overshadow the nebulous meaning, Chipper leaned down to his best friend's ear and slowly and quietly whispered the words. "*God's grace is greater than our needs.*"

No response.

Chipper wasn't surprised, since the phrase seemed trite, if not downright empty. After all, what exactly was God's grace? 'Grace' had 12 definitions in his dictionary (he had, of course, looked it up to help decipher the code, but no such luck).

Backing away, he sensed the need to slip out of the room and leave Jay alone. He had worked himself up over nothing. The so-called magic words were a dud. And he left the room without another syllable to his broken pal.

After hugging Mama Justice in the front room, Chipper walked outside and turned down the driveway to his car. Glancing toward Jay's bedroom window, he thought he could see a form moving, though it was difficult to tell through the venetian blinds. After he closed his car door, he felt more protected for a longer stare.

It looked as if Jay was unrolling a poster and thumbtacking it to the blank space above his desk. Chipper hoped it was the picture of Palmer on the 18th green, tapping in the putt to win his first Masters in 1958, the magic day that the gallery became Arnie's Army.

Perhaps confession, as alleged, was good for the soul. Then again, how could seven stale words reverse Jay's two months in the catacombs?

Twenty-nine

The jukebox stood in the corner of the high school gym like an alien robot, resonating with the heartthrobs of students gathering before classes.

Amy had closed her fourth deal with the Wurlitzer distributor. She started with the country club, then Tate's Drive-in, the bowling alley, and now the gym. She made a successful, heartrending plea to the school board to allow the jukebox, promising—beyond her powers—the good behavior of the students.

Jay and Kelly were seated by themselves on the top row of the bleachers, intertwined in such a way that a crowbar would bend if used to disentangle them. Their lips separated only after the final line of "Hey Paula." Jay seemed remote since his return last week from hibernation, but the smooch factor with Kelly was a refreshing constant.

Chipper watched the twosome from the edge of the crowd. As he turned in search of Amy, he came face-to-horrible-face with Tim Richardson who was almost unrecognizable from last week's savage beating by his former friend Tucker Doogan. One eye was half-open now, the other still shut, and every shade of color from purple to yellow replaced the flesh tones of his face. Chipper felt a peculiar anti-Tucker bond to the guy, the same guy who had left him with a similar look several months earlier.

"How are you, Tim?" he asked.

"Okay, I guess," he answered through frozen lips. "I've felt better."

"I heard what Tucker did."

"You and everyone's mother."

"Sorry."

"Yeah."

After an uncomfortable silence, purple-faced Tim continued, "I should tell you how surprised I was with your fighting at the initiation."

"Thanks." Chipper was caught off guard.

"I…I just wanted to let you know that I could taste the blood in my mouth. I knew you shoulda won, according to the strict rules, that is."

"No big deal. My letter jacket looks the same, and it fits just as well."

He touched the letter E on his chest as he spoke.

The distorted purple head nodded, giving Chipper the impression he had more to say.

"What is it?"

"You gotta know something, Chipper."

"What?"

"Stay away from Gail Perdue, for your own good. She's poison."

Chipper backed away a few steps.

"Watch her," continued Tim. "She's after you. Talks about you all the time. Just sorta works it into the conversation."

He wanted to hear more, but he also wanted Tim to stop. He wanted to ask if Tim really scored the first night, but he didn't want to know. He wanted to know why Gail stopped her pursuit so abruptly after the fights, but he didn't want to ask. He wanted to ask why everyone thought Gail and he were a secret item when he never even talked to her. Then again, he didn't want to know.

"Tucker says he'll kill anyone who goes out with her. I used to think it was just a threat, but look at me."

Chipper felt a cool sweat on his forehead. While he knew he should scamper at the sight of Gail, he felt a yearning to rescue this angel in distress. Clearly, the little girl he had worshipped years ago was troubled by something horrible. She needed a good man. The last thing she needed was someone like Tucker Doogan.

"Remember, Chipper," Tim said, "the next time you see Gail: she's got you in her crosshairs."

Thirty

Jay's shot ricocheted off the fat elm at the corner of the putting green, then bounced toward the miniflag with the 5 on it and rolled within three feet of the cup. After a three-month layoff and only one week of practice, he was still tough to beat.

Chipper's shot found its mark on the fat elm, but the ricochet went wild into the graveled parking lot. He conceded the hole. "Penny for your thoughts, " said Jay.

"Amy shooting 79. She's done it twice now, you know."

"Ah...I knew that'd be getting to you."

"I don't get it."

"What don't you get?"

"A woman's world versus a man's world."

"You're afraid she's going to beat you?"

"No. Well, in a way," Chipper said. "That's what bugs me. I think everything Amy does is cool, then I turn right around and it makes me nervous inside."

"Like what? Give me a for instance."

"Well, the first time was when she took over the jukebox with that Wurlitzer deal. I mean, she was only 14 when she did that. And now, here we are with her making straight A's and talking about going to medical school. Jiminy, my dad wouldn't let my mom go to medical school. And now shooting 79. There's days when that score'll beat me."

"But that's why you like her."

"It's part of why, but it's also why she scares me. I mean, how do you prove you're a man if your girlfriend can do everything you can do?"

"Do I need to explain the birds and the bees to you?"

"Naw, I don't mean it that way. But look at you and Kelly. You all are happy together and there's no competition."

"Kelly and I enjoy a relationship of mutual trust, held together by a love that..."

Chipper wondered how Jay could stand there talking like a robot, knowing that about six hours from now, Jay and Kelly would be humping away in the back seat of Old Blue in a wet and wild frenzy, with Jay inching ever so much closer each night to complete penetration. Even now, it would take an Olympic judge to determine if entry had already occurred, due to the ambiguity of the anatomy. Jay claimed to stop each time on the brink. But what defined 'the brink'? They still considered themselves virgins, and they intended to keep it that way. Chipper guarded these amorous confidences with his life.

"...allowing us to mature together, to grow old together."

"Thank you very much, Ann Landers."

"Heck, I didn't mean to sound..."

"Just kidding," Chipper said. "It's your shot."

Jay set his ball on top of a cement block that was ten yards from the green and choked up eight inches on the club. His shot picked the ball cleanly off the block, lifting it over a mud hole and onto the green. Chipper bladed his attempt into the mud trap, giving the hole and the match to Jay.

"You're Horse. Penny for your thoughts."

"Well, to tell the truth...I've been worried about you, Jay. You know, about your dad and all. I hope you're okay."

"I guess I'm all right. By the way, tell Mr. Ashbrook thanks for the tip. Dad always said the Devil's overrated. It's the battles with yourself and with God that cause the problems."

"Oh, yeah?"

Jay was looking at him strangely, but with the hint of a smile.

"You remember my name is short for Jacob?"

"Of course. Like in the ladder."

"Yeah, well, years after the ladder incident, Jacob got into a wrestling match with God, or one of His angels, that lasted all night. In the morning, the angel dislocated Jacob's hip, but turned around and blessed him by changing his name to Israel."

"I guess I kinda forgot that story."

"Well, it's assumed that Israel limped for the rest of his life even though he'd been blessed. The way I figure it, my blessing was having Dad for 17 years. Most guys never get a dad like mine. On the other hand, I figure I'll be limping for the rest of my life."

"So," Chipper said, "should I start calling you Israel?"

"Ha...but funny you should ask. I do feel a whole bunch older now, and I think I'd like everyone to start calling me by my real name: Jacob."

Chipper smiled, but remained both curious and cautious. Jay—uh, Jacob—had a distinct tone in his voice and a new look on his face. What did it really mean?

"Okay, Jacob," he said. "Let's play nine."

Thirty-one

WINTER 1967

Cold weather could not stop them. If it was unbearable, they played at least the front four holes. If it was worse than unbearable, they hit a few tee shots, chipped on the practice green, then huddled by the furnace in the pro shop for the rest of the afternoon, practicing their putts on the carpet. The important thing was to play every single day. Two shots per man per round.

As Peachy teed his ball, Chipper scanned his shivering teammates. In spite of their frozen faces, it seemed that the winter winds were ricocheting off their chests, protected by letter jackets. The leather sleeves of their armor restricted the golf swing, however, so it was critical on each shot to peel the jacket at the last minute—swing—then don it again before the chill knifed its way through two sweaters and a tee shirt.

Quasimodo. Pause. Cross with the circle at the top. Wiggle to the left. Wiggle to the right. Backswing, overswing, downswing. *Crack*. "Aw shit, missed it." Master's pose.

Peachy's tee shot went high in the air, less than 180 yards up the middle, barely across the creek.

He turned to the other four and grinned. "The Peach skied it," he said.

Buster, who had perfected the art of playing in a fivesome with Peachy using zero communication, looked the other way. L.K. was the only one to comment, "Looks like your best drive to me. I have a hard time telling your good ones from your bad ones."

"Screw you, L.K."

Things were pretty much back to normal.

As Chipper took off his jacket to swing, the heartless wind pounded his chest, making it a chore to breathe. Puffs of smoke left his mouth like exhaust fumes. Twenty-four degrees, said the weatherman, yet they weren't *complete* morons for playing on days like this. Some of their early spring matches would take place in temperatures less than 40, and with wind gusts over 30 mph.

Chipper launched his drive up the middle of the fairway, then scooped up his letter jacket before the ball had a chance to hit the ground.

"Jeez, Chipper," L.K. said, "that driver's starting to love you."

"Nice hit," said Jacob.

L.K. walked to the tee, still a bit unsteady these days, waddling back and forth like a bowlegged cowboy. But he could swing full now, almost like before. His drive zoomed 290 yards up the right side of the fairway, unaffected by the north wind, and landed near a shrinking patch of snow. Buster and Jacob both clobbered the ball, but still fell shy of L.K.

As the five letter-jacketed golfers lined up in rank to begin their march down the fairway, Peachy stopped in his tracks, as if gum had stuck to his cleats.

"Hey, you jerkoffs, have I shown you my new Norelco cassette player?"

"Cassette player?"

"Norelco?"

"Is that an electric razor?"

"Naw, look at this."

Peachy held up a black leather box about twice the size of his trademark transistor radio. He opened the cover, revealing the contents.

"So, what is it?"

"Looks like a big transistor."

"My dad brought it home from Vegas. It's called a 'cassette recorder.' It plays music on little tapes with a built-in miniature reel-to-reel."

"You gotta be kidding," said L.K.

Peachy pulled a flat plastic box from his pocket and handed it to Chipper. The team kept walking as if they were in a rugby huddle, holding and gawking at the curiosity.

"It plays like a record," said Peachy as he grabbed the Sonny and Cher tape back from Chipper. "This one's prerecorded. I mean it's like a record. There's only about a hundred tapes available now, but Dad says they're eventually gonna replace records. He's invested a shitload in the company."

"That's pretty stupid," L.K. said. "Nothing'll ever replace records."

Peachy opened a trap door and pushed the cassette in place, closing the lid. With one punch of the button:

Drums keep poundin' rhythm to my brain

"Amazing," Chipper said.

"No foolin'," said L.K.

Buster stared at the contraption without speaking.

"Can you record stuff, too?" asked Jacob.

"Yep, here's the button for recording." Peachy removed the Sonny and Cher tape, tossed it in a kangaroo pouch on the side of his bag, then pulled out a cassette that said "Norelco C-60" on the front.

"Behold, gentlemen, 60 minutes worth of the Beach Boys. Been recording them off the radio, from my 45s, and from my LPs. I'm gonna do the Beatles next, then Diana Ross and the Supremes, then the Doors."

"Why don't you just wait and buy them?" asked L.K.

"First of all, dumbshit, who knows when they'll be available? The cool thing is that you can record just the songs you want. It's not like with your hi-fi, where you have to lift up the needle to skip the crummy ones."

They arrived at Peachy's ball first.

Quasimodo with a 3-wood. Cross with a circle at the top. Wiggle left. Wiggle right. Overswing back, downswing. *Crack*. Master's pose.

His low hook sought the left rough, which was no different from the fairway in winter. He was a short-iron from the green, and still a good 10 yards from Chief Crazy Hawk's property.

Peachy lugged his clubs onto his right shoulder, then arranged the cassette recorder to hang like his old transistor from the front of the bag. After he punched the play button, the freezing golfers walked up the fairway to the Beach Boys. The intro thumped:

Ah one—and ah two—and ah three—and ah four ee and ah one —

From his short-lived career playing the marimba in Junior Symphony, Chipper easily dissected the rhythm, but he was not familiar with the instruments and their artificial sound, sort of like a high hat cymbal being struck with a drumstick, a rattling bass guitar with a broken speaker, and a snare drum.

It's automatic when I...talk with old friends

"Follow the leader, assholes," yelled Peachy. "We'll keep warm." And he began dancing up the fairway. One-two-three-kick...one-two-three-kick...spin...rear back like a parade horse, holding on to the golf bag.

The others laughed, but the syncopated beat was captivating.

Suntanned bodies...lazy sunshine...California girls—Beach Boy staples.

Chipper began marching with Peachy, easily picking up which beat prompted the kicks and fueled the spins. When it was clear that Chipper had the dance step down pat, Peachy added a dip and a pause, followed by a quick spin.

Do-do-do...do-do-do

The continued doo-doo-doo's brought L.K. and Jacob into the fold, both a bit awkward—too jocky to be good dancers—but able to keep the beat anyway. Buster walked along the edge of the fairway, ignoring the childishness.

The music slowed into a smooth rhythm bridge, causing Peachy to plant himself like an elm in the middle of the fairway. He held his golf bag as if it were a girl on a ballroom dance floor, stroking his woods like the soft hair of a lover.

After the bridge, it was up tempo, as Chipper, Jacob, and L.K. joined in again.

Do...doo...doo-doo-doo

Forward plunge with golf bags pointed down...rear back like a parade horse. Forward plunge. Rear back.

They looked like four oil wells on the Oklahoma landscape, pumping for crude.

On the fourth tee box, Chipper realized Peachy was in the lead... literally. In this miserable weather, he was even par after three and he was leading the group for the first time in history this far into a round.

Between replays, Peachy announced, "You sumbitches, I'll bet all four of you a cheeseburger I'm still in the lead after four."

"You're only one up on Jacob and two up on the rest of us," reminded Chipper.

"Easy money," said Peachy, "easy fuggin' money."

After his drive, Peachy turned on the recorder again.

"Turn it off," said L.K., "and you got a bet."

One corner of Peachy's mouth lifted into a sneaky grin. It was clear he believed the cassette music was a weapon that was weakening his opponents.

"Aw, let him play his music," Chipper said. "He'll turn it down."

After their drives, Peachy flipped on the recorder, and the team strolled down the fairway, now in near perfect unison. That is, except for Buster whose head was pointed to the ground, taking his steps to avoid the beat, almost on purpose.

After Peachy's triple-bogey on the fourth, the boys enjoyed their cheeseburgers in the warm pro shop. Peachy seemed not so much disappointed at the monetary loss as he was with the failure of his secret weapon. Everyone had made par on the hole except him.

"One more hole guys," said Peachy. "I'm feelin' lucky. I'll double the bet this time. And I won't play the same song anymore."

Chipper sensed that Peachy saw his luck pass with the first song, perhaps to be revived with a new one.

"Shit, it's too cold."

"C'mon L.K., you puss. We'll play number five, then back to number nine green, like a par three."

Reluctantly, the four pusses joined Peachy on the Number 5 tee box. He turned the cassette player down, but not off. Chipper could hear the haunting tune hobnobbing with the winter wind as Peachy addressed the ball:

Little surfer, little one

Crack.

"Well, shit, the Peach shanked it."

But it wasn't really a shank. Not the kind that veers immediately right. It was more of a blade-shank-combo, sending the ball, surely gashed, 10 feet off the ground toward the right rough and creek. A loud knock rocketed through the crisp air as the ball hit the creek's wooden bridge, sending it sharply back left toward a bare spot fronting the green where it hit a rock, reversing the pathway back to the right where another wild hop sent the ball heading straight for the pin.

Peachy began jumping up and down like a kid locked out of the bathroom. "Jiminy fuggin' Christmas, the sumbitch is headed for the hole!"

The ball was jet-powered, and it would clearly roll across the green to the trees beyond. Unless it hit the flagstick.

"Hit the pin, you fuggin' sumbitch!"

The ball scooted across the putting surface, kerplunking the metal flagstick. Then it disappeared, as if the earth just opened its mouth and gulped down a hard-boiled egg. The shot was so foul that Chipper halfway expected the ground to belch the rotten egg back onto the green.

Peachy was screaming obscenities in a piercing cry never heard before by human ears. L.K. buried his head in his hands. Buster muttered the F-word over and over in disbelief, as if a certain number of "Fucks" would shield him from the horrible truth.

"That's gotta be the ugliest hole-in-one in the history of the game," Chipper said.

"The odds are 13,500 to 1 for an amateur," said Jacob. "I read it in *Sports Illustrated.*"

"Ugly is the word," said Chipper. "Ugly."

"Yup," seconded L.K.

Peachy was halfway down the fairway jumping, screaming, kicking his heels in the air, howling, and running in circles.

"I'm gonna call the *Tribune*," Peachy yelled to the empty course. "I want my mug shot on the front page again."

"That makes me so sick I wanna puke," Buster said, grabbing his bag and heading for the clubhouse.

"Me, too," said L.K. "I'm callin' it quits. Who'd thought that Peachy would be the first one of us to ace?"

"C'mon, guys," Chipper said. "An ace is an ace. Peachy has to finish the round to make it official. You know, before you can turn in the reporting form to *Golf Digest*."

"You play with him, buddy," said L.K. "We're apeshit crazy to be out here in weather like this."

Chipper looked at Jacob, pleading with his eyes.

"I'm cold," Jacob said, "and it's almost dark. You'll never make it. We'll sign the form for *Golf Digest*. We'll all sign." He left with the others.

An ace, Chipper knew, was a once-in-a-lifetime triumph for Peachy, and that someone needed to be with him for the final four holes before dark. They would have to run between shots.

Thirty-two

"Overall, a damn shitty round," Peachy said as he tapped in his putt for a 7 on the final hole. "But no one's taking away my fuggin' ace. No one."

"Congratulations, Peachy. It was ugly for sure, but it counts."

"Damn straight," he said as he pushed his glasses back up his nose. "The Peach got himself a hole-in-fuggin'-one."

Chipper offered him a handshake. Peachy hesitated, as if to remember a wager, then smiled and shook hands.

"Those other shitheads can kiss my ass," he said.

"Well, it's awful cold and darn near dark," reminded Chipper.

"They can still kiss my ass...even Jay. Excuse me, *Jacob*. He's not the same any more. Have you noticed? And he's one whipped sonuva bitch."

In fact, Chipper *had* noticed. An unsettling distance had accompanied Jay's passage to Jacob, and this new chap was with Kelly every free minute that he wasn't on the course.

"Well, screw 'em all. I got my ace and I'm going home." With that, Peachy joined the darkness.

When Chipper reached his car, he saw a note under the wiper blade. *Good*, he thought, assuming a message from Amy. After all, it was her birthday, and he was overdue in delivering her present—a promise ring. Slipping the white card from beneath the wiper, he read:

I'm waiting by the jukebox
Ready to play our song

Our song? "I Loved You a Thousand Times" was Amy's favorite, "Daydream" was his favorite, but they didn't have a joint favorite.

He tried to talk himself out of the jitters as he walked up the outside steps to the club dining room. Then, as the door creaked open, he confirmed his fears.

Seated in an overstuffed chair beside the jukebox, both feet on the floor and hands folded in her lap as if attending a junior high etiquette class, was Gail Perdue.

She stood and smiled.

Chipper felt rippling flesh crawl from the back of his neck into his arms and legs. With her snow-white hair pulled into a ponytail, her boyish figure, and low-cut tennis shoes, she looked like she was in the fourth grade again, back when they exchanged vows. She was wearing a white jumper with mod polka dots—black dots it seemed, here in the dreary dance hall.

"Hello, Kyle," she said.

His vocal cords jammed as he walked toward her.

Finally, "What are you...what's going on, Gail?"

She didn't take a single step, frozen, while he drew close to her. Could she be a day over 13, so young and oh-so innocent? Her lips, with a frosty coating of lipstick, parted into a smile. Pinpoint dimples appeared as her beautiful white teeth glowed in the dark.

"Our time is almost here, Kyle, so we need to talk."

"Our time?"

"You know what I mean."

"I do?"

He stopped a few feet away from her and tried to assume a casual pose. *Right hand in pocket. No, both. No, just the left hand. Cock your knee. No, the other knee. Scratch the back of your head. Keep cool, you idiot.*

"Yes, you do. All the time I was in California you wrote to me of our destiny together. Destiny, Kyle. It was your word...your favorite word."

"We were kids, Gail. Just little kids."

She took two steps forward, lost her dimples, then her doe eyes grew twice as large.

"I never was a kid, Kyle. Remember that and you might understand."

He cleared his throat.

"We do have a destiny," she continued, "and we need each other to fulfill it."

He shook his head 'no'.

"Yes, we do. We belong together. Every boy I date...it's the same story. They want to go all the way. I mean, right on the first date. When I say no, they tell lies, start rumors. It's awful. I hate it. I hate them.

You're the only one, Kyle. I need you."

He felt himself taking a step backward, but her hand reached out to him, suspended in midair, forever. As if some alien force had control, his arm reached out for the suspended hand. And they touched.

Gail smiled for the second time.

She moved close to him, and he felt the shivers melt away.

"One dance," she said.

"What?"

"One dance, and you will see...it will be our song."

She held onto his hand, pulling him gently to the jukebox.

Oh, no, he thought. *This is Amy's jukebox. Don't touch it. It belongs to Amy.* Gail seemed to be reading his mind and laughing at his resistance.

She plopped a quarter into the jukebox. Every clink of the coin dropping through the machinery felt like nails being driven into his wrists. He couldn't see the song number she punched, nor did he want to. It was Amy's jukebox, and he couldn't believe this was happening.

Gail turned to face him, moving so close that the straps of her jumper tickled the flannel of his letterman's jacket as the music began.

When the twilight is gone...

It was the Platters. How *could* she? Amy's jukebox. Amy's favorite group. It was wrong. Dead wrong. Yet when the music began after the intro, he felt the alien force wrap his arms around her, then she molded herself inside his embrace.

Their feet began to move in a slow rhythm while the Platters wailed their longing prayer.

She pulled her head away and released her arms locked around his waist. Reaching for her ponytail, she unclipped something and the snow fell about her face and onto his arms. When she clamped her arms around his waist again, he felt his breath escape. She was barely squeezing, but he was still about to suffocate in the vice.

He tried to scare himself into running by thinking of Tucker Doogan's threats, Tim Richardson's swollen purple face, and the rumors, but none of the thoughts would stick any better than an approach shot onto the concrete greens of August. And Amy's green-eyed jukebox just stood there, staring, horrified.

Gail pulled her head away again and smiled for the third time. This time, the smile was brief and coy, relaxing to the point where her inviting lips remained barely parted. She let her eyelids close. He could almost hear the sound of her lashes as they fluttered shut.

The remote-controlled force pushed his head close to hers. *Stop*, he pleaded to the alien, but it was so much easier to surrender, then his lips touched the sweet taste of the frost on hers.

As they sank into the overstuffed chair, he slipped his tongue deep inside her, feeling an intoxicating urge to consume her...forever. The entire world shrank to this one fluffy chair, swallowing him and this captivating, virginal girl who needed him so much. No one understood her, no one treated her fairly, and no one could love her like he could. Why had he tried to keep these feelings so buried, for so long?

As the two of them squirmed on their sides in the enormous chair, he mirrored the location of her roving hand. When her hand moved to his inner thigh, he advanced his hand beneath the hem of her dress. When her hand moved to stroke between his legs, he stole a spot on the silky surface of her undies. And as she lowered the zipper on his jeans and slipped her hand inside, he felt the overpowering need to trumpet his eternal love. He pulled his lips away to form three words—the ones he used to tell her when they were kids. Those old magic words that were about to explode.

Suddenly, she jerked away as if she'd been electrocuted. "Noooo!" she screamed.

My-y...prayer

Gail shot up from the chair, crying, but he could see no tears.

"No, Kyle, not yet," she said. "It must be sacred. It must be when...when we're together...forever."

She was pulling her hair back into a ponytail, groping for the barrette that held it there earlier. Unable to find the clasp, she let her hair fall back down, wiped her eyes, and then ran for the door. In her hurry to escape, she shut the front door on her white jumper with the black polka dots. The door opened, then shut again, and the dress disappeared. For some crazy reason, he was not worried about Tucker Doogan, or the rumors, not even Amy—he wondered only if the door had left grease on her polka-dot jumper, and he couldn't seem to shake that thought.

Chipper felt his hands still trembling as he smoothed his hair and pushed the doorbell at Amy's house. It was nearly 10:00 o'clock, but he figured she was still awake.

Amy's mother offered a polite smile as she answered the door, but it wasn't the usual beaming future-son-in-law smile he was used to.

Guilt was oozing out of his pores, so he wiped his brow. Nothing was wrong with Amy's mom. He was just imagining things.

"Come in, Chipper."

He stepped through the doorway into the living room. What was going on? Amy's grandparents were there, along with aunts and uncles, filling every chair and sofa in the living room. Amy was seated on the opposite side of the circle. She wasn't smiling, though she still looked pretty in a yellow sundress with spaghetti bows on her shoulders.

The somber audience was dead quiet. Chipper imagined that his jukebox rendezvous had been televised directly into this living room.

"What's going on?" he asked. "Why's everyone here?"

The family members began exchanging mortified looks. Amy stared directly at him like a blank page.

"What's happening?" he persisted, beginning to feel like a balloon in a room full of razor blades.

It didn't make any sense why the family was gathered so late at night. And on a weekday.

"Well..." began Grandma McNeil, "...after all, it *is* Amy's birthday."

The alien force sucked the breath of life from him, and he knew he was going to die on the spot. He felt the blood rush up to his face like a thermometer about to explode, then drain back down to his feet, leaving swirling spots before his eyes. His field of vision squeezed down so that he could only see Amy through a long, dark tunnel. Her lips were quivering, her jaw was tightening, and even at 20 feet he could see water filling the troughs at the bottom of her eyes.

"Have a seat, Chipper," he thought he heard someone say. The forces of doom that greeted him had nothing to do with the jukebox—he had simply made the worst social blunder of his life, forgetting Amy's birthday, in front of God and family.

Amy stood up from her chair of honor, never moving her eyes away from him, ensuring that the penetrating power of those invisible beams were burning deep into his flesh. Her whole body seemed to be shaking. Suddenly, she bolted past him toward her bedroom, her mascara-filled tears leaving black trails down her cheeks like engine oil over the wing of a jet airplane.

It was going to be a cold winter.

Thirty-three

Through the echo of dreams, Chipper heard a telephone ring in the distance. Was he awake? Was the horrific spectacle at Amy's house just a link in a long chain of nightmares? The phone rang again. He was awake, and he realized the calamity at Amy's was for real.

He opened one eye to see his younger sister tiptoeing into his room, bringing the princess phone on its tether.

"It's Jay," she whispered.

"You mean Jacob."

"I guess so."

"Thanks." He took the phone from her and motioned her out of the room.

"Jacob? What's up, man?" It was not like his chum to call anymore, especially this much beyond his Ozzie and Harriet bedtime.

"If anybody asks, such as my mom," he began between panting breaths, "I'm spending the night at your house."

"What? What are you talking about?"

"If anyone asks, I'm spending the night with you. Got it?"

"Got it."

Click.

Chipper rolled to his back and let the phone rest on his chest. Jacob never violated curfew. What was going on? Tonight must be the night. That was it. Jacob and Kelly couldn't wait any longer. His friend was out of breath trying to hold back, and he just couldn't take it any more. At this very minute, he must be whisking Kelly away to the Boomer-Sooner Motel in Norman where rooms were rented to college kids by the hour. They had come too close, too many times. Certainly, they were going beyond the brink tonight.

Thirty-four

SPRING 1967

Chipper strolled to the 18th tee box at the Pottawatomie Golf and Country Club, relieved by his early victory in the match, though burdened by the private stew in which he'd cooked himself.

Seventeen hundredths of a point. That's how the dominoes began to fall. Amy had taken more college level courses than he; so, at semester, her grade point beat his by seventeen hundredths of a point. Even if he scored straight A's again this final semester, Amy would do the same. Jacob would be Valedictorian, Amy Salutatorian, and he would be nothing.

On the heels of her 4.36 grade average, Amy announced she was going pre-med. This led to spirited discussions about a woman's place, and Chipper had to fight the nagging remembrance that he was critical of his own father's similar stance, yet now he was repeating these paternal arguments, almost against his will.

Then Amy shot a 75. Not just any 75, but one with two shots out-of-bounds. Erase those drives, and she would have had a subpar round. Unthinkable.

Their final day as a couple tormented him still. The conversation went from Salutatorian to shooting a 75 to Amy's forgotten birthday to 'Have your lips ever touched Gail Perdue's?' so quick it made his head spin. It had been almost two months, and he wondered where she was and what she was doing almost constantly.

Keeping up with Gail's rendezvous-on-demand, once a week at 10:00 p.m., was becoming a strain. At first, he agreed that their trysts should be secret, fearing for his life. But Tucker Doogan completely ignored him at school, giving Chipper the notion that he and Gail could relax and go public. Whenever he suggested this, though, Gail's face would stiffen, then she'd dream up some new hideaway for their just-shy-of-whammy lovemaking.

His two frictioned moods—despair at the loss of Amy and delirium at the very image of Gail—rubbed together like two sticks of wood and sparked a baffling blaze for every tick-tock of the day.

Jacob, L.K., Buster, and Chipper, with opponents, were detained on the 18th tee box, waiting for some hackers to clear the creek in front.

Peachy had to lag behind in a twosome when the schools played five men. Pottawatomie, a town smaller than El Viento, was barely able to muster five. A legendary first man, Smokey Ray Divine, was followed by a fair-to-middling second man, but then three duffers ensured El Viento's sixth straight team victory.

Chipper was playing his best round of the season, albeit on an easy course. A few holes back, he had daydreamed about being medalist, but he knew it could never be. Even at his best, he was still a fourth man.

Smokey Ray Divine teed his ball, then squatted on the ground like a television Indian, holding onto his driver for support with one hand, shielding his eyes from the sun with the other, while he waited for the group ahead to clear.

"Those goobers oughta know they're supposed to stay outta the way when there's a match going on." Smokey Ray could articulate rapid-fire like a disc jockey, even with a coffin nail in his mouth. And he always had a smoke.

Raymond Hathaway Divine was an honorary member of the El Viento team. As a solo star from the nearby town—a man without a team—Smokey Ray had played Jacob and the rest of them in Oklahoma junior tournaments, and now high school golf, on countless occasions.

Noted for playing the game in a cowboy hat with a rattlesnake band, Smokey Ray was always within lethal striking distance in any tournament or match.

Chipper had spotted the button on Smokey Ray's headband earlier, but now he could read the words: Hell No We Ain't Going. He wasn't sure what it meant, but he remembered how Smokey Ray couldn't let go of Barry McGuire's "Eve of Destruction" two summers ago. In a world of polo shirts and matching socks, Smokey Ray was from another planet. Peachy considered him a god incarnate.

When Smokey Ray stood up to swing, Chipper was always startled by his short, squatty stature. His arms hung so low to the ground that it seemed a good hot sun might soften and elongate the limbs until his knuckles scraped the dirt. It was hard to figure how he fared so well on the links. His thin, straight hair poured like a yellow waterfall beneath the cowboy hat onto his neck, and it reached the length of a felony at El Viento High. His eyes were tiny black dots, like a snowman's, only colder.

Smokey Ray flicked his cigarette one foot away from his ball, demonstrating the same deadly accuracy that allowed him to attack the flagstick with his long irons. A wispy ribbon of potential grass fire wormed its way to the sky, a smoke signal marking his ball. He didn't take practice swings, and he spent zero time over the ball. If he took his stance while you blinked, you missed the shot.

Chipper turned to look at Jacob's 'clutch' face, and missed Smokey Ray's shot, hearing only the unique crack of his driver, a sound that seemed to pop louder than other golfers.

"Oh, baby, make me wet," said Smokey Ray. "Yesiree, baby, make me wet, make me cum."

The ball easily cleared the creek some 240 yards out on the fly. Most golfers had to lay up and play it safe on this par 5.

"Yesiree, baby, you did it. Three hundred yards. I'm all wet. My King Kong dong will be sticking to my 'wear before I'm through tapping in my eagle putt."

Smokey Ray trapped his grounded cigarette between his driver and his left shoe, then lifted the butt into the air, spinning, catching it in his mouth. It was a stunt that Peachy had tried on numerous occasions, yielding clusters of lip burns, then a self-imposed ban on the "disgusting habit." It didn't matter how the cig landed in Smokey Ray's mouth, though, he never got burned.

Jacob addressed his drive. With the white zinc oxide on his nose, he looked like a Sunday school teacher on a picnic compared to Smokey Ray with his shirttail out, his cowboy hat, and his scraggly blond sideburns that were trying to grow down his cheeks like patches of advancing grass onto a cart path.

Jacob's drive cleared the creek, but landed in the left rough.

One other important thing about Smokey Ray. Along with Ritchie Cosgrove of Castlemont, he was one of only two golfers in the state that, sometimes, could whip Jacob's butt.

After L.K.'s power drive beat them all, followed by his opponent's creek shot, the first and second men took off down the fairway. The fast-walking, fast-talking Smokey Ray was in the lead, his straight yellow hair slapping against the back of his neck like a mudflap on a semi.

Buster sidled up to Chipper, a curious move since Buster counted it crowded if he were within three feet of anyone other than Carol.

"Say, Chipper," he whispered, looking suspiciously to each side for clearance, "I've gotta question."

"Sure, what is it?"

"Well, Smokey Ray made me think of it. Joking about 'make me wet'. Just curious, you know."

"Uh-huh, what?"

"You know that clear stuff that...uh...comes out your...uh... thing...you know...uh...when you first get excited? I mean, just thinkin' about it...sometimes..."

"Yessss," said Chipper with caution. Buster could go 18 holes without saying a word. This was already a filibuster.

"Well...does that stuff have...does it like have those sperm cells in it? I mean...can you..."

"Yes," said Chipper in anticipation. "You can get someone pregnant with that stuff."

Buster scooped the bottom of his nose with his forefinger then began massaging the back of his neck.

"I just kinda wondered."

"Sure."

Buster backed away a few steps to a more comfortable zone. Chipper tried to act like he wasn't paying any attention to his teammate, but out of the corner of his eye he watched Buster milking the grip of his driver, and he could see the leather turn dark from the sweat of his palms.

The first and second men moved out of range.

Chipper's drive hit the far side of the creek at 240 yards, stalled...then rolled back into the ditch. The chance for his first even par round evaporated. He slammed the driver back in his bag.

Well since she put me down I've been out doin' in my head

Chipper turned around to see Peachy and his opponent on the 17th green, Peachy's cassette recorder playing while he sang to the music. Gus, as usual, was caddying for his guru.

Chipper lifted his bag onto his shoulder and started down the fairway, motioning back for Peachy to turn down the music.

Peachy's competition was poised over his putt when Chipper spotted "The Move." Even at this distance, Chipper could see Peachy reach for the cassette recorder to crank up the music just as his opponent's putter met the ball:

Help me, Rhonda, help, help me, Rhonda

Peachy turned toward the 18th tee box and grinned, signaling Chipper with a slash of his forefinger across the throat, then pointing to his brainy forehead, to let Chipper know he'd just psyched out another one.

What a waste, thought Chipper. Peachy won his match three holes back. Of course, for Peachy, the sport had dimensions not really explored by most who played the game. Peachy seemed to enjoy little private victories that no one else understood. Whether it was tapping a toe while standing in his opponent's line, or making clicking sounds with his tongue during someone's backswing, Peachy used clubs in his bag of weaponry that were not regulation. If Peachy could just figure some way to somehow channel his 'psych-out' energy to a 'psych *in*...'

An idea suddenly popped into Chipper's head.

It was a tiny acorn of a thought, for sure, but it might be worth a try during their next practice session.

Thirty-five

The Stingray was backed up to the wooden fence marking the perimeter of Tate's Drive-in, allowing Peachy and Chipper a prime spot for parade review. Evenings were still cool enough in April that the true athlete could cloak himself in his letterman's jacket without looking ridiculous. A steady stream of cars inched their way through the circle drive while Chipper and Peachy leaned against the Vette in their crimson letter jackets, pretending not to notice the passers-by as they took role.

"Smokey Ray might come to El Viento tonight," Peachy said.

"Oh, yeah?"

"Yeah. I guess for a victory lap after thumping Jay's butt today. Or else, looking for chicks."

"It's *Jacob*, Peachy, not Jay."

"Yeah, sure. So sue me."

It hurt whenever Jacob lost. In the back of his mind, Chipper remembered that his friend needed a great season. Limited golf scholarships at OU mandated glory. And Doc Jody's limited insurance policy mandated a scholarship in excess of the piddling academic ones.

"Maybe we'll see *Jacob* and Kelly, tonight," Peachy said a sarcastic snarl. "Hah, just kidding," he added.

"No one sees them anymore." *Not since the midnight phone call*, thought Chipper.

"He's one whipped sumbitch."

Chipper felt abandoned. Jacob and Kelly were gone. Amy was gone. The world was changing. He thought back to when they were kids. Even before the girls. The days were easy—simply cruising down the center of the street with Jay on one side, Peachy on the other, both of them like horseshoe magnets pulling him to their side. The magnetic forces were equal, neutralizing each other such that the walk was straight and simple. Now Jay was gone.

"I've been thinking, Chipper..."

"Yeah, what?"

"I've been thinkin' about your problem."

"My problem? Who said I've gotta problem?"

Peachy leaned one stiff arm onto the hood of his car and turned to look at Chipper over the rim of his glasses, like an old man escaping his bifocals.

"You're frustrated, man. You're just flat fuggin' frustrated."

"About what?"

"About everything. Is it gonna be Gail? Should I go back to Amy? Will I get into medical school? How do we win State? Shit, man, you need to be more like the Peach. You need to *relax*."

Chipper thought quietly for a moment. He didn't *feel* frustrated.

"Life for the Peach is like walking on stage for graduation. You walk up the steps, cross the stage, take your diploma, and you're off the stage. If there's a god, and I do mean 'if', then He might say something like 'damn good job, Peachy' as He hands me the diploma. That's it. Nothing more. Nothing less."

"There *is* a god, Peachy."

"That's not the point. The point is that you, Chipper...you're not satisfied just walking across the stage to get your diploma. You want all sorts of honors tagged onto it. You want God to hand you the diploma and then turn to the audience and say, 'This is the guy that saved L.K. Taylor's life, then taught him how to chip. This is the guy that befriended Buster Nelson when no one else would talk to the jerk. This is also the guy that cured Peachy of his shank. Yesireee, folks, this is the guy that's responsible for the El Viento State Championship Golf Team'."

"So what's wrong with that?"

"Nothing's wrong with it; it's just an observation. The thought of life being meaningless, just a walk across the stage, is so horrible for you that you've just gotta accomplish something—something that says you were on this sweet earth. Not that anything's wrong with that. There's a lot of good things that happen because of suckers like you, but your pats-on-the-back will have a hefty price tag. And that price tag is frustration. It may be frustration that leads to the cure for cancer or world peace, who knows? But it's frustration, just the same. As for me, the Peach will simply take his diploma and say 'thank you very much'."

"Well, thank you very much, Mr. Philosopher," Chipper said, bowing slightly at the waist. "But I don't really consider it a problem." He was perturbed at the sly implication of selfishness. After all, he had given his heart to the golf team.

A low rumble in the street became deafening as a menacing black '40 Ford with chopped top and tinted windows pulled into the circle drive of Tate's.

"What the hell is he doing here?" Peachy murmured. "Damn."

"Never seen him do *this* before." Chipper straightened his blood red letter jacket and stood as tall as he could while Neander T rolled slowly before the row of cars backed against the fence and between speakers.

"The sumbitch is looking for somebody to kill," hypothesized Peachy.

Horror of horrors, Neander T's Carsophagus stopped directly in front of Peachy's Stingray.

It was five seconds, perhaps ten, though it seemed like forever that the bloodcurdling auto and its invisible driver idled in front of the Vette.

Chipper's life almost flashed before his eyes, until it dawned on him that Peachy was probably the target. After all, who knew what shady gambling deals, or worse, that Peachy could get himself into? He began breathing again as the car moved slowly ahead, freeing the congested teenage traffic that was backed into the street.

"Shit, I hate that bastard," Peachy said. "What's he doing here? He's supposed to be in the city, street-fighting or something."

"Why in the world would he come here?" echoed Chipper. "And why would he stop in front of us?"

"Oh, it was probably nothing," Peachy said in a feeble attempt at bravery. "I bet he just stopped to open a beer, or to cop a feel on Juanita Sue, that Apache chick he screws."

"Have you ever seen her?"

"Yeah, incredible body. Solid muscle. Not bad looking, except her sharp teeth are all spaced apart. Makes her look like she could tear the flesh off buffalo bones. I wouldn't want to tangle with her."

"Me, either."

"Hey, look at that," Peachy said. His forefinger was shaking as he pointed across the circle drive. The Carsophagus was starting to pull onto the main drag, and Chipper could see the ham-sized arm hanging out the narrow window beneath the chopped top.

"The scorpion."

"Yeah, you can see it from here. I still say the tattoo glows with a black light."

"Who cares?"

"I care," said Peachy with a mischievous tone. "I care."

The boys rested against the front of the red Stingray, looking like identical hood ornaments in their red and white armor. Chipper noticed that his hands were still trembling as he snapped and unsnapped the buttons of his jacket.

A green '51 Pontiac stopped in front of them and all windows rolled down at once. Six, maybe seven, girls were inside, all juniors and seniors.

"Hey, Chipper," yelled Darla Jenks, "did you hear that Drew Masters won Pep Club Beau?"

"Sure," he lied. "So what?"

"So it helps to be dating the Pep Club President, doesn't it?" The girls began laughing and congratulating each other on their torture techniques.

Drew Masters was Student Council President. Amy had been dating him for the past month. Not that Drew wasn't an okay guy. But he wasn't a letterman. And he was kinda short for Amy. And too awkward with girls. And for that matter, a goodie-two-shoes.

"If you and Amy were still a couple, you'd have won," Darla continued, driving the point to his backbone.

He smiled, even pretending to laugh.

From the back seat of the Pontiac came, "How's Gail?" Laughter. "Have you seen her tonight?" More laughter. "Why would you see her at Tate's?" A mixture of giggling and nervous laughter.

"For your information, " Chipper said pleasantly, "I'm not dating Gail." It was clear that too many people knew too much.

The girls exchanged looks then began snickering again.

"Amy sure thinks so...and so do a lot of other people. Oh, well, we just wondered if you'd heard the news. I guess Drew and Amy will be going to the prom together." Another one added, "Won't they make a cute king and queen?"

The rope inside Chipper's stomach knotted one thousand times as he tossed his head back and laughed at the girls as if he were in complete command of the situation, master of his fate.

The windows rolled up to muffle the continued laughter, and the green Pontiac resumed its position in the cavalcade of teens.

Hundreds of cars passed through the drive-in over the next hour. Chipper and Peachy didn't budge from their prime real estate as they watched the green Pontiac come back through at least six more times. Chipper wanted to assure them he was unfazed.

The flashing blue neon light spelling out T-A-T-E'-S was getting old. In fact, the whole scene was getting oldsville.

"Ready to go?" he proposed.

"Yeah, let's do it."

As they turned to open their doors, Chipper heard honking and yelling from the street. An all-too-familiar-candy-apple-red-customized hot rod was jumping the curb and bullying its way into the line around Tate's. When no one made room, the hot rod forced its own lane, honking at the other cars to get out of the way.

Chipper froze. Peachy's eyes popped wide open as he stared at Chipper. The hot rod pulled in front of Peachy's car at an angle, then the driver shot out of his seat. It was Tucker Doogan. Homer and Eddie trailed.

The flying wedge was after him again.

"Oh, shit," muttered Peachy.

Chipper dug his heels into the asphalt and prepared for the attack. Another broken nose, some stitches, two black eyes...he was ready.

Homer and Eddie each grabbed an arm and held them behind his back. He was already defenseless and they'd only just begun.

Tucker didn't say one word, but his boiling red face, beaded with sweat, gave a ferocity to his owlish appearance that Chipper had never seen before. This time, he meant business.

Quietly, Tucker reached inside his letter jacket and pulled out a weapon. He pressed one thumb against the black handle. A simultaneous *click* and a flash of silver meant death by switchblade.

"Hold the candy ass sonuva bitch still," he ordered.

Chipper felt his arms tighten behind him as he prepared to die.

Tucker grabbed the collar of Chipper's jacket and raised the knife high in the air. Chipper caught a glimpse of the blinking blue neon reflected on the shiny metal blade, as screams of terror reverberated through the drive-in.

"I told you to stay away from her, you candy-assed sonuva bitch."

The knife plunged to his chest.

Funny, he thought, *there's no pain*. He looked down, halfway expecting to see blood spurting out, but Tucker Doogan had driven the blade into his letterman's jacket, right over the letter E. Tucker then began sawing the letter off the jacket, away from his heart.

He struggled, gasping for air, but there was none.

"Candy ass golfers don't deserve to letter. It's not even a fucking sport," Tucker shouted as he cut away the final attachments of the letter, removing it completely from the jacket and holding it up in the air like a scalp. Whooping and hollering, he began running in circles around the drive-in, holding the letter above his head to make sure everyone witnessed the humiliation.

When Homer and Eddie let go of Chipper's arms, he thought the limbs would just drop off and hit the pavement. He wanted to melt, to vaporize, to disappear, to be transported by aliens, anything...anything at all to escape this moment. He couldn't endure the agony. Some things in life were too hard, and this was the worst humiliation he could fathom. Indeed, death was preferable. *Give me my diploma,* he thought. *No pats on the back, no nothing. Just give me my diploma and get me the hell off this stage.*

Tucker circled back, shoved the letter into his face and pushed him onto the hood of Peachy's car. He felt Tucker's fist punching him in the stomach over and over until he thought he would throw up. Then it was over. He opened his eyes to see his letter lying beside him on the hood of the car, like an innocent bystander. He could see Peachy cowering against the back fence, gripping the lapels of his letter jacket.

As Chipper raised himself up off the hood of the car, he realized Tucker and his henchmen were gone. Traffic was moving again. Only now, he was the circus freak extraordinaire as the passing gawkers eyed him and commented on the poor, pathetic creature and its hideous fate.

He remembered from Mr. Ashbrook that perseverance meant continuing to walk forward even though a knife was in your heart. But what if you were *dead* and still walking? What was the word for that? A zombie?

Several vehicles back in the line was the car of Drew Masters... with Amy, sitting close. Through the glass, he could see her worried look as she stared at him. She was opening her mouth as if to speak, but Drew's arm encircled her shoulders, drawing her attention back, protecting her from the zombie. She looked forward, through the windshield, away from Chipper, then dropped her eyes to stare at her lovely hands crossed neatly in her warm lap where he had rested his head so many times before.

Chipper looked down at the hole in his chest, where his heart should have been, then took off his jacket.

Peachy was silent.

Just give me my diploma, he thought, as he fought back the bubbling and rumbling inside that threatened to erupt with fury or tears or both.

Chipper lost all track of time. He sat in the car with Peachy, doors locked. He was waiting for a convenient time to leave, when no one would notice. But that time would never come. He would always be noticed...forever. Every move he would make would be analyzed unto eternity. People would be telling this story forever.

The helplessness bothered him the most. There was nothing he could do. Oh, he thought about knives, guns, and grenades, but only for a flicker of a second before vetoing the schemes as ludicrous. There was simply nothing he could do. On the other hand, he couldn't live with this humiliation. Something had to give.

The passing cars were more like a freight train now, just a repetitive blur. He didn't see if Tucker passed through again. Or Neander T, or the green Pontiac, or Amy. It was just a blur.

Except for the pickup.

No one drove a pickup through Tate's. Especially not a beat-up pickup, and one painted in such a crazy, haphazard pattern that it drew more attention than neon. Primarily yellow, but with designs and swirls of bright purple, orange, and green, forming child-like sunbursts and flowers. It was like a traveling cartoon, and Chipper had never seen anything like it before.

Peachy rolled down his window and shouted and waved. The pickup pulled up to a speaker, then the driver jumped out, waving his cowboy hat with the rattlesnake band in the air.

Smokey Ray Divine had arrived.

Thirty-six

With each bump in the road, Chipper felt his caboose plop in and out of the gaping hole in the leather seat of the pickup, the inner springs prodding him into longing for the comfort of his Thunderbird. Smokey Ray the pilot and Peachy the copilot were absorbed in discussing nuances of love while he, the beer-sipping navigator, was on the lookout for a candy-apple-red hot rod. With these two horseshoe magnets to his left, he was glad to be riding shotgun, closest to the door.

"The Pottawatomie poon-tang's all dried up," Smokey Ray said.

"Shit, I knew that's why you were cruising El Viento tonight. I knew it. Well, it ain't much better here."

"Yeah, a man's gotta keep searchin' for new pudenda."

"Uh...yeah. So much...pudenda, so little time."

Chipper gazed out the window, shying from the topic.

Sometimes, it was hard to tell Peachy and Smokey Ray apart. They both thought God was in our imaginations, they both punctuated their sentences with cusswords, they both considered a second date to be a serious relationship. But there was a difference.

Chipper saw it one of the first times they ever played golf with Smokey Ray. They were about 13 years old at the time, playing in the Oklahoma Junior. Peachy had finished his round and was caddying for Chipper who was being pounded in his match by a scrawny Ray Divine.

In the middle of the 14th fairway, Peachy spotted a tarantula crawling from one rough to the other. Grabbing a wedge from Chipper's clubs, he let the bag drop and charged for the spider with war-like whoops. Poised over the tarantula with his golf stance, early Quasimodo, Peachy prepared to send the spider and its legs flying in eight different directions.

Smokey Ray, puffing on a cancer stick, yelled "Stop!" as he rushed to the scene. Kneeling down before the spider, he held out his hand, whereupon to the horror of both Peachy and Chipper, he coaxed the critter onto his palm and let it creep up his arm. Chipper could still remember having the worst attack of goose bumps in his life. The creature stalked all the way up to Smokey Ray's shoulder and stopped. Smokey Ray just stared it stiff with his beady black eyes riveted on the multiple eyes of the tarantula. Chipper figured the varmint probably saw six or eight terrifying Smokey Rays. With a threatening hairy gesture, the spider reared back on its hind legs, lifting its front legs in the air with a slow motion dog paddle, showing off its fangs as it readied to leap onto Smokey Ray's face. Smokey Ray didn't budge, prepared to hold his position forever. In fact, his eyes narrowed a bit and his jaw muscles tightened as the two creatures squared off.

Chipper fully expected Smokey Ray's face to be smothered by eight hairy legs, his skin melting after the bite, followed by seizures and a grisly death.

His stare finally penetrated the tarantula's threat, its legs dropping back to the skin of Smokey Ray's shoulder. He still didn't move a muscle. Then the spider backed down his arm. *Backed down*, mind you. It didn't take its eyes off Smokey Ray while it back-stepped down his arm, right into the hero's palm. Smokey Ray stood up and escorted the tarantula to the safety of the rough where he let it go free. Peachy stood by dejected, gripping his pitching wedge, denied his pleasure.

"Scientists," Smokey Ray said from the driver's seat, "have figured out there are 24 steps, you know."

"Yeah? From zero to all the way?"

"When you touch her hand, step one. If she interlocks her fingers with yours, step two."

"Right, I get it. But in poker, your opponent isn't even blinking. Harder to read."

Chipper realized that with each beer, the foamy liquid became easier to swallow. The fizzle didn't burn his throat any more, and a few hefty gulps were easy. And the pain of Tate's Drive-in seemed further away, buried beneath the empties on the floorboard.

"Slipping your hand from her back to the side of her boob, step six."

"Uh-huh."

"If you skip six, you're dead. A frontal assault on the boob and it's over."

"Damn straight. I agree."

"She might go apeshit."

"You betcha."

Chipper thought back to that day in the third grade when his mother coached him to believe that people who used cusswords had a struggling vocabulary, and that the words served as crutches—that a gifted, creative mind could always think of a better word for the situation.

"But the goddam fuggin' criminal shame of it all, is that there ain't enough time to mount all the fillies in the world."

"Maybe fuggin' not," Peachy agreed, "but I know plenty who are willing to skip steps 10 through 24 and go right for the poke. Gotta love 'em, dammit."

Chipper realized he could polish off one-half can of Jax with a single gulp, and that the floor of the pickup was nearly covered with tin tombstones. Peachy and Smokey Ray were starting to get funnier and funnier. Gee, Smokey Ray's vocabulary wasn't so bad. And what was such a big deal about getting the letter cut off your jacket at Tate's, anyway?

Chipper assumed church key control. The hissing pops he created by opening the cans alternated with the backfire explosions of the jalopy pickup as they cruised the streets of El Viento. Two for them, one for me. Two for them, one for me. One for them, two for me.

"Yeah, Peachy, I had to quit wearing jockey briefs...my prick kept getting tied in a knot."

Chipper laughed.

"Well, you won't see me wearing Bermuda shorts anymore," returned Peachy. "I keep hanging out beneath the bottom of the leg."

More laughter.

He wasn't sure where the words came from, but Chipper heard himself saying, "Hell, I can't even sleep on my stomach anymore. When I get a boner, I fall off the log and it wakes me up at night."

Silence.

Peachy and Smokey Ray stared first at each other, then at him in disbelief. Chipper smiled as the two comrades broke into howls of laughter.

"When you finish that one, Chipper," Smokey Ray said, "we'll pull off and get my home brew out of the cooler in back."

"Pull over, Smokey Ray. I'm ready."

At roadside, near the bowling alley, Smokey Ray jerked a blanket from a hidden cooler in the pickup bed, like a magician saying "Voilá," revealing the stash of home brew. All three boys were crouched in the bed of the truck as their six arms began pulling out the canning jars with brown, frothy fluid inside.

A crescendoed zzooom followed by a decrescendoed vrrooom caused them to lift their heads from the brew stash like three zebras at a watering hole after smelling a lion.

The familiar taillights of the candy-apple-red hot rod grew smaller with distance.

"That's the motherfugger who cut up Chipper's jacket," said Peachy.

"So that's the fuck-jaw, huh?"

Chipper stared at the taillights as they turned into the bowling alley, circled, then headed back down the strip.

Peachy was flexing his muscles, pounding his closed fist into the open palm of his other hand. "Yesiree, that's the fuck-jaw. The one and only."

Chipper felt his nerves twist to braids as the headlights got closer on the other side of the divided highway. Tucker Doogan slowed the hot rod, looking their way. Peachy and Chipper hit the deck. Smokey Ray stood up and stared back with the same face that had greeted that tarantula years ago. His head pivoted at the neck so that his beady eyes were locked onto the multiple eyes in the hot rod.

"Does the motherfugger think he's got a souped-up slick-ass set of wheels?"

The two boys stood to join their pilot. "Uh, yeah," Chipper replied.

"Loves that car," said Peachy. "Also thinks he loves Gail Perdue, but I bet he'd rather stick his prick in the chrome tailpipe of that machine than in Gail Perdue."

"So he loves that car," Smokey Ray said, his eyes drifting upward as if to look at a light bulb above his head. "Grab the brew, let's go ride 'em, cowboys," yelled Smokey Ray, holding his hat in the air as he jumped over the side of the pickup. Chipper and Peachy followed the lead, scrambling into the cab.

"Wanna Camel?" asked Smokey Ray, offering his pack by flicking his wrist with just enough force to send one cigarette up for the taking. Chipper declined, but Peachy took the bait while Smokey Ray served himself. He struck a match on an abrasive strip he kept near his hatband so that it looked like it was the rattlesnake skin that started the fire.

The engine started with a roar, then Smokey Ray floorboarded the truck, sending it into a fishtail as it accelerated onto the highway.

Chipper grabbed the dashboard as Smokey Ray jumped the median in a bounding U-turn that sent them hot on the trail of Tucker Doogan.

"Motherfuggin' sumbitch," yelled Peachy, sharing Chipper's sentiments.

"The gentleman needs to learn a lesson," Smokey Ray said with absolute calm.

Peachy and Chipper looked at each other with widened eyes.

"Uh...Smokey Ray...what do you...what are you planning to do?" managed Chipper.

"I'm going to see if I can improve this guy's communication skills."

Peach gulped. "Uh...Smokey Ray...you don't have to live in the same town as this guy."

"Oh, not to worry, cowboys. Just duck when we get close."

"Looks like he's turning onto Country Club Road."

"Yeah."

Since the hot rod was not aware of the threat, it was easy for the yellow pickup to catch up. They followed at a safe distance, closing the gap after two miles south to where the new interstate was under construction. The on-ramps and off-ramps were finished, but none of the concrete was poured.

Smokey Ray began to tailgate the hot rod. The territorial foul was recognized, evoking three obscene fingers by Tucker, Eddie, and Homer in the convertible hot rod.

Tucker and his gang-of-two passed beneath the interstate bridge, then turned left up the on-ramp. Smokey Ray never quit kissing their rear bumper, while the hot rod accelerated. As they entered the dirt-layered highway, the yellow jalopy began passing the candy-apple hot rod on the right.

At the same time, Chipper and Peachy realized the threat of their own discovery and bent over at the waist, leaving Smokey Ray as an apparent solo pilot.

Smokey Ray was smiling and puffing the cigarette in his left hand, while steering with his right hand draped over the wheel. He looked straight ahead as the vulgar shouts from the hot rod threatened his future existence on earth.

Chipper's head was between his knees as he thought about Tucker Doogan's spinner hubcaps, and how they looked the same as those on Stephen Boyd's chariot in *Ben Hur*. He thought how nice it would be to have a bullwhip right now. Or a gun.

"Cowboys, behold the first lesson in communication."

Smokey Ray turned his head out the window and began loudly:

"Nor shall death brag thou
Wander'st in his shade
When in eternal lines to time
Thou grow'st."

The words made no sense, but they were delivered with such

warning that Chipper hoped the message was never delivered to him.

From the hot rod came, "Oh, yeah, and so does your mother."

Smokey Ray leaned down and spoke in a hush to his two half-bent companions. "Shakespeare...on immortality. It's all in the delivery. These bozos can only hear insults right now."

He turned his head out the window again.

"Thou whoreson Zed!
Thou unnecessary letter!
You are not worth the dust
which the rude wind blows in your face."

"Fuck you back," Tucker shouted, "you goddam motherfuggin' sumbitch. Pull that piece of crap off the road so I can beat the shit out of you."

Smokey leaned down to translate. "Shakespeare, again. King Lear. I've just challenged them."

Chipper looked at Peachy who was looking back over his kneecap, eyes about to blow out. "Shakespeare?" they said quietly to each other.

Smokey Ray continued.

"Be not afraid, though you do
see me weapon'd;
Here is my journey's end, here
is my butt,
And very sea-mark of my utmost
sail."

"I told you, you goddam piece of shit to pull your goddam car off the road so I can teach your goddam ass a fuggin' lesson."

"Othello," said Smokey Ray.

"Othello?" Peachy and Chipper whispered to each other.

"Seems our young friends are not so inclined to improve themselves. 'Tis they that intend to teach me the lesson."

At this point, Chipper began to appreciate the sobering effect of fear. Who was this guy driving this pickup? Who in the world was Smokey Ray Divine and where did he come from?

Smokey Ray turned his head to the hot rod again as he roared with the same threatening voice, "Let's talk of graves, of worms, and epitaphs; let's choose executors, and talk of wills. And if thine hate bellows forth in not nippy tarn skippy noot 'n nurn, then take your flot gipsom drim down the dribble wibble flaggot fribble."

Smokey Ray leaned down and said to his cowboy friends, "More Shakespeare, plus a voice I heard once when I was hallucinating."

"Voices?" asked Peachy.

"Hallucinating?" gasped Chipper.

Chipper noticed that Peachy's trembling hands were trying to clutch his legs to hold them still. His own hands were just as shaky. He thought he was about to puke.

"That does it, you mealy-mouthed fuck-jaw. Your ass is grass, and we're gonna mow your butt down to your asshole, whoever the fuck you are."

The pickup slowed.

Smokey Ray was smiling. How could he do that? He was about to get them all killed, and he was smiling. Chipper wondered if he could scrunch any closer to the floor of the cab, joining the empties.

As calm as if he were lounging in a hammock watching a beautiful sunset, Smokey Ray transferred his cigarette to his right hand, grabbed the steering wheel with his left, then took a long, slow drag. A thin stream of smoke spewed from his tightened lips with the exhale. As the trail of smoke began to die, he popped a few smoke rings with his tongue, but they were quickly whisked away by the night air roaring through the open window on his left.

"Pull your goddam piece of yellow junk off the road, you fuggin' little pissant." Tucker Doogan's voice was loud and Chipper could picture his boiling red face.

Chipper recognized the upcoming stunt immediately, as Smokey Ray curled his fingers into a contorted hand that served as the crossbow to his burning cigarette. A deadly accurate crossbow. Just like his trademark flick of the cig to the grass during a golf swing.

"My friend," Smokey Ray replied, "we are, all of us, off the road... already." He moved his cocked right hand to the window and fired.

Chipper found the courage or overwhelming curiosity at that instant to raise himself enough to see the sparkling trail of the cigarette as it sizzled toward the hot rod like a pop bottle rocket. He could almost hear the thud of the missile as it splashed between Tucker's eyes, exploding into a shower of fireflies about his face. He could see both of Tucker's hands jump from the steering wheel to cover his eyes, then the candy-apple-red hot rod begin to weave.

Chipper sat straight up and saw Homer lean across Eddie to grab the wheel, sending the beloved chariot into even greater swerves. He could barely hear the shouts and screams of the riders as the hot rod fell behind, the headlights veering back and forth in wider and wider arcs.

"Yesiree, cowboys, we're all of us off the road," said Smokey Ray, still smiling and calmly reaching for another cigarette.

Peachy was finally upright, adding his perspective to the careening hot rod behind them. "Holy mother of shit!"

The headlights disappeared, then appeared again out of the blackness of the night.

"A 360," yelled Chipper.

"No, shit," said Peachy, his head also twisted to the rear.

Smokey Ray never looked back.

For a second, it appeared that the headlights would stabilize, but they drifted to the side of the road before tipping at a diagonal, whereupon the two white dots sank into the earth, leaving only a coffin-black night behind.

Chipper stared at the lighted red dirt in front of them being sucked beneath the lone pickup on this highway of tomorrow. The lump in his throat was so big he couldn't swallow, or speak. Even Peachy was silent, neither of them wanting to appear like the terrified candy asses that they really were, especially not in front of the great Smokey Ray Divine.

Without warning, Smokey Ray whipped the pickup around in a 180, reminding Chipper of the Tilt-o-Whirl at the amusement park as he watched the lighted path of red dirt spin before his eyes.

After returning a half-mile, Smokey Ray skidded to a halt and jumped out of the pickup, at the point where the hot rod headlights disappeared. Chipper and Peachy remained in the cab, stuck like two popsicles that were starting to melt before someone stuck them in the freezer.

Smokey Ray walked in the beam of his own headlights to the edge of the highway. It appeared to be an overpass.

"Sunuvabitch! Sunuvabitch!" came the distant cries from the valley. "You goddam sunuvabitch! I'm bleeding to death!"

Smokey Ray, basking in the headlight, removed his cowboy hat, held it up in the air, and with the grace of a toreador, bowed at the waist to the over-the-edge opponents.

He put his hat back on and walked to the bed of the pickup. "They're alive," he said as he passed the cab.

Peachy and Chipper moved for the first time since their bone-chilling freeze. Chipper felt a canning jar land in his lap and saw another fly through the air for Peachy. Home brew, tossed by Smokey Ray. Chipper untwisted the lid and gulped. It was a rare blend of turpentine and castor oil, enough to thaw a glacier.

"Drink it slow to capture the taste," cautioned Smokey Ray as he sipped his jar and shifted into gear, setting the pickup in motion.

Back at the bowling alley, they stopped to use the john. Chipper assumed their pee would be flammable. As Smokey Ray and Peachy ran ahead, he slowed and let them disappear behind the blond wood bathroom door. Pulling a dime out of his pocket, he walked to the pay phone by the pinball machines and made an anonymous call.

"Slim Harper's Funeral Home and Ambulance Service. Can I help you?"

"A car went off the overpass at the interstate construction site... into Four Mile Creek."

Click.

Then he slipped through the door marked "Men."

Thirty-seven

Crouched on the back of the electric golf cart like two gargoyles ready to spring to life were Peachy and Chipper, while Smokey Ray drove the Waterman's electric cart in circles on the first tee. Peachy's dad, of course, knew nothing of this nocturnal outing. With one hand stabilizing the cooler of home brew, Chipper avoided dizziness by staring at a reference point—the logging chain hanging from the split elm that formed a canopy over the tee box.

All those failed attempts, he thought. *Jay and L.K. touched it every time. But not me. And not Peachy*. As they circled beneath the logging chain again and again, it seemed that the chain, hanging perfectly still, was mocking him. *I win and you lose*, it was saying. *I can rest here motionless and still beat you, you candy ass son of a bitch.*

"Looks like the front is about here," hollered Smokey Ray. "Maybe we'll get sucked up by a cyclone. If we're lucky."

A lightning strike was followed so quickly by a crack of thunder that Chipper could only mutter, "One thousand one, one thou..."

"Shit, that was fuggin' loud," said Peachy.

Smokey Ray steered away from the first tee to the pro shop then wheeled back again pointed toward the split elm.

"One final bucking bronco," he called, referring to their wild bounces over the tee's raised ground, "then we'll head for cover."

Chipper looked at the logging chain, barely lit by the floodlight on the nearby practice green. *You candy ass loser*, it repeated.

Smokey Ray stomped on the accelerator, generating a whirring hum of electricity, as if the switch had been thrown to charge up

Frankenstein's monster. The borrowed cart lurched toward the first tee. Chipper glanced at Peachy, who also seemed to have his eye on the logging chain.

As the vehicle hit the edge of the tee box, Chipper timed his leap to capture the full catapult effect of the golf cart. He was airborne and could almost feel the red cape fluttering behind. Out of the corner of his eye, he saw another form soaring through the air toward the same target.

His hand reached first, and it was destined to grab, not touch. He felt the cold interlocking loops of metal as precious gold in his palm, and he seized the moment. Peachy's body collided with his in midair, and they fell to earth together. But he could still feel the treasure in his hand.

"You broke the goddam chain!" Peachy yelled, brushing himself clean of dead grass. "You broke the fuggin' goddam chain. It's only been hangin' there for centuries. Since the beginning of time."

Chipper laughed. He didn't care. He had silenced the tormentor and he was, if anything, proud. My, how this home brew seemed to improve perspective. Normally, he would need to deal with all sorts of icky feelings.

Smokey Ray circled back to pick up his fallen compatriots. Chipper jumped on the back of the cart, swinging the chain above his head like a lasso, then he roped it over the elm branch as if it were the leg of a steer.

"There, no one will notice," he said, leaving the chain draped in its original spot over the ancient sign that the founding fathers had placed there.

"Oh, hell no," Peachy said. "No one will notice that there's two ends draped over the branch...both half as long as the old chain."

"Hey, what's with you, Peachy?" asked Chipper. He was surprised at the righteous tone in his buddy's voice. "We're friends, aren't we? Best friends?"

"There's some things you don't mess with. I mean...I mean the chain's been there for friggin' ever."

"Sit down, you squirrels," Smokey Ray said. "Let's beat it to the bridge on four."

Chipper felt the raindrops hit him in the face, followed by a gush of wind that forced him to grip the side for support. The threesome puttered down the cart path to the dry creek bed, parked beside the bridge, then hauled the cooler from the back. Chipper and Peachy carried it to a nice dry picnic spot beneath the bridge where the three trolls could carry on with their celebration of life.

"You need another brew," said Chipper to Peachy who was obviously falling behind, as evidenced by his lost sense of humor.

"The chain's been there forever," he said again, wiping the rain from his glasses with his tee shirt.

Smokey Ray took a jar of home brew, twisted the lid, and downed it with a single gulp. "I can open my gullet and pour it in, without pausing to swallow," he said, revealing yet another incredible talent.

Chipper tried it, but the brew spilled around his mouth onto his shirt.

"Don't waste it," shouted Smokey Ray. "It's my precious."

"Your precious?"

"Yeah, haven't you read Tolkien?"

"Who?"

"What?"

"Tolkien."

Smokey Ray and Shakespeare. Smokey Ray and Othello. Smokey Ray and Tolkien. Chipper thought it must have something to do with culture, or maybe another Shakespeare story. Maybe Smokey Ray read the Great Books, and this was one of those Greek plays.

As the three boys huddled under the wooden bridge, Smokey Ray began telling tales of Bilbo, Gandalf, and Middle Earth, all of which seemed to come from this guy named Tolkien.

Hail started to pound the bridge. Slowly at first, then at machine gun pace. Chipper could feel his pulse quicken with the noise. Drops of rain were filtering through the wooden bridge, causing each of the boys to dodge to a dry position. Within minutes, the ground was covered with hailstones, some as large as golf balls.

Smokey Ray gulped another brew, swallowing only once. Peachy and Chipper exchanged looks of amazement.

"Hear that roar?" shouted Smokey Ray. "Like a pissed-off dragon?"

A freight train sounded in the distance as the wind died. The boys froze. The freight train was getting louder. But the real train tracks were on the other side of town. And they realized, all at the same time, what was happening.

"Nature's vacuum cleaner," said Smokey Ray.

"Omigosh," Peachy said. "I hope we're in a good spot."

"Yeah," said Chipper. He thought of Amy, and wished he was with her.

"Yesiree, cowboys, we've got ourselves a cyclone," yelled Smokey Ray as he jumped to his feet and ran from beneath the bridge into the open fairway. The hailstorm was over, the rain had stopped, and Smokey Ray perched himself on the lip of the creek, shouting to the winds that were gathering again. "Come on down here, you sumbitchin' twister!" He held his cowboy hat in one hand, a home brew in the other. "I'm Pecos fuggin' Smokey Ray Divine, and I'm gonna ride yer ass. Now come down here and gimme a ride!"

The roaring freight train was deafening now, with the wind picking up terrifying speed. Lightning flashed and thunder clapped. Smokey Ray stared at the sky, trying to make the heavens part.

As he saw Smokey Ray at the brim of the creek, dueling with nature, lightning strikes within a hundred yards illuminating the image, Chipper realized he was witnessing history. And, for a moment, he could forget that his heart throbbed its last, his lungs went limp, and his life was quite possibly over.

Within seconds, the roaring stopped. The winds died. Smokey Ray's arms fell to his side.

"What a rush," he said, sniffing the air. He lowered his head to the ground as if paying homage to the elements.

"Did you see it?" asked Peachy, emerging from the bridge.

"Naw, never saw it."

"Makes it scarier not being able to see it. Almost, doesn't it?" asked Chipper.

Smokey Ray looked at him, puzzled, as if he didn't know the word 'scary'. "It's a dark night," he began. "What we don't see might not even be there."

"What...what do you mean?"

"What do you *think* I mean?"

"You sayin' there *wasn't* a tornado?"

"Had to be. I heard it," Chipper said.

"I heard it, too," added Peachy.

"The mind is a strange and wonderful place," said Smokey Ray. "You only heard it after I mentioned the dragon sound. Maybe it was a twister, maybe it wasn't."

"Bullshit," said Peachy. "It was a tornado, and it was close."

"Real close."

"Maybe so...maybe not," said Smokey Ray, stooping to the ground to pick up a hailstone. He tossed it up and down in his palm, looking first up to the sky, then across to the out-of-bounds bordering the first hole.

Chipper was crushed that the tornado was being labeled a phantom.

"Say, do you 'spose the Chief is in bed?" Smokey Ray asked. It's past midnight."

Chipper knew what Smokey Ray was thinking. He talked about it every time he played the El Viento course. The number of golf balls in that field staggered the imagination.

This time, Chipper realized he wasn't afraid. Not after Tucker

Doogan. Not after a sure-as-the-world tornado. What was there to be scared of now?

He took the last swig from the last jar of brew, inhaling deeply as if to purify his system of the last remnant of fear. Why was Smokey Ray always taking the lead? Maybe he should be the one. He knew what Smokey Ray was plotting next—a romp through golf ball heaven. But Chipper was the veteran of those fields. So was Peachy. They'd been over the fence last summer. The balls were there. Hundreds of them. *Thousands* of them.

Chipper looked at Peachy who returned the stare, though his friend's eyes seemed a little crossed. Chipper hoped he didn't look as silly. Smokey Ray wasn't budging. He wasn't making his move. It was time for Chipper to lead the charge.

"Let's bring 'em home, guys," Chipper shouted as he broke for the barbed wire fence. Let's go get some balls." With the hailstones crunching beneath his churning feet, he wondered if the others were following. He looked over his shoulder as he neared the border. Peachy emerged from the trees on the Number 1 fairway, but no Smokey Ray. "What the...?"

"Maybe he's really just another chickenshit like us, when it comes down to it," said Peachy, gasping for air.

They paused at the barbed wire.

"I can't believe he's not coming," Chipper said. "How could he...how could he fight off Tucker Doogan and a tornado, then chicken out at Chief Crazy Hawk's?"

Chipper gave a final look to the darkness before he slipped between the barbed wire. He held the wires apart for Peachy, this being a more graceful entrance than the previous summer.

They both hit the ground on all fours and began scooping up the white balls that were covering the earth. But the hailstones were the same size as golf balls, and every golf ball that they grabbed turned out to be ice melting in their hands.

"Shit, I don't believe this," said Peachy.

"Me, either. I haven't found one ball. I mean, all of these...all of these are hailstones."

"Shit, oh dear. Let's get out of here."

"No, Peachy, they're here. They *gotta* be."

"But I'm not finding anything."

Chipper started to grope wildly, picking up ball after ball, only to find hail and more hail.

"There aren't any goddam golf balls here. It's all hail."

"Where'd the balls go?"

They searched for what seemed like five horrible minutes.

"Where are they?"

"The hail's melting and I'm still not finding any."

"Where the hell are the goddam golf balls?" Chipper said in a near shout.

"I gave them to my nephew..." came the low, hollow voice of Chief Crazy Hawk. He was standing over them, a .22 rifle aimed directly at Chipper. "You dogs...you white dogs, out here crawling on all fours..."

The Chief's dark face with Grand Canyon crevices scowled at him with the scary look of a man whose cold heart gives him the freedom of his pleasure.

Chipper prepared, once again, to die.

But the crevices became shallow as a look of recognition came upon the Chief's face. "You," he said, jabbing the rifle at Chipper, "you know my nephew. My nephew Buster Nelson?"

Just as quickly as terror had struck, the mention of Buster's name seemed to be a lifesaving link. *Buster Nelson? What? What did the Chief say? His nephew is Buster Nelson?* This was some sort of dream. The home brew had to be a hallucinogen or something. The brew was why Smokey Ray heard voices. That was it. He was hallucinating.

Chipper sprang to his feet, the whole world spinning now, but the Chief jammed the rifle in his chest. "Back on all fours, white dog."

"We're sorry, Chief," begged Chipper as he hit the dirt. "We're sorry. Yes, yes, we know Buster! I mean, Buster Nelson is our friend. I mean we're on...we're all on the same golf team!"

"I know this. That's why you are not dead right now. You're DeHart. You've been fair to Buster."

Peachy slithered a little closer to the ground.

"But that's not the only reason I spare your young life tonight."

Chipper was relieved to hear the phrase, 'spare your young life.' He couldn't believe Buster was related to the Chief. *Why hadn't Buster said anything? Especially last summer when he pretended to be a trespasser like the rest of them?*

"The reason I don't shoot you..." the Chief said, lifting his rifle to aim at the windmill near his house. A gunshot broke the stillness and plunked the windmill blades to motion. *Not bacon bits...bullets!* "The reason I don't shoot you is I see you as your father's son."

Chipper was stunned. More hallucinations, no doubt.

"Everyone here thought Doc Jody walked on water," began the Chief, aiming his rifle back at Chipper. *Why didn't he ever aim at Peachy?* "But I say you don't need to go halfway around the world to heal the sick. When Buster's old man—may he rot in hell someday—beat my sister nearly to death, Doc Jody was on hospital duty...Thanksgiving Day. He don't come in. Family too important. But I say, 'What about *my* family?' I call every doctor in town. Only your father," the Chief said, nodding at Chipper, "come in and care for my sister. He took her to the city himself in ambulance."

Chipper tried to remember which of the countless Thanksgiving dinner exits this had been, but there was no telling.

"He stays with her 'til she dies. Now, that scum Nelson, murderer of my sister, walks a free man. Whites fear no trouble when they marry a squaw, beat her silly, then kill. But I remember your father. One good white man."

Whether this was a dream or a hallucination, he would be waking up soon. Waking up to the belittling, criticizing, dictatorial man he knew as a father. Was the Chief really talking about the same man? Leonard DeHart, M.D.? So this was what his dad was doing when he wasn't there for ball games, for Cub Scout trips, even for breakfast in the morning. He would never think of his dad the same way again.

"Stand proud and tall, boy," said the Chief, motioning with his rifle for him to rise. "Stand and try to fill the shoes of the father. Do not come back on my land. You will not find golf balls here. I collect them for Buster. What he doesn't use, he sells to pay for this silly game you call sport. His lowlife father won't give him money. It's all I can do."

Peachy, a shadow of the night, stood along with Chipper, trying to look invisible.

The benefactor, thought Chipper. Jacob thought it was Mr. Ashbrook. Jacob was wrong.

"I'm sorry we got on your land, Chief."

"My name is John. John Harjo. My grandfather was proud chief of the Cherokee Nation, but I am not."

"Well, Mr. Harjo," Chipper said, backing slowly away, "we'll stay off your property. I promise. And so does Peachy."

The Chief's eyes widened as he spun to look at Peachy, principal tormentor of Buster Nelson. Peachy's jaw dropped at the disclosure, and he looked simultaneously betrayed and destroyed as he fired daggers at Chipper.

Chipper regretted the words the second they slipped through his lips.

"Peachy Waterman?" asked the Chief as he raised his rifle and pointed it at the Peach.

Peachy let out a howl that would frighten wolves as he took off in a staggered dash for the barbed wire, every 10 steps hitting the ground and rolling, a technique that could be learned watching any good war movie.

The Chief, John Harjo, lowered his rifle to his side and looked at Chipper to offer a wink, barely detectable in the night.

"Watch over Buster," he said. "He lives in danger."

Chipper turned to the barbed wire, but was struck with the most peculiar sensation. He felt a mystical safety here on the Chief's side of the fence, while he actually feared the world on the other side. A remote memory, swirling green translucence, from his childhood. He couldn't pinpoint it, but something was being conjured up by the devilish events of the night. And particularly odd was the comfort he felt on this forbidden land.

"Fill your father's shoes," the Chief called to him.

The rain started again, harder than the initial front.

Thirty-eight

After puke number three, sporting a life-threatening headache, Chipper trudged downstairs to face the Grand Inquisitors. There would be accusations of drinking...denials...repeat accusations...followed by more forceful denials.

His mother and father were quietly eating breakfast, and his sisters excused themselves as he entered the room, their eyes lowered to the ground. Trouble was brewing; he could smell it. Squirt, their wiener dog, was parked in Chipper's chair, tail tucked.

The largest breakfast he had ever seen was spread before him. His usual can of shoestring potatoes was emptied on a plate—he preferred eating them out of the can—surrounded by cantaloupe, strawberries, French toast, a waffle, two eggs, and four pieces of bacon. Plus milk. Ugh. He wanted to puke a fourth time, but he had to act completely normal.

"Kyle, honey, your dad has something to tell you."

Uh-oh, here it comes, he thought.

"Kyle, last night I had to go to the emergency room to sew up three boys hurt in a car accident."

"Oh, really?" he deadpanned.

"Yes, I think they're boys in your class. Tucker Doogan, Eddie Charles, and Homer Nundley."

"Yeah, they're in my class. What happened?" He had committed himself now to a lie.

"They'd been drinking, or else they wouldn't have ended up in trouble."

The silence lasted forever as Chipper feigned innocence, popping strawberries in his mouth to plug the barf that was threatening from the other direction.

"Oh?"

"Yes, they claim someone in a strangely painted yellow pickup ran them off the road. They had never seen the truck before. Can't say as I place a yellow pickup in this town."

Squirt, forced from his chair, jumped back into Chipper's lap, and began begging for the potatoes, just like always. Nope, nothing unusual about this morning. Nosirree. His mother sipped coffee, staring to the neutral zone between the two conversationalists. "No, not a yellow pickup in this town," mused Chipper. "Not that I can think of."

He stuffed a piece of French toast in his mouth as he realized he needed to steer the discussion. "Say, did anyone hear about a tornado last night?" he asked. "Heard it hit the golf course."

"Nope," said his dad, ending all conjecture and debate. "No tornado last night."

The morning stillness was broken only by the sound of Chipper gulping his orange juice.

"The truck was yellow, with funny symbols and signs painted on the side, sort of like artwork."

"What do I know about this, Dad? Are the guys all right? I mean, they're alive, aren't they?"

"Sure, they're alive. But Tucker broke his nose on the steering wheel, and they're all cut up pretty bad. The car's gone, though."

"Gone?"

"Yeah, it landed in Four Mile Creek, but the storm came last night before it could be towed. The creek flooded and the car is gone."

Chipper covered a smile with a big chunk of waffle, dripping in maple syrup.

"Shame," he said. "A real shame."

Leonard DeHart, M.D., wiped his napkin across his face, grunted one of those noises parents make when they stand, and left the table. Chipper pretended to be unfazed by it all, sharing his bacon with the rotund Squirt. His mother sipped her coffee.

After his dad left the room, Chipper's mom stood to clear the dishes. With the plates in midair, she leaned down and kissed the top of his head. What was that for? She hadn't done that since he was a little kid. Not since the time he nearly drowned looking for crawdads with some older boys whose company had been pronounced a no-no.

"Amy's mom called last night while you were still out. Told us about the scene at Tate's. Amy told her mom, but we're not supposed to know."

Chipper felt like that little kid again, hunting for crawdads. Bubbling and gurgling tears at the bottom of a deep well were trying to erupt, but he stuffed another giant strawberry into his mouth to stop the uprising.

"Amy told her mom she was worried about you, so she left her date and tried to find you, but couldn't."

He felt warm inside that Amy still cared. "What else did she say?" he asked, hungry for more.

His mother answered over her shoulder as she walked to the kitchen with the plates, "She never could find you, but she thought she saw you once, riding in a yellow pickup with Peachy. A yellow pickup with funny paintings on the side."

Oh, but to disappear.

And in a repeat flash of the same green translucence he had imagined last night on the Chief's property, he felt his lungs filling up again with the chilly water as he nearly drowned...and the calm bliss that came with it. And for the first time since the crawdad incident years ago, he remembered the perplexing terror that greeted fresh air, and why he wanted to return to the icy green tranquility. Then he felt the strawberry beginning to work its way out of the well, forced by the bubbling and gurgling below.

Thirty-nine

"Never again, man, never again."

"Same here. The Peach was puking all morning. Three times total."

"Me, too. Four times."

Peachy dropped his clubs on the practice tee.

"I've never been so sick."

"Me, either."

Chipper was in charge of the cassette recorder and the earpiece, along with the potential selections.

"Here it is, sun going down," Peachy said, "and I'm just to the point where I can play golf. Dammit, never again."

"And how 'bout that Smokey Ray? Where in the world did he disappear to? I think he conned us into going on the Chief's property."

"Hey, you sounded the charge, buddy."

"I know, but it was like he *knew* there were no balls there. He wanted to get a kick out of watching us die young."

"He did know," said Peachy. "I'm telling you, the guy's a fuggin' psychic. He's got powers you and I will never have. Look at the way he got to Tucker and his goons. Man, that's supernatural. It's enough to make you believe in God-given powers."

"Speaking of God-given powers, Peachy, let's pray this works."

Chipper strapped the cassette recorder onto Peachy's belt then ran the earpiece beneath his shirt to fit like a hearing aid.

"What do you wanna try first, Chipper?"

"Let's try the Mamas and the Papas."

Peachy took a 5-iron and teed his ball. Chipper stood behind him and prepared the recorder, flipping the ON button.

While I'm far away from you, my baby

"Now, Peachy, this song is in four-four time, and the rhythm is tricky. It goes one, two, three-ly four lol-ly, one, two, three-ly four lolly, because of the triplet pattern. Got it? Backswing on one, two, and three, stop on 'ly' and downswing on four."

"What the shit are you talkin' about, Chipper?"

"Okay, okay, let me listen. We'll go by the words. Chipper rehearsed the choreography in his head. "Backswing slowly on 'While I'm far', then downswing on 'away'. Hold the follow-through until the word 'baby'. You get it?"

Chipper punched rewind and they ran through the song again, Peachy taking practice swings with surprisingly graceful timing. Of course, he got it. After all, Peachy was the dance king. Chipper wondered why it took him so long to propose this obvious cure for Peachy's shank. Rhythm was the elixir, and music ushered the rhythm.

"Okay, get ready to hit," instructed Chipper. "Ignore this part. It's the bridge or something like that. Okay, get ready."

While I'm far...away...

The ball shot from the tee in a perfect arch.

"Jeez, that felt pretty fuggin good," said Peachy.

Remarkable. A trace, still, of Quasimodo, but there was no cross with a circle at the top, just a slight wiggle to the left, and very little wiggle to the right. The backswing didn't have a chance to overswing, since the music forced the club down by the fourth count. More importantly, there was no 'awshit' at the end, replaced now with 'jeez.'

"You've done it, man. Just keep doing the same thing over and over. Hit some more."

Whisper a little...prayer...

The ball soared again after a smooth downswing on the word 'prayer.'

Peachy pushed his glasses back on the bridge of his nose, simultaneously raising his eyebrows Groucho-style. "I'm a badass mutherfugger," he said. "The Peach is gonna be a contender."

Forty

The ball was sailing on target. Judging from the way Buster cocked his head, it seemed that the shot-maker was pleased. If he won the hole, he would end up a 3-0 victor (front nine, back nine, total 18) and El Viento would win 8½ to Castlemont's 6½.

The critical approach shot from 120 yards hung forever with the arc of a pitching wedge before floating down to the pin like a tiny parachute. Buster would be putting for a bird, while his opponent was in the trap, and would be struggling for a par.

Buster tilted his head some more, awaiting the verdict.

From Chipper's angle, walking up the rough, the descending shot looked to be homing in on the cup. He heard a *clank* then the ball disappeared. It was nowhere on the green. Did it land directly in the cup? An eagle?

A mixture of groans and moans came from the handful of spectators. *Shouldn't they be cheering?* The groaning continued as the few folks clustered on the back of the green, including Mr. Ashbrook and Coach Dresden, turned toward the parking lot.

What was going on?

Buster held his position mid-fairway, while Jacob and L.K. came walking down the hole, heads to the ground, as if to tell him Old Yeller had just been shot.

Buster dropped his club, then held both hands shoulder high, palms flattened to the sky. "What the...what the hell happened? Where's my ball?"

L.K. was looking to the ground, shaking his head. His limping was almost imperceptible. Jacob's chin was higher. He looked back and forth, his eyes shifting from Chipper to Buster to Chipper to Buster, as if to enlist Chipper in delivering the grievous news about Old Yeller.

The number one man and number two man stopped in front of the number three man, Buster Nelson. The Castlemont jerks were walking ahead to the green.

"Out-of-bounds," said Jacob.

"Out-of-bounds? What the hell are you talkin' about? The sunuvabitch was headed for the cup!"

"Out-of-bounds," echoed L.K.

"The shot was great...almost perfect," began Jacob. "It—you're not gonna believe this—it came down directly on top of the flagstick."

"Ricocheted right off into the parking lot...out-of-bounds," added L.K. "Odds are a million to one."

"I heard it," Chipper said as he joined the others. "I didn't know what the sound was. All I knew was that the ball disappeared." He spoke with bubbly enthusiasm, as if the uniqueness of the shot was actually neat enough to erase the disastrous consequences.

The Castlemont jerks were gathering near the bunker, smiling and yes, even snickering.

Chipper readied himself for Buster's explosion. He figured this would be worth at least one broken club. Nobody would fault Buster in a zillion years. Especially not him and not Peachy who were both losers today. Not Jacob. Not L.K. It was a total fluke. It was also El Viento's first loss of the year.

The muscles in Buster's face began to ripple, first at his jaw, then up to his forehead, down his nose, then to the lips, which began to scrunch together before sending the ripple back to his jaws again. It was like earthworms burrowing in the deep layers of his sodden face. He squinted as his face turned pre-explosion red.

Here it comes, thought Chipper, backing away. But the explosion never happened. Buster stooped down to pick up his clubs, then said with a forced calm, "I'd be hitting five. Let me know if he muffs his sand shot." And he walked in a diagonal off the course toward the locker room.

Mr. Ashbrook and Coach Dresden left greenside and walked toward Buster as he reached the clubhouse. It did no good. Buster ignored them both and kept walking out of sight.

"It's not fair," said Chipper. "It's one thing to go out-of-bounds on a bad shot, but to hit a perfect shot and go out-of-bounds...it's just not fair."

"A lotta things aren't fair," muttered L.K.

The Castlemont jerk blasted out of the trap, landing eight feet from the hole. He sank the putt for a winning par. After dropping another ball, Buster would have had to hole out from the fairway to win the match. By forfeiting the hole, he lost the nine, tied the 18, while Castlemont won team play 8 to 7.

"Coach Dresden's gonna be pissed," said L.K. "He shoulda tried. I bet even Mr. Ashbrook's gonna be pissed."

"I've never seen him not explode," Chipper said. "I don't believe it."

"All that anger just collapsed on itself," added Jacob. "Like nuclear fusion instead of fission."

"Yeah, something like that."

"He shoulda at least tried to hole out."

Chipper led his two teammates up to the fringe where his own ball was resting, lying three. A chip and a putt for a par was almost automatic.

L.K. carried Chipper's bag for him, while Jacob walked over to talk to Ritchie Cosgrove, the top ranked golfer in the state—the golfer that Jacob had just defeated 2 to 1, capturing medalist honors with a 69 on his home course.

Stone-faced Ritchie Cosgrove had thick lips that never smiled and never smirked, opening only to say, 'You're up' to opponents and 'Nice shot' to his teammates. Surely, he was just as intense the day he was born, probably telling his mother 'Nice shot' in the delivery room. For a guy of medium build, it was a mystery how he could hit the ball as far as L.K. But on top of that, he had the skilled irons of Smokey Ray, the short approaches of Chipper, and the putter of Jacob. He would be a star at Oklahoma State next year, then later a pro. No doubt about it.

And like all Castlemont jerks, he drove a funny-looking car with a foreign name. It made no sense. These guys in their matching white polo shirts with navy trim, all rich as Kennedys, and not one of them drove a Corvette. How could it be cool to drive those weird boxy cars with silly names and unknown logos? Oh, well.

But today, in spite of the pug-nosed, thick-lipped, top-ranked Ritchie Cosgrove, Jacob Justice was the victor. Even L.K.'s 70 tied the great Ritchie. But the medal scores meant nothing. This was match play—and peculiar match play at that, at least when it came to the 3-point scoring system. One point was awarded to the player (and team) for a front nine win, another point for the victor on the back nine, and yet a third point for the total 18. Ties split the points in half. Under this method, a player could stomp his opponent 5 & 4 on the front nine, lose the back nine by only 1 down, and pick up a measly 2 points to 1 victory. In five-man, two-school matches, there were 15 points for the taking, and the madness behind this method was in softening the agony of defeat. A 0-3 loss was the same whether by one hole per nine, or by humiliation on every hole played.

Although his loss was settled back on the 16th hole, Chipper had casually played out the final holes and turned to shake hands with the fourth man from Castlemont who just shot an even par round. With his open palm suspended in midair, Chipper watched Mr. white-polo-shirt-with-navy-trim-and-the-boxy-little-car-with-the-funny-logo walk right by and ignore the offering of sportsmanlike conduct.

Chipper felt his second, fourth, and fifth fingers starting to curl into his palm, leaving the third finger boldly extended. He fought against his curling fingers as they formed the universal sign of denigration when he saw Mr. Ashbrook looking directly at him. With his hand still extended in midair, he ran after the Castlemont jerk.

"Nice match," he called out.

The jerk turned around.

"Nice match," he said again. "Congratulations."

Looking perplexed, the jerk's eyes dropped to Chipper's outstretched hand. His right arm didn't budge.

Chipper smiled.

His arm still didn't move.

Chipper dropped the putter from his left hand, then grabbed the right arm of his opponent and forced the reluctant hand into his.

"I said, 'Nice match'." He pumped both arms up and down as if he were drilling for oil. "We'll see you next month at State," he added with a slight taunt, probably not justified from someone who had just cranked out a triple-bogey on the 15th and a double-bogey on the 16th to lose all three points.

The Castlemont jerk said, "Yeah, nice match" then turned to walk away.

"Shitheads," Chipper whispered to L.K. "All of them. Shitheads."

L.K. chuckled as he lifted Chipper's putter from the green. "We'll get them later...at State."

"Yeah, later. We're still 14 and 1 in matches this year. Two shots per man per round." He thought to himself how he'd just been beaten by five strokes over the 18 holes. Even the victories today by Jacob and L.K. couldn't come close to neutralizing the 15 strokes he could lose in three rounds of medal play to Castlemont at the fourth man position. He shuddered at the prospect.

Peachy, with caddie Gus, was still on the course, coming up number 18. Completing the last group was the fifth jerk from Castlemont who had somehow lost a point to the Peach.

"Did you hear about Peachy's front side?" asked Chipper.

"I heard a 37. Is that right?" asked L.K.

"Yeah," he replied. "His best nine ever."

"How'd he do it? Do you think that tape recorder did anything?"

"I dunno. We'll find out."

The caddie stood at attention a yard away from Peachy's ball. Gus was hitting puberty a little late, still only five feet tall, but at least well past his four feet nine inches of last summer, looking more and more each day like a Goofy head on a Pez dispenser. Gus was thrilled by the possibility that with two more inches, his feet would reach Peachy's pedals on the Vette. It remained to be seen if Peachy would fulfill the 'I'll-let-you-drive-it-someday' promises he had made over the past two years to inspire his lackey.

A little too much Quasimodo, thought Chipper. *Oh, no, remnants of a cross with a circle at the top. Wiggle to the left. Wiggle to the right. Backswing, overswing, downswing.* The ball squirted right with a shank that sent the projectile scooting for the Number 5 tee box and beyond. Chipper could hear 'awshit' from 150 yards away.

"I guess that answers your question about the tape recorder."

"Yeah. Looks like the curse is here to stay."

Gus picked up the clubs and the two of them headed south, 90 degrees from the direction of play.

Chipper looked around the green again. Mr. Ashbrook was rubbing the loose skin of his neck between his forefinger and his thumb. Mr. Dresden was shaking his head in disgust. Old Sarge was there as well, smiling while he drooled tobacco juice like a giant grasshopper.

"Did you ever think about why no one comes out to watch golf, L.K.?"

"No, not really."

"I mean, here we are, one of the best in the state, playing the top-ranked team in Oklahoma, and there's not a high school kid here. Not one supporter. Parents don't even come."

"Well, I know why my dad won't. Sissy sport, remember?"

Chipper pictured the man-mountain and understood. After all, he'd killed Nazis in hand-to-hand combat on the beaches at Normandy. Then, more importantly, after the war, he'd played tackle both ways for the new coach Bud Wilkinson and was All-Big Six, helping the Sooners to the conference championship. Of course, a shoulder injury ended his pro career before he ever played a single down with the L.A. Rams. But it didn't seem to matter to the folks around here. Who in Oklahoma cared about pro football anyway?

"Tell me, why does he think it's a sissy sport?"

"'Cause the girls play it as well as the guys, he claims."

"Well, the best pro guy can beat the best pro girl."

"Only because of the long game. The power. Think about it. The girls are just as good inside a hundred yards."

Power, thought Chipper. *Maybe that was the only difference. Why all the head scratching for definitions?*

Peachy blasted out of the bunker next to the fourth green, still 150 yards away, lying who knows and who cares.

"How's your brother doing, L.K.?" The subject hadn't come up in months. No one else even knew.

"Not so good. He keeps getting pneumonia. At least, that's what the doctor in the city says. He tells Dad we gotta get Benny out in the fresh air, or he'll die. He's gotta take deep breaths, not lie around in his bed all day in the dark."

A shiver went down Chipper's back. It was like the ones he'd felt watching the movie *House on Haunted Hill,* when he realized that the skeleton coming out of the acid pit wasn't really alive, but due to the trickery of puppeteer Vincent Price to cause the "accidental" death of his wife. And he wondered if...if maybe, L.K.'s dad left Benny in the room all the time on purpose just so he would...go ahead and die.

"You gotta get your dad to get him outside. Maybe he'd bring him to our next match."

"Never!" shouted L.K. who cooled as quickly as he flared. "I mean, he'd never do it. Trust me. I'm telling you. Never."

"Just a thought."

"Dad's getting weirder about it, not better. As time goes on, he stays in his room by himself more and more. Doesn't even eat with the rest of the family. I'm scared. He started going downhill after my snakebites. You know, everything seemed to hinge on my football career. I'm not kidding. He didn't even want me wasting time with basketball or baseball."

"Why not?"

"Nobody can be a star at two sports, he'd say. After my accident, he never talked about sports again. I don't dare mention the golf team. It just makes him mad."

"Man, I don't get it."

"To tell you the truth, Chipper, in a way—don't ever tell anybody this—in a way, I'm glad the pressure's off. There's more to life than football. And Dad never would've been satisfied. If I'd made the OU team, he'd expected All-American. It never would've ended."

Poor Benny. He didn't stand a chance. He was going to rot and die in the dark bedroom at the Taylor household on Reformatory Plaza.

Poor L.K. His father was going to be permanently disappointed. Chipper was beginning to realize how lucky he was to have a dad that didn't smack him when he lied about a yellow pickup.

"My mom's getting worried," L.K. continued. "I know, because I saw her sneak a Bible last week onto the reading table by his armchair."

Wow, thought Chipper. *That's* like feeding rubber meat to a lion and not removing your arm from inside the cage. He remembered the story about the crushed Communion glasses.

"I expected him to rip it into shreds, but he didn't. Then again, he barely comes out of his room, so who knows? Maybe he tore it into pieces and flushed it down the toilet."

"I'm sorry, L.K, I shouldn't have brought it up."

"Don't worry. You're the only one who knows, the only one I can talk to."

Chipper nodded to reinforce the confidentiality.

"I'd like to get a golf scholarship, then I'd get the hell out of El Viento, away from my father. Maybe I could be a club pro somewhere. Set up junior tournaments and work with kids. You know, like Mr. Ashbrook did for us."

Chipper hoped L.K.'s dream would happen.

Peachy scored an 8 or a 9, it didn't matter, and he walked away from his Castlemont opponent without saying a word. He pulled out a fiver for Gus who trotted the money over to Sarge who then laughed and stuffed it in his pocket.

"Peachy, you're not betting on our matches, are you?" asked Chipper.

"Hell, yes," he replied. "I shot a goddamned 37 on the front side. I was on fire, man, the Peach was hot. The music was groovin'. No shanks. Best I ever played. It's not like I was throwing the match. I was betting on me to win."

"You shouldn't bet on matches, Peachy," L.K. said. "It's against the rules and it's going to get us in trouble. As a matter of fact, let me put it this way: Peachy, don't do it again or your face'll be hamburger."

"Sure. Fine. Okay."

Removing the tape recorder from his belt, he said, "I don't know what happened, Chipper. The music worked great on the front nine. I mean I got a little tired of the same song over and over, but other than that, I can't figure it. Shanked it on 11, and it was downhill after that."

"What do you think you shot on the back nine?"

"Near 50. Hell, maybe over 50. But dammit, I got a point from that little bastard. A fuggin' point from Castlemont. I never thought I'd do it."

"Still, I can't figure it, Peachy. You didn't do anything different?"

"Naw. Nothing. I mean, well, I started listening to the words. Now that I think about it, I started kinda singing with the music. But I don't know what that would do. It was working, I'm telling you. I mean, after all, a 37. A sumbitchin 37."

Chipper didn't know what to think, but he felt they were very close to a cure.

"You know, Peachy, my mom's got some old 78s of classical music. Maybe we should go with an instrumental. No words to distract you."

Peachy's ornery grin wilted, and he seemed to shrivel about two inches in height, his chest not so puffed out, his body no longer fidgeting. "My mom had some 78s, too. I've still got them."

"Your mom?" asked Chipper. He and L.K. exchanged glances. Peachy never admitted even having a mom before.

"Yeah, my mom. I'll get them out tonight. You come over later, Chipper. We'll go through them."

Peachy strolled away without offering a word of explanation..

"Peachy's mom?" said L.K. "What's the world coming to? I didn't know any mom would claim him."

"As long as I've known him," Chipper said, "he's never talked about his mom." He wondered if maybe all moms have old 78s.

Forty-one

He blew the ink dry on his logbook entry:

April 28, 1967: This is a crazy world. Cassius Clay, who calls himself Muhammad Ali now (shades of Jay to Jacob), refused to join the Army today, so he's been stripped of his title and may go to jail. And Elvis is an old man, but he's going to marry a 21-year-old with a mountain of hair that could well prove to contain the legendary spider nest. El Viento almost upset Castlemont (well, some things stay the same).

I still care a lot about Amy and I think she cares, too, but I can't face her knowing what Gail has on tap for the night before state tournament. Gail promises our dates are supersecret, especially given my near-death experience.

Two more matches before conference. Then Gail. Then state.

His hands trembled as he closed the log. Why did he ignore the bulletins from his brain telling him to run from Gail? Bulletins that were like a clanging burglar alarm while he continued to stuff precious silver into a knapsack.

He was late to Peachy's, but the Apology had to come first. He couldn't remember having done anything like this before, but his conversation about L.K.'s dad earlier in the day left him hounded by guilt and compelled to carry out the plan.

He grabbed the stack of 78s on his bed and tucked them under his arm. Starting for the door, he felt his feet sink into wet cement and the concrete harden at his ankles. He hadn't felt this tug for many years—this invisible force that held him in his room. As a kid, he would kiss Gail's picture for strength to leave the room, but that seemed silly now. As his pulse quickened, though, he tried to think of that old fourth grade photo of her. Nothing happened. He could hear his own breathing deepen as he tried to move his feet. He looked to his open closet where he could see Amy's framed photo, face down on the top shelf. He pictured the upright photo in his mind, Amy's soft smile with the crease-dimples, U-shaped at the top, supporting her rounded cheeks that looked like golf balls sitting on dimple tees. And he felt the concrete about his ankles start to break into pieces. His breathing slowed, and his heart stopped hammering on his breastbone. As he walked out the door, it seemed the old monkey on his back was getting heavier.

Usually, he would step only on the stairs that didn't squeak. But this evening, he stepped on each and every step down to the first floor. He turned around the corner of the banister and saw his dad, legs stretched out in the La-Z-Boy Rockin' Recliner. Chipper marched to the doorway where his dad's face was covered by the latest issue of *Field and Stream.*

Great, thought Chipper, the shield was up. He wouldn't even have to look his father in the eye. They could carry on entire conversations through *National Geographic, Scientific American, Field and Stream*—they were all equally effective.

"Dad?"

"What is it, son?"

"A few weeks ago, you know, when Tucker Doogan and those guys got hurt?"

"Yes, what about it?"

The giant, gaping mouth of a striped bass was about to swallow the hook on the front cover. He thought about the fact he could care less about fishing or hunting or hiking or camping. If there wasn't a final score at the end of the game, it made no sense to him. It wasn't worth the time. Men—32, Fish—0. Big deal. He wanted a level playing field and he wanted a final score. As a result, he had little to discuss with his dad.

"You know that I lied to you about the yellow pickup..."

"Yes, I know."

The *Field and Stream* shield dropped to his father's lap. Yikes! Here it comes. Where did he get this crazy idea?

"Well, I guess you know the story," he continued. "I...I just wanted to say I'm sorry..." He tried to read his father's eyes, but it was a blank stare in return. "...and I appreciate the fact that you didn't yell at me or nothin'."

His dad pursed his lips then began stroking his turkey neck between his thumb and a curled forefinger. It was a habit like Mr. Ashbrook's. His dad was getting old.

"I appreciate that," he said. After a long pause that seemed to last forever, he continued, "I know it's tough growing up, Kyle. There's a lot you have to deal with."

He'd never heard his father sound so agreeable, so concerned, so sincere.

"Your mom and I have been worried about you, but we don't feel like there's anything we can do. We just want you to know that we're here for you."

"I'm all right," Chipper said. "I'm fine. You don't need to worry." He preferred they stay out of his private life. Especially, when it came to girls...and bullies...and threats on his tender, young life.

"I know we don't have much to talk about, Kyle. I'm sorry it's turned out that way. I never played any sports. I always figured my son would be an Eagle Scout like me. I know I haven't been around for you."

What was going on? He came to apologize, but now it sounded like a reverse play—his dad was apologizing to *him*.

"It's okay, Dad, it's all okay," he said. "I still want to go to medical school. There'll be plenty we can talk about then." He wanted the *Field and Stream* shield to go back up. It was time to get out of Dodge. Things were getting too mushy.

Chipper started backing out the door.

"By the way," began his dad. "I ordered you a new lettermen's jacket. It should come in soon at Jensen's Sporting Goods."

Chipper was stunned. "I...I..."

"I know you said you weren't going to get another one."

"Well, it's too warm to wear one now, and you're a squirrel if you wear a high school letter jacket at college. I..."

"Well, I thought you should have one anyway."

He didn't know what to say. His dad raised the *Field and Stream* shield back into place. The conversation was over.

Who was this man? Chipper looked at the reading table beside his dad's chair. Resting alongside the black telephone was a Bible. Was there a Bible epidemic? He thought of his dad stroking the skin of his neck, and he thought of L.K.'s mom sticking a Bible in the lion's cage. Did old folks just naturally bone up for finals? Then there was Jacob. He wasn't old. Of course, there might be a little touch of hypocrisy there. Peachy said he had something important to tell him tonight, and that something had to do with Jacob and rubbers.

At any rate, he felt better and it seemed his dad felt better, too. The letter jacket deal was a real zinger. He couldn't imagine his father taking the time or trouble to help soften the blow of that horrible night at Tate's Drive-in. One thing for sure, the old Godzilla was dead.

Forty-two

Peachy was the only kid in town with a television in his bedroom. A color TV at that. What's more, his model came with The Space Commander 400—a clicker that made an ultrasonic sound, allowing Peachy to switch to all three channels from across the room without having to move anything but his thumb.

"Take it off. Take it *all* off," meowed a sex kitten as Chipper entered Peachy's room. In response, Joe Namath began stroking the shaving cream from his face, while "The Stripper" played as the background music for the commercial.

Peachy and Gus were turned away from him, huddled over Peachy's desk, fiddling with some weird contraption. Above them, on an otherwise barren wall, was a poster of a recently dead comic named Lenny Bruce who no one in the world had ever heard of, except Peachy. Even Jacob couldn't hold forth on this unknown joker whom Peachy had enshrined.

David Rose and his orchestra continued, muting Chipper's sneaky entry.

"What do you mean it's all symbolism?" asked Gus of his hero.

"The whole thing," Peachy answered. "The whole egg-eating contest. I'm telling you, when Paul Newman lies down on that bench and stretches his arms out, he's forming the crucifix. It's a standard movie symbol. Look for it, I'm telling you."

"Gosh, Peachy, how do you know all this stuff? I mean you don't even make good grades."

Chipper was within three steps now, preparing to scare the hell out of them both, when he got his first good look at the contraption. A red battery the size of a milk carton attached to a thingamajig, which then attached to a tubular loop of glass. It looked like a portable neon light spelling the letter 'O'. "What the hell..." he began.

Both of the electrical engineers spun around to greet him.

"Damn, Chipper, come on in. Didn't even hear you."

"What the hell...?" Chipper repeated.

"It may not look like much, my friend, but it spells fame and fortune for the Peach."

"What is it?"

"It's a portable black light," Peachy said, nodding to Gus who nodded back. It was easy to see they were quite pleased with themselves.

"Where'd you get it?"

"We made it. I mean we did the hard part, putting it together and all. Getting the black light itself was easy. We went to that new store in the city called Guevaro's—it's a head shop."

"What's a head shop?"

Peachy smiled knowingly at Gus, letting his pupil realize once again that making good grades has nothing to do with how smart you are.

"A head shop is where hippies buy all their paraphernalia. They shine black lights on fluorescent posters then look at them while they're tripping on LSD or smoking hash. Head shops are all over the place in California. Guevaro's is the first one in Oklahoma. Man, you shoulda seen some of the weirdos there."

"When did you do all this? I mean, *why?* What's this for?" Chipper was baffled. He usually knew when Peachy was working on one of his stunts.

"It's for the all-time, big-time, coup d'état. It'll be my tour de force performance. The grand finale of my senior year."

"Speak English, Peachy. What're you up to?"

Gus began to giggle then hid his smile behind a closed fist.

Peachy held up the contraption and seemed to offer it as a sacrifice to dead Lenny Bruce on the wall. "Behold, the scorpion searchlight!"

Chipper stopped breathing.

"No, Peachy. Not Neander T. Don't screw with that guy."

"Gus here has already collected over $200 in wagers, an amount I am guaranteed to get, dead or alive. But the payoff is if the scorpion tattoo on Neander's arm glows with the black light. It's five to one odds, daddy-o. I can't lose. If it doesn't glow, I get the 200 bills for trying. I only have to get within 10 feet, in front of three witnesses. Then, if it glows, like I think it will, everyone has to cough up the rest. That's a thousand bucks, and people are still investing. People will also be talking about this for years to come."

"Peachy, have you lost your ever-lovin' mind? The guy is a killer. You could die."

"Naw, I don't think so. The way the Peach has it figured, it's your run-of-the-mill, pissant bullies like Tucker Doogan who pick on the little guys. You take your true crazy killer types like Neander T, and they could care less about pipsqueaks like you and me. We're no more of a concern to Neander T than that little fly buggin' Anthony Perkins at the end of *Psycho.* There's symbolism there."

"Symbolism, shit, you're gonna get yourself killed, you idiot."

"A thousand bucks and legendary status, my friend," Peachy said. "Why, Gus here gets ten percent. That'll be more money than he made all last summer working the pro shop for a buck twenty-five an hour."

Gus nodded his confirmation then said, "Gotta go, Peachy. It's getting dark and the headlight on my bike is broken." He scratched his rust-colored hair and waited for Peachy to okay the departure. When he got it, he started out the door.

"If you bring in another 50 bucks on the bet," Peachy called to him, "I'll start teaching you to drive a standard."

"Man, cool. See ya."

Chipper buried his face in his hands. "Peachy, you're crazy. How...where...just how do you plan to get close to Neander T?"

"You're not gonna believe it."

"Uh-oh."

"Cornfield, five miles west on highway seven."

"What?"

"Neander's parking spot. It's where he screws that Apache bitch."

"What are you saying? How do you know?"

"I didn't believe it either. Gus heard it from Andy who got it from Arth who learned it from Fletch. Fletch got the word from Tricky Jack, Dylina, and Mal-Mal. They claim to have seen it with their own eyes. Picture this. There's a circular swath cut in the corn. In the middle sits Neander T's car, bouncing up and down as he pumps Apache Sue. After it's over, the massive arm with the scorpion tattoo falls out the window and hangs there for 10 minutes while they smoke a cig, or do whatever it is you do after barbaric bone-jumping."

Chipper shook his head in disbelief. In spite of the well-known song cheerfully pronouncing corn as high as an elephant's eye, he had never seen such a cornfield in Oklahoma. Then again, he had never seen a tornado, either. Not for sure, that is.

"That's when you plan to sneak up with your scorpion searchlight and shine it on his arm?" asked Chipper.

"Ten feet. Three witnesses. I figure you, L.K., and Jacob. Everybody knows that Jacob has never told a lie in his life, and no one will dare argue with L.K."

"Why me, Peachy? I'm not sure I want to be part of this."

Peachy put his arm around Chipper's shoulders. "Because not only are you my closest friend," he whispered, as if there was actually someone that might hear them in the huge, empty house, "you, and you alone, can fully appreciate the magnitude of this conquest."

Was Chipper supposed to feel complimented? Inspired? He wasn't. He thought Peachy was nuts. Surely, none of this would happen.

"I don't want to talk about this anymore, Peachy. It's not funny. It's dangerous."

"Well, who knows, when the time comes, I may not do it. May not even need to do it."

Chipper eyed him, wondering what he meant by "May not even need to do it."

"Won't bring it up again, my friend," Peachy said, setting the contraption back on his desk. "Not tonight, at least."

"Good, the subject is closed," Chipper said. He tossed his mother's 78s onto Peachy's bed. Strauss, Verdi, Bach, and Rachmaninoff spilled across the bedspread.

"Wow," Peachy said. "Those are your mom's, huh?"

"Yeah, remember she's Concertmistress of the symphony," Chipper said proudly. "These are the pieces I used to listen to at night, back when I was trying out my subliminal stuff."

"I do remember that miserable failure."

"Oh, well, the music helped me get to sleep, even if I didn't learn much."

"I need help with my shank, not getting to sleep. Hey, here's the Lone Ranger song."

Peachy pulled the album from its cover and walked to his hi-fi in the corner between his bed and desk, under the watchful eye of Lenny Bruce.

"Supposedly I'm getting a stereophonic for graduation," Peachy said, "and I'm betting it won't have this lever for playing 78s. If this plan works, I'll have to hang onto my hi-fi."

Da-da-dum
Da-da-dum
Da-da-dum-dum-dum

"Now," he said, "let me tell you about our long-lost friend Jay. Excuse me...Jacob."

With a Hi-ho Silver in the background, Peachy related how he stumbled (he called it) into Jacob's locker when the door was ajar, discovering a box of rubbers in the Puritan's gym bag.

"It wasn't the single packet all you hopeful virgins carry in your wallet until the rubber rots. It was a full box. Like the old man would have at home. But Jacob doesn't have an old man anymore. So is he screwing Kelly on a daily basis, or what?"

Da-da-dum
Da-da-dum
Da-da-dum-dum-dum

"Yeah, you're right, Peachy. I don't know how he goes on pretending they're not. I don't even let myself think about it."

"Well, you know it, and I know it. But we don't tell anyone. Remember, everyone thinks Jacob is a saint, that he's the most honest guy in El Viento. He's got to be the key witness on the scorpion sighting, so everyone will believe and I'll get my money."

"Fine, but I don't want to talk about Jacob and Kelly screwing any more."

The hurt went deep. Hurt that he was shut out. Hurt by Jacob's hypocrisy. And jealous that Jacob beat him to the cherry punch.

"C'mon, let's get to work here," Chipper said. "The William Tell Overture is too loud. We need a soft song. A soothing song." Chipper lifted the record from the turntable and put it back in its cover.

"So...are you and Amy speaking yet?"

"Oh, we've been speaking all along."

"I mean are you talking about dating again?"

"Naw, nothing like that."

Peachy picked up a Rimsky-Korsakov album and pretended to be reading the back as he spoke. "I'm not one to intrude on affairs of the heart. In fact, I don't believe much in love. Not for me anyway. Don't see much point in it. But if there was ever a girl who was more than just a girl...if there was one that I thought was really cool, and I'm talkin' cooler than cool, I think that one would be Amy."

Chipper took it as a compliment, but he wasn't really sure why. He'd known Peachy idolized her at a safe distance for years.

"For what it's worth."

"Thanks, Peachy, I appreciate that."

Conference tournament first. Then Gail. Then state.

"Well, while we're having this deep discussion about women," Peach said, "I guess I caught you off guard today mentioning my mother."

"Uh, yeah, to say the least."

Peachy tossed the Rimsky-Korsakov album back on the bed, and got down on his knees as if to say his prayers. Reaching beneath the hanging bedspread, he pulled out a stack of record albums. The top ones he brushed away were all the standards—Beatles, Dave Clark Five, The Birds, Donovan, The Doors, more Beatles, Dylan—that every guy in El Viento owned. But at the bottom of the stack were three albums clearly out of a different era—*Coppelia, Swan Lake,* and the bottom one, *The Nutcracker Suite.*

"What are these?" asked Chipper.

"They're ballets...my mom was a ballerina."

"A ballerina? You're kidding. That's cool."

"Well, my dad has a *different* word for her. But since he says all women are whores, I'm not sure that means much. To me, she was a ballerina."

Peachy's voice sounded different. No accented phrases, no crescendos for dramatic effect, no cussword punctuation.

"She danced with Maria Tallchief, so I'm not talking about just *any* ballerina."

Without knowing a thing about ballet (except for the fact that Bud Wilkinson once had the Sooners schooled in ballet principles), every kid in Oklahoma learned that next to Will Rogers and Jim Thorpe, Maria Tallchief was the most famous Okie.

"She was good, really good. I was in the Nutcracker deal once as a kid. Didn't do nothin'. Just sat on stage at the Civic Center in the city. But I remember watching my mom, floating around on stage like an angel in white. She had layers of this white mosquito net around her waist that opened like a parachute each time she flew back to the ground. I can still hear the sound of her feet hitting the stage in those ballet shoes. It was weird that she would be flying through the air so high, yet when her feet touched, it made such a soft little sound."

Who was this guy talking? Surely not the Peach.

Peachy lifted the *Nutcracker* album and fingered the vinyl disk out of its cover, taking care not to touch the grooves. Placing it on the spindle, he checked the speed selector lever again to make sure it was on 78. He lifted the needle manually and set the arm down on the first band.

"This is the overture," he said, listening. "But it's too jumpy." He lifted the arm and placed it on another band. "Let me try this one." Chipper had the feeling that Peachy played the record frequently.

As Peachy moved the arm from band to band, Chipper heard Russian dancers, then music for cobra charming, then a tremolo flute dueling with a plucky harp. This was not music to cure a shank by. Even Peachy was shaking his head no.

Suddenly, a flowing harp caused the two boys to sway like the cattails in Number 1 creek during a gust of wind. Peachy looked at him, nodding in quiet deference to the music.

Chipper looked at the band position, then at the back of the album cover. "'Waltz of the Flowers'," he whispered. "Six minutes, 39 seconds. This might be the one, Peachy. Six minutes, 39 seconds is nice and long. And no words."

Peachy was transfixed, his eyes glued to the spinning disk. Chipper was scared to speak another word.

The music waltzed on as Chipper counted out ¾ time and pictured Peachy swinging his irons. One-two-three, two-two-three for the backswing, then downswing on the first beat of the third measure. Smooth and easy for six minutes, 39 seconds.

Peachy didn't twitch a muscle. He didn't even blink. He seem mesmerized as the record went around and around.

"I was six years old when she left," Peachy muttered. "Never saw her again."

Chipper dropped his head to the ground as if to say, 'Please, you don't have to tell me any more.'

"Christmas Eve, we would open one present. She gave me a little red car once. I loved all my toy cars, but that was my favorite. The red one."

Peachy gulped. Chipper gulped in return.

"The next morning, I went down to open the rest of my presents and Mom was gone. Just like that. Never saw her again."

Peachy was starting to sniffle, and Chipper tried to focus on the song's rhythm to keep from sniffling with him.

As the music swelled, the cattails were blowing wildly and Chipper tried to think of something to say, something to lighten the moment. His mind was blank.

"Christmas morning, do you believe it? Christmas fuggin morning, she leaves." His eyes were red, and Chipper was certain he could see tears starting to form as Peachy's voice rose with the music.

"And you know what makes me maddest?"

"What?"

"It didn't bother the old man one bit. He called her a whore and went on about his business. Told me never to mention her name again. Well, I'll tell you somethin'. It bothered me. It damn sure bothered me."

Peachy's voice was louder than the music now, and the tears that had welled in his lower lids were now drifting down his cheeks. "It damn sure bothered me, all right. I wanted my mother, dammit. I wanted her back. I prayed every night for years for God to bring her back. I prayed that she would come home and take me with her, wherever she went. But she never came back. So much for prayer. So much for God. And my asshole dad would smack me every time I mentioned her name."

He was bawling now, and Chipper took a few awkward steps toward him as a gesture of comfort. He'd never seen Peachy cry before. Ever.

"I'm sorry, Peachy, I never knew. What was her name?"

"Her name?" Peachy looked at him funny-like. "Why...I only knew her as...Mom."

Seated on the edge of his bed, elbows on his knees, Peachy dropped his head and sobbed.

When the music came to its grand finale, Peachy shot up from the bed, grabbed Chipper by the collar and pinned him against the wall, his face inches away.

"Don't you ever, *ever,* ever tell anyone you saw me cry."

"I won't, Peachy, honest I won't."

When it came to physical threats, Peachy was in a class with the Pillsbury Dough Boy. But this time was different. Maybe this was the way he was when he knocked out Buster Nelson in the letterman's fights. His teeth were clenched, his face was red, and Chipper could almost picture smoke pouring out his ears and horns sprouting on his forehead. It was scary to know someone this long and never see them foam at the mouth before. Peachy's grip didn't ease. His tears seemed to sizzle away from his cheeks like water tossed on a hot pancake griddle.

"Ever."

As he looked into Peachy's fiery eyes, it occurred to Chipper that with all his personal preoccupation about dads and what makes a man, he'd overlooked an important and powerful truth: a guy needs his mom. And this powerful truth was revealed to him all in the span of six minutes, 39 seconds.

Forty-three

As he tapped in his third putt for a personal worst of 85 in hometown competition, Chipper snatched his ball out of the cup, trying to figure how this demon had been launched from hell. And why did this demon choose the conference tourney to take possession of his 7-iron? A bad round was usually caused by his poor drives, not the miraculous 7-iron. He'd even bladed three approaches, something he hadn't done in years. What had gone wrong? He'd even tried humming *The Nutcracker,* but 'up and in' turned into 'up, up, and away'. He'd still qualify for State, but he was worried.

"I played like crap. How'd everyone else do?" he said, as Jacob and joined-at-the-rib Kelly greeted him at the edge of the green.

"Not bad. Not good," Jacob replied. "L.K. was even. I was two over. Smokey Ray's the leader in the clubhouse with a 70, but you're *not* gonna believe this..."

"What?"

"Buster had an eight-footer for a 69 and the conference medalist."

"And?"

"And he blew it."

"So, he tied Smokey Ray?"

"No, I mean he *really* blew it," Jacob said. "He three-putted. Missed a one-footer for par."

"Shit. Damn. What happened? Did he kill anybody?"

"Nothing," Kelly said, joining in. She brushed the black, wind-whipped hair out of her face. "Nothing at all. That's the weird part. He just picked up his ball and walked off the green as calm as if he was picking the morning paper off the lawn. Didn't say a word to anyone."

Jacob looked at Chipper. "Exactly like a few weeks ago when his ball hit the flagstick. No tantrum, no yelling, no broken clubs."

"Hmm. Conference champ sure woulda helped his scholarship chances. I didn't know until recently that he even wanted to play college golf."

"Well, anyway," Jacob continued, "no one's going to come close to us today. We've got the team championship in the bag, even if Smokey Ray won medalist."

The mere mention of Smokey Ray's name made Chipper fear a jail sentence, or worse.

"Hell, then there's me," he said, "burning 'em up with an 85. I don't believe it."

"It's okay," offered L.K., joining them at greenside. "It'll come back at State. We've got a week. Just forget it."

The crowd was beginning to thicken around the 18th, in anticipation of the final golfers. Chipper estimated that there were 60 or 70 there, mostly players.

"Here we are," he said, "about to accept the conference trophy, and the only spectators are a bunch of old country club geezers. There's not one student here."

"Hey, give me a break," said Kelly.

"Oh, I'm not counting you," he replied.

"And what about me?" came a voice behind him.

It was Amy.

She struggled for a grin. He'd forgotten how the corners of her mouth turned up, as if they were drawn on, always smiling. She didn't have to work hard to look happy.

"Congratulations, champs," she said to the three boys, but looking mostly at Chipper. "It might be a stretch, but pretend I'm representing the pep club today. Sure, no one else showed, but hey, I'm the president. I speak for all the girls."

He also forgot how she bobbed her head when she spoke, each accented word punctuated with a confident nod. And, oh, those dimples.

But he felt awkward. They hadn't enjoyed an extended conversation in months. He could feel Kelly's eyes burning through the back of his head. And Jacob's. And L.K.'s. And even Gail's, wherever she was.

Amy waited for him to keep the conversation alive. He knew very well it was his turn to speak. Kelly expected it. Jacob expected it. L.K. expected it. And Amy...waiting.

A million words flew through his brain, but he choked on all of them as they tried to squeeze through his throat.

"Good to see you again, Amy," he said finally, starting to turn away.

The corners of her mouth, drawn on as they were, drooped. And the crinkles at the corners of her eyes disappeared as well.

She lifted her golf bag onto her shoulder and turned to the rest of the group. "Well, are you guys off the course now? It's about time. How's a gal to improve her game when there's a tourney hogging this place?" She tossed a final glance in Chipper's general direction, her golden hair twirling about her neck, before walking toward the Number 1 tee box where the logging chain remained detached from its companion elm branch.

His ex-friends were dead silent. He stared at the ground to avoid any further discussion. If he stared long enough at the tree root beneath his shoe, this whole sticky situation might go away. He knew every one of them wanted him back with Amy, but dammit, they didn't have to stand there so quietly about it!

"Seventy-seven, a fuggin' seventy-seven," came the familiar voice of Peachy. He was waltzing off the 18th green. Chipper hadn't even noticed him.

Peachy fiddled with the cassette controls at his side and pulled the earpiece from its hiding place beneath his long, sandy hair.

"It's the lowest fourball score ever," said Coach Dresden, approaching the team. "Two hundred ninety-four. Do that on a city course, do that at the Lake Heritage Course next week, and we'll take the state trophy home with us."

The thunderbolt stunned everybody at once. Jacob. Kelly. L.K. Coach Dresden. And Mr. Ashbrook, who also joined the group, scratching his head at the prospect. Then, Peachy and Chipper turned to face each other. It was impossible but true—Peachy had just outqualified Chipper for state.

"Oh, my God," said Kelly, never beholden to Peachy's good fortune.

"This has never happened before," Coach Dresden said. "We've never qualified five players. I'm not sure I know what to do."

"It's up to the coach," said Mr. Ashbrook, an authority on everything with the word 'golf' in it. "All five can play for medalist honors, but you have to declare in advance who's on your four-man team."

Chipper had outscored Peachy in every match this year. Even in the last two matches where "The Waltz of the Flowers" gave Peachy his two best rounds in competition. How could Peachy go to State ahead of him? Everyone knew Peachy's game was a fluke. *The Nutcracker* gimmick couldn't last. For a moment, Chipper felt like grabbing Peachy's tape recorder and smashing it to the ground. Peachy must have sensed the bad blood, because he clutched the recorder and took a few steps back. His eyes tried to apologize, but his mouth stayed shut.

"Let me think about this overnight," said Coach Dresden.

Chipper was dumbstruck, stupefied, mortified.

The awards ceremony took place without incident, though Buster didn't show for his runner-up trophy. Peachy and Gus had positioned themselves well away from Chipper during the presentation, then sped off in the Vette before the applause stopped. L.K. also vanished after the ceremony, whispering to Chipper that there was trouble with his brother Benny.

"'Think about it?'" Chipper said to Jacob. "'Overnight?' What the hell is there to think about? This is the first time in history that Peachy has ever beaten me. At anything."

"It'll be all right," Jacob replied as they walked down the outside concrete steps to the locker room door. "Coach Dresden knows better. Mr. Ashbrook does, too. There's no way they're gonna let Peachy take the fourth spot."

"I never shoulda done it. I can't believe it. It was *my* idea, for God's sake, to use the tape recorder. Hell, I've been his main instructor on that shank for *years.* To tell you the truth, it was kinda fun to fight the shank when I thought nothing would really help. I never dreamed the sunuvabitch could ever beat me!"

They entered the drab locker room, and Chipper whiffed the familiar odor of sweat and mildew, covered by the percolating scent of Old Spice.

Chipper's locker was near Jacob's, but he was too angry to think about attempting a shakedown for illicit rubbers. Especially since the accusation was from the unreliable Peachy. First, an 85. Then everyone makes him feel guilty and awful for being rude to Amy. And now this—Peachy beats him. For chrissakes, he was the main motivator, the guy that taught L.K. to chip, befriended Buster, cured Peachy's shank, and raised Jacob from the dead. It wasn't fair. It just wasn't fair.

"Look at this," said Jacob, darned near yelling. He was standing about 10 lockers down, in front of Buster's locker at the end of the aisle.

Chipper joined Jacob in staring at the battered door.

"What the..."

"I dunno. The lock is still on."

Deep indentations, 20 or 30 of them, spread across the front of the door, though it was still hinged in place.

"Gosh, it looks like someone took an ax to Buster's locker."

"Yeah. An angry someone."

They looked at each other, bewildered at first, then fearful at what they both knew was probably true.

"I'm just glad I wasn't nearby when it happened."

"Same here."

Forty-four

Chipper grabbed the customized wooden steering wheel on his '60 T-bird and eyeballed the instrument panel to enjoy the power imparted by the mere reading of the top speed: 140 miles per hour. So what if he only got nine miles per gallon out of the 390 cubic inches? Would he ever love a car this much again in his life? Power steering, power brakes, power windows, and a power seat on the driver's side. Just the sound of the word "Thunderbird" made him swell inside. The Indians said that the bird was both thunder and lightning, that it blocked the sun as it flew overhead.

"So what is it you're trying to tell me?" Chipper asked. He turned to look at Jacob in the black leather passenger-side bucket seat as they pulled away from the stop sign.

"Well, before you pick up the other guys, I want to explain something."

"Okay. What?"

"I want to explain why I haven't been hanging around with the rest of the team."

"You don't have to explain anything, Jacob. We understand. You're whipped."

Jacob shifted in his seat, reached up to swipe his fingers across the silver push buttons of the radio—without changing the station—then turned down the volume.

"It's more than that, Chipper. But you're right. It's about Kelly and me."

Uh-oh. Here it comes, thought Chipper. *True Confessions. Jacob and*

Kelly were going all the way. And Jacob, with his new religious fervor, was suffering the guilts. The guilt was building, building, building, and now, finally he couldn't bear it any longer. He would have to confess to his good buddy Chipper, Old Trusty. Chipper prepared himself to forgive the secrecy, forget the transgression, and bless the ongoing sin.

"We're married."

"What?!!"

His foot jumped to the brake pedal and he pulled the car to the shoulder of Rock Island Road. "You're what? You're married? What are you talking about?" He felt his head spinning. Surely, he was entering the Twilight Zone.

"Chipper, I know you feel like the world is tipping on its axis greater than its usual twenty-three and a half degrees, but Kelly and I are married. We've been married some time now. No one knows. Not even our parents. Until now. You're the only one. I needed to tell you so you'd know why I've been away from the team. Kelly and I spend every minute we can together."

"When? I mean, how?" Chipper sputtered. "How can you do something like that and no one know?"

"Remember last winter when I called you and asked you to cover for me?"

"Yeah, I remember. I figured..."

"Well, Kelly and I couldn't wait. We knew we were about to do it. Every night we got closer and closer. And sometimes during the day. We didn't want to do it unless we were married."

"You got married just to do it?"

"Naw, you know Kelly's the one for me."

"How do you know that for sure? You've never had so much as a coke date with another girl. For gosh sake, you went through puberty together."

"I'm lucky, I guess. I knew it from the very beginning. They say marriages are made in heaven, and that's what I think about Kelly and me."

Chipper was bordering on furious, but trying not to spoil Jay's excitement. *What about Sigma Chi? Roommates at OU? All our dreams since we were kids? All gone in a flash. All gone with the news bulletin.*

Chipper stumbled over his words, "Well, yeah, but..." Surely there was a good reason to speak now or forever hold his peace. "Yeah, but... but...well...congratulations. I love Kelly like a sister. You're right, it was meant to be."

"We drove to Louisiana that night. Shreveport. You can get married there when you're 17. Then we drove right back the same night."

"Did you...like, get a motel room or something?"

"Didn't have time, or the money. We did it right in the back of Old Blue, parked behind the Chapel. It was only proper, you know. We'd been warming up in Old Blue for years."

"So...how was it?"

Jacob chuckled, then beamed like a little kid with a new pogo stick. "Great, it was just great. The synchronization of the parasympathetic and sympathetic nervous systems is really incredible."

"Yeah, sure."

The box of rubbers spotted earlier by Peachy was no longer contraband. The near total absence of Jacob for the past few months was explained. *Why would he want to be with the guys when he could be doing it?* Chipper was jealous, and he knew it. But it was okay. *Conference was over. Next Gail. Then State.*

"And no one knows?"

"No one. You're sworn to secrecy."

"I swear."

He could keep secrets. After all, he and Peachy had never told anyone about Chief Crazy Hawk being Buster's uncle. And he had never told anyone about L.K.'s brother Benny. Oh, except for Amy.

"Let's go get Peachy and L.K.," Jacob said. "My mom said our celebration dinner will be ready at 8:30."

"I'll try to look happy at dinner," Chipper said, "but it won't be easy. I'm not gonna rest till I know who's playing fourth man at State. Anyway, I'm happy for you and Kelly."

He grabbed the wooden knob on his gear shift, and threw the transmission into drive. For the hell of it, he peeled out and left rubber on the concrete, guzzling gas by the gallons.

Forty-five

With Peachy now in the back seat of the Thunderbird, Chipper headed to Reformatory Plaza to pick up L.K. As usual, L.K. would be standing on the porch, waiting. No one was allowed inside the Taylor household.

Peachy was strangely silent. In fact, the entire carload was deadsville. And the population of deadsville—three to be exact—knew why. Peachy had shot 77, Chipper an 85.

Along the straightaway of Country Club Road, Chipper could zoom to 110 miles per hour late at night when there were no other cars. But it was too early for that. Hell, on old Highway 6 east of town, he could hit the magic 140 when he needed to let off steam. He felt like pushing it to 140 now.

"What the hell is that?" Peachy asked, sitting upright from the sunken leather seats in back.

"I don't know," said Jacob.

"What are you two talking about?" Chipper asked.

"Up there on the right, at the club. On Number 9 green. There's a pickup."

"Yeah. Its lights are on."

"Look. Someone's out in front of it."

"What the hell...?"

"Slow down, Chipper."

He pulled into the circle drive at the country club for a good look at the black Dodge pickup. And the person standing in its lights.

"Holy mother of shit!" Peachy said. "It's Buster."

"Jeez, you're right."

Buster's dad's pickup was parked on the fringe of the green. The headlights were on and Buster was stooped over, addressing a ball with his putter. The flagstick was still in. Buster didn't even look up.

"What the hell's he doing?"

"I dunno, but let's get out of here," Peachy said. "He's nuts."

Chipper looked over his shoulder. "Dammit, Peachy, shut your mouth."

The Thunderbird crept slowly alongside the pickup. Buster still didn't look up. As they emptied the car, Chipper assumed Buster would take notice. He was wrong.

"Hey, Buster, whatcha doin'? Kinda late to practice, isn't it?"

Buster stared at the ground, stroking a one-foot putt toward the hole.

"Gotta make this putt," he mumbled to himself. "Gotta make this putt." He stroked one after another, mumbling all the while: "Gotta make this putt."

As the bizarre chanting continued, the three intruders exchanged glances, looking for guidance. Chipper walked to the edge of the green.

"Gotta make this putt. Gotta make this putt."

"Buster, it's us. Chipper, Jacob, Peachy. It's the team, man. We were on our way to get L.K., then to your house. Remember? We're celebrating with a late dinner at Jacob's house. His mom is cooking up a storm."

"Gotta make this putt."

"Buster?" He stepped forward onto the green.

"Stay the fuck off my green," Buster yelled. He had a nutso look in his eyes Chipper had never seen before.

"Let's get the hell out of here," Peachy whispered.

"Buster, it's us," said Jacob.

"Why...why is it *your* green, Buster?" asked Chipper, trying to apply slick psychology, but knowing damn well he didn't have the foggiest idea what the hell he was saying or why. "Isn't this the club's green?"

"Fuck no. It's *my* green, so stay the fuck *off!*" Buster held his putter in the air with a stance that indicated he was quite comfortable with assault and battery.

"Why is it your green, Buster? Tell me, why is it your green?"

"Whatever hates you, you hate back. And when you hate back, you own it, and it owns you. Isn't that the way it works?" Buster spoke in a flat, spooky tone, like Slim Harper at the funeral home. He didn't move. His putter was frozen in the air.

"Why does this green hate you?"

"Why the fuck do you have to ask me something like that, Chipper? Isn't it obvious? Isn't it fucking obvious?"

"No," Chipper said, somewhat relieved that Buster addressed him by name. Until now, he wasn't sure that Buster even recognized them. "No, it's not obvious to me."

"So, I have to fucking *explain* everything to you?" Buster swung his putter around his head then threw it aimlessly into the dark night. It was lost in the stars, but Chipper heard a thud in the distance. It was the same thud they'd heard for years playing golf with Buster, but tonight the sound seemed to rattle around in Chipper's head.

Buster jerked the flagstick out of the cup and pointed the quivering tip at Chipper.

"Does this make it simple enough for you?"

"No, I still don't understand, Buster. But we've got dinner waiting..."

"The flagstick, asshole, the fucking flagstick. My ball hits the tip-top of the goddam sunuvabitch. Million to one odds, Jacob said. Well, bullshit, it's not a million to one if you're Buster Nelson. If you're Buster Nelson, you're fucked. Do you hear me, you sons of bitches? You're fucked!"

Chipper tried another step onto the green, but Buster thrust the flagstick at him like the Black Knight jousting his enemy. "Stay off my fucking green, I told you already."

"Buster, we're your friends, your best friends. We're only trying to help you."

"And if hitting the tip of the flagstick wasn't bad enough," continued Buster, oblivious to the appeal, "today my goddam gimme putt circles out the back lip, and I lose the fucking tournament. And you have to ask me why the fuck this green hates me? What kind of friends are you if you can't figure that out?"

"You're right," Chipper said, trying another strategy. "It's been a bad green for you. But it's not gonna do any good to fight it tonight. In fact, you probably shouldn't be standing on it either."

Buster looked down at his feet, lifting them one at a time.

Chipper took a baby step off the froghair and onto the green. Buster stared at him like a caged animal, not sure if the approaching human was planning to free him or slay him. Chipper couldn't sense Jacob and Peachy behind him, and he was scared to look. For all he knew, they had scampered back to the car.

"Don't come any closer, Chipper. I'm warning you." Buster jabbed the spear at him again.

"It's a bad green, Buster. Just a bad green. And it's a bad flagstick. You need to drop the pin and let's go."

Chipper inched forward with more baby steps.

"Stay back, goddammit. Stay the fuck back!"

Buster raised the flagstick in the air like a javelin and held his arm cocked, ready to impale Chipper.

"You got screwed, Buster. No doubt about it. Odds were a million to one. And that little one-footer, hell, that could happen to anyone."

"Well, it *didn't* happen to anyone. That's my point. It happened to Buster Nelson. The green, the Number 9 fucking green. It's got me by the balls, but I'm getting ready to get even, goddammit. Now don't get any closer."

Chipper raised a hand of friendship, palm up, as if trying to befriend a barking dog. But with each step closer to the tip of the flagstick, Chipper could see Buster cock his arm farther back like a ratchet until he looked ready for the kill.

Why the hell were his feet making him walk up to a madman? Only one step away, Chipper stretched his arm until his fingers touched the red flag with the white number 9. He formed a tight fist around the blunt point of the flagstick where Buster's ball had landed, a million to one.

Buster's face melted, his hand released the pin, and he fell to the green in a sobbing heap.

For the first time, Chipper looked back to see that Jacob and Peachy were still there, though both were motionless, eyes wide and jaws slacked.

He looked back at Buster on the ground, rocking himself like a baby, curled in a ball, boohooing, not 20 yards from the spot where Jacob had fallen with the news of Doc Jody's death.

"What can we do for you, Buster?"

No response. Only more crying. He stooped to one knee and touched Buster's rocking shoulder.

"Tell me what we can do."

The bawling turned to whimpering.

"Do you want me to call Carol?" Chipper offered.

"Carol? Carol?" he asked, looking up at Chipper.

"Yes, do you want me to call her?"

"The old man is gonna kill me. The old man is gonna kill me. Gonna kill me," he said over and over in rhythm to his rocking.

"Why's your dad gonna kill you?"

Buster quieted a little, but kept rocking and weeping.

"Gonna kill me, gonna kill me, gonna kill me," he continued.

"Why, Buster, why?"

"Pregnant. 'Cause she's pregnant. Gonna kill me, gonna kill me."

Chipper sighed and looked back at the others who were joining him now, circling around Buster right there on Number 9, six feet from the cup.

The crying was over. Buster was silent.

Jacob and Peachy each took an arm, lifting Buster off the tormenting green and holding him on his feet. The foursome hobbled toward the fringe, Chipper moving ahead to open Buster's pickup door.

"I better drive you home, Buster. Here, Jacob, take my keys and follow us."

Jacob and Peachy helped Buster into the shotgun spot.

Before closing the door, they had to position his lifeless body upright in the seat. Buster's head flopped back, eyes closed.

"I'm not a boxer," he said with a raspy whisper. "Never was, never will be."

The three team members looked at each other as if they'd just guessed the answer on *I've Got A Secret.*

"What...do you mean?" asked Peachy, the victor in their one-punch match.

"We moved away from El Viento when I was little, when Mom died." Buster sighed, but continued, "I didn't know why we moved away. By the time we moved back here, Dad was whippin' me regular. I had black eyes my first day at school. How else could I explain it? What else could I say?"

"You never boxed?"

"Only as the punching bag. Shoulda been obvious at the letterman's fights. My life's been fallin' apart ever since that fight."

He started to whimper again, but caught himself before it turned into full-fledged blubbering, the kind of crying you have to count against yourself when you're trying to become a man.

"Does your dad...does he still whip you?"

"Not so much anymore, now that I'm bigger. I think he's starting to get scared. But when he gets drunk, which is pretty damn often, he comes looking for me, calling me a goddam son of a squaw."

Chipper looked at Peachy. They were sworn to secrecy about the link to Chief Crazy Hawk.

"Since we've moved back to this town, I've heard the whispering, the rumors, people saying the old man beat my mom to death. I was too little. I don't know what happened."

Buster sat upright in the seat, his eyes beginning to open. "But I can tell you this. That goddam asshole is capable of anything. Once, just once, I'd like to let him have it. I'd like to throw a punch and knock him cold."

He pounded his closed fist into the opposite palm as he spoke. "Then I'd take Carol, get married, and get the hell out of El Viento forever."

"Why do you think he's gonna kill you? Because of Carol? I mean, her being pregnant and all?" asked Chipper.

"He hates Carol. He hates the thought of me being happy. He calls her a cunt behind her back and a bitch to her face. I live pretty much at her house now. I hate the motherfucker. I hate him with all my guts."

"Why don't you leave, Buster?" Peachy said. "Graduation's not that far away. Get your degree, get married, and get away."

"Kelly says Carol's been checking on some colleges," Jacob added, "especially the ones that offer golf scholarships."

Buster sighed again and looked down at his fidgeting fingers, no longer in a fist. "That's why I needed to win the tournament today."

"Hell, Buster, you're a damn good golfer," added Peachy, of all people. "In just about any other town, you'd be first man on the team. Hell, who knows, you might take State."

"Carol being pregnant is gonna piss off the old man really bad."

"Don't tell him," Peachy said.

"He already knows. Carol's dad called him today. I've gotta go face him now. Gotta pack my bags and move out till graduation. I can't take it anymore."

Buster was working his way back in control. Back in his shell. At least he wasn't acting wacko anymore. He wasn't crying anymore. He wasn't pounding his fist, and he wasn't sighing as he talked. But the more Chipper thought about it, the more it bothered him. All those horrible feelings—the anger, the hatred, the fear, everything that was so crummy in Buster's life—it was all exposed there on the final green for about 10 minutes. And now it was gone. Completely gone. Buster was back to Buster's normal. But it was too quick. It was the same normal they witnessed the day Buster's ball hit the top of the flagstick. It was the same normal earlier today when he missed the one-foot putt. Then Chipper remembered the dents in the locker door, as if an ax murderer had been furiously practicing his craft.

"Thanks, guys. Sorry to be a trouble," said Buster as matter-of-fact as you would say to a group of guys that helped push-start your car. "I'm sorry for the tantrum. I think I'm okay to drive myself home now."

Chipper tried, but Buster gave him a go-away look that let him know that his place was in the Thunderbird with Jacob and Peachy.

Forty-six

Mrs. Justice wasn't upset in the slightest that it was after 9:00 when the team arrived. She used the conference trophy as her centerpiece and built the meal around it. Spinach and T-bones for blood and biceps, she said. Potatoes to provide the energy for the grueling second day of State when they would play 36 holes. Carrots for the eagle-eye vision needed to judge distances and to read the difficult greens at the Lake Heritage course. Black-eyed peas for good luck.

L.K. put huge portions on his plate, while the others watched in amazement. Plenty of food was left. The only shortage was in the rationed conversation.

Chipper's head was still spinning. Jacob was right—the world was tilted too far on its axis. He looked at Jacob now. The son of a gun was married. Jeez. He thought of Buster who was missing this great meal. The subdued Buster who was about to get married, albeit prodded by a 40-gauge shotgun. And Peachy, the asshole, was trying to take his spot on the team. Plus, who knew what was going on with L.K.'s brother Benny? Or L.K.'s surly father?

Oh, how he wished they could all step into the Justices' den again, with Doc Jody singing "Heart of My Heart."

He could picture Amy by his side, talking about the perfect marriage that Doc Jody and Mama Justice had created for themselves.

Now Doc Jody was gone. Amy was gone. The only thing still the same about the den was all those golf trophies on the wall, never dusty thanks to Mrs. Justice.

The telephone rang.

Chipper's thoughts raced back one year ago to that first night when Gail phoned him here at the Justice home. Surely, not again.

Mama Justice called from the kitchen phone, "It's for you, Chipper. They're asking for Kyle."

Oh, no. Just like before. His parents were the only ones who called him Kyle.

Pushing himself from the table, he left the silent party for the kitchen. Jacob's mom handed him the phone, offering her usual smile.

"Hold, please," came a woman's voice at the other end. He waited anxiously.

"Kyle, this is your father."

What was happening? He told them earlier where he would be tonight, and his folks were supposed to be at home.

"I'm calling from the emergency room," his father continued.

"What's going on?"

"Buster Nelson is here."

Chipper gasped for air that seemed remarkably thin compared to the atmosphere that used to surround the player piano.

"Why? What for?"

"He got into a fight with his father."

"And?"

"And they're both hurt."

"How bad?"

"We sent the father on to the city. He's got a broken jaw. It'll have to be fixed over there. They'll need to wire his mouth shut."

"And Buster?"

"He's fractured his fourth and fifth right metacarpals."

"Meta-what?"

"Metacarpals. His knuckles. He fractured his metacarpals slugging his father. It's a common fracture in fights. We call it a boxer's fracture."

"A boxer's fracture?"

"Yeah, it's an awful situation there at the Nelsons. Buster told me the story. He's going to be okay. We'll make sure of that."

"His hand, Dad, is it in a cast?"

"Yes, for six weeks. Buster told me you needed to know right away."

"Is there anything he wants me to do?"

"No, he just wanted me to let you know, and also to give you a message."

"A message?"

"Yes. He says someday he'll repay you. For being nice to him, I think. He says that someday you'll get double in return. I haven't the slightest idea what he means by that. He wouldn't explain."

"Thanks, Dad." *Double in return?*

Chipper walked back to the table and slipped into his chair. How would he choose the right words? There they were, gearing up for State, getting themselves primed and ready—L.K. stuffing his mouth with T-bone and spinach, Jacob mixing his carrots and potatoes, Peachy gawking at the good-luck black-eyed peas, captivated. How would he tell them? Was there a gentle word for 'devastation'? A kind alternative to 'catastrophe'? How could he relay the news that their quest was over? They couldn't win State without Buster. They couldn't win State if they had to count both Peachy's score and his own score. Peachy simply didn't have 54 good holes left in him, not even propped up by "The Waltz of the Flowers." Counting his own score was iffy enough. After all, the great Chipper scored an 85 today.

Well, hell, good for Buster, he thought. *Damn good for Buster.*

Mama Justice returned from the kitchen and set a bright green plate in the center of the table, near the conference trophy.

"These are for dessert, men," she said, reminding Chipper that Doc Jody always addressed the boys as men. He looked at the plate bearing four, folded pieces of shiny, tan dough. "They're fortune cookies," Mama Justice said. "Each of you...take one."

Forty-seven

Peachy, of course, declared it a brainstorm. A stroke of genius. A revelation. And no matter how much the team bellyached, they agreed to play along, if for no other reason than to silence the Peach. What could it harm? Jacob was the most reluctant, calling the lady a fake, sight-unseen. L.K. was in the same camp, though not as vocal. Chipper thought it premature to pass judgment on someone they had never heard of when Peachy insisted they venture into the fifth dimension.

The idea blossomed after the fortune cookie fizzle the night before. Chipper had been disappointed when all the strips of paper inside the cookies made cockamamie statements that had nothing to do with the future. His so-called fortune read: "He who analyzes the mirage becomes the philosopher." What a waste. Peachy's was equally boring, but when he read aloud: "Enjoy the gifted, but seek counsel with the wise," he immediately shouted, "Jenniquita!"

Now here they were, poised at the fence marking her property line on the outskirts of El Viento. Peachy had pointed out that she was the only local Negro who did not live in colored town. Chipper found it strange that she lived in the country by herself, on a farm no less, though it seemed more of a menagerie. Brown chickens, white ones, ducks and geese flittered about the front yard, while a billy goat looked on, tied to a revolving clothesline. The goat stopped chewing to stare at the intruders.

Peachy was in charge of the expedition, as if he were compensating for the unspoken doubt surrounding his ability to maintain his blistering golf game through next week. The magic words in store for them today would hopefully translate to victory and, of course, Peachy would be responsible.

"She's the best around, I'm telling you," said Peachy, creaking open the wooden gate. "Brandi, one of my dad's friends, goes to her all the time. She says people come from all over this part of the country. They say she's better than Jeanne Dixon."

"Bogus," Jacob said. "It's all bogus."

"Fuggin-A, it's the truth."

"Yeah, sure," said L.K., "We've heard it a hundred times the past 24 hours, Peachy. We're here, all right? You don't need to sell us any more of your bullshit."

L.K. and Jacob were sharing the same corner of caution. But Chipper wondered if, deep inside, the others weren't just a little bit scared, like he was, at the thought of entering a stranger's home—a stranger said to be a Yoruba princess from New Orleans, and before that, Haiti. Peachy had been quick to point out there was a difference between the Yoruba religion and voodoo, though it seemed a minor technicality to Chipper, especially when her towering shape appeared at the screen door.

The top of her orange bandanna rose above the door frame, even though the boys were three steps lower than she was. *She must be six-foot-six,* Chipper thought. The foursome paused. She didn't speak. She didn't move. Her arms were folded across a billowy white blouse. Her bottom half was covered by the solid part of the screen door. *Maybe she's standing on a stool.*

Peachy flashed his pick-a-card smile, but his lower lip seemed to be quivering at the corner, saying 'Any card, if you please, ma'am'. The chickens and ducks gathered at his feet as he entered the yard, pecking at his penny loafers like they'd never been fed.

"I've heard of watchdogs, but never watch-*chickens,*" Peachy said half-heartedly.

She didn't smile. Neither did the rest of the team.

Peachy turned around to encourage the others, unconvincingly, that it was safe to proceed. Chipper was glad to be a follower for once. The wooden gate opened only a foot because the bottom dragged the ground. Chipper kicked it softly to make room for L.K., then looked up to see if that maneuver was okay with the lady of the house.

The chickens and ducks and geese escorted the team onto her front steps where she motioned the boys to enter, turning to walk deeper into her shanty. She did not step off Chipper's hypothetical stool, maintaining every inch of her stature.

The screen door creaked louder than the outside gate. Peachy went first, followed by Chipper, then L.K. and Jacob. A surprisingly sweet smell greeted them inside, like clove chewing gum, contrasting with the rummage sale decor. Chipper thought it odd for her to live in squalor if she made such big bucks as the top fortune-teller in the Midwest.

Although she was walking away from them to the corner of the room, Chipper made a quick height comparison. She was taller than L.K. The six-six figure was about right. She wore a multicolored skirt, primarily red, that hung from her high waist to the ground like a tent. It seemed that her shiny gold belt would hit him at chin level, and the shimmering hoops in her ears looked large enough for a gymnast.

When she reached the corner, she turned slowly and lowered herself into a huge chair woven like a basket, with a tall, rounded back. She signaled to them, one at a time, with a flop of her wrist like a priestess blessing her flock. They were to sit down. Chipper wasn't sure which threadbare chair to pick. It didn't matter. They all looked colorless and dusty. He wondered if the candy fragrance could be coming from the flickering candles scattered about. The only other light in the room after Jacob shut the front door was one bare bulb on a table beside her basket chair. On closer look, the table was an elephant's foot. *Surely a fake,* he thought.

"So..." she began.

The boys sat at attention.

"...which one of you telephoned Jenniquita?"

They jerked their heads in a synchronized stare at Peachy. His eyes widened.

"Ah, hah," she said, "your friends tell the truth for you." Her voice was deep for a woman, as if it were in an echo chamber. She had an English accent that crowned her with authority, a dialect not heard much around El Viento. Chipper thought she resembled the Uncola guy smoothly selling 7-Up, seated in the same sort of basket chair, comparing cola nuts and uncola nuts.

Peachy slouched in his seat.

"Go ahead, young man. Tell why you come to Jenniquita today."

"Well..." began Peachy, craning his neck. Chipper wondered why, if she was a fortune-teller, she had to ask. "...you see, we're a team. A golf team. But we lost one of our best players. Broken hand. We're in a big tournament this Friday and Saturday. State tournament. We want to win. Still. Even with Buster out. That's the name of the guy that broke his hand."

"Then you come to Jenniquita for...golf lessons? Hah, hah, hah, hah."

Chipper felt three inches tall, and he hoped Peachy felt smaller so he could squash him like a bug as soon as they got out of here.

"Hah, hah, hah, hah."

They tried to laugh with her, but no one could muster a chuckle.

"Hah, hah, hah. Good joke for Jenniquita. Hah, hah, hah."

Her huge mouth with painted red lips revealed glistening white teeth, many of them framed in gold.

Peachy sat taller in his chair. "No ma'am, we're here 'cause we heard you can see the future."

"Ah, but there is difference between *seeing* the unseen...and *preparing* for the unseen."

Peachy looked confused, as well he should.

Her smile melted and she reached for something at her side. It was a shallow basket, like an upside down Chinese hat, only contoured smooth rather than pointed in the center. From a pocket near the waist of her skirt, she pulled out a small bag and emptied its contents into the basket. Rather than marbles, about fifteen seashells spilled out, identical in shape, salmon and white in color. She gathered them and threw them like dice. Over and over.

The boys were seated in a semicircle before her. She turned to L.K. on her left. He was stony. She stared at him, poker-faced, the only movement being her eyelids that alternated between spooky saucers and probing slits. Jenniquita threw the shells again, then eyeballed L.K. forever.

As Chipper looked back and forth between the two, it seemed as though every time her eyes opened and closed, she burrowed her way deeper through L.K.'s wooden scowl. Chipper could almost see the force fields radiating from her, piercing the air. Beads of sweat were forming on L.K.'s forehead, but then again it was pretty warm without air-conditioning.

L.K. started to fidget, but only his legs were twitching. She must be reaching deep and uncovering the story of the snakebites, he thought. L.K.'s legs were vibrating now. *My God, she's reading his mind!*

Chipper considered running away rather than risk discovery of his major league rendezvous planned by Gail for 10:00 sharp on Tuesday night. Did this woman know his parents? Amy? Would she call them, or were there professional ethics for fortune-tellers, like doctors, where they were bound to secrecy? How silly. Of course, she would know his parents and Amy—even their phone numbers. She was, after all, a mind reader.

The mind reader finished with L.K. who fell back in his chair, panting relief. She turned to face Chipper. He was trapped. Like a rat.

She tossed her shells for a while, then began the stare, the ungodly stare that had set the great L.K.'s legs to shaking.

It was all over for him and his best-laid plans. Within minutes, she would see the entire rhapsody of lovemaking with her gifted eyes. His secret would be exposed for all the world to see. She started squinting and opening wide. Squinting and opening, with a rhythm that tried to rock him back and forth into submission.

A rescuing thought popped into his brain. When those tow-headed, mind-reading, little alien monster kids in the movie *Village of the Damned* couldn't be stopped, the only hope of victory for the townspeople was the mental construction of a brick wall. A brick wall it was, a brick wall it would be. He erected the brick wall in his mind and positioned it at the back of his eyes, at the front of his brain. No one could enter. No one could tear it down. Not even Jenniquita.

Her eyes were saucers, then slits. Saucers then slits. He felt the cosmic beams blasting the bricks, but his wall was solid. The beams tore at the mortar that held the bricks. They made the whole wall vibrate with their force. But the wall stood firm. The wall protected him. Whew!

She turned toward Jacob, the next batter. Peachy was on deck. Chipper sighed and slumped into his chair.

Jacob seemed bored. He was staring at a crucifix on her wall, a curious emblem in the home of a voodoo queen, as Jacob had called her. Then again, he had also pointed out that these religious cults were often amalgamations, assimilating bits and pieces of various legitimate religions.

Chipper was exhausted. He paid no attention to the torturous staring ritual as performed on Jacob and, finally, Peachy. His brick wall had done the trick.

After she put the shells back in the marble bag and into her pocket, the basket at her side, she scanned the room without making further eye contact.

Finally, she said, "A team of warriors enters the battle. One warrior missing." She spoke with her chin in the air, as though she was addressing a room full of ghosts standing behind them. "Gird the loins with scarlet blood, then you will rise to the point most high."

Chipper held his jaw square, but let his eyes roam to the others. Their eyes were lost as well.

"Pardon?" asked Peachy, with a meekness rarely heard.

"Time all gone for Jenniquita."

"But...what did you say? What do you mean?"

"Let's go, Peachy," said Jacob.

"Jenniquita give you what you ask. Now gift for Jenniquita." She held out her hand.

Peachy grumbled as he stood, reaching in his pocket for the $20 bill, part of his $250 sure-thing prize for the scorpion hunt planned tomorrow night at five to one odds. Chipper thought he heard Peachy say, "What a gyp."

They hustled out the door for the safety of the Thunderbird.

On the road home, the foursome discussed the possible interpretations of the prophet.

Peachy waxed eloquently: "Sounded like the same goddam crap that was in those fortune cookies."

"Glad it was your money," chided L.K.

"But then, what if it meant something," Peachy continued, "and we're just too friggin' dumb to figure it out? I mean, what's a loin? Is it the same as a groin? And what does gird mean? Jacob?"

"It's all pretty silly," said Jacob. "Fortune-tellers thrive by making their statements vague. It can mean whatever you want it to mean. What do you want it to mean, Peachy?"

"I wanted her to tell us to do something. Something that will make it happen. I want instructions, dammit!"

"Gird the loins? Jacob?"

"Gird means to surround, with the implication being to prepare for action. The loin is your side, between the bottom of your ribs and your hipbone. Bottom line, it's a weak spot. The Bible talks a lot about girding the loins. Protect your weak spot. Scarlet could mean the blood of the Lamb. If her 'most high' phrase means heaven, then surround yourself with the blood of the Lamb and you'll see heaven..."

"Gimme a break," interrupted Peachy. "We're talking golf here, not some fairy-tale crap."

Jacob continued, "She said 'gird the loins with scarlet blood, then you will rise to the point most high.' If it weren't coming from a voodoo queen, Billy Graham might have said it." He teased Peachy with a smile.

Peachy looked disgusted, then pretended Jacob didn't exist. "I say it's symbolic, but the symbols have to do with us."

"Maybe it means Buster's blood," said Chipper, entering the think tank for the first time. "If we take Buster's blood, symbolically, so to speak, into battle...then the 'most high' means we'll take first place."

"Naw. I say it's a double instruction," said Peachy. "There's two things we have to do. We have to gird the loins with scarlet...and...we have to go to the point most high. Do both, and we win State."

"You seem pretty confident interpreting as you see fit," said Jacob.

"Hey, holy-roller, don't give me any shit. Talk about interpreting the way you see fit. Blood of the Lamb, for chrissakes."

"Cool it, assholes," L.K. said.

Chipper's mind raced through the possibilities. Sure, everyone was talking about what a fake she was, laughing that Peachy coughed up the dough, but here they were, all four of them, scratching their heads to unlock the mysteries of the universe.

Gird the loins, he thought. It sounded like putting on armor for battle. There was no armor in golf. *With scarlet blood*...put on armor of blood. *Then you will rise to the point most high*...the highest place in El Viento was the first tee box at the golf course where the crest of the hill caught the peak wind velocity. Except...except...except for the grain elevators that towered above the skyline like El Viento's Empire State Building. Put on armor of scarlet blood. Rise to the point most high. Blood red. Put on red.

Rise.

Forty-eight

"I'll go along with no more Horse," said Jacob. "'When I became a man, I put away childish things.'"

"From the Bible?" asked Chipper.

"Yeah."

"Who'd ever thought there'd be a time when we didn't play Horse anymore?"

They sat together on the lonely wooden bench by the practice tee, waiting for the others to arrive. "I guess you kinda figure you're going to be doing the same things for the rest of your life," said Jacob.

"Yeah, it was weird when it hit me. I was lining up the shot to bank it off the shed and onto the green, and all of a sudden I realized that Horse wasn't fun anymore. I mean, you being married and all. College around the corner. It's all good, I s'pose, but it doesn't seem right playing a stupid game of Horse. With golf balls, no less."

"I guess not."

Shirtless, in madras Bermuda shorts, they sat with their backs to the wood slats, pounding their 5-irons between their spread-eagled feet.

"Penny for your thoughts," said Jacob.

Old games die hard. Chipper traced his thoughts for the past few weeks to a recurring theme, a topic that kept him company in those rare moments when he was alone.

"Remember that drowning story at the viaduct when I was six?"

"Sure, in the crawdad hole under the railroad tracks."

"Yeah, I'm never sure how much I remember for real, or if it's just been told so many times. But lately, it seems more clear than before."

"You fell in. Your dad pulled you out. What's there to remember?"

"The crawdad hole was strictly taboo. I watched the older boys playing there, leaving with buckets of crawdads. And when I snuck away with them that day, boy, it was fun. Mud squishing up between your toes, plucking crawdads out of the water, our coins overhead on the railroad tracks, waiting for a train to come by and turn the pennies into pancakes. It just doesn't get any better than that."

"So what happened?" Jacob asked. "How'd you fall in?"

"The water was deep only in the center. You caught the crawdads near the shallow edge. When a train finally came to squash my penny, I got so excited that I stepped off into the deep part. The weird thing is I don't remember being scared. To tell you the truth, it was just the opposite. Until recently, that's all I could remember. Then last month, I started to think about it a lot. It seems like it's coming back to me in little bits, and I'm starting to put it together."

"Like how?"

"Well, now I remember green all around me," Chipper said. "It felt good. The water was cold, and I remember the chill on the inside as my lungs sucked up the green. I wasn't scared at all."

"How'd your dad find you?"

"The way my mother tells the story," Chipper continued, "I wandered away with my Sunday school clothes on. It didn't take long for them to miss me. Dad spotted the older boys at the opening of the viaduct and showed up just in time."

"Sounds like you had a guardian angel."

"I remember feeling so good underwater that I didn't want to leave. Lately, I think I remember why. As soon as I was jerked out, I heard a pop that lifted me off the ground. My arm was being held tight, and I was being paddled hard-and-fast all the way home. I don't remember it hurting, I only remember the sound of his hand slapping against my wet britches, like a cap pistol. I was terrified. Every few yards across the field all the way home. Slap after slap after slap. I think it was raining, but I'm not sure. It seems like rain was hitting my face, and I heard this voice, like God, saying 'Stop crying' over and over. And I said, 'I'm not crying, it's the rain.' Everything stopped on our front porch when Mom kissed the top of my head. Honestly, I don't remember Dad being there at all. Just the slapping sound against my butt, lifting me off the ground. I know he saved my life 'cause everyone's been saying for years that he's the hero. But I only remember Mom that day."

"Guess I never heard the whole story," said Jacob.

"No, you wouldn't've. That last part is new. New to me, at least. That's the way it's coming back to me. But I do remember how safe I felt underwater. Sometimes, I wish I could feel that good again. I think that's how I got stuck in my room after that."

"I remember that phase—like the Beach Boy?"

"Yeah, but I was only six. Gimme a break. It felt good, like being underwater, when I was in my room. To tell the truth, I still have trouble..."

"Is that the summer you refused to go back to school?" Jacob asked.

"No. It was sorta gradual until two years later that I had my endless summer, right before the fourth grade."

"How'd your mom get you back to school?"

"She didn't."

"She didn't?"

"No. You're not gonna like this."

"Try me."

"It was Gail."

"Gail?!"

"Yeah, "Chipper said, "'fraid so." He was apologetic in his tone, knowing the group condemnation that was mounting lately. "I'd look at her picture, stuck in the springs of my upper bunk, and I'd think if I didn't go back to school...something bad would happen to her. I always had a funny feeling that I was her knight in shining armor."

"Ugh."

"It's crazy, but it's true. I'd probably be a hermit in a cave right now if it weren't for her."

A flock of blackbirds swirled above them. They flew in a tight-knit grouping, weaving in and out of small and large circles with perfect choreography. In one of the smaller circles, they formed a tornado of black feathers before they widened to a whirlpool, then to a black sheet circling overhead.

"Gail's the reason I ran for fourth grade class president and wrote that letter to the Governor. Our class visit to see the Capitol after that seemed to start the ball rolling for me. One thing led to another."

Jacob continued pounding his 5-iron between his feet. Chipper choked up on his grip, then held his 5-iron like a rifle, pointing it at the circling black birds.

"Did you hear that the OU president's office called the school last week?" Chipper asked. "You know that freshmen group of leaders, the President's Leadership Class, that I'll be in next year? Well, I've been appointed first term president."

"Ah, the leader of leaders."

"Hey, do I detect some sarcasm?"

"No, not really."

"It's like I said. One thing has led to another, ever since the fourth grade, and it looks like it's going to continue at OU."

"And it's all due to Gail?" asked Jacob.

"I know it sounds goofy, but in a way, yeah."

Jacob shook his head 'no'. Chipper couldn't recall a yes or no question.

"What have you done, Chipper?"

"What do you mean?"

"What, as a leader, have you done of lasting importance?"

"Lasting importance?"

"Yeah. And I don't consider painting signs for pep rallies to be lasting importance," Jacob said. "Do you see what I'm saying? You've been class president from the beginning, in no small part due to the fact there are more girls than boys in our class. Then, because of that position, you're elected president of every other club. That, with a straight-A average, gets you President's Leadership Class at OU next year. Now you're president of that. Where does it end? When is it laurels and when is it actually accomplishing something?"

Chipper stood up from the bench, angry at first, but he dropped his 5-iron rifle to the side. Jacob was right. What had he done that counted for anything? He knew that's why he was so focused on the team winning State. He considered it a selfless act until the moment he thought Peachy had bumped him off the team. It was then that he realized that his motives were not selfless at all, and he wondered if an act of human goodness could ever be truly selfless.

Then it occurred to him. "Yearbook," he said. "My being editor of the yearbook. That's lasting importance. My folks say they still refer back to theirs. They say it's lifelong memories."

Jacob seemed to be nodding in the positive, so Chipper continued. "In fact, you're not gonna believe this, but this year's writing class is the best time I've ever had in school. I love science and all, but the writing is, well, it's hard to describe."

"Yeah, I read your short story on human nature being more powerful than any technology. The closing scene in the United Nations was as good as any *Twilight Zone* that I've seen."

"It's more than that. I couldn't put it into words until recently, but it goes along with the crawdad hole."

"What?"

"Well, after that guardian angel experience, Mom always said that it wasn't my time to go. That I was saved for a reason. When I got a little older, she told me to discover my talent, you know, the reason I was saved at the crawdad hole. When I was eight or nine," Chipper said, "I thought that talent was the Bongo Board. I figured I held the world record after balancing for two hours in my room one night. Then there's this guy on the *Steve Allen Show* that stays on it for 24 hours. Then it was the marimba. I was going to be the next Lionel Hampton. Then it was bowling, then real sports, then golf. After a while, I figured out that no matter how good you are, there's always someone better."

"You're just now figuring that out?" Jacob asked. "Don't you watch *Gunsmoke?* Even Matt Dillon got beat once."

"That's what I'm coming to. I don't have to be the best, see, but I have to be different. Something to explain why I didn't die in the crawdad hole."

"You are different. We're all unique."

"You asked earlier what I've accomplished. You're right. You're dead right. Then I remembered the yearbook. It's not out yet, but I want you to read the Foreword. When you read about the compound interest of unselfish community spirit, when you read about searching for meaning in our existence versus existing for our meaning, when you read about...well, there's a whole bunch more. That'll be me talking, Jacob, using words arranged in my own way. That's lasting importance."

"It's probably a good hobby then."

"No, I'm thinking more than that. There are only 12 notes on the piano, or for me the marimba, but think of the different songs that come out of it. Now, think what you can do with a hundred thousand words. I used to believe writing was about using the biggest, fanciest words possible and voicing my opinions all over the place. But in creative writing class, Mr. Lerned says different. He says the fiction writer stays out of the picture. He says use the little words, but put them together like no one else has ever done. In your own unique way. He says I've got the talent for it, that I should develop it. Maybe this is what I've been looking for."

"You're talking like you're nixing medical school."

"Well, can a doctor really be unique by removing an appendix? Is there really a difference between one tonsillectomy and another?"

"Maybe so, maybe not," Jacob replied, "but there is a difference in the way you deal with patients."

"So you're talking about bedside manner, comforting people, that stuff?"

"Yeah, I guess so. Something like that."

"Maybe you can do those very same things with words. With

words that only you can put together in a certain way. A way that gets into another person's heart slicker than a scalpel."

Jacob was looking at Chipper as if he were a stranger, his eyes all squinted together trying to recollect exactly who this alien golfer was standing before him, swinging a 5-iron back and forth like a weedcutter, chopping away at sacred tee box grass.

After a moment, Jacob said, "We were always going to be partners."

"And we were always going to play Horse," replied Chipper.

"Well...if you do become a writer, maybe you'll put all us guys in a book someday."

"I dunno. I'd rather write stuff that's interesting, like Rod Serling does, with a surprise at the end."

From the red Corvette in the parking lot came the familiar shouts of Peachy: "It's a great fuggin' time to be alive, dammit." He began walking toward the practice tee, arms swinging at chest level like one of those Olympic walkers. "As we speak, gentlemen, two outstanding developments. First, the red dye is at work in my washing machine at home, but that's tomorrow's excitement. Secondly, tonight, the Peach gets rich. For tonight, we go a'hunting. Scorpion hunting."

Forty-nine

The corn was nowhere near an elephant's eye. And it wasn't reaching up to the sky, either. Dead stalks were bent at the waist, their husks with bird-plucked cobs pointing to the ground as if they had tried to slurp some water with their dying gasps. This was last year's crop, never harvested, abandoned, victim of the pests that thrived on drought-afflicted yields.

Wispy, overlapping clouds crossed the full moon, begging a werewolf to jump into view. Fortunately, the wind was blowing hard enough to add a whistle to the crackling cornstalks, helping to drown their crunching footsteps. Peachy led the safari. He held the black light/battery combo under one arm like a football while he stiff-armed the cornstalks out of the way with the other. Chipper was next, followed by Jacob, with L.K. at the rear. The Thunderbird was parked on the dirt road at the edge of the field for a quick getaway.

Chipper wasn't as frightened as he figured he would be. Safety in numbers, he thought, especially when one of those numbers was L.K. Taylor. It was 10:00p.m. Peachy swore you could set your watch by it. After all, Gus relayed the info from Andy who got it from Arth who learned it from Fletch. And Fletch said Tricky Jack, Dylina, and Mal-Mal were eyewitnesses.

They had to crouch to stay below the broken cornstalk level. Peachy spotted the car first. He stopped and turned, cautioning with a shush sign, as if the need for silence weren't self-evident.

Rising barely above the level of the abandoned crop was the roof of Neander T's Carsophagus. The flat roof looked like a black surfboard on cornstalk waves. The scene was uncanny, exactly as Peachy had predicted. And with the car top sighting, their footsteps became amplified, and it sounded as if they were walking on potato chips.

"Move forward during the wind gusts," Chipper whispered to the front man. Peachy nodded in return.

"In-fuggin-credible," said Peachy. "Never doubted it, though. Not for a fuggin' second."

Chipper turned around to see both Jacob and L.K. shaking their heads back and forth, rolling their eyes. But they all moved forward in rhythm with the wind.

As they crept within 20 yards of the car, Chipper thought he could hear voices. No, it was one voice. A girl's. Alternating between soft bliss and torment. Back and forth with the sway of the cornstalks. A coo, then an ouch. A yes, then a no. A purr, then a moan. A go, then a stop.

The leader heard the noises, too. As Peachy turned around to face the others, Chipper expected the classic shit-eating grin to communicate that they were listening to Apache Sue getting her brains rearranged. Instead, Peachy looked briefly at Chipper before his eyes darted away. *Peachy's scared,* he thought.

The cornstalks were as sparse as Slim Harper's new hair transplant, and Chipper realized they could be spotted just as easily as they were spotting the customized fenders that completely covered the rear wheels on the Carsophagus.

"A few more yards, Peachy," Chipper whispered, "then you're on your own."

Peachy nodded without looking back.

Chipper slumped to the ground for a belly crawl, inching forward to a point where he could monitor the car. The man-eater grill with its silver incisors made the car look like a Martian monster ready to devour its human prey, then burp the bones back out again.

Jacob and L.K. scooted up close to him, and the three of them watched Peachy advance toward the clearing around the car. Chipper checked his watch. It was 10:05 p.m.

The alternating sounds from the car were getting louder, and it was hard to tell which noises were 'yes' and which ones were 'no.' More breathless panting now, louder and louder. And for the first time, Chipper could hear Neander T, grunting in cadence like John Henry hammering a spike into a railroad tie.

The narrow windows beneath the chopped top didn't allow detail, but Chipper could make out the long, straight hair of Apache Sue swaying to and fro, with the throbbing tempo inside the car. An eerie glimmer colored her mane as if the full moon were beaming down through a hole in the roof, making it hard to believe her hair was black. She was on top.

Chipper became so engrossed by the rocking Carsophagus that he barely noticed that Peachy had worked his way to the edge of the clearing.

Peachy signaled back with an okay sign. He cowered down only six to eight feet from the back bumper of Neander T's car. Waiting for the arm to emerge.

The panting became gasping. The grunting became shouting. The gasping became shrieking. The shouting became howling. Savage sex at its finest.

The four of them were on the brink of what would become a legendary affair: the shining of the black light onto Neander T's scorpion tattoo. For Peachy, a small fortune and great fame. For Chipper, a badge of courage. He wasn't sure what it meant to Jacob and L.K.

After one final synchronized scream, the night fell silent. All that could be heard was the rustling sound of cornstalks in the wind.

No movement in the Carsophagus. The dark figures had been digested and could not be distinguished. Peachy was perfectly still, ready to sneak into action.

"Do you s'pose he'll ever hang the arm out?" Chipper whispered to the others.

"Dunno."

"He may not even be in the driver's seat. It's his left arm, you know. It's gotta come out that side of the car."

Several minutes passed. Peachy was doing a great job of keeping still, barely visible in the cornstalks. He was dressed in blue jeans, a black long-sleeved shirt, and black high-topped tennis shoes. He was balancing the magic light on one knee, like a sidelined football player with his helmet ready to pop back on.

"It's not going to happen," said Jacob. "Get Peachy's attention and let's get out of here."

Jacob was probably right. It was 10:09. This slight encouragement was enough, and Chipper felt himself waving to Peachy to come on back. But like a cat staring at a canary, there was no way to get Peachy's attention. He was simply too close to registry in the El Viento Teenage Hall of Fame.

Chipper motioned harder, careful not to give away their roost. Peachy was a statue. No, there was motion now. Peachy was moving.

But he wasn't moving back toward them. He was moving slowly into the clearing, bent forward, the black light in front at waist level, held with both hands.

"Oh, my god, look," Jacob said.

Chipper was so focused on Peachy that he did not see the arm emerge. But the massive hunk of flesh was resting on the side of the car. It was too dark to see the scorpion, but it was the correct arm. The left arm. The jumbo left arm.

Peachy crept to the back bumper. Chipper felt himself moving his feet up underneath in a squat position, ready to run. He knew he would have to force himself to look at the arm long enough to see if the scorpion lit. Hopefully, Peachy would flash the light on and off in a jiffy, and Neander T would never know what happened. They would all slip quietly away.

Peachy stepped out from behind the bumper, aimed and fired. The purplish glow of the black light bulb permeated the clearing, strikingly evident on Peachy's white shirt buttons, white stitching in his jeans, and the white trim of his hightops, all highlighting and betraying his presence with radiant purple. Chipper squinted at the giant arm, but Peachy was blocking the way.

"Do you see it?" he asked.

"No, Peachy's in the way."

"I can't see, either."

"He needs to get the hell outta there."

"Beat it on back, Peachy," L.K. whispered.

Peachy looked down at the light and started fumbling with the battery. His elbows flew up like chicken wings, as he became increasingly frantic. He couldn't turn the switch off! He started backing away, shaking the light into submission, his every move advertised in purple neon wherever he was wearing even a pinch of white.

Neander T's car door opened. Peachy threw the light, still shining, into the clearing and charged into the cornfield to join his buddies in flight.

As Chipper gave a final glance over his shoulder, he saw Neander T, then the girlfriend, pile out of the driver's door. Something was wrong. Dreadfully wrong.

He kept staring. The girl's glowing, long hair was fluorescent violet. She was clutching a matching violet dress, or a slip, to cover her naked body.

"Who the fuck's out there?" bellowed the monster. His voice reverberated in the night air. "I said 'who the fuck's out there?'"

Chipper felt L.K.'s large hand grab his arm and tug. "C'mon Chipper, let's get outta here."

But the 10,000-volt electrical jolt was followed by a calm inside. A deadly calm. The peaceful calm that one must feel when there is that final resolve to the reality of impending death.

More urgently this time, L.K. said, "Let's go."

Chipper no longer felt connected to his body, and his vision constricted into a long dark tunnel, as if looking through a telescope backward.

"Let's go," said multiple voices tugging now on both his arms.

He broke away and ran in slow motion down the tunnel to the girl with the violet hair who was standing at the end, looking so wide-eyed and innocent. From somewhere, he heard her saying, "If you say you love me, then everything is okay after that."

The ultraviolet glow with its electromagnetic radiation enveloped him in a molasses that made every step a struggle. One goal: the girl at the end of the tunnel, the girl with the violet hair and the violet dress. The rest of the world had dissolved into night, and it was the night that lined the walls of the tunnel.

Even though the girl with the violet hair didn't seem to be getting any closer as he moved toward her, he knew she could hear him speak, "Tomorrow night. Ten o'clock sharp. We were supposed to blend our souls together, you said, so that our spirits could merge. We would become one with infinity. We would occupy our destiny, you said. That's what you said." He reached to touch Gail's neck, but felt himself being lifted in the air, then dashed against the open door of the car, slamming it shut.

He looked up from the ground to Gail's lifeless eyes. Her lips didn't part. She didn't say a word. Maybe her eyes were trying to say something, but he couldn't tell for sure.

He felt himself being lifted up again, this time smashing across the hood of the car. It was painless.

As he rose to his feet, Gail was slipping the violet dress over her violet hair. Then she moved to his side and whispered, "I love you, Kyle. You've come to save me. I knew you would. I always knew you would."

He backed away from her and felt himself being lifted to the sky, then tossed over the hood of the car onto the ground beside the black light. He knew Neander T was swarming all around him, but he could neither see him nor hear him. He could only see the bewitching image of Gail Perdue, exposed, shining like a purple beacon, her formerly white hair and her oh-so white dress altered in hue by the mystical ultraviolet light.

He was choking. He knew it must be Neander T's giant hand around his throat. The scorpion was about to sting. Then he heard the words, "Apologize to her, or you die, motherfucker. Apologize to her."

He nodded 'yes,' and the near-fatal clutch eased from his throat. He fell to his knees, then a kick forced him onto his back. He saw the black light beside him again, along with a solitary rock, half-hidden in the trampled cornstalks.

"I'm sorry, Gail," he said. "I'm sorry..." He sat up and secured his feet beneath him in a crouch. "I'm truly sorry...that you're a whore."

Chipper grabbed the black light, smashed it on the rock and prepared to jab the broken edges into Neander T's face. The broken edges would kill, claimed Peachy. But a blow to Chipper's jaw sent him stumbling back into the cornstalks. He couldn't hang onto his only weapon as the busted light fell from his hands. The purple cast was gone. Death was imminent and he was prepared. He was drowning again and the icy water that filled his lungs was surprisingly welcome as it turned warm.

Gail was standing by the car, her hair white again, as well as her dress. She did not move. She did not plead with the large, dark blob that approached him now for the kill.

He looked up to see Neander T's brutish face move close, both arms raised in the air, when suddenly the beast was pulled back, a python arm wrapped around its neck. It was L.K. The same L.K. who had fought only once before, against L.D. Washington in the renowned lettermen's initiation.

Neander T's arms and legs flailed in all directions to pull L.K. off, but the coils around his neck only tightened. L.K. took his free hand and bent Neander T's head down so that his chin smushed into L.K.'s squeezing arm. The flailing slowed within 30 seconds, then Neander T slumped to the ground.

"The sleeper hold," L.K. said.

The tunnel was gone, and Chipper could see that Jacob and Peachy were standing beside L.K. Gail was inside the car, tinted windows rolled up. Chipper stood up, nursing his jaw with the flat of his hand. He could open and close his mouth and his teeth still fit together. Every square inch of his body ached as he moved toward the others.

Neander T twitched on the ground a while, then slowly started to rouse. A tiny stream of blood trickled from one nostril as he raised himself to a sitting position.

L.K. moved down face-to-face with the previously invincible Neander T. "Don't ever...ever...bother my friends again. Understand?"

The creep nodded. The biggest toad in the pond was now a tadpole.

Chipper left the clearing for his Thunderbird, never looking back at the site of the carnage. Never looking back at the girl in the car.

As the foursome walked abreast through the cornstalks, it occurred to Chipper that the predictability of the scene had been uncanny. Too much of a fluke. The scouting reports were perfectly accurate, down to the exact minute. Every Monday night at 10:00 o'clock, they said. Yet, he and Gail had been meeting every Tuesday night at the same time. Were there others? Was there one for every night of the week? And how could Tricky Jack, Dylina, and Mal-Mal have witnessed the Monday night ritual of Neander T without realizing it was Gail, not Apache Sue. And if the eyewitnesses knew it was Gail every Monday night, surely the rest of the gossip brigade knew. His teammates knew. Everyone in the world knew, except him. What a fool. What a fool, indeed. And was this whole stunt tonight just a way for the team to beat some sense into him?

"I have a question for you, Peachy," he said.

"Shoot."

"Did you guys know it was Gail that Neander T was bangin' out here on Monday nights?"

"Hell, no, man. We had no idea. I'm sorry you had to see that."

Chipper looked at the other two who were staring at Peachy as he talked. When his eyes met theirs, they both looked down to the ground.

"So, did you mutherfuggers see the scorpion light up?" asked Peachy.

"No," said Jacob. "You were blocking our view."

"I couldn't see either," L.K. said.

Chipper was still too numb to join in.

"Well, shit. If I don't have witnesses, then I don't collect the big bucks. Oh, well, I did pretty damn good anyway, what with 250 bucks. I pulled the entire sumbitch off, just like I said I would."

"Two hundred thirty bucks. Remember, you had to pay the voodoo queen 20."

"All right, 230 then."

"So, did it?"

"Did it what?"

"Did it light up? Did the scorpion glow?"

"I'll never tell, assholes. I will never tell."

Fifty

With his arm braced against the concrete wall of the viaduct, Chipper stared into the murky green water oozing around the tips of his loafers. The scene of his near-fatal trespass was different than he remembered. Twelve years had passed since his family moved away from this side of town. The crawdad hole seemed smaller now.

Blades of tall grass and reeds encroached the water's edge where the pool stretched beneath the railroad tracks. With this new vegetation obscuring the view, not to mention the foamy scum on the surface, Chipper could not imagine anyone looking for crawdads here.

The embankment to the railroad track above was steep. The weeds and wildflowers that held the dirt in place didn't seem to mind that the water pooled a good distance away at the viaduct, and the cactus plants that grew like plates on end didn't care if it ever rained. Chipper noticed a closed flower bud on one of the larger cactus plants. He heard somewhere, probably from Jacob, that the petals of the cactus flower open only at night. Every night at the same time. He had no reason to doubt his friend's word.

And when did Gail start opening only at night? Every night at the same time. When did she sell her soul? Or did she have a choice? He wouldn't even let himself think about her scuzzy father, or the rumors. Had she envisioned Chipper as the ideal, but still a trophy she could never enjoy?

From his wheat jeans pocket he pulled Gail's fourth grade photo. Why give it a last look? The image would be burned in his mind forever. Nothing he could do today would make it disappear. But he couldn't help himself. Flipping it over, he looked at the large dark eyes of the fallen angel. Bedroom eyes, everyone said, even when she was little. He remembered asking his mother what 'bedroom eyes' meant, and he could still recall that the muddled answer made no sense. The glow about her face was gone.

Gripping the photo between both thumbs and forefingers, he ripped it in half, severing the bedroom eyes from her thick, shiny lips. He carefully put the two pieces together and ripped again. And a third time. And a fourth. He tossed the pieces into the water where they floated like 16 white lily pads.

Using a fork-tipped branch he found on the ground, he swirled the water in a circle, creating a whirlpool to suck the torn pieces below the surface. Some of the pieces spun out of the edge of the vortex, but he could see one bedroom eye staring at him as it sank to the bottom.

He slapped the branch against the escaping pieces until all of them were drowned. It was all so clear now. Why was he unable to see it before? How did everyone know except him? What a fool.

Walking the hundred yards back to his car parked in front of his old house, Chipper thought only of Amy. Was his plan to win her back working at this very moment? Rumor held that she and Drew Masters were an item now, prom and all. It made him sick to think about it. What a buffoon he had been.

His plan was corny, but he had to do something. State tournament was only four days away, and he wouldn't play well if he was brain-wrecked.

Borrowing on Amy's favorite song, "I Loved You a Thousand Times," Chipper had found her name in his logbook 412 times, recorded faithfully over the years. He had driven to the city where an office supply store was allowing customers to use their so-called photocopier—a new machine that would make copies just by placing a book on the glass. At ten cents a copy, he left with a heavy manuscript and an empty wallet. He then wrote I Love You on 588 pieces of typing paper and submitted the 1,000-page apology to Amy's doorstep the night before.

He felt his Thunderbird blocking the sun as he flew to her house for the response. He knew her heart had to be softening by the minute. The verdict would be: Drew Masters out, Chipper DeHart up and in from the fringe. Like always.

"If you think dumping this box of trash at my door is going to change what's happened this year...well, Chipper...you've underestimated me."

"Hold it, Amy, don't shut the door just yet. Let me come in for a minute."

"One minute is all," she said, opening the threshold. "As soon as Mom gets home, we're leaving for the city to get my prom dress."

Ouch.

"Let me explain..."

"You can't explain, Chipper. That's the problem. You can't explain because you don't understand it yourself."

"All I know is she made me feel crummy about myself, and you always made me feel good."

"Well, even a lab rat can find the cheese. Congratulations, you finally made it to my door."

"Give me a break, Amy. I was damn near killed."

She sighed and shook her head as if to say, 'You poor, pathetic imbecile.'

"So I heard."

"Give me a chance is all I ask."

"Yeah, like my mom gave my dad once? He finally left her...some three or four lovers later."

"People can change. I can change."

"It's not that easy. It takes more than just changing your name from Jay to Jacob. It takes commitment."

"I know."

"No, you don't. Just because a housefly escapes a Venus flytrap doesn't mean it won't get caught by the next hungry trap. There are over a thousand Venus flytraps out there, Chipper...there are more than a thousand Gails. A thousand 'I love yous' won't last a lifetime. You can't put a number on it, commitment is infinite."

Chipper was mildly annoyed at the biologic reference from his pre-med ex-girlfriend, but he shook off the fact that he had just been demoted from rat to housefly.

"Think of me more like a dog," he said.

"What?" She started to laugh, but quickly covered her mouth with her fingertips, not wishing to show even a speck of pleasure.

"A dog. A few whacks on the rear and a dog finally learns. He changes. I've been a real dog this year and I've taken my whacks."

She sighed and shook her head again, this time to say, 'You poor, pathetic bozo.' He could sense he was making headway—from imbecile to bozo.

"Commitment isn't always fun, Chipper. It means sacrificing, saying no to things. It's a decision in your head more than your heart. You're a dog all right. Your heart drags you around on a leash."

Maybe he wasn't making headway after all. He flashed to the time

Kelly told him he played on a golf course without flagsticks, a charge he never understood.

"I don't get it, Amy. I need you. I love..."

"Don't say it. Not unless you know what you're saying. Let me tell you something: you don't know what you need. You'll only learn what you really need *after* you make a commitment, not before."

Chipper was stymied by the riddle. He wasn't going to get it up-and-in from the fringe as he had hoped.

"You've got me all confused, Amy. I don't know what to say."

"Then say nothing. Try it; it works sometimes."

He opened his mouth once more to tell her he loved her, but she shook her head 'no.'

"I know what you're about to say to me," Amy said. "I know you better than you know yourself. You like to believe in things you can't see. Well, I'm the type that makes you see those things. So you've gotta ask yourself if you're happier seeing or believing."

Amy's mother pulled in the driveway, putting an effective end to his efforts.

"You'd better go, Chipper. Good luck at State on Friday."

He backed away from her, nursing the machine gun wounds in his chest. But he thought he could see a peculiar glistening in her eyes. More importantly, he convinced himself that her pupils were dilated, the universal sign of pleasure in the world of biology. According to Peachy's old man, that is.

Seeing or believing? What was she saying?

And with his hasty retreat, a vision began to dog him: a vast rolling green, a putting surface—but without a cup. No target, no flagstick, no purpose. Try as he might, he couldn't see the flagstick.

Fifty-one

Prevailing opinion held that there were only two colors for jeans in the world—blue and wheat. The infiltration of wheat began in the late '50s with Levi's 501s, forever dividing the blue world of adolescent males. Sure, there were off-brands that made a black jean. But any self-respecting Levi devotee would swear allegiance only to blue or wheat. As far as Chipper knew, this was a worldwide phenomenon. Only Mr. Greenjeans had violated this rich tradition, green jeans demonstrating the radical nature of any color besides blue and wheat. After all, kids had grown up watching *Captain Kangaroo* in black and white, so the mere mention of the word 'green' was sufficient to paint the character as an oddball. Yes, there was a profound sense of comfort in the world of blue and wheat. No surprises. No change. No fear. No disruption in the harmony that pervaded the hallowed halls of secondary schools everywhere. No disruptions in the status quo.

That is, until Wednesday, May 3, 1967.

When Chipper stepped into the basement utility room, next to the infamous poker room, Peachy and Gus were huddled at the door of the electric dryer like Dr. Frankenstein and Igor waiting for the Creature to come alive.

"How do they look?" Chipper asked, interrupting their preoccupation.

"Fuggin' great," said Peachy, pushing his glasses back onto the bridge of his nose as he stood straight. "They turned out damn fuggin' great."

"Damn straight," echoed Gus, flashing his silver front tooth.

"Let's see 'em. Are they dry?" Chipper looked at the three empty boxes of RIT dye lying on top of the washing machine.

"Just about." Peachy popped open the door, and the humming of the dryer stopped. He reached in with his left hand and pulled a giant wad of bright red clothes from the opening. "Presto, chango...behold! From wheat to red, I give you the uniforms of the El Viento golf team."

Chipper couldn't believe it. The tangled mass of red jeans wasn't just red. We're talking really, really red. Not a trace of burgundy. No rust. No maroon. All red. American flag red. Scarlet red.

"Wow. I...I didn't expect them to be that...red."

"That red shittin' dye really works, doesn't it?"

"Cool," said Gus.

"I'll say," Chipper said. "Have Jacob and L.K. been by to pick theirs up?"

"Naw, all five pairs are right here," Peachy said as he began unwinding the twisted red legs. Carol brought Buster's wheats by. She says he's gonna come to the tournament, even if he has to cut class."

"Good."

"Carol said they're taking off the night of graduation. Buster's old man probably won't be out of the hospital even then."

"They should get away without any trouble. Where are they going?"

"They don't know yet."

"Uh, Peachy, I think the caddies ought to get to wear red jeans," pleaded Gus.

"Hey, I told you twice already, punk. Only the A-team, only the players."

Gus looked at Chipper as if appealing to a higher authority.

"Yeah, Peachy's right. Only the players. Next year, Gus."

"Which ones are yours?" asked Peachy.

"The 30 by 34s."

Peachy checked the rawhide label for the numbers, then handed Chipper his once-wheat jeans.

"I can't get over how well the dye worked."

"Me, either."

He held the ruby trousers up to his waist. "These are gonna blow everyone away."

"Yeah," Peachy said, "imagine trying to sink a putt when you're playing with some asshole wearing red jeans."

"I saw red trousers in a pro shop in the city once. You know, in the old geezer section. And I've seen red Bermudas. But I've never, ever, seen red pants on the golf course."

"Or anywhere else."

"This is gonna be like...like making history," Chipper said.

"Glad we went with the long pants."

"Me, too. L.K. never wears anything but long pants because of his legs. And we gotta be dressed alike."

"Somebody mention my name?" L.K. asked as he joined them in the utility room. "Jiminy shit, are those bastards ever *red.*"

"Oh, my gosh," said Jacob, two steps behind L.K.

"Step right up, gentlemen," Peachy said. "Get your uniforms, right here."

"Gird your loins with scarlet," added Chipper. "Then on to the point most high."

L.K. and Jacob claimed their jeans and held them to their waists. L.K. suddenly dropped trou. The others followed. In seconds, they wiggled into their red britches and stood in a circle around Gus. He spun around to look at each of them. "Jeeze, do you guys ever look cool."

"When you're cutting edge, there's a fine line between being cool and a fool," Chipper said.

"Doesn't matter," said L.K. "It feels good to be in a uniform again."

"Maybe we ought to check with Mr. Dresden, or the school, before we do this," said Jacob.

"Are you shittin' me?" Peachy said. "We ain't checkin' with no one."

"I agree," said Chipper. "Let's just do it."

"This is so cool," repeated Gus.

"As a matter of fact," said Peachy, "I don't think we should wait until the tournament on Friday. I say we wear these sumbitches to school tomorrow."

The group fell silent. Like tossing a basketball in the air to begin the game, it's sometimes difficult to follow the tip-off as the ball changes hands from player to player. So it was with Peachy's suggestion. Who had control of the ball? Exchanged looks were followed by a scramble of words: 'We'll get killed,' 'cool,' 'laughingstock,' 'studly,' 'hoods will punch our lights out,' 'L.K.'s the only safe one,' 'can't stick by L.K. all day,' 'we have different classes first hour,' 'get my butt whipped,' 'girls gonna laugh at us,' 'football players wear their jerseys on game days,' 'football players will punch our lights out,' 'people will be talkin' about this forever,' 'gird your loins.'

As the ball bounced to a stop, the consensus was: "Let's do it!"

Fifty-two

Chipper was living that recurring nightmare where you've forgotten your clothes and you're sitting at your desk at school in your underwear. Only this was worse.

Sixteen minutes after the hour. Eternity. Stuck forever in Philosophy 1. Eyes were burning holes in him from all directions. Classmates, all of them, were staring. When Chipper caught one set of eyes, they would dart away. He'd catch another, and they'd do the same. And by the time he got back to the first set of eyes, they would be staring again.

Mrs. Kipling was making every effort to keep the class under control. She liked Chipper, stating privately that he had a knack for philosophy. This morning, it was almost as if she were calling on the students that were staring the hardest at his red jeans. Calling off the dogs, so to speak.

"Peggy, can you tell the class who is most identified with the origins of structuralism?"

Peggy Ann Wintermute was caught in a frozen stare at Chipper's red jeans.

"Peggy?"

"Yes, ma'am?"

"Did you hear the question?"

"Uh, yes, ma'am. His name was Saucer, or something like that."

"Saussure, yes, the linguist. He observed the component parts of systems are binarily organized..."

Peggy returned her stare to the red jeans as Mrs. Kipling continued her discourse.

Chipper could remember the good old days when these people seated around him were his chums. They were strangers now, gawking at a zoo animal. It was only 16 minutes and 21 seconds after the hour.

"...but it was many, many years before structuralism caught on with the intellectuals. Can anyone give me the name of the anthropologist who brought structuralism into the limelight? Belinda?"

Belinda Lou Patterson was staring at Chipper's red jeans.

"Belinda Lou? Did you hear the question?"

Belinda, startled from her trance, turned to Mrs. Kipling while straightening her bangs. "Uh, no, ma'am. I mean, I don't know. Even if I heard the question, I don't know. This stuff is all so...I mean, is it really relevant?"

"Why, most certainly. Is there any greater love than the love of knowledge, the love of understanding, the great love of wisdom?"

Brian Templeton, sitting behind Chipper, whispered, "I hear Candy Warren is a great love. She puts out love for everyone."

Chuckles were interrupted by Mrs. Kipling's biting authority. "All right, Brian, you seem intent on speaking. Why don't you answer the question? Who brought structuralism into the limelight?"

"Uh...I dunno, Mrs. Kipling."

The teacher straightened her shoulders, holding her lecture notes in the crook of her left arm, using her free hand for heartfelt gesturing. "The answer is Claude Lévi-Strauss."

The entire room stared at Chipper's jeans. His embarrassment was nearly fatal. *Whose idea was this, anyway, to wear the jeans to school?* The jeans were meant for climbing to the point most high. It was already a stretch to expand their scope to the golf course. Now, here he was, sitting in a sea of future philosophy-haters and the discussion had suddenly taken a turn to Lévi-Strauss, of all things.

"Mrs. Kipling?"

"Yes, Brian?"

"Was, by chance, this Lévi-Strauss a...Communist?"

"Well, Brian, some people believe his ideas had Marxist overtones. Why do you ask?"

"I just wondered if Lévi was *red!*"

The class broke into riotous laughter. Chipper tried to laugh along, but inside he was dying. Who would save him from this moment? How silly to have been worried about thug attacks. He had seriously underestimated the torture of sitting in a classroom while your ex-friends laugh at you in your underwear.

It was 42 minutes after the hour when Miss Dotterly, the principal's secretary, entered the room and handed Mrs. Kipling a note. The laughter ended.

Mrs. Kipling looked up from the note and nodded in Chipper's direction. It could have been anybody she was nodding to, but Chipper knew it was for him.

"Chipper, it seems you're wanted in Mr. Horton's office."

It was hard to believe a call to the principal's office was so welcome, but Chipper jumped from his seat. Hoots and catcalls were muffled beneath cupped hands as he made his exit. The hallway was refreshing. He didn't think he could take it anymore in the classroom. Maybe his teammates felt the same way. They should all go home and change after first hour.

As a student leader, Chipper was used to being called to the principal's office. After all, there were important affairs of state to be addressed. There would be his speech at the Junior-Senior Banquet the week before the prom. He would also have to make some introductory comments on Senior Awards Night. And, of course, he'd be accepting many of the awards himself.

"Suspended?!"

He heard the cry as he passed through the reception area and into Mr. Horton's office. It was Peachy, yelling in protest.

Seated next to Peachy, in a bright red row of six legs, were L.K. and Jacob. An empty seat awaited Chipper.

"Chipper, come sit down," Mr. Horton said. He had a deep voice that made your insides squirm even when he said 'Good morning.' "I was informing your cohorts here that the four of you are suspended for two days. For disrupting classes. This stunt is outrageous. Peachy, I'd expect this from *you.* But Jacob, L.K., Chipper...*what* were you boys thinking?"

Chipper was stunned. How could this happen? A fine line between cool and a fool, he remembered. What were they thinking, indeed? He should apologize, accept full blame, and throw himself at the mercy of the court. After all, this could jeopardize his selection as outstanding senior boy.

"We're sor..." he began.

"Mr. Horton," L.K. interrupted, "these are our uniforms."

"What?" Mr. Horton turned to L.K., as did the teammates.

"I said 'these are our uniforms.' The golf team. And we're proud to wear them. We're contenders, Mr. Horton. We're going for the state title."

Mr. Horton adjusted his glasses and scanned the full length of L.K., all six-foot-four-inches. L.K., the greatest El Viento athlete that never was, sitting there in red jeans, in the principal's office, accompanied by three candy ass golfers, also adorned in school colors. Mr.

Horton had been a star athlete at El Viento a hundred years ago, so Chipper figured he might listen to L.K.

"The football players wear their jerseys on game days," L.K. continued, "and it's not considered disruptive. This is what we plan to wear on game day at the state tournament. Only instead of these dress shirts, we'll wear white polo shirts. Like I said, it's our uniform. And we plan to bring a trophy back."

"Well, boys, I see your position on this, I really do."

Mr. Horton was softening.

"But in spite of our enthusiasm, some degree of discipline..."

Still softening.

"...other students, not involved in athletics who are trying to learn..."

Mr. Horton was beginning to sound more like he was convincing himself rather than the golf team. He rambled on and on.

"...respecting each other, without interference..."

First hour was about to end. Chipper began watching the second hand on the clock behind Mr. Horton tick away. The automatic bell system would ring at 10 till the hour. Thirty seconds away from his final verdict.

"So the suspension has to stand," he concluded. "I'm not going to enter it into your official records, but that's the way it has to be. There were too many complaints, too quickly. I have to answer to a lot of people."

"Thank you, sir," said L.K., standing to shake hands with the principal. The others followed suit. As they filed out, Mr. Horton called after them, "Good luck at the tournament. Get in a little practice this afternoon." Then he winked.

Some victories are hard to define as such, but Chipper felt good inside.

The bell rang, and classrooms emptied into the halls as the four uniformed athletes emerged from the principal's office. The initial response was mixed. Since their early morning entry was sneaky, this was the first time the entire student body got to gander at once. Thank goodness for L.K. The comments would have been brutal without him. Even so, Chipper could hear a few "faggots," "pricks," "jerkoffs" murmured as they pushed their way down the hall.

Then, the word "suspended" spilled into the crowd and spread like a grass fire ahead of them, parting the sea of humanity and allowing easy passage of the foursome down the hall, marching side-by-side. The cursing and blasphemy ended, a few hurrahs and cheers began, accompanied by nests of applause. Finally, a rousing ovation. Standing, of course. Ah, the recognition that accompanies punished defiance.

Only 10 yards from the outside doors, Chipper's heart sank. Drew Masters had a smiling Amy pinned against the wall. His extended arm, locked at the elbow, was braced against her locker and prevented him from falling into her embrace. One buckle of the elbow, and he'd be there. She was looking into Drew's eyes, standing with one knee bent so that her foot rested against her locker. The spreading applause engulfed the so-called couple.

Amy dropped her foot to the ground and straightened herself upon spotting Chipper. Her jaw fell so far open at the sight of the red jeans that Chipper could see her chewing gum against her molars. She froze. Chipper nodded, enjoying the bravos, the cheers, the glory of the moment. And there stood that boring Drew Masters in his wheat jeans.

He could see with peripheral vision that Drew Masters was plopping both hands on his hips. Chipper was passing Amy now, parade left, and he turned his head to smile, waiting for a signal. Was there any sign of hope? Some little gesture that all was well?

Amy rolled her eyes and looked away.

Fifty-three

In years past, Mr. Ashbrook would pace in front of the boys as he spoke. Today, he stood with his feet nailed to the ground, underneath the giant split elm on the first tee box. His gnarled fingers cradled the Sherlock Holmes pipe as he let smoke escape through a wry smile.

"Of all the crazy shenanigans, you fellas take the cake. Just when I thought I'd seen it all. Where'd you get those red britches anyway?"

"It was Chipper's idea," said Peachy.

"Yeah, but Peachy dyed them," Chipper quickly replied. "They used to be wheat-colored jeans." He was unsure as to why he needed to toss blame.

"And how long is the suspension?" asked the old man.

"Two days," said Chipper. "I think Mr. Horton forgot we're out of school Friday for the tournament anyway. So it's really just today."

Mr. Ashbrook scooted the pipe stem to the corner of his mouth where he seemed to be gnawing at the bit.

The boys stood in their traditional semicircle before him, directly beneath the repaired logging chain. Each of them held a driver, preparing for 18 holes on this day of suspension. Each of their loins was still girded in scarlet.

"Did Buster get a pair of those things?"

"Yes, sir," Chipper said, "but he didn't wear them. He told me he'd wear them tomorrow, though. He's gonna cut class and go to the tournament."

"One of you could sure use him as a caddie. Let him judge your distances for you. But I don't think we can ask him to do that."

"No, sir. It's...well, kinda beneath him. And you know how the B-team counts on caddying for us. It's already decided who caddies for who."

Mr. Ashbrook puffed a few seconds before he spoke. "I suppose so. I guess you're right. Well, anyway, three weeks ago if you told me Buster was going to be out with a broken hand, I'd said there's no way in tarnation to win State. But after seeing Peachy come around, I hope to eat my words."

Peachy grinned and nodded to the others that he deserved the tribute.

"Peachy, I've combed the rule books, and there's nothing that says you can't play with that thingamajig strapped to your waist. I don't know how it's working, but go ahead and do it, son."

Peachy adjusted his earpiece then saluted Mr. Ashbrook like a buck private who just passed inspection.

"If you can shoot in the 70s, son, even if it's 79 for three rounds, there's a chance, a wee chance. Jacob, you'll need to hug par like a bear hugs a honeycomb. You, too, L.K. Mid-seventies for you, Chipper, and you'll need the driver. That course is too long for you to backslide to your 2-wood."

Chipper looked at Peachy who was pretending undying devotion to Mr. Ashbrook, clinging to every word with phony enthusiasm. How long would the magic of the music hold? Surely, a song for ballerinas couldn't soothe the savage shank forever. Chipper knew it, the others knew it, but fortunately, Peachy believed in it. And for the first time as a golfer, Peachy believed in himself.

"By the way, Chipper, I've come to appreciate this whole new perspective on your game," Mr. Ashbrook said, interrupting roving thoughts.

"Sir?"

"This business about your never shooting even par."

"What?"

"You didn't hear me?"

"Uh, no, sir. Sorry."

The master frowned at his pupil.

"I said I've reviewed your score cards, and this business about you blowing the last few holes to ruin par rounds simply isn't the case."

"It's not? It always seems like I blow it at the end when I'm playing well."

"Sometimes you do. But just as often you blow it early, make a nice comeback, but still shy of par. It's almost as if you work to avoid shooting even. I've not seen a golfer with your talent never shoot an even par round."

It was more like predestination, Chipper decided. A predestined rut. An antipar rut where he couldn't even fantasize himself playing as well as Jacob. He was a little embarrassed that such a disclosure was made in front of the others, and he felt himself wishing for a Norelco recorder that would play ballerina music.

"Shitfire. What the hell do we have here? Four pissants dressed in fairy costumes?"

Sarge was decked out in a pansy-purple Banlon shirt, yellow shorts and blue socks. *An odd one to comment on fashion,* Chipper thought.

"Ethan, are you still wasting your time with these punks? They can't win shit with Buster Nelson's arm broke."

As usual, Sarge was followed by his squad, middle-aged, middle-bulged, and cutting in front of the team. Sarge's lower lip swelled with tobacco. He let a glob fly with a *ptooey* that landed at Peachy's feet. "I hear you're pretty hot shit, Waterman. Lately, that is. I sure hope you're not hacking away again before sundown."

"Hey, Sarge," countered Peachy. "I'll still—" L.K.'s hand covered Peachy's mouth.

"Gentlemen, gentlemen," said Mr. Ashbrook. "Sarge, you and your boys go ahead and tee off. We'll wait."

The old man turned to the boys and tried to relight his pipe. When he failed to get the embers glowing, he lifted the pipe from his lips and held it waist level in his palm, arm bent at the elbow.

"I told you fellows once upon a time that some men are jealous... jealous of your youth." Mr. Ashbrook moved his sunken blue eyes through the semicircle, one-by-one, making sure each of them was listening.

"They're fighting pot-bellies and balding heads," he continued, "and they're losing. They're getting older like folks have done since Adam and Eve. And they don't seem to know what's in store for them. At least they don't act like it. In another 20 or 30 years, they'll barely be able to get dressed because their joints will hurt so much. They'll be scared to go to public places for fear of catching a cold that might turn into double pneumonia. They won't be able to pee more than a dribble, and their kids will take their automobiles from them, saying they're a danger to the public. When you fellas wanna get in touch with each other, you only have to pick up the phone and put your finger in the dial. But when I wanna talk to one of my boyhood chums, I have to offer up a prayer and hope there's a heaven.

"My young men, this is no fairy tale. No one lives happily ever after. It's tough near the end, and Sarge's gang will soon be longing for the days when their only worry was their bellies growing over their belts, and why in tarnation their hair bothered turning gray before it fell out.

"Did you fellas ever notice how old folks tend to be in two corners? Those that are sweet and kind, and those that are mean and cantankerous? Not many in between."

It was a rhetorical question, but Chipper felt his head nodding up and down.

"Well, somewhere along the line, you make your choice. The dreams you have as kids don't just fade as time goes by—they'll be pounded, stomped, crushed, chewed up and spit out. And you've gotta choose as to how you're going to react.

"And as I stand here today, running off at the mouth, you think it's not going to happen to you. Growing old, I mean. But it is. And when you get to be Sarge's age, and your stomach is starting to balloon out, don't you fellas go and get mean and persnickety. And when you get my age don't go and get bitter. You practice getting in the groove right now, being grateful. That way, when the tough times hit, you can thank the Almighty that He gave you the luxury of these years with your head full of hair, your back straight, and your bellies flat."

Chipper knew he was hearing something called wisdom, but Mr. Ashbrook was right when he said it was hard to believe it would happen to them. He couldn't picture the team as old men, or even middle-aged. He scanned the semicircle, noting the white polo shirts tucked neatly into scarlet jeans. Even Peachy, with his marshmallow body, was smooth at the beltline. Their bellies were absolutely, unequivocally flat. And surely, flat they would always be.

Fifty-four

First in line, Chipper grabbed the side rails of the ladder and put one foot on the bottom rung. He was surprised that the metal ladder felt so cool on this warm spring night, less than 12 hours before tee-off. Thank goodness there was no blowing wind to add greater hazard.

"Gird the loins with scarlet blood, then you will rise to the point most high," he repeated, as if anyone needed to hear Jenniquita's words for the umpteenth time.

"Don't look down," warned Peachy. "It'll make you fall."

"Thanks for the encouragement."

The grain elevators looked like sticks of giant dynamite standing on end. The first challenge had been how to carry their chosen clubs up the 10-story ladder that was attached to the outside of the concrete silo. Sliding the club shaft down a leg of their red jeans didn't work because then they couldn't bend their knees. Holding the club in one hand didn't work because of the insecurity in grabbing the side rail. Finally, Jacob figured out to take off their belts and each guy slide his club through the back belt loops. They left their belts in a pile at the base of the ladder.

Chipper took about 20 steps up the ladder before he paused. He didn't look down.

"Here I come," he heard Jacob say below.

After 20 more steps, he paused again. Even though there was no metal cage around the ladder like the one at the water tower, he felt reasonably calm.

"I'm starting up," yelled L.K.

Chipper was worried about the strength in L.K.'s calves, but L.K. didn't seem to be bothered. The mission continued.

Halfway up the ladder, Chipper hesitated. Peachy should have hollered by now. Maybe he had wised up and was going to leave the tape recorder on the ground.

Chipper couldn't resist; he had to look down. Partly to see what Peachy was doing, partly because he was warned not to. He snuck a test glance at first. Then he turned over his shoulder again and looked back to planet Earth.

L.K. and Jacob were almost up to his step, but Peachy looked like a little red ant on the ground. His tiny arms grabbed the side rails. "I'm coming, you mutherfuggers." Everything was A-okay.

Looking west, Chipper realized he was already higher than the cement company on the other side of the railroad tracks. He stared down at the giant piles of gravel and sand where they had played as kids. The mountains looked like molehills. He felt his head start to swirl, so he decided not to look down again.

He climbed the rest of the way without stopping. The exit from the ladder to the top of the silo was easy, but he heard strange, heavy breathing in the quiet night air that turned out to be his own.

He was joined in short order by L.K. and Jacob. "That wasn't so hard," said Jacob, though his eyes seemed to be wider than usual.

"How're your legs, L.K.?"

"They did fine. No trouble at all."

Chipper looked over the edge of the ladder and saw that Peachy was barely halfway. A mumbling arose from below.

"Mutherfuggin sonuvabitch, mutherfuggin sonuvabitch."

Peachy's chant was in rhythm with each step on the ladder. After 50 more rounds of 'mutherfuggin sonuvabitch', Peachy joined the others on the flat asphalt surface. "If you want my opinion," he said, "I say we stop here." He was huffing and puffing, adjusting the shoulder strap of his tape recorder.

Chipper turned to face, for the first time, the real challenge. Just like Fletch, Tricky Jack, Mal-Mal and other ancient explorers had described. The ledge. A ledge like the one in that old black and white movie *Lost Horizon* where they had to pass one at a time to make it to Shangri-La.

A one-story house, or workshop, or office, or something, sat on top of the double row of silos, almost occupying the entire roof. There was plenty of space on the east and west sides of the structure, but it was flush on the north, while set back 18 inches on the south. To get from the west to the east side, during these illicit after-hours, you had to cross the ledge. It was about 18 inches wide, 15 feet long, and it passed in front of windows that looked one way into the structure, the other way to certain death.

"We don't need to go any higher," said Peachy. "Let's hit these sumbitches right here." He started to reach for the golf balls in his pocket. Each member of the foursome was carrying six—two shots per man per round.

"We gotta keep going, Peachy," Chipper said. A firm tone sometimes worked on Peachy. Sometimes it backfired. "If we stop here, we're not as high as the water tower. Look." He pointed south to El Viento's water tower, the favorite Mount Everest for schoolboys. Thanks to a safety cage that surrounded the water tower's ladder, spray-painted initials appeared at the top as fast as teenaged lovers switched partners.

"Are you sure?" Peachy asked. "Looks like we're above the water tower to me."

"We're 20 feet below the tower, Peachy," Jacob said. "I checked. Remember, if we're going to do this, we're going to do it right."

"Yeah, Jenniquita said to go to the point most high," reminded Chipper.

The point "most high" was a nearby silo that stretched another 40 feet skyward. The connection between the two sets of silos was a metal staircase, broad enough for three or four people, and with side rails. The stairway was nothing more than a chip shot. The hard part was crossing the ledge to get to the stairway.

"Should we leave our clubs in our belt loops?"

"No, hold them in your hand."

"Do we face the building?"

"No, we should go with our backs to it."

Peachy put his hands on his hips, but remained silent. It was clear that the majority vote was over.

Chipper slipped the old 5-iron, formerly used for Horse, from his belt loops, and walked to the rooftop shack where the ledge started. With his back to the wall, gripping the 5-iron in his right hand, he began sidestepping across. He silently counted a waltz cadence in ¾ time. Long step, short step, pause. Long step, short step, pause. Rather than look down, he patted the wall with his left hand to make sure his heels were as close to the building as possible. Long step, short step, pause. The wall changed to the inset window, then back again to wall.

He was across in 20 seconds. Safely on the east side of the building, he looked down. How stupid. How dangerous. How fun. His heart was pounding in rapid 2/4 time. Once was enough for this stunt. When they were on their way back to the ground, he would tell the others about the easy way down at the other end of the silos (a little-known fact provided to him by the ancient explorers).

Jacob and L.K. crossed with the same technique. Iron gripped in one hand, patting the wall with the other, not looking down until they were in Shangri-La. Chipper shook their hands as they joined him. Peachy stood wide-eyed, still in the snowy Himalayas.

"I'm leavin' the club where it is, in my belt loop," called Peachy. "I can't hold the strap of the recorder and my 3-iron, too. Jiminy shit, what am I doing?"

With the Norelco recorder on his left shoulder like a lady's purse, Peachy turned his back to the wall and started to inch along.

"I can't do it this way," he yelled. "I'm turnin' around, facing the wall."

"Go ahead," Chipper said. "It might be better that way." This was no time to call him a "Chickenshit."

Peachy began sidestepping. All was well. "Mutherfuggin sonuvabitch. Mutherfuggin sonuvabitch."

The peaceful crossing ended prematurely. The grip end of Peachy's club caught the window frame, sliding the 3-iron out of balance as he advanced. When the other end of the club tipped down, slipping out of the loops, Peachy's left hand automatically reached to save it from falling. As he did so, the tape recorder strap dropped off his shoulder, slid down his arm and down the shaft of the iron until it caught the crook of the club where the head met the shaft. Peachy grabbed the end of the club just before the tape recorder and the 3-iron both fell to a 10-story death.

"Godammit!" he screamed. "God fuggin' dammit, sumbitch, mutherfuggin..."

The tape recorder was dangling by its strap at the neck of the club, the same spot on the clubface where shanks occur. Peachy held on with his left hand, opposite from Chipper and the guys, as he faced the wall.

Both Jacob and L.K. yelled at Peachy to drop the recorder.

"Wait a minute," Chipper said. "Pull it back over the ledge, then set it down. One of us'll get it."

"I can't," Peachy said. "My arm can't lift it any higher. It's too fuggin' heavy out there at the end."

"Let it go," repeated Jacob.

"No, not yet," Chipper shouted. "Swing it, Peachy. Swing it around as far as you can twist. Don't let the strap slip off the clubhead."

"I can't. I can't even get it back up to the ledge."

"Sure you can, twist toward me. I'm coming to get it." Chipper started back onto the ledge, his 5-iron in his right hand and his back to the wall. After some sidesteps, he made it to the window, where Peachy's cursing to the end of universe continued.

"As far as you can, twist as far as you can."

Twisting 90 degrees left the tape recorder still suspended beyond and below the ledge, but within reach if Chipper used his 5-iron for the transfer. Their future was in the balance, and it was shaky and slippery. For the first time, Chipper questioned his beloved doctrine of predestination. *Shit, what are we doing?*

"Keep twisting, Peachy."

"Mutherfuggin sonuvabitch, I'm gonna twist my ass off the ledge. Don't tell me to twist anymore! I'm mutherfuggin friggin twisted as far as I can twist my everlovin' sumbitchin..."

Chipper stretched his 5-iron to new lengths as he hooked the strap of the Norelco, then lifted it from Peachy's club. Peachy was right—it was extra heavy way out on the end of the stick. A one-handed grip didn't allow much leverage. As he turned to his left, he saw Jacob at the beginning of the ledge, his club extended while L.K. held onto Jacob's other arm. The team became a bucket brigade, putting out the fire.

Swinging his right arm to the east, Chipper made the transfer to Jacob's club, and finally the tape recorder was hauled to safety. Chipper sidestepped off the ledge to join Jacob and L.K., followed quickly by a rattled Peachy. It was going to be even harder now for Chipper to explain the easy way back.

Peachy straightened the collar on his polo shirt and pushed his glasses back on his nose. "The Peach was in control at all times, gentlemen."

"Sure, sure," said L.K. "But I don't want to be the one to wash your Fruit-of-the-Looms."

"What?"

"Odds are pretty good you've got a fudge factory in your pants."

"Screw you, L.K."

All was well.

"Let's get to the top, men," Chipper said. He led them to the silver stairway that rose to the point most high. The metal stairs were even wider than he thought, allowing them to walk four abreast to the top level. Marching in uniform, he had the same feeling as earlier this morning when they made their historic exit out of the high school, basking in the glory of their suspension.

The full moon was starting to disappear behind thin clouds, but the night was still bright. The foursome walked to the edge of the silo and began pulling golf balls from their pockets, six each, two shots per man per round, all to be cast to the wind. They lined up as if they were at a driving range, then Peachy flipped on the recorder. He didn't plug in the earpiece, so all of them could hear the music as *The Nutcracker Suite* began to broadcast from the tower.

An eerie calm settled over them as the music played, first with the harp introduction, then on to the mesmerizing "Waltz of the Flowers." L.K. hit first, then Jacob, followed by Chipper and Peachy. The balls formed white arcs across the sky, over the railroad tracks, over the cement company, finally plunking and plopping on the empty parking lot of the Piggly-Wiggly below.

Twenty-four shots in all, each followed by bounces and ricochets until the quiet night was filled with bonks and pops and plunks. Peachy didn't shank a single ball, in spite of his brush with death.

In the distant west, Chipper spotted a faint light roll across the horizon. The lightning was too far away to make thunder.

Friday, May 5, 1967: Unbelievable. For the first time in history, a round of state tournament was canceled. Lightning storm lasted until afternoon. Fortunately, not much rain because I'll need the roll on the fairways. It's a long course. Still wondering every minute about Amy. Can't quit thinking about her. We're staying in a crummy motel on Route 66. The A-team is in one room, caddies in the other. State will be just 36 holes this year. All 36 tomorrow.

"Hey, Chipper, are you writing in a diary, like girls do?"

"Screw you, Peachy. Go back to sleep."

Fifty-five

The early morning winds, descendants of Dustbowl days, brushed away the final remnants of haze that lingered on the Lake Heritage Golf Course. Four sets of footprints in the dew trailed to the first green, where the red-jeaned foursome stood on the fringe.

The ritual of walking the first hole on foreign courses, very much a religious act, was inspired by Jacob. "Becoming one with the turf," he would say. The team usually let Jacob walk it alone, but today was different. You couldn't get too much religion for the state tournament.

Jacob dropped to one knee and, with flattened palm, wiped the virginal surface of the dew-soaked green like a windshield wiper clearing the mist. As he stood again, droplets of condensed water fell from his fingertips back to the green. Chipper halfway expected him to perform a Presbyterian baptism with the sprinkles of dew.

"The greens are soft after yesterday's rain," said Jacob.

"Yup. They're gonna bite like a bulldog," replied L.K., holding his driver under his arm like a rifle.

Peachy was several yards away, kneeling on the fringe, making handprints in the dew like a kid in wet cement.

Chipper looked back at the clubhouse in response to the noise. Car doors and trunks were slamming, golf clubs clattering, cleats crunching on the asphalt, all in the distance, but with remarkable clarity. The pretournament cacophony reminded him of an orchestra warming up with random notes prior to the first curtain.

Chipper looked at his watch. Six-fifteen a.m.

"We'd better head back. Jacob, you're in the first group, you know."

"I know," he said, drying his baptismal hand on his scarlet jeans. "Let's go."

"Peachy," Chipper said, "Coach Dresden has you at third man for a reason, in Buster's place. So good luck." It galled him that he would be playing behind Peachy, even though fourth man was his spot all year long. "You and I tee off on Number 10, that little par 3. You go at 6:45. I'm in the last group."

"The Peach is hot. I feel it in my bones."

As the foursome marched back up the fairway, retracing their dewprints, Chipper looked at the crowd assembling at the first tee box. Over 130 kids would play today, representing the 23 schools that had four qualifiers, plus the stray players like Smokey Ray Divine who qualified as individuals without their teams.

Red jeans were not so bizarre on the golf course. Granted, there were a few double-takes upon arrival this morning, but nothing after that. Besides, the Castlemont jerks had their navy Bermudas, navy visors, and white polo shirts with navy trim. A Tulsa team wore matching green caps, and Norman High School wore orange polos with black trim. For sure, the red jeans didn't draw the same gasps as in philosophy class.

At the rim of the crowd, Chipper spotted a fifth pair of red jeans. The ex-golfer was waving, a white plaster cast on his forearm.

"It's Buster," he said.

"Yeah, and Carol's with him."

"Gee, our own gallery."

"When Coach Dresden and Mr. Ashbrook get here, then Kelly, we'll have a gallery of five, not counting our caddies," said Jacob.

"Let's see now," said Peachy, "there's 10,000 people in El Viento... five are here. That'll be..."

"Point zero five percent," said Jacob.

"It's not important," L.K. said, stroking his jaw. "It doesn't matter if anyone is here or not. It's only important to play well, to win."

Chipper caught a glance from Jacob. They remembered the days when the great L.K.'s father attended each and every sporting event where the future star played. But those were true sports. And that was before the snakebites. It was history now, and L.K.'s dad was nothing more than a phantom. And was brother Benny on his way to ghostdom as well?

Buster met them at the front of the tee box, raising his plastered arm like a full-blood Indian. "How."

Could it be? He was smiling.

Carol gave Chipper a hug around the waist. "Good luck, guys, pour it on," she said. He thought about the little baby in her belly and refigured the gallery count at five-and-a-half.

Peachy extended his hand to shake Buster's, then the two of them realized that Buster wouldn't be shaking for a while. Nervous laughter broke the tension.

"You and Carol seem pretty bubbly today," Chipper said. He felt uncomfortable not asking about Buster's father. Then again, he would feel worse by asking.

"Bubbly?" repeated Buster. "Well, I'm getting my diploma early. Just found out yesterday. Carol and I are getting married next Saturday, then we're moving to South Carolina."

"Hey, congratulations," said Peachy.

"South Carolina?"

"Yeah, Carol's gonna finish high school there, while I head to Parris Island."

"Parris Island?"

"Yeah. Marine basic training."

"What? Marines? Basic training?"

"That's right. I'm a new man since I popped the asshole's jaw. I wanna start my life over."

"Start life over? With the Marines?"

"There's a war brewing, guys. We need good men."

"But...the Marines?" Chipper couldn't believe it. Then again, Buster looked like a totally different guy. He was all smiles, his arm around his true-blue pregnant fiancée.

"Hey, Peachy, we've gotta get to the 10th tee." It was Gus, carrying Peachy's clubs. Denied the privilege of red jeans, he was sporting a red Banlon shirt and a red visor.

Booger Yarkey, Chipper's caddie from the B-team, walked beside Gus. Booger was a small, polite freshman who shot in the mid to high 80s, having played only one year. Coach Dresden had great hopes for the little guy.

Booger rarely spoke more than one word at a time. Nature cursed him at birth with a spot of albino skin above his upper lip, no pigment at all, shaped like a teardrop dripping from his left nostril. From a practical standpoint, it looked like a booger. Chipper didn't even know his real name. When Booger talked in one-word sentences, he'd brush his nostril with a knuckle as if he could somehow wipe away the mark that tortured him.

"Peachy, go ahead to Number 10 with Gus," Chipper said. "I'm gonna watch Jacob tee off."

The first and second men would play the front nine, while the third and fourth men would start on the back nine. The good part about teeing off last, Chipper figured, was the fact you didn't have 65 competitors standing around the tee box for your opening drive. Peachy wouldn't be so lucky.

An old man with leathered arms dangling from a yellow tee shirt held a clipboard, a sure sign of authority. He was pacing between the tee markers.

Jacob pulled the driver from his bag and tossed the headcover to Wilson Parker, his caddie, who made a nice one-hand catch. Wilson was a senior who couldn't break bogey if his life depended on it, spending his entire career playing B-team matches, never having a shot at a letter. Long and lanky, he creamed his nose with zinc oxide, like Jacob. It was comical to see them together, this Ichabod caddie mimicking his master with the identical clown nose.

Chipper spotted Smokey Ray Divine. He was across the tee box, already looking at Chipper with a crinkled grin. He lifted his cowboy hat with the rattlesnake band and nodded to Chipper, then slowly lowered the hat to his head. It was as though he was saying, 'no need to thank me for destroying your enemy, cowboy, for now I'm going to destroy your friend, Jacob Justice, in 36 quick holes.'

Ritchie Cosgrove from Castlemont was warming up with half-swings beside Jacob. Ritchie lived in his own world, separate from everyone, even the other Castlemont jerks. It was a quiet world of steel nerves, 320-yard drives, a deadly putter, and subpar rounds ever since he was 14, all of which predestined him for the PGA Tour. Ritchie's confidence was frightening to Chipper, and he wondered if Jacob felt the same aura when he was around this golfing machine.

The old man with the tan arms and clipboard looked at his watch.

"Gentlemen," he said loudly, "it's time to play golf."

Two shots, per man, per round, thought Chipper.

"The first group teeing off will be Ritchie Cosgrove of Castlemont, Jacob Justice of El Viento, and Doyle Crimble of Tulsa Edison."

The wind was only five to ten miles per hour, but it was still early. The Lake Heritage Golf Course was the windiest in the city, given the nearby body of water for which it was named. But it still couldn't come close to the winds at El Viento.

Ritchie Cosgrove's drive started the tournament by cracking through the morning air, well over 300 yards up the middle of the par 5.

Jacob looked back at Chipper and smiled. Apparently, he wasn't intimidated by Ritchie's aura. He teed his ball and pointed to the fairway like Babe Ruth, a gesture stolen from L.K. Chipper looked in L.K.'s direction to see if he minded. The great athlete didn't. L.K. was smiling, standing next to his caddie Frank Harris, the only teenager in El Viento who listened to western music. Buster and Carol were a few steps away. "Crush it, Jacob," said L.K., offering the only words spoken on the tee box.

Jacob's smooth swing ended with a pop that might have split the cover off the ball. It sailed higher and flew farther than Ritchie Cosgrove's. What's more, he played it to the right, giving him a better second shot on the dogleg hole. Unbelievable.

As Chipper was about to slip to the back of the crowd and move to the Number 10 tee, he felt a death-grip on his upper arm. "What the...?"

It was Gus. "Chipper, come quick. We're in trouble. Big trouble."

"What's wrong?"

"Come quick."

"Grab my bag, Booger," Chipper said. He followed Gus out of the horde of first and second men.

"What are you talking about, man? We haven't even started."

"Batteries," cried Gus, tears starting to stream from his eyes.

"Batteries?"

"Batteries. Peachy's tape recorder is dead, and I forgot the batteries."

"Oh, shit. Did you check the pro shop?"

"Yeah, they don't sell 'em there. I even tried to buy them out of their flashlight, but they were D's. We need C's."

"I thought you had extras."

"I do—I mean I did. But I left them back at the motel."

"Dammit, Gus. What does Peachy want to do?"

"You talk to him, Chipper. He's mad as hell."

Another old man with tan leather arms, yellow tee shirt, and a clipboard, was standing on the Number 10 tee box. Peachy was pacing frantically at the back of the crowd of third and fourth men. He stopped cold when he saw Chipper and Gus, trailed by Booger.

"I can't do it," cried Peachy, "the sumbitch forgot my fuggin' batteries."

"Stop it, Peachy," Chipper said, grabbing the mushy upper arm of his friend. "Stop it. You've heard that song hundreds of times now. Think about it. Listen to it."

"I can't."

"You can."

"I'm tellin' you, I can't."

"Now look. Give Gus the keys to your car. He can go back to the motel and get them."

Chipper turned to Gus. "Do you remember where you left them?"

"Yeah, in a sack under my pillow."

"If they've cleaned the room, go to the manager."

"Wait a minute," said Peachy. "Gus ain't gonna drive my Vette. Let him take *your* car."

"I can do it, Peachy," insisted Gus.

"Gentlemen, let's play," said the old man in the yellow tee shirt. "First up, Peachy Waterman of El Viento, Monte Guilford of Castlemont, and Tim Timberling of Muskogee."

"Oh, jeez, mutherfugger, goddammit, Gus, take my fuggin' keys and get your ass in gear. And get the shit back here as fast as your skinny little butt'll travel."

Gus plucked the keys and sprinted to the parking lot. Peachy hoisted his bag onto his shoulders and barged through the 60-plus golfers gathered around the Number 10 tee. At least this hole was an easy start. A 150-yard par 3, one bunker at the back. Peachy rarely went long, always overestimating his strength. He pulled the 7-iron from his bag.

"Use the six, Peachy. It's farther than it looks." Chipper was careful to lay blame on the illusion of distance rather than a deficiency in Peachy's wimpy arms.

Peachy complied, but scowled while he pushed his glasses back onto the bridge of his nose. He giraffed his neck, eyeballing the parking lot and his stupid caddie.

Chipper turned around to the *vrooooom* of the red Corvette as Gus started the engine. The names William Tell and Lone Ranger came to mind as Gus began lurching through the parking lot, a neo-novice with a standard transmission. Lurch...lurch...lurch, lurch, lurch. Lurch... Lurch...lurch, lurch, lurch. Would he ever bring the car to a gallop? Could he save the duffer in distress?

Peachy handed the silenced tape recorder to his teammate and swaggered to the tee box.

"Think about the music," Chipper called after him. "Remember the melody."

Peachy straightened the collar on his shirt, hitched his red pants, and teed his ball. Placing the clubface to the ground, he assumed a pose that bore only a faint resemblance to Quasimodo. Wiggle to the left. Wiggle to the right. Backswing, overswing, downswing. The ball squirted laterally, a direct shot to the parking lot.

Peachy turned, facing Chipper and the crowd: "The Peach shanked it."

The snickers Chipper heard seemed miles away. It didn't matter. Nothing mattered. Like a baseball catcher walking to the mound to calm the frazzled pitcher, Chipper made his way to the front of the tee.

"Out-of-bounds," called the old man with the clipboard.

"What?" Peachy yelled. "Out-of-bounds?"

"The parking lot is out-of-bounds, son. Tee up another one. You're hitting three from the tee."

Peachy's two shots per man per round had been gobbled in a jiffy by the asphalt jungle where the state's top golfers, half of whom were currently laughing at Peachy, had parked their cars.

"Holy mother of shit. If I'd known that was out-of-bounds..." He caught himself. He knew the shank was uncontrollable.

"Think of The Nutcracker, Peachy," Chipper said, backing away to join the gallery of chuckling contenders. "Play it in your head."

Peachy reached into a red pocket and pulled out another ball. He teed it closer to the ground than the first, then he began fiddling with his grip, making some sort of last minute adjustment. He smiled at Chipper, as if he'd found a flaw in his handling of the club.

"He's not doing it. I can tell," said Chipper to his caddie. "He's not listening to the music. I can tell by the look on his face."

Quasimodo. Wiggle to the left. Wiggle to the right. Backswing, overswing, downswing. The ball squirted right, adding another two strokes to the parking lot.

Peachy turned to the crowd and pronounced with theatrical grace: "The Peach shanked another one."

It was over. All hope was dashed to bits by four shitty little C batteries in a goddam sack under a friggin' pillow in a pissant little motel on Route 66. The dream was dead. He'd kill Gus when this day was over. No, he'd kill Peachy. Several hundred strokes from now, he'd walk up to Peachy and place the shaft of his driver to that squawking throat like Buster had done once upon a time, then press down until the wind was gone. All Peachy had to do was listen to the music in his head. But instead, he panicked. Chipper looked at the tape recorder and, for a moment, thought about smashing the contraption into Peachy's face.

"Hit another one, son," the old man said with a snarly tone in his voice that implied 'You disgusting excuse for a golfer.' "You're hitting five from the tee."

Hitting five and he's still on the tee box, thought Chipper. He couldn't bring himself to walk out to the mound again. Lowering his head to his open palm, he wanted to cry.

The tee box gallery was silent. Funeral silent, except for the breeze that seemed to be gaining strength. It was a rhythmic whistling, to and fro, this peculiar sound. To and fro, to and fro, in and out, in and out.

Chipper looked between his fingers. Peachy was stooped over at the waist, hands on knees, arms locked at the elbows, huffing and puffing with increasing force. The old man dropped the clipboard to his side. "Are you all right, son?"

In and out. In and out.

"Oh, my God," Chipper said.

"What?" said Booger, touching his knuckle to his nose.

In and out. In and out.

"Oh, my God. I don't believe it." Chipper started back through the gallery toward Peachy.

In and out. In and out. Peachy stood up straight, like Dracula out of his coffin, and closed his mouth after the final inspiration. His face turned red.

"Oh, my God."

Chipper was sure Peachy's eyes met his own, right before they rolled back in his head. The shanker fell to the ground, flopping about, arms and legs twitching in a fit so real that the crowd let out a collective gasp. There he was, the Peach, at one with the turf. At one with himself.

Chipper rushed to his side. "Stand back. Stand back, everyone. He has these spells. Give him some room."

As the old man with the clipboard approached, Chipper ordered, "You, sir, go call an ambulance." The tournament official hustled off to the pro shop without protest.

The fish-flopping stopped. With his intimate knowledge of this special disorder, Chipper knew that Peachy was awake now, playing dead.

"Stand back," he ordered again to the pressing crowd. "Give him some air."

Chipper dropped to his knees and pretended to minister to the stricken hacker. He lifted Peachy's eyelids, loosened his collar, and gently slapped his cheeks. "He'll be out for 10 or 15 minutes," he announced to the stunned crowd. "Happens after every fit. He kinda goes into a coma."

No one moved. Every golfer on the tee box riveted their eyes on Peachy and his dutiful teammate. The twosome was planted squarely between the markers on the Number 10 tee box. Peachy, hitting five from the tee, was lying low as long as he possibly could.

Chipper began fanning Peachy with the green towel from his golf bag. He tried to picture how far Gus might be right now. The motel was only a couple of miles away. If the manager was cooperative, it should be a snap. Every time Chipper looked at his watch, the hands seemed frozen in the same position. He began to mutter the Hi-ho Silver song to hurry Gus through the return trip. Ba-da-dum...ba-da-dum...ba-da-dum, dum, dum. Lurch...lurch...lurch, lurch, lurch. Peachy lay perfectly still. No one in the crowd said a word. No one moved.

Chipper looked at his watch for the trillionth time.

A siren wailed in the distance. *Oh, man,* he thought, *this could get out of hand.* He didn't think an ambulance would arrive this quick. Gus should've beaten the ambulance back to the golf course.

But when he turned to the siren, it wasn't an ambulance at all. Racing up the two-lane road to the Lake Heritage Course were the spinning red and blue lights of a black and white police car—in hot pursuit of a speeding red Corvette.

"Oh, shit," said Chipper as he stood to his feet.

Gus wasn't stopping. His head was barely visible above the dashboard.

The siren grew louder, more menacing, more threatening. Chipper looked down at Peachy who cracked one eyelid.

"C'mon, Gus, you're close," Chipper said. "Don't stop."

The red Corvette spun into the parking lot, weaving in and out of the lanes, followed by the flashing lights of the police car. With unbelievable skill, or luck, Gus found an opening in the barrier and steered the Corvette onto the course toward the Number 10 tee. The police followed close behind. Gus was a dead man, but it didn't matter. Peachy could carry his own bag. That is, if Gus had found the batteries.

The Vette skidded to a halt behind the tee. Gus jumped out, tossed a brown paper sack to the ground, and held his hands in the air to surrender. Chipper could see he was crying. Scared to death. Shaking like a dog trying to shit a peach pit. Two policemen jumped out of the car, one with a pistol pointed at Gus. In a split second, the B-team caddie was spread-eagled across the back of the red Corvette. Another criminal brought to justice.

In the commotion, Chipper slipped in front of the Vette and rescued the brown paper bag. Concealing it in the crook of his arm, he turned from the scene of the crime, denying any association with the reckless reprobate who had just been apprehended by the authorities.

The crowd was drifting like curious cattle toward this newest piece of action, leaving Peachy alone on the tee box. Chipper fought his way against the migration.

Opening the bag, he found the precious treasure—four C batteries—and he scrambled to place them in the recorder.

Another siren in the distance. Over a gentle hill, he spotted an ambulance barreling down the two-lane road into the parking lot. The crowd was getting so thick around Gus and the cops that he couldn't see what was happening. The ambulance pulled alongside the police car, and the siren wound down to silence. The flashing lights on both emergency vehicles pulsated against the morning sky, drawing the first and second men from the Number 1 tee box to join the crowd.

Chipper took a deep breath, held it, then he closed the battery compartment and tested the recorder. "The Waltz of the Flowers" sounded its cue. Whew! Peachy opened his eyes. It was a miracle!

"You okay, Peach?"

"Does the pope shit in the woods? Is a bear Catholic?" He rose from the phoenix ashes and dusted himself off. "Strap me in, captain, the Peach is on the comeback trail."

Chipper hooked the Norelco onto Peachy's belt in the back, then helped his friend thread the earpiece beneath his white polo shirt. With his shirttail out, most of the recorder was covered, leaving the rectangular outline for people to wonder: 'Is it a hearing aid?' 'Why, yes, it's an aid,' he always replied.

Peachy shook Chipper's hand, then turned to the ambulance attendants who were approaching the tee box. "All is well, gentlemen, go on home now," he said. "All is well. Just a little sunstroke."

The old man with the clipboard was leading a group of golfers back to the tee box. Chipper approached him and explained Peachy's entire medical history, along with the fact that he'd be just fine now. Just peachy. The old man wasn't so sure, but he turned to the crowd behind him. "Let's play ball."

As the crowd split, half returning to the Number 1 tee and half to the Number 10 tee, only L.K. and Buster remained, chatting with the police. Poor little Gus sat in the back seat of the patrol car, probably shackled, his life in ruins, given his upcoming 16th birthday and driver's exam. Buster strolled away from the cops toward Chipper.

"They thought he looked too young to be driving," Buster said. "When they tried to pull him over to check his age, Gus bolted. Eighty miles an hour all the way to the golf course in a 35-mile-an-hour zone."

"He'll be grounded for life."

"I'm going to the pro shop to call his folks," said Buster. "Then I'll go caddie for Peachy."

Chipper was shocked at the offer.

"That idiot couldn't pick the right club if his life depended on it," Buster said. "Someone has to keep him from under-clubbing. He may hate my ass, but he knows my knack for distances."

"He doesn't hate you, Buster. He acts that way when he's afraid."

"Anyway, I'll catch up to him after I make this phone call."

On the tee box, the resurrected Peachy was addressing his ball, lying four, hitting five, listening to the music.

Quasimodo was gone. The wiggle to the left was nearly imperceptible. His backswing was shorter. Downswing was smooth. The ballerinas in their white mosquito-net tutus jumped through the air, then thumped on the stage as their shoes landed on the ground. Peachy's shot arched beautifully through the sky, floating down to the green, where it landed with a distant thud, 20 feet from the cup. He held both hands in the air, fists clenched.

Chipper heard clapping near the clubhouse behind him. He turned and saw that Coach Dresden and Mr. Ashbrook had just arrived.

"Helluva shot," said Coach Dresden.

"Nice shot," said Mr. Ashbrook.

L.K. whispered in their ears, probably something to the effect that Peachy was putting for a triple-bogey, because they looked at each other with eyebrows raised, then at Chipper, at the ambulance, at Gus in the police car, and back toward each other, their mouths open and cavernous.

Peachy lifted his bag to his shoulder, still holding his arms up in a V, signaling victory to the astonished crowd.

Fifty-six

Chipper went with the easy 6-iron, rather than trying to crush the seven. By the rhythm of his swing, by the vibration-free crack of the club against the ball, by the slight draw and the high arc toward the hole, he knew it would be a good day. Maybe a great day. He was fond of predicting his final score from this first crystal ball of the day. He would shoot a 76. Maybe better. Call it predestination or whatever, he was usually right.

The ball hit the far edge of the green, bit like a bulldog, then rolled back to the smack-dab middle of the putting surface, 10 feet from the cup.

"Shot," said his caddie, touching his knuckle to his nose. This was, of course, the abbreviated Booger version of the more elaborate compliment, 'Nice shot.'

Unlike the course at El Viento where you could see nearly all nine holes at once, the Lake Heritage Golf Course camouflaged its 18 holes with a rich forest of tall oaks and aged pines. Chipper couldn't find his teammates. Accustomed to hand signals and helpful club members, he usually knew the whereabouts of each player and how they stood with par. He felt alone. Was golf a team sport or a solo sport? He'd never been able to answer that question for himself.

The midmorning sun ushered more forceful winds that whipped down the fairways in gusts, as opposed to the constant flow of the tree-deprived El Viento course. More than once, Chipper's approach shots were perfectly adjusted for the wind, only to have a calm interlude as the ball went airborne, leaving him slightly off target. It was okay, though. For him, a chip was as good as a putt.

He maneuvered his 7-iron shot from the fringe of the 16th hole. The ball hopped along the grass, settled into a smooth roll, and curled into position 18 inches from the cup. Easy par. One over for the day as he neared the quarter-mark.

"Shot," said Booger.

On the Number 2 tee box, the 11th hole for Chipper, he was squeezing the grip on his driver, preparing for the kill, when he spotted two pair of red legs charging from the seventh green to the eighth tee. The upper halves of the two bodies were blocked from view by a row of flowering trees. Peachy and Buster were too far away to yell, so he watched the four red legs churn beneath the white flowers of the trees until they passed from sight. It was a good sign to see their rapid pace. When Peachy was on a roll, he walked like he had ants in his pants.

Shadows pulled in tight with the midday heat. Chipper wiped his brow with the green towel attached to his bag.

"Luck," said Booger, meaning 'good luck,' as he handed Chipper the Golf Craft "Touring Pro" putter, with the golden head and the flared grip. He was putting for a par, four feet from the cup. He couldn't wait to look at the scoreboard to see what the others had shot. This putt would give him a 76. That score was expected at El Viento. It was great at Lake Heritage. For him, that is.

He set the putter behind the ball, the black dot on top of the clubhead aligned perfectly with the center of the ball. Somewhat akin to Peachy's 'wiggle to the left,' Chipper tilted his putter grip forward two inches as a prelude to the rigid rhythm of his swing. Tilt, back, putt, all in 3/4 time. As the ball rolled toward the cup, he knew immediately that his stroke was too firm. The ball rimmed the lip, leaving him with a tap-in for a 77.

"Round," said Booger. Chipper didn't know if that meant good or bad.

He reviewed his scorecard with a freckled kid from Tulsa who was bugged all the time, even after good shots. Freckles had him down for a 77. It was certified correct when Chipper signed the card. He turned to the last member of his threesome, Steve Brownelle, a big guy with a flattop and glasses from Altus. Chipper had him with an 81. The big guy agreed and signed the card.

They handed their cards to one of the old men with the yellow tee shirts and clipboards who added the numbers to the large scoreboard in front of the clubhouse. Chipper decided to wait for the team totals to be calculated before starting the final 18.

The lowest number on the board was a 70. His eyes worked back to the names where he found Raymond Divine, alias Smokey Ray, as the owner. Jacob was on Smokey Ray's heels with a 71. Ritchie Cosgrove also bagged a 71. Three or four 72s beat L.K.'s 73. Then he spotted Peachy's 83.

"Eighty-three for Peachy. See that, Booger?"

"Yup."

"Without his four penalty strokes at the start, he'd had a 79."

"Yup."

"Peachy's hot, Booger. I'm tellin' you."

"Hot."

He waited for the old man's hand to back away from the scoreboard. El Viento's total was 304, averaging 76 per man. Seventy-five per man won it last year. Okay, so they were only improved by one shot per man per round. Peachy's four penalty shots alone made the difference.

Castlemont was the leader at 295. Chipper groaned. The team would have to make up 10 strokes in 18 holes—more than two shots per man per round. It was hard to imagine. It was even harder to imagine when Chipper saw the other team totals. Tulsa Edison at 299, Muskogee and Altus at 300, Lawton Ike at 302, and John Marshall at 303. El Viento was in seventh place. It was anybody's game.

For a moment, he had the same crushing sensation he'd had when Peachy's second tee shot had scooted into the parking lot. But it was stupid to let the scores get to him. He couldn't influence anything besides his personal game. He panned the rolling horizon, searching for another pair of red jeans. He was still alone.

Four holes into the back 18, Chipper spotted the double set of red jeans again, standing in the middle of the fairway waiting for the green to clear. The Castlemont player, jerk of jerks, Monty Guilford, was taking practice swings, knocking clumps of dirt toward Peachy and Buster.

Chipper watched Peachy as he turned and walked toward the jerk, held out his hand and took the club from the reluctant player. Peachy shook the jerk's club against his own ear. Chipper could almost hear the dialogue:

"I thought I heard a funny noise in this club on that last hole."

"What?"

"A funny noise, you know, like something loose inside. It sounded like a marble rolling down the shaft when your club was up in the middle of your backswing."

"Gimme that club back."

"Sure thing."

Monty Guilford hooked his next shot into the woods, pounding his defective iron into the ground, probably swearing at Peachy. This was all hypothetical, of course.

His long irons were on fire this afternoon, hitting more greens in regulation than he could ever remember. This novelty of putting for birdies had a certain appeal. Two birdie putts neutralized his two bogeys, and Chipper was even par after 12 holes of the final 18. He was thrilled.

His 3-iron approach from the knee joint of the Number 4 dogleg rose like a 5-iron into the head wind, then plopped onto the front of the green. Chipper clenched his fist with pride.

"Shot."

"Damn straight," he replied.

Two fairways over, on the back nine, he caught his first glimpse of Jacob. He wasn't sure which hole his friend was playing, but it had to be near the end. Jacob had teed off with the first group, Chipper with the last.

Jacob saw him, too, and waved. Red jeans had a way of drawing attention like June bugs to a porch light.

Jacob spread his palm in a line parallel to the ground. He was even. But even to what? Even for the day? The 18? Or even for the individual lead?

In a move that surprised himself, Chipper was able to return the gesture with his own smooth wave parallel to the ground. He was even so far on the final 18.

Jacob held a victory fist in the air to acknowledge receipt of the message.

"Even," said Booger.

Fifty-seven

From the back of the Number 9 tee box, Chipper's shadow touched the twin red markers at the front. The 36th and final hole stretched before him, and his threesome would soon wrap up the tournament. A birdie on the previous hole again rendered him even par for the second round. He was ecstatic, but cautious, still ignorant of his teammates' scores.

For the past three holes, a dark squall line had been encroaching the blue sky, though clearly not a threat for the tournament finish. Such a thunderstorm, however, could make wind directions fickle.

He snapped off blades of grass with his fingers, held them high in the breeze, and released. They fluttered to the ground at an angle.

"Still coming from the south," he said.

"South."

"About 15 miles an hour."

"Yup."

"I'd rather deal with a head wind or tail wind on this hole. The drive is tight."

"Tight." Booger nodded in agreement, handing Chipper the driver.

Only 395 yards and a slight dogleg left, the par 4 still screamed trouble, with tall oak trees abutting the fairway in a narrow constriction, giving the hole something of an hourglass shape. Even the big hitters had to thread their drives carefully to get by the waistband. For Chipper, a well-hit drive would be even with the constriction, at the level of the navel if the hole were a woman's figure. To cap the challenge, a feeder creek off Lake Heritage ran across the fairway some 180 yards from the tee, forming a bikini line across the hips of the fairway. The drive had to go 200 yards on the fly to clear the creek.

The big guy from Altus and Freckles from Tulsa were perched on their drivers, held like walking sticks, waiting for the threesome in front to clear the fairway. Neither had played well this 18 and Chipper was pleased. Both of their teams were in contention at the halfway point.

"Buster," whispered his caddie.

"Where?"

Chipper looked up the cart path that ran along the right-hand of the fairway. The red-jeaned Buster was waving his cast in the air.

Gentlemen's rules dictated that spectators behave like a gallery at a professional match, keeping a comfortable distance from players and their caddies. But Chipper knew a message was on the way.

"Go see what he wants, Booger. Find out where we stand. I mean, do we have a chance?

Booger laid the green and black bag at the edge of the tee box and met Buster on the cart path. Buster lowered his head to scribble on a scorecard, finally speaking again to Booger who hightailed it back to Chipper.

"Bogey," said Booger between breaths.

"Bogey?"

"Bogey," he repeated.

"Bogey? Whaddya mean?"

"Bogey."

"Dammit, Booger, quit saying 'bogey.' Talk in sentences. What are you trying to say?"

"Bogey wins it."

"Bogey? Wins? The championship? The team championship?"

"Yeah, bogey."

"What...how..."

He couldn't believe it. What happened? Everyone must've done super. They must've done better than super. Even Peachy. And here he was even par. And a bogey wins it? Unbelievable.

"Hit it, DeHart," said the big guy from Altus. "They're clear."

Chipper looked at the hourglass fairway and gulped. If all they needed from him was a bogey, he could baby-up to the creek with a safe 5-iron. Another iron would send him within 50 yards of the green. On in three. Two putt for the victory. A little on the candy-ass side for a finish, but still an easy victory. His first even par round would be spoiled, but the team mattered most, after all. Didn't it?

"Red," said Booger.

"What?"

Booger pointed at the cart path, which was starting to fill with spectators, most of them wearing red, streaming from the clubhouse like little corpuscles along an artery. Chipper followed the flow of red up to the final green where maybe 200 spectators stood. At least half of them were wearing red.

"What the..." He could see Jacob, L.K., and Peachy leading the way down the cart path, easily identifiable in their scarlet trousers. Others behind were wearing red shirts, red skirts, red shorts, though they were too far away for positive identification. Where did they come from? He hadn't seen any supporters all day besides Kelly, Carol, Coach Dresden, and Mr. Ashbrook.

That settled it. Candy-ass golf was out.

But maybe the 2-wood was safer than the driver. More control. Like he used to do all the time. Then he remembered his conversion to his driver, the day Doc Jody died. It would have to be the driver for a clear shot to the green.

"You're up, DeHart, hit away," said Freckles, the Tulsan whose real name Chipper had forgotten by the third hole.

He teed his freshly cleaned ball, then plucked at the grass again before he stood straight. The angle was the same. The wind was steady from the south. He planned a slight fade so that the wind would neutralize any overcorrection on his part. He knew crosswinds, and he knew them well. Crosswinds were all he ever played at El Viento, and his drives were accurate when played slightly against the flow.

With the crack of the ball, he knew the drive was precise and accurate, hope confirmed. The ball soared to the right side of the fairway. It would be perfect.

But the ball sailed farther to the right than he planned, then continued toward the trees. What was happening?

"Wind," said Booger.

Chipper noticed instantly that the wind had stopped. 'No wind,' his caddie meant. Then a swirling cool breeze hit him in the face, temperature plummeting with a stock-in-trade Oklahoma front. The new northwest wind carried his ball into the wooded waistband. On any other hole, it was a great drive. Not on this one.

"Oh, God," Chipper said. "I'm in trouble."

"It's a bitch over there," said the big guy from Altus. "I was in jail there in the morning round."

"No problem," lied Chipper. He glanced at Booger whose eyes took a nose dive.

Buster was still on the cart path near the tee box, his casted arm shielding the sun from his eyes as he tried to follow the ball. He turned and shrugged his shoulders.

After the group finished their tee shots, Chipper led his caddie to the cart path. Since this was the only avenue over the water, it allowed a moment to mingle with the gallery, that is, Buster. The others were farther up the trail.

"I think you might be okay," said Buster.

"Did you see it?"

"Well, not where it stopped, but you're in the middle of those trees. I don't think it made it through to where the fairway widens again."

"Even so, at worst, I'll lose a stroke hitting out of the woods. Down in three for the win shouldn't be too hard."

Chipper and Buster walked side by side down the cart path, the caddie a few steps behind.

"You're having a helluva round, Booger tells me."

"Yeah, even I don't believe it."

"Everyone on the team ripped up this second 18. It's incredible."

"Who's the closest? Who's on our butts?"

"Castlemont, of course. Their guys are all in. They shot 301 on the back side for a 596 total. Better than last year."

"Jeez! What the hell did we do? I mean...how..."

A congregation was forming in the trees near the cart path, mostly in red and white.

"What's going on?"

"I don't know."

Chipper and Buster broke into a sprint, leaving Booger to struggle behind with clubs clattering. As he arrived on the scene, Chipper heard the two worst and most formidable words in his young life:

"Unplayable lie."

"Unplayable lie," echoed someone else.

"Unplayable lie?" he asked, his heart drooping to the ground. It couldn't be true. He still couldn't see his ball.

Surrounded by skyscraping oaks, his teammates were standing in a central clearing where he ought to have the opportunity to pop a shot back to the fairway. What were they talking about? Sure, grass was sparse, but he didn't mind hitting off the dirt. Half the fairways at El Viento were nothing more than dirt.

Then he saw it. The Loch Ness Monster surfaced and disappeared again. Out of the base of a smaller tree in the clearing was a surface root, rising like the fabled serpent into the air and back into a sea of rusty dirt. Beneath the half-inch diameter root rested his ball, wedged beneath the Monster. The odds were a million to one.

"Betcha you can punch it out of there to the fairway," said Peachy.

But the rim of trees lining the fairway was tight. Maybe he could punch it from beneath the root, but there was no assurance it would get out of the forest. Even if it did, the trees on the opposite side of the fairway blocked access to the green. The most obvious direction to punch it out was straight ahead, but a bushy cedar the size of a Mack truck would swallow any ball headed that direction.

"Unplayable lie has three options, each with a one-stroke penalty," said Jacob. "You can go back to the tee, hitting three..."

That didn't sound good. He'd have to drive the bottleneck again and, in effect, score a birdie to win. Par to tie.

"You can drop the ball back on the extension of an imaginary line running from the hole through the unplayable location..."

That didn't sound so good, either. The farther back he went along this line, there were more trees, then the creek.

"Or, you can drop two club lengths away, no closer to the hole."

"That's the best option," said L.K. "Take the penalty and punch it to the fairway. You'll be lying three."

"That's down in two for the win. A hundred yards out. I'm not even sure I can punch it out between these trees. A lateral punch still doesn't give me a clear shot to the green, and there's that giant cedar blocking my best shot forward."

"Is there a play-off for a tie?" asked Peachy.

"No," answered Jacob. "A tie's a tie."

Great. Three lousy options, thought Chipper. He crouched to his knees to inspect his ball wedged between the root and the dirt. He hoped to see a crack of daylight between the white dimpled cover and the root. No daylight. The ball was jammed. It was hopeless.

Booger was still 10 yards away, his trotting now trudging, his panting heard easily above the clanking irons in the bag.

Chipper looked into the eyes of his teammates. They must have shot tremendous rounds, each of them. And here he stood, jammed by a root, getting ready to turn over part, or all, of the championship to the Castlemont jerks. He should have played it safe with the iron off the tee. Or the 2-wood. He clenched his fists over and over, growing more and more frustrated. More and more angry. The sound of his teammates arguing the best option faded to the background, joined by distant thunder rolling closer to the hills around Lake Heritage.

"It's the rocket shot." Out of the gallery, the mellow voice was smooth and full, like the tones of a marimba.

Amy stepped forward.

Chipper heard a howl and turned to see Booger sprawling to the ground, golf bag still slung over his shoulder.

"Ankle," cried Booger.

"Oh, no," said Chipper.

"Gopher," his caddie said, pointing to the hole in the ground that had buckled his knee. Chipper looked toward Amy, then at the ball wedged in the unplayable lie, then back to his caddie coddling the twisted ankle.

"Amy," sighed Booger, as his finger swooped the bottom of his nose. He pointed to the vision standing nearby.

She took the green and black bag from Booger, tossed it onto her shoulder, and directed the ex-caddie to the gallery. Booger struggled to stand, then limped to the sidelines.

"It's the rocket shot," Amy repeated.

"What?"

"It's the rocket shot."

He looked to the ground again. The serpentine root protected its egg with maternal conviction. Surely, Amy wasn't suggesting...

"Chipper, did you hear me? Buster says you're a 155 yards away. It's your 7-iron, Chipper," said his new caddie.

He was dumbstruck. The cooler breeze announcing the storm whipped Amy's golden hair about her face. He had never seen her look so intent. He couldn't let himself think about anything other than this shot.

"Swing away," she said, as more thunder echoed in the distance. "Swing like the root wasn't even there. It's nothing more than the rocket shot. You simply ignore the top ball. In this case, the root."

Jacob, L.K., Peachy, and Buster were silent, looking at each other in disbelief. Could they all have been so shortsighted?

"But the root has to break for the shot to work," he said. "You've got to have a follow-through."

"That's right." She handed him the 7-iron.

"Lemme use the six. I'm afraid it's gonna ruin the club."

Amy didn't move. Her outstretched hand held the 7-iron, unwavering.

"The six," he persisted.

She didn't flinch. "The seven is your number, Chipper. It's your club. It's the one with the magic."

As he took the clubhead in his palm, she held onto the grip. For a moment, they held the club together, and Chipper thought he could feel a current resonate through the shaft of the club into his arms. The deep green of her eyes sent shivers through his skin as he stared at his former girlfriend. He longed to see the dimples. Finally, one corner of her mouth turned up, and a one-sided dimple emerged. She released the grip.

Turning to face the shot, he realized, for the first time, an opening—an escape route that was invisible when he was considering little sacrifice shots. Above the cedar directly in front—the shrub that would have devoured any attempt to punch a baby shot directly toward the hole—and below the tall branches of the huge oak trees, was a window toward the green. Though he couldn't see the flagstick through the cedar as he addressed the ball, he knew it was straight ahead. The portal to the green was the right height for a well-hit 7-iron. He would have to swing away. And if he was off to the left, right, up or down, he could end up in worse shape than he was right now. The root had to snap. He had to complete the follow-through. The trajectory had to be perfect.

He looked again at his teammates. Unlike Amy, they seemed bewildered.

The club will be ruined, he thought. Then again, he wouldn't be playing college golf. So, did it really matter?

He set the club face to the ball...and the root. He couldn't believe what he was about to try. Was he stark, raving mad?

The squall line eclipsed the late afternoon sun. The course darkened as the thunder grew closer. The wind was almost cold.

Rocking back and forth to distribute his weight, he gripped the club with full strength.

One last look at Amy, he thought, before the swing. *I'll look into those green pools and she'll inspire an effort in me never before achieved.*

But when he glanced back, Amy wasn't looking his way at all. She was staring above the cedar, below the oak branches, through the clearing where he needed to fire his shot.

He gazed back at the ground, his ball, his 7-iron, the root. He would try once more to look into her eyes.

But she was still staring at the clearing, her eyebrows raised and her lips barely parted, like the soprano in the church choir waiting her turn to hit the high note.

He followed her line of vision to the clearing. No visible green. No flagstick. No assurance there was anything beyond this window other than thin air. He needed to trust that this was the blind passage to victory. He had to commit. He had to believe before he could see.

He bowed his head to the ground. At first, his arms were paralyzed. Then, silent lightning lit the course as if Providence snapped a Kodak Instamatic. Rumbling thunder sang bass to his backswing...downswing. *Whack!* The sound of the shot was so loud it drowned out nature's ruckus.

Chipper forced his follow-through to the sky, head still down, where he saw the broken root. The ache in his arms was crescendoing, like hitting a crowbar against a utility pole. The pain finally paralyzed, and he felt the club drop from his hands just before he fell to the ground in a ball of nauseous agony. Writhing on his side, he saw the bent 7-iron lying by the broken root. Amy was picking up the club.

The swell of the crowd noise was distant at first, then mushroomed to the point Chipper thought he was in the middle of the gallery.

"Unbelievable," "Damn straight," "My god," "Mutherfuggin' sumbitch" came the sounds of his teammates. He looked up from his side to see them hopping up and down, embracing each other. Buster was squeezing Carol, Kelly was kissing husband Jacob, and L.K. was suffocating Peachy in a bear hug. He rolled on his back to see Amy still staring at the window, walking ahead out of the trees.

Lifting himself to his knees, he crawled to the edge of the forest where he could see—for the first time—the green and the flagstick. A red and white gallery was cheering louder than the threatening storm. Amy turned to him and smiled. Both dimples were in gear now.

Against all rules of gentlemanly conduct in the noble game of golf, Chipper felt himself smothered under the dogpile of his teammates.

He peeked from the bottom of the heap to see a little white dot on the green, superimposed by the base of the flagstick. He could spot an old man—it was Mr. Ashbrook—ringside by the green, holding two hands high in the air, palms facing each other, one foot apart.

Fifty-eight

After the tap-in for a 71, Chipper kissed his caddie. More importantly, she kissed back, like it used to be. He surrounded her waist with his arm, and they bid the final green farewell. If there was applause, Chipper couldn't hear it.

"So you just called everyone you could think of?"

"Yes. And I told them to call five friends. Like a chain letter."

"There must be a couple of hundred people here from El Viento," Chipper said.

"At least."

"Well, barring some screwup on the scorecards, we're the champs."

It dawned on him that in the heart-pounding thrill of the final hole, he still hadn't heard the news on the individual champ. "Did Jacob win? Did he beat Ritchie Cosgrove?"

"They tied," she said.

"Tied? For the state title?"

"No, they tied each other."

"What? Who won?"

"Guess."

"Don't do this, Amy. I dunno. Smokey Ray?"

"Nope."

"Amy, tell me."

He gently grabbed her upper arm to make her stop walking.

"L.K.," she said with a two-dimple smile.

"L.K.? I...never..."

"He had a 69 on the second 18 for a 142 total. Beat Jay and Ritchie by one shot. Smokey Ray by four shots."

"L.K.? I don't believe it."

His teammates had gathered beyond the fringe near a large sand trap. L.K. was beaming.

"You son of a gun," Chipper said with outstretched hand to L.K. "No one told me until now. Congratulations."

"We didn't want to rattle you."

"Peachy, you lucky S.O.B. What did you get on the back 18?"

"Seventy-friggin'-seven. No luck involved. The Peach was hot. Seventy-friggin'-seven."

"Yeah, sure," said Buster. "He was so confident that I had to leave the course on the back nine to get more batteries, just in case. Peachy bogeyed two out of the three holes I was gone, just thinking about the batteries running down."

"Ah, bullshit. The Peach was hot."

"And Chipper, a subpar round for you finally," said Jacob.

"Yeah. I still haven't shot even par, I guess. Second place okay for you, Jacob? I mean, the scholarship and everything?"

"I'm great with second. L.K.'s not going to OU. I should still have first crack at the scholarship there."

"The trophy presentations are going to be in front of the scoreboard," announced Amy.

"They better hurry before it starts raining," added Kelly, joining the group with Carol.

The temperature continued to fall, as if Old Man Winter had one more round to play in late spring. The sky was dark, like sunset. But when Chipper checked his watch, it was only 5:30.

He felt a hand on his shoulder, encouraging him to turn.

"Helluva final shot, Chipper." Mr. Ashbrook smiled.

"Way to go," echoed Coach Dresden.

"It was the rocket shot, Mr. Ashbrook," he replied. "The ball was beneath a tree root. It was Amy's idea."

The old man's eyes sparkled as he turned his attention to Amy the caddie, then back to Chipper.

The B-team caddies, minus poor pitiful Gus, circled the A-team at the foot of the steps leading to the trophy table on the wooden stage. Chipper had been relieved to learn that Peachy's dad, Peach Waterman Sr., was able to spring Gus from jail with a single phone call to one of his friends in high places. Still, the sacrificial caddie would not make it for the trophy presentations.

Chipper looked at his watch again. It was still 5:30. He held it up to his ear to make sure it was still ticking. And as the tick-tock continued against his ear, he thought back to his orchestral days when the conductor moved him from the marimba to the chimes for the "Great Gate at Kiev," doling out a great passage of time with the repetitive majesty of church bells. The chimes rang and rang and rang.

What if Peachy screwed up his scorecard somehow? What if they didn't add right? Was it possible there could be a mistake this late in the game?

The wind was whistling through the microphone as one of the old men in yellow tee shirts began announcing the third place finishers, then the runners-up. Jacob walked on stage to share second place with Ritchie Cosgrove. The two great competitors shook hands. Then L.K. joined Jacob on the platform, collecting the individual champ trophy. L.K. didn't gloat or anything. He just scratched the back of his head and put his arm around Jacob's shoulders.

The chimes in Chipper's head continued their bong, bong, bong, while the microphone began screeching with feedback on top of the roaring distortion caused by the wind.

It didn't matter. Chipper could read the lips of the old man as he mouthed the name of the state championship team: "El Viento."

He squeezed Amy's hand before letting it go, then felt her kiss on his cheek. Holding on to the wooden rail, he would be the last to climb the steps. He made sure Buster went before him to claim the trophy with the team.

Suddenly, without turning around, he felt an enormous presence behind him, moving through the crowd to the steps leading to the stage. He wanted to spin to the rear to double-check this eerie sense, but the sight of the three-foot golden trophy, four golfers perched at equal heights, drew him up the steps.

Peachy was already holding the trophy, bowing like a maestro to the noisy applause of the gallery. L.K. touched one of the four golfer statues, holding his personal trophy in the other arm, like the Heisman. Buster and Jacob stood by their side.

Chipper felt the hulking form follow him to the center of the stage. As he reached to touch the trophy and join the others, he saw L.K.'s face turn white as a ghost. The bursting smile on the champion's kisser vanished.

Chipper turned around to greet the colossal form behind him. It was the spitting image of L.K.'s father...but how could that be? Chipper snuck a peek at Amy, standing on the ground, beaming. Was she behind this? In the arms of this man's man, cradled like a baby, was a sickly kid, a dead ringer for Benny. Reality seized the stage.

Like Abraham carrying his son Isaac to the altar for sacrifice, the towering man walked to the center of the wooden platform.

No one moved. No one spoke. Cold drops of rain began to pelt the earth. Chipper finally forced his hand up to gently shake Benny's fingers of bone, then he let go. He was afraid to look at Mr. Taylor.

L.K. stepped forward and presented his individual trophy to Benny who embraced it like a teddy bear. The thin white skin around Benny's lips spread into a smile that could thaw a heart of ice.

L.K. and his father were locked in an unfaltering stare. Neither of them moved. Benny smiled at them both, stroking the golden golfer at the top of the trophy.

No, those were not tears streaming down Mr. Taylor's cheeks. Surely, it was the rain pounding his face. Tears would not come from the Nazi-killer at Normandy, the quarterback-killer from Norman. Not from the man who shook his fist at God and lived to tell about it.

And no, those were not tears running down L.K.'s cheeks. Not the great L.K. Not the greatest would-be athlete of all time. These were men. And with mortal men, the rain can hit your face and make it appear that you are weeping.

L.K.'s python arms embraced his father, then Benny, into a huddle. The three Taylors lowered their heads. No, they were not sobbing. Not these men.

Chipper pulled his shirt collar over his head to protect himself from the chilly rain. His turtleshell sanctuary blocked the rest of the world as he stared at the Taylors before him.

He noticed Mr. Taylor's hands, one cupped beneath Benny's shoulders, the other supporting his legs. On the side of each massive fist, Chipper could see clusters of semilunar scars, each and every curved white line matching a broken Communion glass swept away years ago into a sacred dustpan.

The realization shook him like the flagsticks at El Viento in mid-March, and he knew the exact words he would use for his final entry in the logbook:

It isn't strength that makes the man, for the Almighty parcels strength in various sizes, as if life's passageways will be scaled to match. Nope, it's not strength at all. It's harnessing the strength...by listening to the music.

And he wiped the drops from his own eyes, even though it wasn't raining anymore.

Epilogue

NINETEEN YEARS LATER

April 4, 1986

A. DeHart, M.D., Chairperson
Board of Directors
El Viento Golf and Country Club
561 Country Club Drive
El Viento, Oklahoma

Re: Estate of John Harjo

Dear Dr. DeHart:

The Last Will and Testament of John Harjo (a.k.a. Chief Crazy Hawk), Deceased, named the undersigned as Executor.

The purpose of this communication is to inform you of certain terms of the Decedent's Last Will and Testament which bequeathed certain property to your Club.

The Decedent's Last Will and Testament provides that the ownership of the following described property, bordered east by Country Club Road, south by Interstate-40, west by federal prison land and north by the existing Country Club Golf Course, is to be transferred to the El Viento Golf and Country Club. This bequest is conditioned upon 105 acres being utilized to double the existing course from 9 to 18 holes. Any property not used for this purpose is to be sold at public auction, with a portion of the proceeds therefrom to be used for the development and maintenance of the additional 9 holes.

$100,000.00 of the proceeds of the sale of the surplus property is to be used to fund the establishment of the Buster Nelson Foundation. The Foundation will provide a college scholarship each year for the member of the local high school golf team who demonstrates the greatest potential in leadership, academics, and service.

Your husband, Mr. Kyle DeHart, is designated as the Chairman of the Foundation, and will oversee the selection of additional Foundation Board members. The Buster Nelson Foundation is established to honor the Decedent's celebrated nephew, Buster Nelson, killed in action January 21, 1968, along with fellow Marines at Khe Sanh during the Vietnam conflict.

I have taken the liberty of notifying Walter ("L.K.") Taylor, Professional Golf Association, Palm Beach Gardens, Florida, as well as Jacob Justice, D.D., Ph.D., Professor, Dallas Theological Seminary, of the establishment of this Foundation, and the relevant terms of the Decedent's Last Will and Testament. The Decedent's Last Will and Testament does direct that these gentlemen, together with myself, be included on the initial Board of Directors of the Foundation.

Very truly yours,
Peach Waterman, Jr., Esq.
Attorney at Law

Acknowledgments

Great appreciation goes to my family for accommodating antisocial behavior ("he's disappeared into his study again") during the years required to bring *Flatbellies* to life. My wife Barbara helped with manuscript preparation and stepdaughters Susannah and Emily served as early critics. We then had the joyous experience of being gathered at home when word came that my manuscript had been accepted for publication.

My first draft was typed from dictation by Anita Owen who believed in its eventual success from the beginning. I am very grateful that Wrennie Landau then urged me to whittle, dissect, and augment my story until *Flatbellies* took its present form (what's one more year for a rewrite anyway?).

Flatbelly Andy Bass and his wife Linda served as resources/readers throughout the evolution of the story. And thanks go to other flatbellies that provided fodder for my fiction: Arth, Fletch, Dylina, MalMal, and Tricky Jack.

It takes a dedicated soul (or a literary masochist) to critique someone's unpublished, typewritten manuscript when there's only a snowball's chance it will ever become a book. So I offer my thanks to those who took on this heretofore thankless task: Frank Harrison, Jeff Wood, Dee Harris, along with neo-flatbellies Jamon Herndon and nephew Thomas Hyde.

My deep appreciation goes to the crew at Sleeping Bear Press who made the leap of faith to take on a new writer (new, that is, after 23 years of warm-up writing). Thanks go to editor Danny Freels for his immediate enthusiasm, which he then transferred to publisher Brian Lewis. Then, when we settled down to work, I truly appreciated Danny's careful and diplomatic "tweaking" of my manuscript, understanding the possessiveness an author has for chosen words. And as the process continued, I am indebted to those at Sleeping Bear Press who took the manuscript to its finished product: Lynne Johnson and Jennifer Lundahl.

Finally, a word of gratitude for my parents who gave me a small town heart for a big town world where it's "never too windy to play golf."

Acknowledgments

[illegible]